FIRST KISS

"A kiss with somebody else is nothing," Lainie clarified raggedly, trying to pull away a little. "But with you—I'm—it's too important. I've thought about it too long. I'm not ready. You just got here." What was she saying? She pushed back the words that kept tumbling out, helter-skelter. Around him, she couldn't think.

He was so still that she finally looked up from her confused embarrassment.

"Lainie."

Determination and desire made his dark face sharp as he bent over her, and his arms, the hardest arms she'd ever felt, wrapped around her and pulled her to him so tightly that his overall front cut into her breasts. His eyes clung to her mouth. He never looked away from their trembling curve, and he never said a word.

He just kissed her.

"Lisa Brown is a magician, and *Sleeping at the Magnolia* the spell she weaves. Dark as old secrets, hot as a southern summer night, seductive as a dangerous man's eyes, this is a book that will pull you in and not let you go."
—*Eileen Dreyer*

Books by Lisa G. Brown

Billy Bob Walker Got Married
Crazy for Lovin' You
Sleeping at the Magnolia

Published by HarperPaperbacks

SLEEPING AT THE MAGNOLIA

Lisa G. Brown

HarperPaperbacks
A Division of HarperCollinsPublishers

![HarperPaperbacks logo] **HarperPaperbacks**
A Division of HarperCollins*Publishers*
10 East 53rd Street, New York, N.Y. 10022-5299

This is a work of fiction. The characters, incidents, and dialogues are products of the author's imagination and are not to be construed as real. Any resemblance to actual events or persons, living or dead, is entirely coincidental.

ISBN 0-06-108214-7

HarperCollins®, ![logo] ®, and HarperPaperbacks™, are trademarks of HarperCollins*Publishers* Inc.

Cover illustration copyright © 1997 by Robert Steele

First printing: December 1997

Printed in the United States of America

Visit HarperPaperbacks on the World Wide Web at
http://www.harpercollins.com

❖ 10 9 8 7 6 5 4 3 2 1

For my daughters, Autumn and Dakota
(If you ever do what the girl in this book does, I'll lock you both in the closet until you're fifty. In fact, you can't read this book until you're fifty.)

Come all ye fair and tender ladies,
Take warning how you court your men.
—Appalachian folk ballad

SLEEPING AT THE MAGNOLIA

Prologue

"You better come down off the top of the world, Mr. Rawlins, and answer the phone," the youngest of the construction workers, a boy barely out of high school, bawled up at the man who straddled the top beam of the big warehouse that was under construction.

Colley Rawlins squinted down at him, lifting the orange hard hat he wore to run his hand through his too-long black hair and push it back off his hot face. "Tell Mrs. Simmons to take a message, and I'll call whoever it is back later. Right now I'm busy."

"Well, I would," the boy said apologetically, "but she told me not to take no for an answer." He shielded his eyes against the bright sun of the sticky Kentucky afternoon, and at Colley's frown, he rushed his next words. "It ain't Miss Rachel," he informed Colley and every member of the interested crew. "It's your grandpa."

His grandfather.

He couldn't refuse the call; they all knew it.

After a moment's pause, Colley nodded. "I'll be there in a minute." But he didn't move until the boy turned and vanished in the direction he'd come from. Then Colley spoke to the supervisor who stood on the nearby construction platform that the men were using to put up the long, heavy rafters like the one he sat on. "It's sturdy, just like it needs to be. This place has to hold a lot of tobacco."

"My work's always up to your standards, Mr. Rawlins, and you set some tough ones. That's not a complaint. I just want you to know that I'm willing to do what you want done. I'd like to be around to build all of the Rawlinses' tobacco warehouses."

"I reckon this will be the last one for a while, Kello," Colley said shortly in answer to the supervisor's indirect question. "The old man wanted three in Kentucky, and this is the third. He makes those decisions. I just do what he says and buy the tobacco to fill them for him every year."

Kello hesitated. The long-haired, sweaty man across from him was not the normal rich boy. He might be only twenty-four or twenty-five, the youngest of the Rawlinses, but he was as hard as nails. He put on no fronts and he despised a kiss-ass. That much the older man had learned.

"I hear that Mr. Harding has asked you to be his partner in building a horse-breeding stable somewhere around here." Blunt honesty, that was the key, Kello decided quickly, before Colley could get away. "I'd sure appreciate it if you'd consider me for it. I've got two kids to put through college," the contractor answered humorously, hoping he'd not pushed it too far.

He couldn't quite put his finger on why he got so uptight talking to a guy who wasn't much older than his own son. Maybe it was because Colley was like his grandfather Albert, whom Kello had met a time or two in person—self-made, independent, rough around the edges.

"I don't know yet about the stable," Colley said slowly, "but if it ever gets built, I'll recommend you." Kello nodded a little, relieved. That was another thing about the man he was working for: he meant what he said.

Some people couldn't stand him. A few crazy gossips even whispered that he'd already killed a man, which was exactly the sort of wild story that would get told about people like the Rawlinses.

But all the supervisor knew, all he was interested in, was that the boss's word was like his money: very, very good.

Colley unhooked one long leg and swung it over the rafter so that he sat on it instead of straddled it. The makeshift ladder was right there at his feet, waiting for him to climb down, but he couldn't for a minute.

Riding this beam high against the brilliant blue sky, the sun beating fiercely down on his shoulders, he might have been a kid again, high in the tree house in Lainie's backyard. Free.

But it was only an illusion. Always, he had to climb back down.

He hated telephone calls from the old man. They brought him too close to home. Too close to her. And when that happened, he wanted to tell AT&T where they could get off. Reach out and touch, they said—but he couldn't. She wouldn't let him. Her mother wouldn't let him. His own grandfather wouldn't let him.

So why was Albert Rawlins calling? Colley had done his duty: he'd gone home earlier in the spring to help with the planting of the tobacco. He'd go back in the fall to help with the cutting and the stripping. He always did, and he always hung around just long enough to find out whether or not there was anybody she was serious about.

Not yet. It hadn't happened yet, at least not that he'd found out.

But it would, and soon. Lainie would find somebody and get married, and the only way he was going to survive the happy event was to stay a long way away from her.

Was that what his grandfather was about to tell him? The old man would get a lot of pleasure out of imparting the information.

"Damn it," he swore to himself and reached for the ladder.

Past the construction site, he took long steps across the rich bluegrass of the field beside the warehouse, avoiding the puddles where it had rained the night before and filled the ruts that the heavy equipment had made in the ground.

The makeshift trailer where the office of the construction crew was temporarily housed said Kello and Brothers, Contractors, on the side. He pulled off the hard hat and yanked up his stained T-shirt to wipe his throat free of sweat. When Colley finally swung the door open, a gust of cold, air-conditioned air hit him in the face.

"Here he is, Mr. Rawlins," Mrs. Simmons, the secretary, said soothingly into the phone. "Yes, sir. It did take him a while. But maybe he was hard to locate." The woman's face bore an odd mix of reproach and relief as she turned the phone over to Colley, and he tossed the hat into a nearby chair.

"Is that you, boy?"

He'd know Albert Rawlins's voice anywhere, the gruff overtones, the smoky sound of the West Virginia hills.

"Yeah. What are you calling me for?" he demanded. He ignored the shocked, silent reprimand on the secretary's face at his rudeness to the one on the other end of the line and turned his back to her. She couldn't know that there had never been much love lost between his grandfather and himself.

"Gettin' right to the point, are you?" Albert's voice was

wry. "But that's all right. So will I. I want you to come back to Indian Springs, Colley. Now. To stay."

Surprise ran right down his back, and then dread. "You want me to? Three years ago, you couldn't get me out of Tennessee fast enough. Nowadays you want me around just when you've got to have me to help with the tobacco, or to do some kind of dirty work." Yeah, that was the right term. The last deal that he'd gotten Preston out of down in Atlanta certainly qualified as dirty.

"Things are changin', I reckon."

This is about Lainie, isn't it? he wanted to ask. But he knew better than to mention her name to Albert.

"So what's changed?" he said at last, carefully.

"Your uncle James is raisin' hell, to begin with. He claims you did wrong by Preston when you settled his affairs in Atlanta a month ago. He wants to talk to you. I'm keepin' your cousin here with me for a while, and that ain't helpin' matters."

Out of the blue, Colley laughed. The thought of his suave, city-loving cousin being forced to hole up in a one-horse town like Indian Springs was a joke—on Preston.

"Reckon you think that's funny. You want to know what I thought was funny? When I talked to Paul Harding the other day, he told me how you've learned faster about breedin' race horses than anybody he's ever worked with. A born natural, he called you. He says he's lookin' at blueprints for the stable you're plannin' to build with him. First I've heard of it, boy."

That was the problem. Harding was as free with his tongue as he was with his fortune. Colley understood now and swore silently to himself.

"You don't like the idea of the stable?" he asked his grandfather evasively.

"We agreed, Colley, that when you got ready to put

down roots, they would be here, in the Springs. Tobacco warehouses are one thing. We need a few right in the middle of Kentucky if we're gonna stay on top in that business. You or an overseer can handle the buying in just a few visits a year now that all the warehouses are in place. Your job's done with them. But I know you. You'll spend all your time with a stable. That's where your heart is. So I ain't interested in you buildin' one two hundred miles from me."

"I've spent most of the last three years around Danville, old man," Colley answered in angry contrariness. "You raise hell every time I come back to the Springs if I stay too long. So where did you expect me to build it if not around here?"

"I never meant for you to stay gone forever, all over a damn woman."

A damn woman.

At last Lainie Thorne had found her way into their conversation.

"You sent me away because of her. I've stayed away for the same reason. What's different now?" He managed to sound calm on the phone. Colley knew better than to let any real emotions show where she was concerned.

"She's no worry of yours any longer, is she? You got another woman now. That's different, and I'm glad of it."

"Is that something else you and Paul Harding have been talking over?" Colley demanded in rising anger.

"He just let me know pretty plain that his girl had an eye for you, and wanted to know what I was goin' to do about it. I been checkin' up on her. Rachel, is that her name? I hear she's a high stepper, and she don't hold men on very tight strings. That's the kind you need. Let her understand that you belong in a different place. Tell her that you expect her to learn to belong here, too."

"Look, old man, I can make my own decisions," Colley

said hotly. "Maybe I'm not a goddamned millionaire, but I've made money on my own."

"My goddamned millions will be half yours someday, boy. That ain't too bad for a kid that started his life as a bastard in the shantytown. You know you don't want Preston to have it all, or James. And you can't stand there and tell me you don't miss home, Colley. I know you better."

Miss home.

Home.

It was a word he didn't use because it meant too much. Maybe it always did when a man grew up as he had, not sure where he belonged for so many years.

Albert Rawlins might be eighty, but he was as shrewd as ever. He knew where his grandson's weaknesses were, just where to hit him the hardest, and he never hesitated to do it.

But he couldn't know the real depths of the pain Colley felt.

He couldn't realize just how much his grandson had missed the Springs. Why, Colley himself didn't understand. The people there didn't like him, didn't trust him, didn't want him.

But the Timms Fork River always recognized him. Widow's Creek welcomed him. It sent its cold waters around his feet in a glad greeting every time he returned. The tobacco fields lay rich and fallow, the distant hollows reached longingly for him with drifting, foggy fingers.

He'd grown up there, on Rawlins Farm. It was where his mother had borne him, where River Charley had taught him. Where he'd learned about places like the Magnolia and the women of it, women who belonged to a gentler world than he'd ever known.

Lainie Thorne was one of them.

Something was very wrong where she was concerned.

His grandfather was certain that she was out of his reach now, or he'd never have made this call and this demand.

"All right, Devil." He slipped unconsciously into usage of one of the nicknames for the old man that the shantytown people on the river called him. It was the only name Colley himself had known him by as a child. "I'll be there, soon."

"When?" Albert persisted.

"It'll take me a day or two to get business settled here. I'll have to make plans to have the horses shipped to the Springs, and then I'll drive down."

He was really going home, where his life was.

Where his woman was.

Part 1

Wilder Days

1

The devil never sleeps.

That was what Great-Aunt Olivia always said, and on that hot night in June, Lainie Thorne thought that maybe her aged relative had it dead to rights.

Something was certainly stirring up trouble, and Old Nick seemed as likely a scapegoat to hang it on as anything else.

The Magnolia Hotel kept its dining room open late only one night a week, on Wednesdays, so that the prayer-meeting crowd from the Baptist church, the Church of Christ, and the Holiness Pentecostal Tabernacle could stop by for home-made pie and coffee after the preachers got through with them.

The place was crowded on this particular Wednesday; for one thing, it was the only eating establishment still open at eight o'clock in the Springs, and for another, it had rained most of the day, so that tobacco farmers and kids who might normally have stayed late at the community swimming pool had wound up going to church for spiritual help and then on to the Magnolia for a little socializing.

And just to make the old hotel a little more lively, three or four men who looked as if they'd be a lot more comfortable at the country club were present. Normally their type found the place too dull, too down-home and old-fashioned for their tastes, but the group tonight had brought their own excitement with them.

They'd come in with none other than Preston Rawlins.

Great-Aunt Olivia had been absentminded all day long; twice she had mistaken her niece Deborah for her mother, who'd been dead forty years. That was why she was the only one in the place who wasn't staring and whispering, bowled over by the surprise of the newcomer's appearance. She just plain hadn't noticed him.

Olivia wouldn't have known him anyway, even on one of her good days. Preston Rawlins had done his best never to set foot in the little town of Indian Springs until now. He might have visited his grandfather, Albert Rawlins, out on the nearby farm a time or two during his growing-up years, but nobody in town had ever seen much of him until the last few weeks.

He'd been raised in Nashville, where his father and his uptown, high-society mama resided. Teresa Cooper-Rawlins had no intention of bringing her son up to be a rough, uneducated backwoodsman like the old man. She had largely kept Preston out of Albert's reach.

But the townspeople all knew that if his grandfather ever decided that Preston should come to the Springs, his father James would send him, and all his mother's plans and her family's genteel money would take a backseat to the raw strength and power of the old man. It was just always better not to antagonize Albert Rawlins.

They surmised that such was the reason that Preston was finally in the Springs now for an extended visit.

"He says he only wants a glass of tea, and you to bring it to him," Dana, the girl who worked part-time as a waitress, who'd been Lainie's best friend through all of high school, whispered in the other's ear as they met at the swinging door of the kitchen.

"He's got his nerve," Lainie returned dryly, but she flushed a little and shot a glance at the noisy table of men in the corner. She wasn't the only one; Miss Bella Foster and three of her cronies were viewing them with intense disapproval.

"He's got just about everything else, too," Dana whispered fervently. "Is he not the most perfect thing you've ever laid eyes on? Can you believe that something that looks like that is sitting at one of the Magnolia's beat-up old tables?"

Lainie had no answers. She just had questions. What was Preston Rawlins doing here? And why, why was he singling her out in front of all these people?

But she smothered a laugh as across the room his blue eyes met hers and he raised his eyebrows teasingly, wiggling them as if to ask why he hadn't been waited on yet, daring her to come on over. Beside him, an older man—his name was Tate, Lainie knew from a slight acquaintance— said something, and the other two with them listened and laughed as well, eyeing her admiringly.

Lainie flushed, and the big room was suddenly too hot. Actually, the room really was hot. The Magnolia had no air conditioners at all; only the windows, wide open on the black night, and the big ceiling fans with their slowly twirling blades provided relief from the mugginess.

She had to do something, and the obvious choice was to stay calm and cool, walk over to that table, and give him his tea. Then she'd—

"Oh, my God," Dana said quickly, clutching at Lainie's arm. "Look."

Lainie followed her gaze to the open door, the one that led into the dining room from the wide hall just outside—and if a knife had been stuck into her heart, she couldn't have felt a sharper pain. She was barely aware when Dana faded into the background, somewhere behind her.

Colley Rawlins.

Colley was standing in the door of the dining room.

She didn't know what stunned her more—the sight of him, who'd been gone for so long, or the sight of him in the Magnolia.

He wasn't supposed to be in the Springs. He stayed away these days, except for two months or so every year. She always knew when he was coming back—in early spring, at the beginning of the tobacco-planting season, and in the fall for cutting and stripping—and she always made it a point to stay out of his way. That was the way it had to be.

He wasn't supposed to be here now. Most of all, he wasn't supposed to be in the hotel. He knew she didn't want him to come.

Could she be dreaming? He couldn't have arrived so quickly, so quietly, after all these years. There ought to have been a warning.

He couldn't just be standing there.

Her frightened, shocked gaze dropped over him.

When had Colley ever worn an expensive black suit, so well-tailored to his frame that it seemed to be part of him? And a coffee-colored T-shirt, a shade or two lighter than his skin, just under it? He looked as elegantly understated as something in *Gentleman's Quarterly*.

This surely wasn't the boy from the shantytown, the one who'd grown up barefoot and ragged.

Yet—the face, the build, they were his.

The man standing there was as opposite from Preston Rawlins as night was from day. In fact, he looked like night personified—tall and lean and dark, his heavy, straight black hair falling to his shoulders, his cheekbones high and lean beneath his coal black eyes.

But they weren't really black. In the sunlight, in the very brightest sunlight, the kind that shone at midday in hot cornfields and on tall tobacco, they were a rich brown.

Lainie remembered that much, in the flashing instant before he caught sight of Preston at the far table and started toward him determinedly.

"Co-Colley? Is that you?" Aunt Olivia was as surprised as the rest of the people in the room, but she alone seemed glad to see him. She followed him a little ways into the room, folding her handkerchief into the belt of the delicate organza of her white dress.

He hesitated a minute in his long strides across the room, finally pausing to look back. "Yes, ma'am," he answered reluctantly.

Lainie as well as the rest of the people in the dining room sucked in a communal breath at his admission.

"I—I hadn't seen you in so long," Olivia said with a slow, glad smile. "Where's Lainie? She'll be wanting to talk to you. Boy, where have you been?"

Lainie checked her impulsive, jerky move forward. She wished it were as easy to stop the sudden pounding of her heavy pulse and the rise of blood to her cheeks.

But the man never glanced in her direction. His hand caught for a minute at the neck of his shirt, and that hand and his throat proved like nothing else could have that he really was the boy from the river. They shone dark and sleek, like some renegade Indian's. "Miss Olivia, I came to talk to somebody. But sometime soon, maybe I can come again, and we'll sit down together."

"And have some of my fruit tea," she said with pleasure.

"And have some of your tea, I reckon," he said gently.

Lainie had to shut her eyes for a split second, not at the sight of him, but at the sound. She had always loved his slow, richly accented voice. It was the way Albert talked. Somebody once said it was the sound of the coal country, where he had come from. It had been bequeathed to Colley, that habit of flattening vowels and drawling out syllables. Preston didn't have it; his raising and his education had prevented it.

It took the newcomer only four long strides to reach Preston's table, and no effort at all for Lainie to hear what he said, because the whole room had gone deathly still, waiting for a confrontation.

"You know what I've come after," he said flatly to the blond man seated there in front of him.

Preston flushed a little in the face of all the interest of the room, but he was calm. "I don't know what you're talking about."

"Yeah, you do. Nadine saw you take it. She said she tried to stop you, and you pushed her to get away."

"I told Grandfather that housekeeper of his is a basket case, and now I'm telling you. She's lying," Preston said flatly.

"Now what reason would Nadine have to lie?" Colley asked in humorless amusement. "Just to get you in trouble?"

"More likely she'd lie to keep you out of it," Preston retorted. "She's from the same shantytown where you grew up, isn't she? I guess that breeds loyalty."

"Where I grew up has got nothing to do with this. You took the whistle. My whistle. I want it back," Colley said with determination. "Don't make yourself a thief over it."

Lainie caught back a whimper of sound.

There was a long, shocked pause. Then Preston laughed in attempted amusement, but he was angry at last. "You're crazy, Colley. All of this excitement over some whistle? What is it, the only heirloom my uncle ever left that mother of yours?"

Colley never moved.

"Now look," the older man at Preston's table said abruptly, coming to his feet, "you can't just walk in here and threaten Preston over some damn toy. You may spend a good part of your life throwing your weight around for Albert Rawlins like some hired gun, and the poor white trash in this town may be scared senseless of you, but you're talking to us now. To us. Do you understand? So butt out."

"Since you're doing his talking for him, mister, are you going to do his fighting, too?" Colley answered, quiet and cool—but he dropped his hands to his sides and let them curl into loose fists.

"No—no!" Lainie cried the words before she even knew it, breaking from Dana's grasp to take a step toward them. She knew what Colley looked like when he was about to wreck havoc on somebody, and he had that look now.

Both of the men reacted. Preston came to his feet, furious; Colley jerked and finally faced her.

Three years.

It had been that long since she had looked him in the eye, and an electric shock swished down her when she did now.

He didn't say anything, but a tide of red blood was rising from the neck of his shirt up his dark face, giving him a bronze look. It was funny how that happened to him, how a man so dark skinned could flush like that. He'd done it as a boy when he was embarrassed or moved by intense emotion.

She didn't want the rest of the Springs to hear what she had to say, but there was no choice, not if she meant to prevent a confrontation right there in the middle of the prayer-meeting crowd.

Struggling for composure, she found her voice at last. "I don't know what you're doing in town tonight, but you know not to come here, Colley. Not ever," she said, but the lowness of her tone was in vain.

"Why, Lainie," Aunt Olivia exclaimed in dismay.

"Please, Aunt, you don't understand," Lainie pleaded. "Just let me handle this."

"But you were the one who brought him to the Magnolia the first time. I remember it clearly. You took his hand and led him right to me," her great-aunt pleaded.

Colley made a funny sound deep in his throat, and it was the turn of the girl in front of him to blush. "That was a long time ago," she said defensively.

"Just yesterday, surely."

"What about him?" he demanded brusquely, motioning at Preston. "Albert's his grandfather, too. He's a Rawlins, too."

"Except I'm the real thing. Hell, Colley, I don't know what you are," Preston flung back at him.

"I want to know, Lainie," Colley said insistently. "Why is he welcome here, and I'm not?"

"You know what this is about. It's personal, between you and me, Colley," she whispered for him alone.

He looked at her then, and she'd forgotten just how intent his gaze was, how his eyes slanted downward at the corners and made him look serious and sad. "There's nothing between us, Lainie. Isn't that what you told me? But it doesn't matter. I'm not leaving until I get what I came for. I'll get it, too, even if I have to beat it out of him."

Behind her, Lainie heard Bella's muffled cry as Colley

made a sharp, lunging motion toward Preston, pulling him up out of the chair he sat in with one jerk on the front of his shirt.

For a moment the two of them seemed to freeze there in front of a good part of the upright citizens of the Springs, locked together in a silent struggle.

"Please," Lainie begged, turning to Preston as a last resort, "if you've got the whistle he wants, give it to him. He means to hurt you if you don't."

"You'd better listen to what she says," Colley panted. "She knows me better than you do."

"Oh, for God's sake," Preston choked out in disgust, yanking away from his cousin's hold on his shirtfront. "Here. Let me find the damned thing." He fumbled a moment in first one pocket and then another before he finally brought out a leather cord. On it, a whistle dangled, its dull sheen speaking of antiquity and genuine silver.

Preston shoved it at the other man. "You can't take a joke. It was just a trick, you idiot."

"I know what it was," Colley said implacably, lifting the cord over his head, letting it drop around his dusky neck so that the whistle fell onto his chest. "And I know you. I'd never have seen it again if I hadn't come after it. That's your kind of trick."

"Colley, honey, what in the world is going on?"

The voice that came from the door was high and sweet, a woman's voice. All eyes turned from the two men to the apparition standing there.

Lainie knew suddenly why Colley looked like he did: he was the match for the gorgeous woman who'd called his name. She wore something simple: a short, well-fitted skirt and a deeply veed, sleeveless vest with a burlap-weave that picked up the gold in her brown hair and made the simple chain around her neck gleam. But she was so fashionable,

so expensively dressed, that Lainie wanted to hide somewhere in her white summer slacks and T-shirt. She had to
restrain herself from tearing off the apron she wore.

Who was this woman?

Something hot—it couldn't be jealousy—stung her
heart.

"Nothing, Rachel. I told you it'd be better if you waited
in the car," he said, with a trace of irritation.

"I would have been happy to, but the local fuzz pulled
up behind the Porsche, and I thought maybe you needed
protection," she drawled, and stepped aside to let the man
behind her through.

"Way! What are you doing here?" Lainie demanded
blankly of the big. sandy-haired man in the trim police uniform.

"Dana called me on the kitchen phone while I was down
the road at the station," Way explained, looking from one
face in the room to the other.

"Well, I didn't know what was going to happen." Dana
defended her actions from behind Lainie.

"Colley." Way acknowledged the other man with nothing
more than the one word. "So you're back. I heard you
were, for good this time."

For good. Colley was back for good? And nobody had
told her yet? Lainie thought in frantic panic.

"What you really mean is, for bad, don't you, Way?"
Colley asked ironically.

"I was going to give you the benefit of the doubt, but it's
not looking like I can. I'm waiting for the answer to the
lady's question here. What's going on?"

"Nothing, Officer," Preston answered unsteadily. "My
damn cousin overreacted, like he always does, about nothing. But it's settled now."

"He's right. It's finished, but I don't call it a nothing.

Somebody gave me the whistle, somebody that I used to know," Colley answered. He never looked at Lainie as he turned away, but his voice was completely different when he spoke to her great-aunt. "I'm sorry, Miss Olivia. I never meant to break up the Magnolia."

"I—I'm not angry with you, Colley," she said at last, looking sideways at her niece. "I want you to stay a while, and Lainie does, too. You know she does. She always loved you. I don't know why she won't admit it now."

Colley turned for a minute and looked right at the flushed girl opposite, letting his eyes sweep her just as she had inspected him a few minutes earlier.

"I know all about what Lainie wants. So I'll be going. You take care." And after a moment's hesitation, he bent and kissed the old lady's cheek. "Rachel, are you ready?"

The woman in the doorway took two or three graceful steps until she was nearly face-to-face with him and could lock her left hand under his left elbow, letting her long, red-tipped fingernails rest proprietarily on his black coat sleeve. "I think I need to use the little girl's room before we leave. Would you mind waiting for me in the car? I don't think it'd be safe for you to wait here, Colley, darling. They don't seem to like you."

He moved uneasily. "Hurry."

Before he could get away, she dropped a kiss on his cheek. More scandalously, she let her free right hand brush across his coat back—right down over his hips.

Bella Foster gasped in delicious outrage. Lainie stood stoically still. Colley himself protested in a low voice, "Rachel."

She laughed, a rich throaty sound, and he took several long strides out the door, leaving her alone with the others in the dining room.

"Damn bastard," Lloyd Tate swore viciously into the silence of the dining room.

"Please," Rachel said calmly, "you're talking about the man I'm going to marry." She glanced around the little room, at the dropped mouths and shocked faces of the small-town people who didn't know what to make of this woman, or the man with her. Then she looked right at Lainie, and there was a challenge in her gaze. "Maybe I don't need to use the bathroom after all. It was interesting to meet all of you, to say the least," she said on a gurgle of laughter, and she vanished out the same door Colley had exited through just minutes earlier.

"She's the bitch to be his match," Lloyd finished explosively.

"Sir!" Bella said reprovingly. "Just because we have rid ourselves of one heathen does not mean that we want another one to take his place."

"Save your outrage, ma'am," he answered furiously. "Come on, Preston, I'm getting out of here. And if I meet your cousin in the dark, one of us won't live to tell about it."

Preston Rawlins took one long, considering look at Lainie. "Let's go."

It wasn't until he, too, had vanished from sight that the room broke out in a loud confusion of sound and avid gossip.

"Albert Rawlins has brought that boy back home," Bella told the entire dining room. "And he's not changed one bit. I don't care what fine clothes he's wearing tonight. He'll always be a brat from the river."

A tiny little pain, hot as blue fire, encased Lainie's heart for an instant. "Please, could you—I don't mean to be rude, but . . . it's getting late, and this has upset Aunt Olivia."

"Well, of course, Lainie," Matt Cassidy reassured her soothingly. "Let's hurry up, folks."

Old Ben Sanders cackled as he rose from his table. "Surely we got better manners than the Rawlins boys, tearin' up jack at a place as calm as the Magnolia, and over something as silly as a whistle. Can you beat that? Yep, Colley Rawlins is back in town. Looks like things are goin' to get lively again."

I can't believe Colley kept that old whistle, thought Lainie quietly, not after all these years.

She couldn't stop the hurt completely, after all, no matter how much she tried. Everything hurt where he was concerned. Why did he have to come back?

The place was emptying fast; only Bella and Alma were still gathering up their Bibles and purses and Wednesday-night study books. Way waited until even they had gone before he spoke to her.

"I only heard yesterday that Albert had brought him home to stay. Colley and Preston both—two Rawlinses in town this summer. I hope we survive it. No, what I really mean is, I hope you do." Way looked worried.

"I'm not your baby cousin anymore, Way. I'm grown up," she protested. "You don't have to protect me."

"Sure I do. You've got no father to do it for you, and we both know why."

"I don't want to talk about it tonight," Lainie said on a harsh in-drawn breath. "Besides, Colley has a woman friend. He's not interested in me anymore."

Way laughed without amusement. "Say that enough and maybe you'll get to believing it, girl. But I know better, and so do you. He didn't have to come here tonight, but he did. Maybe it really was over the whistle, but I noticed he took a good, long look right at you. His fancy girlfriend saw it, too. Colley's interested. He always will be. Take care." Way hesitated, then did something he might have done twice in their entire lives. He bent and brushed an embarrassed kiss on her forehead.

Stoically, Lainie watched him go. Then she turned back

to the kitchen. Dana was loading the old dishwasher as she came in. "Just let me finish, Dana. You go home early."

"But all the tables still have to be cleaned off."

"I'll do it."

"Well . . . if you're sure. But I feel like a rat leaving you with this mess. I guess the only good thing is that your mother stayed late at church to meet with the Ladies' Auxiliary and missed it all." Dana pulled off her apron, folded it on top of the washing machine in the little room off the kitchen, and crossed to the open back door. She paused with one hand on the screaky black screen. "Thanks, Lainie. Maybe I'll go home and do my nails," she said whimsically, examining their stubby lengths, "or take a long bubble bath. That woman with Colley tonight made me feel like a grubby kid. I don't like the feeling, and I don't like her."

"I didn't, either," Lainie whispered, more to herself than to the other girl, who had already stepped out on the back porch.

Alone in the big hotel dining room, she stacked dishes and carried them to the kitchen, then straightened tables.

And she thought. *Stop thinking,* she told herself, but she couldn't.

His hands at his throat had been dark and quick, just like he was, and they had reminded her of what it felt like to have him touch her.

Of what it was like to touch him.

Oh, not when he was dressed like he was tonight, all covered up and civilized, but when his arms had been bare and warm around her, and he'd been wild and urgent in his embrace. His mouth had not been stern, like it had been thirty minutes ago, but sulky and beautiful.

She thought she'd folded those memories away forever. Now here they were.

When had she ever felt the leap of jealousy like the one she'd felt tonight when that woman he called Rachel had touched him?

I can't bear it. I can't bear it, she cried to herself, holding herself around the middle as she leaned against the dishwasher and felt its chugging against her side, its noise the only sound in the quiet hotel.

Why did he come back? Why did he come here?

How will I ever stand to see him ma—she had to make herself think the word—married to another woman?

I've got to leave, she thought in desperation, *or I've got to get a grip. Even if sight of him with that old silver whistle about his throat hurts my eyes and stuns my heart.*

They met on a day so bright it hurt the eye and stunned the heart.

The boy knew a lot about her before she'd even glimpsed him. He'd been slipping from the circle field, the one closest to the shack where he lived, to watch the construction of the white house high up on the hill. It wasn't all that hard to escape; he was tending tobacco all by himself, and it was a fast run down the cool slope into the dark hollow where Widow's Creek gurgled along. The house sat high at the top of the hill on the other side of the creek.

That clear water had been his happy playmate for all his life, his only companion besides old Charley, but he was tired of it. He wanted people, real people, and Charley wouldn't let him play often with the children who lived in the shantytown down on the farther edge of the river. "They got no use for you, Colley," he used to say sternly. "Won't do you much good."

And he had learned that Charley was right. The two of them lived apart from the others on the farm, still close to the river, but back up a tiny hollow hidden by trees and brush, one that he had to wade the creek to get to. It was more, though, than the fact that Charley tried to keep him isolated; the others stayed away from them, too, watching his and Charley's movements suspiciously from a distance.

Once, when he tried to approach one of them, the mother had come after the little boy. "You stay away from that one, Joshua," she'd told her ragged son. "We don't mess with the Rawlins by-blows. Devil said to leave him be, and I don't aim to have trouble with Devil."

He knew who Devil was: he was the Man, the tobacco king who owned the big farm, the white-haired one in the overalls and big boots who made Colley afraid when he stepped so heavily, leaning awkwardly on his stiff right leg as though it were a staff. Fortunately, Devil never did much more than look, and he never paid much attention to Colley and Charley, anyway, other than to bring them their share of the money when the crops came in, the same money that Charley would later spend down at the little store out where the farm boundary met the river road. It was Devil's store, just like it was Devil's farm and they were Devil's workers.

But he didn't know the other word that the woman used. "What's a by-blow?" he asked Charley curiously.

The old man had looked up from the calf he was trying to bottle-feed. He had the calf caught under his strong left forearm, the bottle in his right grasp, his Roman nose glistening with sweat. "Something you're not," he answered shortly. "And those people in those shacks, they don't know anything. They're afraid of you because you're different. You're getting out of this shantytown someday. Them, they're lost souls that got doomed by their own lives, condemned to work here on this farm because they can't do better."

"You, Charley?" Colley asked curiously. "Is that why you came here?"

The old man turned away. "I came with Devil to this place fifty years ago, looking for a place to hide," he answered at last. "I found it here."

He wore a funny brown hat that crooked over one eye, so Colley couldn't see him at all when he asked half in fright, "And me? What am I doing here, Charley? I don't remember why."

Charley stepped away from the calf. "There," he said to it. "If you don't live now, it's not my fault." He held the hat up with his two forefingers to run his other three over his nearly bald head. "And it's not yours, either, Colley. You just came along at the wrong time and in the wrong place. It's up to us to put you back where you belong. To turn the terrible into the glorious." Charley could sound like that sometimes, like he was preaching a fancy sermon, his words long and impressive. He was an educated man, as good with books as he was with the big horses that Devil had a weakness for. "Now, stop asking so many blamed questions and get the hoe. You're as curious as a cat about things you don't even need to know."

Colley's curiosity was what led him to find the house; he had no reason to cross the creek this far down, but he'd stumbled on the sound of hammers and saws one day and hid to watch them build the place. He never went close enough to talk to one of them; that was something he instinctively knew not to do, just as he knew better than to tell Charley where he'd been.

The house was nearly completed when he crept there one day and saw the little girl.

Sight of her stopped him in his tracks.

She was sitting high in the fork of a giant oak tree, on a flat wooden platform that a big man, apparently her father, was putting the finishing touches on, and her dark curls tumbled around her face in spite of the fact that her hair had been pulled up into some kind of little topknot.

"Princess Sally likes this new house, Papa," she announced.

The man paused in his hammering and took three nails from between his lips to answer. "Elaina," he said sternly, "you're old enough to outgrow this make-believe. There is no Princess Sally, for the last time."

The little girl didn't say anything for a minute, then she told him, "Can't I just say there is, even if there's not?"

"We've talked about this. It's time you gave up these pretend friends. You have real ones."

"But they're at school, and school is out."

"Then occupy your mind for a few weeks with other things, and stop pretending. Now let's go back to the house." He looked around as he prepared to come down the short wooden ladder he'd tacked to the side of the oak. "I may have built this playhouse too close to the woods," he said with a touch of worry. "This was such a perfect tree that I couldn't resist. But you're just a little ways down the hill from the kitchen window, and I'll run a fence and we'll get a dog. You'll like it better when you're older."

"I like it now," she said decisively. "And I'm already eleven."

"Yes, you are. Plenty old enough to—"

"To stop playing with Sally."

"That's right. So that we won't have to take you to some shrink to try to figure out why you're refusing reality," he teased suddenly, making his voice sound proper and horrified.

"What's a shrink?"

"Something I've not got the money for, not for you or the princess."

By now Colley had recognized the man, and the recognition made him shiver. It was John Thorne, the overseer for Devil's big farm. He had little to do with the horses, but he was the one who gave the orders for the tobacco and the corn and the hay fields, and he was the one who ran the big tobacco warehouse. Thorne was quiet and even until it came to the shantytown people, whom he hated without reason. He gave his orders to them without even looking at them, as though they hurt his eyes, and at any small infraction on their part, he penalized them. He rode the farm in an open Jeep, and the hatred of the field hands followed him like a tangible thing.

Colley had few dealings with him; Charley relayed most of the man's instructions to the boy.

He never forgot that first glimpse of the two of them; it was the first time he'd ever seen a child like that, so pampered, so taken care of, so valued just for her existence instead of what she did in a field or around the farm. And he loved the platform, so high up in the clouds from his position at the bottom of the hill.

He thought of them, of her, for days, and he slipped away twice more to try to find her.

Instead, she came to him.

Deep in the month of July, on a sweltering, brilliant afternoon, he left the lonely field that he'd been sent to tend that week in desperate need of the cooling water of the creek. The iciest, deepest spot was the big blue hole that lay between two wooded high banks at a curve in the stream; just beyond that narrow, dark, cold curve, the creek opened up and began its flow into the waters of the Timms Fork River just beyond.

Colley had barely topped one of the rocky banks to look over into the water he was about to plunge into when he heard someone singing, her voice high, uncertain, and sweet.

"Hang down your head, Tom Dooley, hang down your head and"— There was a pant for breath—"and cry. . . ."

He saw her with a start of disbelief. The little girl from the white house was down below him, wading the creek, so far from home, struggling to balance on the mossy rocks along the edge.

The sunlight tagged after her lingeringly through the shifting patterns of shade that the trees made as they leaned out over the water, and listening air caught the sound of her "ouch!" when she stepped on a too-sharp rock. "Don't step there," she told nobody at all. "It hurts."

He saw the black, ropey movement of the snake as it came toward her in the water, and it didn't mean much to him. This was a creek; there were snakes, that was a fact of life; they weren't poisonous, and if you ignored them, they ignored you.

But apparently no one had ever told the little girl and her airy friend that much. The second she clapped eyes on it, she began to scream—and then she ran, splashing water high in the air, water that fell back on her in prismed droplets.

She couldn't have known that the ankle-deep creek just dropped away to nothing around that curve.

She went under like a rock; from high above her, he caught sight of her terrified, shocked face as the water sucked her down.

It took a minute for him to realize that she was fighting the water, that she couldn't swim. Everybody could swim, except the little girl.

Instinct pushed him. He leaped feet first into the waters after her, shouting, "Hey—hey—" as if she could answer his call from somewhere down there at the bottom of the blue hole.

She fought him as much as she fought the water; Colley

finally hit her across the cheek as they came up for the fourth time, and she opened her eyes wide to try to see him. Blue, or maybe purply blue orbs, as deep as wildflowers, watched him as he grabbed her around the waist from the back and yanked her toward the big rock at the creek's edge. She clutched at it frantically as he pulled away from her.

"You're okay," he gasped, swimming to the other side of the rock and levering himself up on it. "Here, grab my hand, and I'll pull you up."

Prying her fingers from the rock's edge wasn't easy; she kept making panicked, whimpering sounds. But he got her to safety without difficulty; working like a dog on the farm made him strong. Once on top of the rock with him, she rolled away into a tiny, shivering, miserable ball, watching him warily.

"You're not even choked," he offered admiringly. "You held your breath the whole time."

Now that she thought about it, Lainie discovered she was holding it again, and she released it in a puff.

"I was watching from that bluff," he offered in the stark silence, "and I saw you go under. You sure don't know anything about creeks. They get deep sometimes. This one finally goes into the quarry way down around the next bend. And I never saw anybody that couldn't swim."

Lainie looked at the creek at the edge of the rock and began to cry. "I want to go home," she said in tremulous belligerence.

"Okay," he said quickly. "Only, don't cry. Only babies cry. You're not a baby, are you?"

"No—but I still want to go ho-home," she wailed, hiccuping. A shiver started in her abdomen and fanned out, until she was shaking from head to toe, and big goose bumps stood out on her arms and legs.

He frowned at her. "Here, you better get out in the sunshine. You're about to freeze."

She didn't move.

"C'mon, I'll help you," he said at last, reaching out to take her arm.

She jerked away, then clutched the rock as she came too close to the water again. "I don't want you to. You—you hit me."

He looked at the circling red place on her cheek. "I'm sorry. Anyway, I had to. You kept hitting me, and all I was trying to do was get you out of the water."

Another shiver. "Aren't you cold?" she demanded, examining him in wonder. He was as skinny as a rail in his sopping wet, blue-jeans shorts; she could count all of his ribs under his sun-dark skin. And his black hair hung clear down his back, clinging to his shoulders.

"No, I'm never cold. But you are. You need the sun. Over there. Will you follow me if I show you a way out of this creek bed?"

Lainie considered the spot he'd indicated. It was another rock, but flat and smooth; it protruded from the steeply upward slope of the hillside just to the side of them. The sunlight blazed down on it, and daisies waved in the long grass around it.

"It looks like a throne," she observed with another chattering shake. But still she didn't move, her fingers trying to dig into the limestone beneath her.

"A throne?"

She relaxed a little. "Don't you know what that is? It's a fancy chair for magic things. Things like princesses and kings."

"It is," he said quickly. "A throne for—for witches. Good ones. And listen," he said persuasively, "if you'll go sit on that rock over yonder, I'll show you how to make a whistle. A magic one. It'll be the loudest one you've ever heard."

Lainie looked at him and wavered. "I'm not s'posed to talk to strangers."

"Well, what's your name?" he demanded.

"Elaina Marie Thorne."

"So now I know who you are and I know where you live, too," he said smugly. "You live at the big house on the hill up from the creek, the one with a big round porch with ceilings as blue as the sky. And sometimes, you sit in the big tree nearly at the bottom of the hill, close to the creek."

"How'd you know that?"

"I've seen you there. I live with Charley, on the other side of the creek," he plunged on, "so I reckon that means that we're not strangers anymore." Then he pointed out reasonably, "Anyhow, I yanked you out of the water. That ought to make us friends."

She looked up around them again, at the high bluffs beyond them on each side of the blue hole. "It's scary here. And there was a snake."

He said soothingly, "Nah, it's not really scary. Hey, listen, I've turned flips in the air off that bluff and gone under the water lots deeper than you did. You were making such a ruckus that you scared away that poor old snake and didn't go too far down."

"I didn't want to go down at all," Lainie objected. "I can't swim."

"I saw that right off," he told her humorously. "I guess you're mighty little to be swimming."

She stiffened immediately. "I'm eleven. I'm just small for my age. How old are you?"

That gave him pause, and he frowned, considering. "I'd say I was maybe fourteen."

She stared. "You don't know how old you are?"

"Well, not for dead sure. But River Charley knows, and I think that's what he says. He knows almost everything. He keeps trying to push all he knows into my head. He's making me work algebra and read the whole Bible this summer."

Lainie relaxed. She was pretty sure that Mama would approve of somebody who was reading the Bible cover to cover. "Mama calls me just Lainie," she offered.

"That's a good name," he answered. "Mine is—" He hesitated; he wasn't supposed to be down here, talking to this pampered little girl.

"Well?" she demanded. "What is it?"

"I can't tell you," he said slowly, thinking hard, "because if I did, I couldn't talk to you. I'm magic, too, and nobody can know the names of the—the people like me who live in the woods. If you was to call out my name by accident where bad people might hear it, then I'd just turn into nothing but smoke."

She drew in her breath and stared at him big-eyed. "I don't believe you," she whispered shakily. "That's a lie."

"Okay, it's a lie. Just don't get to crying again," he said hastily. "I told you, I wouldn't hurt you. I'll take you home to your mama and daddy. Okay?"

"You promise?"

"I swear it," he said solemnly. "Just wait and see." Quickly standing up, he said, "I'm gonna go sit on that big old rock. Since we're not strangers anymore, are you coming, too?"

Lainie straightened slowly. "Well . . . okay." She looked down at her cotton shorts and matching shirt. "I bet I'll get in trouble," she said dismally. "Mama was taking a nap, and I was supposed to be, too, but I went to my tree house, and when I saw the creek, I just meant to take a little walk in it. She'll be mad when she finds out that I fell in the water."

"If you dry off on the rock for a few minutes, she won't know," Colley said reasonably.

"Oh." That sounded reassuringly calm and very practical—not unnervingly supernatural at all. "You're smart," she said with a trace of admiration.

He flushed hot and red, the color running up under his brown skin and making his dark eyes glow. "No, I'm not. Charley says I can't sit still long enough to get book smart."

It was a short distance to the big rock, and Lainie plopped down on it thankfully. Then her thoughts returned to what the boy had said earlier.

"I want to see a magic whistle," she said slowly, not sure if she should bring up the subject of witches and smoke again.

"You can't see it," he explained patiently. "It's something you hear."

"Okay, I want to hear it."

"You'll have to close your eyes. Tight. Don't go peeping, now."

Lainie obediently scrunched up her eyes so tightly that she saw little yellow dots against the blackness. She felt the boy moving beside her.

"Now you can look," he whispered at last.

When she did, he was sitting beside her, his hands folded over each other. Holding her eyes with his, he slowly raised them to his mouth, pursing his lips against the heels of his thumbs, right where they pressed together. His cheeks puffed out, and he blew into his hands.

A shrill whistling noise came from his cupped palms. He made it once, twice, three times.

"I can do that," Lainie said promptly.

"Yeah? Let's see you," he challenged.

Putting her lips to her hands as he had, she puffed. Nothing. She tried again with the same dismal results.

"See?" He grinned at her frustrated face. "It's magic."

"Mama says that only Jesus is really magic," Lainie protested.

"I don't know about Jesus," Colley retorted, laughing. "But I'll give you a hint about how I make the whistle." He opened his hands. Inside his palm lay a thick, broad shaft of old fescue. He pulled in his breath dramatically. "Look, it's witch grass," he teased.

"It is not. It's just plain old green stuff. And I don't believe it's what made the whistle, anyway. When I get home, I'm gonna tell Mama what you said and—"

He stood up hastily. "Now you listen to me, Lainie. You can't be telling Thorne—or anybody—about me. I'd get in a lot of trouble. Hell, Charley would have my—"

She stood up, wide-eyed. "You swore."

Colley looked confused. "What? Oh, never mind, but you can't tell. If you do, I'll get into trouble. I couldn't come back. Anyway, so would you," he pointed out desperately. "You'd have to tell them you nearly drowned in Widow's Creek."

Lainie and he stared at each other while she pondered his words. They had the ring of reasonable truth. "I won't tell," she said slowly, and it might have been the first time she ever made a conscious decision to do what her parents were sure to object to.

"Good," he said, relaxing. "That's good, Lainie. Can't anybody else ever know about me, or see me, except you, no matter what happens."

Neither of them seemed to realize that there was an implicit understanding that they would meet again.

"C'mon, and I'll show you a short way to get back to your house." The boy started off down the field that lay just beyond the hot rock, his hair gleaming like black satin against the rich green of the tall sunlit grass. The light in the field danced around him for an instant, dazzling Lainie, making her blink her eyes.

"You know what?" she whispered. "I don't really believe

in magic. I"m too old. But I think maybe he could be a real witch."

Lainie moved to follow him, not even noticing that her invisible friend didn't answer. The princess couldn't; she was gone forever, drowned in the cold depths of Widow's Creek, done in by the warmth and brilliance of the witch boy.

The moon was vanishing just over the edge of the trees, that was how late it was.

Mama said sleepily, "If you're bound to make up another pretend friend, why couldn't it be somebody nice and calm?"

"But he's not pretend, Mama," Lainie protested from the pillow beside Deborah's. "Just like I told you. He can jump off bluffs into water, really deep water, and he can make grass whistle, and his hair is shiny black."

"Lord, it's no wonder you're waking the house up with bad dreams about water and snakes. You've got the wildest imagination of any little girl I've ever seen. Now go back to sleep. I'm here in your bed with you and it's past one o'clock in the morning."

"But the witch boy—"

"Honey, if you'll go to sleep, I'll make you a promise. I'll tolerate this witch boy of yours as long as he's not as spoiled rotten as that little princess is," Deborah said humorously, half asleep. "If he gets as high-handed as she does, like having to have her own place set at our supper table, I'm going to burn him at the stake. That's . . ." She paused to yawn. "That's what . . . they do . . . to witches. Burn them alive."

"Really? Or is that a story?" Lainie asked in quick, quiet alarm.

"You're the one with the stories. That's really the truth. . . ." Deborah's voice trailed off, and her eyes closed.

Lainie sat up very, very carefully, so she wouldn't wake her mother again, and looked out the window opposite. The steep slope of the land on that side made visible only the top of the tree where her tree house was. The leaves on it had been turned to silver by the stealthy moon.

"I won't tell anymore that you're real." She whispered the promise to the distant witch boy, and she kept it for three summers.

2

Lainie leaned her forehead against the old black screen that Dana had stepped through an hour earlier and looked out on the night sky. The rain that had hung over the Springs all day disappeared as quickly as Preston and Colley had vanished from the dining room, and now the night was clear and star-spangled.

The air that was pushing its way through the window screens of the kitchen was cooler than it had been, and the last of the cleaning was done.

She was tired; it was past time to go home.

Shutting the back doors, checking the front ones, she stopped long enough to gaze at the stupendous, bloodred moon that hung so low that it seemed to sit right down in the wine-dark waters of Widow's Creek as the stream bubbled its way through the shadowy yard of the hotel.

But Lainie had too much on her mind to do more than glance at the awesome globe.

The problem was, she was in over her head.

How much longer could she hold the Magnolia together? She couldn't tell Mama and Aunt Olivia how serious things were.

As if that weren't enough, Colley was back. How could she hold herself together?

And then there was Preston.

What in the world had she been thinking of to let herself be amused by him? To be flattered by his attention and attracted to his good looks?

She had known better than to let Mama know about their summer flirtation; at least she'd had that much sense.

But it had seemed harmless enough, just fun, the kind of fun she never got to have anymore until tonight.

Until his damned cousin had shown up.

And as she stood there at the open double front doors, frozen in her thoughts, she suddenly heard it—the creaking sound of someone stepping quietly up on the old wooden boards of the porch.

Her heart tripped.

Someone was carefully winding his way to the doors, moving through the row of rocking chairs. She couldn't tell herself that it was just the groaning of the ancient old hotel as it settled into its hundredth year. It was the sound of footsteps.

Nobody ever bothered things here, she reminded herself quietly. This was Indian Springs, after all, where people went to bed with the chickens.

Except tonight, Colley Rawlins was back in town.

She risked one squeaking movement of the screen to crane her head around its edge, trying to see who was coming; the bright red glow of the moon shone through the massive maple trees, lighting the uneven length of the porch.

She didn't see the figure distinctly, but she heard enough.

"'I come to the garden alone,'" the intruder was quietly humming.

"Mama!" Lainie sucked in a long sigh of relief, swung open the door, and tripped over an old rocking chair that some visitor tonight had left pulled out too close. It rocked vigorously, slamming into the wall behind itself.

"Good gracious, Lainie, did you hurt yourself?" Deborah Blackburn Thorne asked in concern as she came into full view.

"Yes, ma'am," Lainie returned with reluctance.

"What in the world are you doing here all alone, honey? I wouldn't have gone to church tonight if I'd known Dana couldn't have stayed late to help clean up."

"I told her she could go. I guess I just wanted to be alone for a while."

Deborah stopped just where the steps led down to the yard, one hand clutching the rickety old railing. For a minute she didn't say a thing. Instead, she just looked at the moonlit figure of her only child there in the middle of the long porch.

"I heard what happened," she said at last, quietly.

"You mean—"

"Colley's back. He came to the Magnolia." Deborah took a step toward Lainie until she stood in her own pool of moonlight, her face open and honest. Deborah Thorne was beautiful in spite of all that the years had done to her, beautiful in the way that the Madonna might have been, serene and perceptive. "Part of me wishes that it had happened tonight, this change I can feel in you, Lainie," Deborah said slowly. "Then I could blame it on Colley and understand it. But there's been something wrong with you all summer. You're too young to carry the kind of load that you're under, I know that much."

"I'm twenty-one, and getting older all the time," Lainie said flippantly. She hated the tone of her own voice, but she couldn't let Mama know what was really going on with her and with the Magnolia. Not yet. Not until she understood things herself and had found a way, any way, to solve the problems.

"You're not with Way, or with Dana much these days," Deborah persisted. "I don't know where you are half the time. What's wrong, Lainie?"

"Look, Mama, I'm old enough to choose my own friends and to live my own life without being policed. I know what I did three years ago; I'm doing my best to pay for it. But can't I—"

"Lainie, honey, I don't blame you for that," Mama protested, her voice rich with distress. "You don't have to—"

"Deborah, did you find her?" The strong, clear voice cut into the conversation between mother and daughter. It came from the yard.

Deborah moved down onto the first step. "She was just late locking up, Susan."

"That's good." Susan McAlester strode into the same spill of moonlight that the mother and daughter were bathed in. Her shadow fell behind her, and it was as long and broad-shouldered as a man's. She was six feet tall, built like a weathered Amazon.

Twenty-five years ago, after her husband died in an accident at the old quarry and she had no place to go, Susan had come to work at the Magnolia. Over the years she became a companion, someone to live with Aunt Olivia as she grew older.

Susan had no other family, so she made the Blackburns hers. There was little money to pay for her companionship anymore; now she gave it out of love, just as she lived with Olivia because the other woman's house was home to her.

"I'd better get back," she said.

Lainie followed Susan with her gaze as the woman turned. In the distance, a fence with a gate in it separated the grounds of the Magnolia from the yard of Aunt Olivia's two-story Victorian house.

Lainie knew it well; it was where she and Mama lived now, too, where they had lived since not long after Papa's death.

Another reason to keep working, to keep the Magnolia open—they were living in Aunt's house. They owed her.

"Aunt's still awake," Deborah said in dismay.

"I don't know that she's going to get any sleep at all tonight. She's asked me twice to go fetch her father, and I can't make the poor lady understand that Lansing Blackburn has been dead since Eisenhower was president." Susan added curiously, "What happened at the hotel tonight to get her so worked up?"

"Two of the—the customers had a fuss over nothing," Lainie finally answered as Deborah clung to the railing in worry.

"Oh." If Lainie had expected Susan to ask more questions, she hadn't counted on the older woman's worry about Olivia overriding all else. "I was thinking maybe I should call Dr. Maxwell tomorrow and drive over to his office to pick up some more of her medicine. I know you don't want me to—"

Deborah interrupted Susan's words quickly. "It's not that I mind you calling. It's just that I know what he'll do. He'll see her, and then pat me on the arm and tell me not to worry about the money, that such-and-such government program will pay for it. I was such a fool. I believed him for a while until I heard what his wife said when she brought some of her friends to the hotel for lunch one day. There's no such programs; he sees her out of charity because she's such a 'dear old lady—a part of the local color.'"

Susan snorted. "You let me handle Dora Maxwell. I'll show her friends some of the local color that's related to her, those crazy Lettisons that live up the holler. First cousins to the old biddy, every one of them."

Deborah leaned over the rail a little more, her voice hushed, as though she didn't want even the night wind to hear her next words. "I'm afraid, too, that he'll tell me again that maybe we need to consider the old folks' home down the road."

"Don't you worry about that. I'm not letting them take Miss Livy anywhere. She'd die away from the Magnolia. That's what I'm here for, to make sure she stays right where she wants to be. I'll have a talk with Dr. Maxwell. He can be trusted."

Lainie thought for just one bitter moment that it was true. He knew too much and didn't tell any of it. A man of discretion.

"I won't let his wife bother me," Susan concluded. "I'm tougher skinned than you are. You come on home, now. It's late. You, too, Lainie."

The woman faded back into the trees and headed across the little footbridge that led to Aunt Olivia's house, glowing like a lustrous pearl in the misty, moonlit setting of the shadowy field beside the Magnolia.

There was a long pause, and a sudden light breeze carried on it the dewy wetness of the night and the heavy smell of late honeysuckle. Deborah sucked in the bosky sweetness and murmured, "Lord, on a night like this one, I dread getting old."

Lainie took a step away, and her mother spoke quietly, without turning from the sight of the moon and the earthy smell of the flowers. "Elaina, you're young. Pretty as a picture. You've got a right to enjoy it. I don't want to hear any more talk about what happened in the past. Put it behind you, just like you have Colley. Don't let him tear you up again. I know there's more bothering you. Maybe you can't tell me because you think I wouldn't understand. You could be right. Sometimes I think the world passed me by here in the Springs. But one thing never changes: God's watching. You be careful."

Deborah turned, looked her daughter over one last time, and reached for the shaky stair rail. "Come on home as soon as you get things locked up. I'll leave you alone, like you wanted."

Lainie watched her mother follow Susan into the dark midnight.

God's watching.

Once she had even found comfort in her mother's favorite phrase, but that had been when she was little, when it was easy to believe. Then her life had been full of sultry Saturday nights when friends and neighbors and relatives had flocked around the front yard of the Magnolia to eat watermelon and talk and smoke. In those days, there had been laughter and hope.

She could wade into the forbidden reaches of Widow's Creek itself . . . because then she hadn't known that there were some things and some people that even God couldn't protect her from.

Like Colley and Albert.

No. She wouldn't think like this. Like Deborah said, the world was passing her by. She was just sitting, watching the people around her go their own way, never thinking once that she was here. Here, at the Magnolia, where time had stopped.

Pulling herself off the wall, Lainie finished shutting the doors and turning off the lights until only one was left. A single lamp burned on the top of an antique cherry table with spindle legs that stood beside the stairs, and she ran through its dim yellow light on her way out the front parlor. Shutting the door, she let the screaky screen bang shut behind her, and the cool night air rushed against her face.

The monstrous moon in front of her seemed to dance on the grass just at the dark edge of the trees between the Magnolia and Olivia's house, catching the tall silhouette of the person who stood there, waiting.

Why were they hovering over her like a bunch of hens tonight? she wondered in quick irritation.

"I'm coming, Su—"

And then the figure moved, and the moonlight fell full on his face. *His* face.

"Oh! Oh, God," she gasped in shock as the long, cool shadow completely enveloped her.

"Not quite God," Colley answered, his voice smoky and dry. "But I've wished I was an awful lot of times, girl, especially where you're concerned. Don't scream."

"I'm not going to," Lainie said unsteadily, but she took a step away from him.

"Don't run, either," he said quietly.

"I wouldn't run, not from you," she denied, and this time she managed to make her voice cool and calm. "You just took me by surprise, that's all." And that was nothing but a lie. Ever since he'd walked out of the hotel an hour or two earlier, she'd known he would show up somewhere.

This meeting was the reason she'd been hanging around the place.

"Tell the truth, Elaina Marie," he said quietly, and she thought for a crazy minute he'd read her mind, "You've been running from me for years now."

"I don't know what you're talking about."

"It started after your father died."

Her heart bumped along the floor of her chest and she moved to jerk away, but he was too quick. His hands caught hers, as quick as lightning, and they burned her with their touch.

Lainie went still.

"I said I wouldn't scream, but if you try to talk to me about that day, about what happened—if you try to explain what you did, I'll wake the dead with screaming," she said fiercely. "I was there. I won't relive it."

"I could stop your screaming," he said without a flicker of emotion.

Her heart skidded into her throat.

He can't scare me, she told herself resolutely; I remember when he was nothing but a ragged kid with scratches down his cheeks and blackberry juice staining his mouth.

"If this is all you have to say, leave me alone, Colley. It might be me instead of Dana calling the police. Way's still on duty," she said flatly.

"And your good cousin would come rushing to your rescue again. Is that what you're trying to tell me?" Colley asked dryly.

"Don't worry. He wouldn't hurt you much. That rich old man you call your grandfather would save you before too much happened. Just like he did the last time."

"I thought you didn't want to talk about it."

She didn't. All she wanted to do was cry. "I'm sorry," she said, choking on the words. "Let me go."

He dropped her hands and she drew a quick, relieved gulp of freedom.

"No, don't leave yet."

"Then walk to the creek," she whispered, "where the moonlight is brighter." If he took that as an admission of fear, then so be it.

But he only nodded and did as she asked.

At the edge of the water, when he turned toward her, the rays of the big moon glittered off the silver at his throat. He still had on the whistle.

"Why are you wearing that thing?" she asked flatly, nodding at it.

His hand went up to find it. "Maybe I'm remembering a little girl who gave it to me to show that we'd be friends forever. Except forever didn't last very long, did it, Lainie?"

"That's the past, too, Colley. I won't let you make me remember the way you used to be. Not now."

But he frowned. "Don't get so high-handed, baby. Maybe you know a lot about me, but I can return the favor." His voice changed and filled with amusement. "I can remember when you ran screaming from a crawdad and I had to catch you by grabbing your ponytail. Then you kicked my shin for pulling your hair. Lord, you could be wild as a mink sometimes."

Heat flushed through her, as well as a dangerous, answering flicker of laughter.

NO.

She couldn't laugh with him anymore. This was Colley.

"Where's your girlfriend?" she demanded, and the question was more to stop herself than it was to stop him.

Colley leaned a little from her, bracing himself against the edge of the wooden bridge across the creek.

"Rachel? She's staying with friends in Cookeville. I guess that's where she is."

"Is that where you took her in your Porsche?"

He laughed. "Can you really see me in a Porsche? It's hers. She picked me up in it, we went out for a while, she dropped me off at the house, and she left. I came here in my truck, but I was smart enough to park it down the road at the swimming pool and walk up here. Wouldn't want Way to see me harassing you."

"Your girlfriend . . . is she the one who dresses you now?" She couldn't stop herself from glancing down him. He'd abandoned the coat. The T-shirt clung to him across the shoulders, and in the moonlight, its rich brown color blended with his skin so well that it made him look almost naked from the waist up.

Colley considered her words, reaching behind himself to hold the rail. The play of his muscles beneath the cotton fabric revealed his movement clearly. "You don't like the way I look?"

Lainie glanced away and shrugged.

"Maybe you liked it better when I wore overalls two sizes too big and no shoes. When the town called me shantytown trash," he said stoically.

Lainie felt her own heart clutch. "Colley, don't."

"Don't what? Don't remember?"

"No. People always remember. But at least you can recall the good things, too." She smiled suddenly. "I wanted to look like you. I've got a few memories of my own. I once tried to get Mama to buy me overalls like yours, but I didn't like the ones she got me. They weren't cut off at the knees for the summer, and she wouldn't let me go without a shirt like you always did."

He relaxed just a little. "Thank God. I couldn't have stood it."

Lainie flushed. "I was eleven or twelve," she protested.

"And already running with a river boy," he said, only half joking.

She had to do something. She couldn't let herself remember how it felt to talk to him, how much pleasure there was in his teasing directness. *Think about who this is,* she commanded herself, *and what he did.* Her voice sharpened. "Is that what you came to tell me tonight? Is that why you were at the Magnolia?"

Colley went still, registering the change in her, and his answer was slow and terse. "I came because of Preston and his pilfering hands. What I want to know is, what in the hell was he doing sitting pretty as you please in your dining room? Your whole family bans me, but he can come when he wants?" There was no laughter in his words now.

Dangerous ground. This was very tricky.

But her voice was scornful and careless when she answered. "Your cousin? What are you asking me about him for? How would I know why he showed up here tonight? He never has before. I don't want him near the place." And that was pure truth. "Go find him if you're looking for another family conversation."

She turned away, and when she did, he caught her arm and she stumbled right into him. She heard the hiss of his in-drawn breath.

One sound, and panic flooded through her in a wild rush. She tried to turn into him, to brace herself against his hard frame enough to push a long way away, but when she did, that smell of sunshine and spice that was peculiar only to him—that scent that she'd practically grown up with—completely surrounded her and panicked her even more.

"Turn loose of me, Colley. Now," she demanded shakily, snatching her palm from his warm midriff.

"I don't think so," he whispered, his voice husky, and with his other hand he forced her completely around so that her back pressed his chest behind her. The movement took her by surprise. "You can just be quiet a minute."

His fingers above her elbow were steel; so was the arm he wrapped around her waist so tightly that she could barely breathe. She knew from childhood the futility of trying to escape his grasp, so she hung between his hands for a moment, a pinned butterfly with him at her back. He didn't make a single move to do more, but she felt the wanting in him as if he'd spoken it.

"There was a time," he whispered raggedly, "when I would've killed to stand here like this, to touch you like . . . like this." The arm rose suddenly, brushing her abdomen, and he let his hand cup under her left breast. "And there was a time when you wanted me to touch you. When you met me yonder, at that old stone cellar, and I touched you here . . . and here . . ."

"Colley . . ." Wherever his hand pressed burned like fire. "Remember—"

The other woman. Rachel, that was her name. But Lainie couldn't make her lips speak the word, and Colley came up with his own.

"John Thorne? It was an accident, Lainie. No, don't fight me. I won't say anymore. I'm not going to beg you again to listen to me. I know it's pointless. Just don't think I ever forget him. I don't. I live with it every day."

He turned her toward him, and the light fell on his renegade's face. The moon was turning to a hot gold now; it traced the delicate white-on-white stitchery that ran along the front bodice of her white shirt as well as the sun might have as she twisted unsteadily in his grasp. But it was better to look right at him. He was too dangerous to have at her back.

"Devil sent for me to come home, Lainie."

"So? He always does when he needs something done. Do you like being Albert Rawlins's hit man, Colley? That's what people around here call you." Hurt him. Hurt him enough, and she would make a clean getaway.

"They've called me a hell of a lot worse," he said dispassionately. "And it never damaged me. But this time, when he wanted me in the Springs, it wasn't like all the other times. He means for me to stay, and I'm planning on it. Do you know how that's different? In the past, he sent me back to Kentucky whenever he got afraid I would notice you again."

Dark richness rolled up inside her—glad, so glad that she still mattered to him—and on its heels came sickness, because the gladness had to die. She couldn't feel it.

"It's too bad that he didn't understand that it was really over. Nothing can ever put us back together," she whispered harshly.

Colley just looked at her a minute. It was strange how his eyes could be so dark and still give his face so much life, so much emotion. In the unbearable silence, she could barely stand to hold his gaze, and her heart was vibrating, taking her breath.

"So what's changed, Lainie?" he murmured at last. "What have you done that's set you so far out of my reach that Devil's not afraid anymore?"

She stared up at him, honest bewilderment in her face. "I don't know what you're talking about. Maybe it's something *you've* done."

Like found another woman, she wanted to blurt out.

He frowned, searching her face again, and still discovered nothing.

A sly, quiet spider might have been at work while they stood there in that taut embrace, because tiny gossamer threads of emotion had woven themselves around them. They were shimmering along her arms, pulling her closer, closer, closer to his sweet, sweet mouth.

His face bent over hers. When his head blocked the moon, when darkness touched her skin, she broke the threads in a sudden violent motion.

Lainie shoved him as hard as she could.

Caught off balance, he stumbled against the bridge, slipped, and sat down right in the cold waters of Widow's Creek.

Colley swore in shock, and Lainie took a quick three steps back, afraid of his reaction. For a long moment, they just stared at each other, and then she couldn't help herself.

She laughed.

Teach him to dress like that Rachel woman's uptown lover boy. She was glad she'd messed up his fancy outfit.

"I told you I didn't like your clothes," she said on a gurgle of laughter.

His face relaxed. He gave a huff of sound that might have been an answering laugh and pushed himself upright until he stood dripping in the middle of the stream.

"If you don't like Rachel's taste in clothes," he said mildly, "then maybe you should dress me."

The idea made her still and mute as he took two or three squishy steps toward the bank.

"No?" he questioned, pausing just below her, just out of her reach. "We'll let the idea go for a while. But I've got one or two more things to say, Lainie Thorne, wet or dry. I'm back. I'm not going to sneak around just so you don't have to look at me, the way I did right after Thorne died. I'm not going to drive clear around town to avoid coming near the Magnolia. It's an open business, and I'll come when I damn well please, just like I did tonight. When I meet you on the street, I'm not going to hang my head in shame. Now, if you can stop yourself from spitting at me every time we're near, we might get by in the Springs without stirring up old gossip."

He shook both his arms and water spattered on her face. She turned her head and he took another step nearer.

"I want a life, Lainie, and a woman to love me."

"You're going to marry her." She forced her numb lips to speak the terrible truth.

"What I'm going to do is—" Quick as a cat, before she

could move, he had her by the arms again, yanking her inexorably right down into the shimmering dark creek.

Lainie realized too late what his intention was. "No! No, Colley!"

But he sat her down hard in the water, right in the very spot where she'd pushed him. It was icy cold, fresh out of some underground spring that had its origin near the old quarry.

"Oh! You—you—"

She couldn't think at all of what to say. He was too near, too quick, too unpredictable.

"Try 'uncivilized savage,'" he advised. "It's what your daddy used to call me. You've called me worse, but I reckon it'll still do in a pinch."

Colley's face wore the oddest mixture of humor and sadness that she'd ever seen as he gazed at her sitting up to her waist in the foaming creek.

Then he turned his back on her impotent fury, and his long, lean shadow followed him as he crossed the bridge to the highway and walked down it, vanishing into the glowing, red-gold moon.

When the moon glowed golden red and nearly touched the earth for night after night, Colley knew that two things were sure: the tobacco was almost ready, and Lainie would go to school.

It was September, and come that month, she always did.

Colley stared at the empty backyard and the lonely looking house through the bright leaves of the maples and the oaks and missed her. He had come to the foot of the hill twice more since he'd pulled her from the water, and he'd found her at the tree house, willing to sneak down to the shelter of the trees over the creek and splash in it with him, hidden from the world.

The season was over. The tobacco in the rows that wrapped around and around the knob of land at the back of the ridgetop was due to be cut. There would be no excuse for him to come back to the circling field again for a while.

At night he lay on the low, hard cot in the little house at the head of the hollow and tried to imagine school. He pestered Charley with a thousand questions—Why didn't he go? Why couldn't he?—until at last Charley told him flatly, "If you're so eager to do more schoolwork, we'll put you at it with geometry."

He liked geometry better than reading the Book of Job, but it was no answer and they both knew it. Finally, Charley became aggravated with the questions. "Ask Devil," he said to Colley harshly, and that quieted him.

It had not been but two weeks since he'd had a big lesson in why he should fear the old man. On that day, he'd seen just what Devil could do when somebody displeased him.

He had come to the shantytown in his boots and overalls, his cap pulled low over his eyes, with a big black whip curled around his hand. He rode in the Jeep with John Thorne, whose face was hard. "Garner was the one I sent to paint the room, Mr. Rawlins. I promised him extra pay for the job. I thought I had picked the best of the lot to go in your home, but with this kind of people, there is no best."

Rawlins climbed awkwardly out of the vehicle and went straight to one of the shacks. It was suppertime, and a crowd of quiet, frightened farm workers hovered behind him as he threw open the wooden door.

"Garner," he said, his voice deadly.

From inside, the man's wife began to cry and scream. "He's sick. He didn't do nothin.' Oh, please, oh, please, Mr. Rawlins."

"You, Garner, you gonna hide behind her like a yellow coward and make me have to drag you out in this yard?"

Devil took a backward step off the porch and out into the yard himself when Garner appeared at last in the doorway, his hands shaking as he grasped the frame on either side of himself. "I ain't done nothin', Mr. Rawlins," he whined, but his face was pasty white.

"You stole my dead wife's diamond necklace, Garner. I don't put much store in shiny stones myself, but she sure did love that pretty piece when she was alive. I want it back." He ran the whip through his hands caressingly.

"You know ever'thin', I reckon," Garner said, and tried to smile. "But this time—"

The whip flashed with a deadly hiss, so quick that Colley, who stood well back and nearly hidden from the shanty people, sensed it more than saw it.

A vicious red stain appeared miraculously across the front of the man's dirty shirt, and he began to cry, clutching at his chest.

"I ain't done nothin', I swear it before—"

Crack! Another stripe appeared, and a woman near Colley began to scream.

The third blow knocked Garner to his knees and bloodied his chin as well, and suddenly his wife flew from the porch, throwing a tiny black velvet bag at Devil. "For mercy's sake, here's the necklace. Take it. Take it and be finished with him," she cried.

Devil dropped the whip to his side, his face as still as if he'd done nothing at all. "Hand it to me," he told the moaning man on the ground in front of him. Garner fumbled painfully at the other man's feet, finally shoving the bag into his outstretched hands.

"This is mine," he told the frightened gathering of people, raising it above his head like a trophy. "I pay you for what is yours. Garner took what never was his. That makes him a thief. You keep your hands off mine."

He limped back through the thundering silence to the Jeep, and his baggy overalls might have been a robe. Just before he pulled away, his eyes fell on Colley there by the trees, and for a minute, they studied each other. Then Colley ducked away in fright. The two men drove right past him, Thorne's face set and blank, and Colley ran out to stare after the rumbling vehicle.

He was still staring when the first rock hit him right between the shoulder blades. It was one of Garner's boys, and Colley flipped around with a surprised grunt to face him. "Get your damn face outta here," the boy snarled. "Go back to that crazy old man."

Colley didn't know what they were so angry with him for, but it was in all their eyes, from the adults to the smallest child. It intimidated him enough that he turned to leave, but the Garner boy suddenly made a sound, as if he couldn't stand things anymore, and jumped Colley from the behind.

It was a furious, hard, vicious fight, and neither one of them followed any rules. They rolled and grunted and bit and kicked, and when it was over, Colley held the other's face into the hard dirt, one bloody hand in the boy's dirty hair, the other one pinching his neck down unmercifully while Colley straddled his kidneys. "I'll beat—the shit—out of you," he panted, blood dripping from his nose onto the other's torn shirt, "if you ever rock me—from the back again. I ain't done nothin' to you."

He had become oblivious to the crowd around him until now, when two or three of them began to move forward, and he looked up to see them advancing on him.

He scrambled to his feet, leaving the sobbing boy on the ground, ready to die right there.

"Leave him," cried Garner's wife. "You ain't goin' to get nothin' out of beatin' the kid up, except more trouble. He's the old man's property, too, and you heard him lay down his almighty rules about what's his. You'll be here on the ground with my man and my poor boy if you hurt that one."

As they hesitated, Colley looked at her through his own sweat and blood, meaning to show gratitude, but she pulled her dress away from him, turned her back, and spoke. "Somebody help me get these two here that the Rawlinses have near killed inside."

They left Colley to turn and stumble home.

Halfway there, just as he hit the creek to wade across it, he heard the voice calling him.

"You, boy."

Devil waited for him, right down below, standing in the gently swirling mist that fell over the wide creek with the coming of nearly every dusk. Thorne had stopped the Jeep, and now he stood just beside it up the hill. Colley stopped, his heart pounding, not because of the overseer but because of the old man.

"Yes, sir?" The cool mist caressed his cheeks, its smoky fingers leaving tiny trails of dampness on his skin.

"You tell Charley to go check on Garner. Make sure he lives, even if he is a piece of slime," Devil said shortly.

"I'll tell him."

He meant to make his escape then, but Devil suddenly took several steps, until he was standing right in front of Colley, and grasped his thin shoulder. Colley felt his heart thump madly, but he forced himself to look right up into the old man's face under his cap brim. He'd never been so close to the Devil before.

"That kid beat you up pretty damn good," the man observed.

Up on the slight rise, Thorne snorted. "This little wretch fights like a crazed animal. He should have his hide tanned for beating that other one's face in the ground."

"You, Thorne, take the Jeep and go on up the road a piece," Devil said slowly. "I'll follow on foot in a minute."

"You better watch him like a hawk, Mr. Rawlins," Thorne called back as he pulled away.

"That boy hit me in the back with a rock and I don't know why," Colley burst out in frustration. "That's why I went after him."

"You don't need to know why. You saw what had to be done, and you did it, all on your own. Ain't nothin' fancy about the way you fight—you mean to win, and that's all there is to it. That's good. I reckon you'd have took on the rest of 'em if Garner's woman hadn't found some common sense."

"You saw," Colley realized.

"I knew they'd have to take it out on somebody, and you looked real handy. So I parked the truck and walked back just to see if they were as low-down as I thought they were. Not to help you, though."

"You ain't heered me askin' you for no help," Colley returned shortly.

The old man's hard hand moved up and caught him by the chin this time. "You know better than to talk like a shantytown brat," he said harshly. "Say it right."

Colley swallowed, and from somewhere inside him, defiance rose. "What's it to you how I sound? I'll talk the way I want."

"Then I'll take it out on Charley," Devil said with a shrug, letting his hand drop. "He's the one who's teachin' you, and if he ain't doin' no better than this, maybe he needs a taste of what Garner got."

Colley stared, wide eyed, his throat closing up. "No—no,

wait. I can—I can say it right," he implored quickly, grabbing at Devil's arm.

"So let's hear you."

"I said, you ain't—didn't—hear me askin' you for help," he stumbled.

Devil nodded. "That's better. What's that god-awful name you took to callin' yourself? Colley?"

"It's what Charley calls me. It's my name."

"It makes no difference to me what you're called. They call me Devil, and I earned it. Not because I do evil to 'em, but because I'm just. Justice is a strange thing. Ever'body says they want it until it gets handed out. Then what they really want is mercy. Nobody's ever been too merciful to me, but I can say that I'm just to them. What I did to Garner was justice. He's a thief and always has been, but they won't tell that around the farm; they'll just tell I beat him, like they'll say that you beat up his kid. Somewhere, that rock will get left out of the story. So you let 'em tell what they will and then wish 'em to hell. Just remember: the Garner woman was right. I protect what's mine, and you're mine."

It was a long, lonely winter, because Colley made it that way.

He thought about what happened, and he thought about what the shantytown people had done. Most of them left the farm not long after the incident, the same way they did every winter. Nobody knew where they went, but they would come back to Rawlins Farm next spring, looking for work. Colley stayed away from everybody who remained, even Charley's lone friend, Nadine, and he didn't go to the creek once to look up at the big house.

Charley, sensing that something was wrong, gave Colley

enough work to keep him occupied. He fed the animals, he cut firewood, he stripped tobacco and cleaned out the barns. Inside the shack at night, Charley's old transistor radio crackled with the blues. He listened to a little station out of Tompkinsville, Kentucky, called WBLU. He'd sit beside the popping fire with his ear bent to the tiny speaker and chew on his worn pipe, holding it in his one hand, sometimes humming with B. B. King.

Often as not, he'd have a coughing fit and finally put down the pipe in disgust. "Can't even enjoy a smoke anymore," he'd fuss.

And then in a moment, he'd turn to Colley, sprawled out on the floor with the book that Charley had forced into his hands when supper was done. That winter, besides the geometry, Colley read history, tons and tons of it out of books that mysteriously turned up in Charley's possession.

Charlie would ask, "What's the Sphinx?" or "Who's Henry VIII?" or "What happened at the Alamo?"

And Colley would answer, based on what he'd been studying. If the answer to whatever single question that Charley asked was correct, then Colley went on with the reading. If it wasn't, then he had to read out loud to Charley the whole passage that he'd just read silently.

When spring came, when he figured he had to be at least fifteen, he finally got up the courage to ask Charley one question: "Is Devil my father?"

It was hard to say the words because they admitted a pitiful truth: he did not know the first fact about his own identity. The only thing he sensed was that his life was somehow tied up with the white-haired Rawlins. But it wasn't in the way he'd thought, even dreaded, because Charley hesitated, then answered his question with such finality that the listening boy knew it was the truth, "No, he's not."

Colley concluded that he was lost, alone, connected to nobody, and the coldness around him deepened.

As soon as he went to the distant circling field high on the back of the ridge to prepare it for the coming season's tobacco crop, the darkness of the winter began to fall away. The pungent, piercing smell of new grass, the sun caressingly warm on his face, the sound of a mockingbird ringing across the clear, dewy morning sky—those vanquished the chill.

And with the warmth, Colley had one desperate need: to see the little girl.

She could make the world right.

He left the field late one May day when the sun was burning hot on his back, bare beneath the ragged overalls. His sweat, as well as that of the two mules that he worked the hillside with, had dropped onto the clods of dirt turned up by his plow, staining the ground darkly.

Colley told himself that he would just go take a dip in the creek, but before he could even get close to the blue hole, he found himself at the foot of the hill standing barefoot in the ankle-deep icy water, looking up at the house.

She was there, and today she looked her age—twelve years old. Grown taller now, with all her rich dark hair cropped close to her face.

He just watched her standing high in the air on the platform in the tree until she turned and saw him down below.

For a minute, she didn't move.

Then her face twisted, and she began to cry, hard sobs that he could hear even down at the creek, sobs that went on as she clambered down the ladder awkwardly, hanging her blue jeans on a nail as she descended.

Straight as an arrow she ran to him, splashing into the creek and into his body, pressing her wet face right to his sweaty, dirty throat.

"Witch boy," she panted, hugging him with her still-skinny little-girl arms while the words spilled on and on like her tears, "I thought maybe you really were just in my head, like the princess used to be, and that you'd gone somewhere, like a dream does, and I couldn't dream you back. Then I knew that was silly, because I touched you, and saw you in the daylight. And I hung a present for you on the tree house at Christmas. I left it there for three months, and you never came, so then I thought, if he's real, he could die. I got afraid that you were dead."

Colley laughed, and the laughter came right out of his soul. Warm, bubbling, happy. He had stepped into the sunny places again.

Wrapping both of his arms around her waist, he hugged her so tightly that he wondered if he'd cracked her bones.

Then he let her go, pushing her away from him.

"You're gonna get dirty," he explained, only to catch her wrist. "Wait a minute, here, let me look at you. What'd you do to your hair?"

"I cut it," she said with a trace of defiance. "Dana had hers cut, and I wanted mine short, too, only Papa wouldn't let me, so I did it myself. Don't you fuss about it, either, cause they've already told me I look like a scarecrow."

He reached out and pulled one of the short curls over her ear. "Nah, you don't look like a scarecrow. It's not that bad," he teased.

She laughed and grabbed a handful of his own mane. "You've still got enough for both of us."

"Charley hates cutting hair, and Nadine says I wiggle too much, so, she just cuts it off straight once in a while and then leaves me alone."

"I never saw any boy with hair like yours," Lainie said.

"If you don't like it, I could . . . I could maybe sit still long enough for Nadine to—"

"No," she answered instantly, standing with it wrapped and tangled around her hand, like a rope binding her to him. "It's the way a witch boy is supposed to look."

"I told you that was a story. I even told you my real name."

"Colley," she said promptly, but added in mischief, "the witch boy." Then Lainie took a deep breath. "You're not going away again after today, are you? You will come back soon, won't you?"

"I reckon I'll hang around for a while this time," he said simply, and inside him, the warmth rolled like a strong tide.

This little girl wanted him to stay. She liked him.

3

The Magnolia had two gravel parking lots.

One of them lay to the front and to the right of the hotel. It was the largest, the one most people used.

The other was smaller and to the back, heavily overhung with shadowy oaks. It could be reached only from a side entrance.

Lansing Blackburn used to call it the "private" area. People who didn't want to advertise their presence at the Magnolia always used the back lot. Lansing hadn't approved of their doings and had not been above stopping what he considered illicit activities, even delivering a strong moral lecture if he felt it necessary, but he'd been forced to let some things slide. He was running a hotel, not a church, he told the townspeople.

The only scandal that ever marred the hotel's history had happened in that back lot in the fifties when Mayor Buford Potter had parked his Studebaker there and gone to one of the rooms with a girl from a traveling circus. Lansing caught the two of them and ousted them in the nick of time, just as Mrs. Potter was pulling in the front. She found the Studebaker and shot it up with her husband's own pistol, but at least the hotel as well as Mayor Potter had been spared a few bullet holes.

On this bright, sunny morning, Lainie got up early enough to be a party to one of those secret rendezvous in the back lot.

It wasn't that she awoke so easily; it was that she hadn't really slept, tossing and turning, trying to shake the misery of the night before.

She stood on the front steps of Aunt Olivia's house and looked out on the freshly washed face of the morning.

So Colley was back. She had discovered that fact and was still alive. Life would go on.

And she wouldn't think at all about Rachel, or about how her own heart felt as if it had finally come to a resting place when she'd faced the youngest of the Rawlinses the previous night.

Lainie focused determinedly on the Magnolia as she crossed the yard to it.

The place was too old and too rustic to do much as a hotel anymore. Even sitting serenely in the middle of its huge, shady lawn just off the two-lane highway that was the main road through town, the long, white, two-story clapboard building looked a little rickety.

It had been there a hundred years, after all. Back in the early days of the century, the little town of Indian Springs had been a fancy resort, known for the mineral water that bubbled rich and sometimes sulfuric up to the ground surface.

In those days, the Magnolia had been the crown jewel of Logan County.

It was famous for its E shape, where the two end wings

held elaborate hotel rooms and the shorter middle one contained the stately dining hall, with Lansing Blackburn's office on the second floor above it.

It and the town had been showplaces.

But now the Springs was small, rural, and forgotten back there in the hills, seventy miles from the nearest shopping center or city, and the people who spent the night in one of the Magnolia's old rooms were either quixotic fools or tourists, or, as Aunt Olivia used to say acidly, "one and the same." They came usually because they'd gotten lost off the beaten path between Louisville and Nashville, and most of the time, the Magnolia supplied them with all the local color they could stand.

But this morning, one of them was waiting in a car in the infamous back lot.

Lainie spotted the unfamiliar green Toyota as soon as she circled to the back door to open the kitchen and get ready for breakfast. It wasn't quite six A.M., and breakfast wasn't served in the dining room until seven thirty.

Who was sitting there, waiting?

Hesitantly, she looked the car over again. Then the driver's door opened, and a tall man with shining golden hair climbed out.

Preston.

Lord, what was Preston Rawlins doing here at this time of the morning? What was he doing at the Magnolia at all? She'd told him over and over not to come.

"I know what you're going to say," he was already beginning as she broke into a run toward him. "What am I doing here. But I can explain, Lainie."

"Oh, can you?" she said wryly. "Well, let's hear it. This should be good."

"It's about last night," he said with a half laugh, squinting down at her in the morning sun. For just a moment, he appeared distracted, letting his hand reach up to brush the dark curls back from her cheeks. "Damn, you're beautiful."

"So are you," she said frankly, and she meant it.

There ought to be a law against men who looked as good as Preston Rawlins, she thought fleetingly, some statute that said if they were too dazzling, too perfect, if their eyes were too blue and long-lashed, if their hair waved like thick, golden wheat back from their ears, if their noses had just the tiniest, most masculine bump in them that roughed up their looks just enough to keep them from being pretty—well, a man like that ought to be locked up for the safety of women everywhere.

In which case, Preston would be doing life, and that would be a shame, because sometimes, he could make her laugh.

But not like Colley.

"What about last night?" She remembered suddenly why he was here.

"I'm sorry, that's what," he said ruefully. "I made a fool of myself all because I was trying to get next to Colley. God, I hate that bastard. I didn't think he'd find out about me taking the whistle—which I did just to make him squirm—until this morning. I didn't mean to bring him or a fight right to the Magnolia, Lainie."

A petty, little-boy thing to do, she thought sharply, but she didn't say it. Who was she to find fault with Preston?

"You weren't supposed to bring yourself here, either," she reminded him instead.

He let his hand drop from her cheek and stiffened. "And I found out why last night, didn't I?"

"That comment's about Colley, too, isn't it?" she said in resignation.

"Why didn't you tell me there was a past between the two of you? You said there was some kind of feud between your family and mine. Quaint, to be sure," he drawled with a touch of angry hauteur. "And I was fool enough to believe you."

"I don't think there's any love lost," she returned, hunting for an answer.

"Except maybe between you and Colley."

An early rain crow called somewhere above their heads in one of the trees as they confronted each other.

"That's in the past," she said quietly. "And it's over, for good. Not that I owe you any explanations, Preston."

"I've been sneaking around to see you for the last four weeks. What do you think I'm hanging around this hole in the road for?" he demanded in frustration. "I hate little towns. I hate farms. I don't get along with the old man. I'm here just to satisfy Dad, to keep Grandfather reminded that he's got more family than Colley."

"Why does that matter?"

Preston raised his eyebrows and said in resignation, "You want the sordid truth? Dad thinks Grandfather's about to leave his fortune to the savage. I don't give a damn. My mother's father left me all he had."

"You're a lucky one, aren't you?" Lainie said, only half joking.

"At least I don't have to kiss up to anybody. I've had to watch my father do it, and it's not a pretty sight. He's paranoid about money. I've told him, nobody with a grain of sense would leave millions of dollars to somebody like Colley, not even Grandfather."

Lainie laughed a little. "That's funny, the shantytown boy, turning out to be richer that anybody in town."

Preston frowned. "Don't count on it. I'm here to stop it and give poor old Dad peace of mind. Nothing could keep me here this long, though, if I hadn't met you. So if you're that important to me, you tell me why it's not my concern that you once ran around with him?" he demanded, returning to his original complaint.

"You and me, we met by accident. We've had fun. It wasn't meant to be serious," she tried to protest.

She hadn't even realized his identity the first time or two she met him. He didn't look anything like the two members of his family she knew. If she had recognized him from the beginning, she never would have spoken to him and started this summer fling.

She'd thought that he was different from the other men of the Springs, and she'd been flattered by the way he took one look at her and came after her with single-minded determination.

"You think it was an accident? Angel, I saw you in town the first day, and when I realized that it was you with a flat tire out on the Gainesboro highway two afternoons later, I stopped so fast I nearly went through my windshield."

"The next thing you know, you'll be saying you let the air out of my tire," she derided.

"Maybe I did," he retorted. "But hell, I took you where you needed to go, didn't I? In my Jag, too."

"Speaking of which, where is your car?" She knew the silver Jaguar by sight; it had become a fixture in town lately, something that every man under fifty admired.

"I may have temporarily lost my mind over you last night, but I'm under control this morning. I couldn't go to the farm after that round with Colley, so I spent the night on Lloyd's houseboat down on the lake. This—this clunker"—Preston thumped the door of the Toyota with distaste—"is a car he rented for the summer, while he's vacationing. I thought it'd be less conspicuous. That seems to be the only way you want me to be."

The challenge in his words made the blood rise in her face.

"You ain't doin' this man right, angel," Preston drawled, letting his hands come out again to cup her face and pull her gaze up to his. "Maybe you didn't know me at first, but since the second meeting, you have. I told you. If you meant to drop me because my last name is Rawlins, you're either late doing it, or you're using me."

"Preston!" She tried to pull her face away, but he wouldn't let her.

"Have you been hanging out with me because you wanted to get to Colley?"

"That's over. I told you. Cold as ashes," she lied without a flicker of emotion. "Besides, I didn't even know he was coming to the Springs again."

"I believe you," he said slowly. "So you're with me because I'm what? Fun? That's not great, but it's not bad. Maybe we could make it better?"

"We don't—" Somewhere she had to make him understand that this was over. She had had a better time with him than she'd had in three long years; he made her remember that she was young . . . but Colley was back.

Just like him to ruin everything.

It was time to face the fact that this man, gorgeous or not, was a member of the same horrible family. It was too dangerous.

Was that why she'd run with Preston a little, because she was desperate for some kind of life, even a risky one?

Lainie didn't think he was going to like any of her explanations. She thought he just might make trouble. He was the kind who was used to getting his way, which was another problem with perfect-looking men.

Why did I let this get started? she thought miserably, and tried to speak again.

But she didn't get a chance. Preston shut off her words by a simple means: he laid his lips on hers.

And that was another thing that was definitely going on her list of illegalities, the way some men knew how to kiss. Perfect.

Colley hadn't ever been perfect. He had kissed too hotly, touched too freely, pushed too hard—

Lainie shoved Preston away. "It's six o'clock in the morning."

He let her go reluctantly. "Don't make it worse by reminding me. Do you know what time I had to get up to see you alone this morning? This is criminal. The last time I was up before the sun was the day I crammed twenty-four straight hours for my bar exam. Lainie, this could be love."

His too-solemn voice made it a joke, but she didn't feel like laughing.

"I've got to go to work," she mumbled.

"Wait. You haven't heard the last reason I'm here," he interrupted quickly.

"Other than apologies and true love?" she asked whimsically.

"We're planning to swim and scuba sometime in the next few days. Maybe on Saturday. Sort of a party. The Gregory twins have to go back to Nashville, so we're sending them off in style. I want you to come with me."

"Who's planning it?"

"Lloyd Tate and I."

"Isn't he a little old to be running around with you and Jack and Mark Gregory?"

Preston made a wry face. "You're only as old as you feel, I guess. He's just somebody to hang around with while I'm here. You don't think Colley and I have much in common, do you?" The question was clearly rhetorical; he didn't wait for an answer. "Are you going to come with me?" he demanded.

"I have to work."

"Your mother needs you to wait tables again?" he said derisively. "Lainie, baby, you've got a million-dollar face. Why are you wasting yourself here in this dump?" He glanced beyond her toward the Magnolia and said dismissively, "It's got some classy antiques, including your aunt, and that's about all. Come with me to the party."

What he said stung, and Lainie retorted a little unsteadily, "You're just a party animal, aren't you? It's all you and your friends think about."

His face darkened and he stepped right up to her. "You mean I'm not serious enough? Well, how about this: we go to the party, and when it's over, we go somewhere alone together, and not just for a night. Come with me out of this nowhere town, Lainie. Live with me awhile. You'll like it. I'll make you like it."

Lainie stared at him in silent shock and finally took two steps back until she was against one of the trees and away from his insistent body. "You don't know what you're saying," she whispered. "Anyway, I couldn't. I have to keep the Magnolia running. We have to make a living. Not all of us have rich grandfathers."

He followed her, reaching to catch one of her hands in his and bring it to his lips. "I'll give you money. How much will it take to set you free from this place? To let you come away with me? I'll take care of it, Lainie, and you, too."

She pulled her hand free. "I'm not going to be a mistress, Preston."

Amusement flickered across his face. "Such an old-fashioned word, for such an old-fashioned girl. No, you're not mistress material, Lainie. That's not what I was offering."

She flushed a little. All her life had been spent right here, in this town, with the same people. Preston made her feel ignorant and backward, and maybe she was. She tried not to let it show, that she didn't know much about his kind of world.

"I just want to show you that life can be good. What's the crime in that? Let me teach you how to live just for the pleasure of it. How to dress." Preston never once glanced down at the cutoff denims and sleeveless shirt she'd tucked into them, but she flinched at his words.

"I have to help Mama, and I'm sorry you don't like my clothes," she said defensively. Unbidden, the thought of Colley and the fashion-plate Rachel from the previous night rose in front of her.

"Your clothes are fine if you're going to be Daisy Mae all your life," Preston said bluntly. "But why, when you can be Fifth Avenue? Let me buy you something, Lainie. Spend some money on you. A swimsuit, maybe, for you to wear to the party."

She pulled her hand away. "I've got one, thanks. And I don't swim well, anyway."

He sighed and ran his hand back through his hair. "Okay, I'm sorry. I've hurt your feelings. I keep forgetting all these backwater rules that little towns still live by. Can't buy women clothes unless you're married to them, right?"

Neither of them said anything for a second, and then Preston whispered, his voice silky, "Would that make you say yes, Lainie?"

Dynamite couldn't have pulled Lainie up faster and sent her backing away again, right around the side of the tree, even more quickly. "What's come over you this morning? You don't know what you're saying," she stumbled. God, how had she ever gotten herself into this? "You're a Rawlins."

"How awful. I should have been a Smith, and you'd like me, right?"

"Stop it. You don't understand," she protested passionately.

"Okay, calm down." He held both his hands up as if in surrender.

"You have to go now."

"I didn't have anything to do with whatever happened between you and the rest of my family, Lainie. I'm not going away just because Colley showed up last night. Now, if I can't get you to agree to more, will you at least see me again? Maybe go to the party with me?"

"I'll think about it," she temporized. Anything to get him out of sight before Mama showed up. Anything to get away from his insanity.

"You know, Lainie, I've been a perfect gentleman so far," Preston said consideringly.

"If you don't count all the times I've had to watch your hands," she returned shakily.

"I haven't kissed and told, have I? But I could."

Instantly, she knew what was in his head, and everything inside of her went on alert.

"You mean Colley. You're threatening to tell Colley about us."

"The old man, too. What would it matter?"

She couldn't tell the truth, so she lied. "Nothing. They'd be angry, but it's nothing to me how they feel."

Oh, God, don't let them find out, she thought in panic. Not now.

"Your mother?"

Lainie couldn't stop the wince. "She wouldn't like it," she admitted. "But she'd get over it. Because what is there to tell? That I went out with you a few times? You're hitting some kind of low. Don't you think I've been out with other men?"

Preston considered her face a minute. "Who?"

Lainie shrugged and hoped she didn't have to answer. The truth was, a good many men in the Springs connected her with Colley and kept a safe distance from the woman he'd branded as his before she was barely old enough to know what was happening.

Her father had known, but she hadn't understood what he tried to tell her. He'd been too upset, too overwrought every time the subject of the shantytown people came up.

"I can't believe I've come to this." Preston released her abruptly and turned with a laugh and a shake of his head. "I'm actually trying to blackmail a woman into a date with me. You'd think I was a monster and I was asking something terrible. What's happening to me? Lainie, honey, there are other women, and they're normal, unlike you."

Lainie didn't need Preston's diagnosis. She knew exactly what was wrong with her: the witch boy was back, and she was afraid.

How dare Colley come back and mark her all over again, just like he had before?

"Wait."

Preston halted just as he started to climb in the Toyota, his tanned legs beneath the blue shorts too long and muscular for the tiny car.

"Can I think about it and maybe call you?"

"At Lloyd's houseboat, like always?" he answered with a knowing twist of his lips. "So we can keep it our little secret?" He shrugged. "Sure, angel. Why not? Every man has the right to be a sucker once in a while, doesn't he? I'm not proud. I'll stay away and give you time to think. I'll wait to hear from you, maybe even two or three days."

Not two, not three, but four glorious days—that was how many times Colley saw the little girl that summer when she was twelve and he was fifteen.

They had a blackberry fight on one of the days that left both of them stained blue and Lainie full of giggles.

Once they made hideous masks, like something the ancients would have created, out of the heavy, claylike mud at the bottom of Widow's Creek, and left them to dry in the hot sun.

On an afternoon in June, he tried to teach her to grapple for fish in the cold places under the overhanging rocks, but she was too leery of the deeper water, so she settled for admiring the pinching crayfish he finally pulled up.

Toward the end of July, on a rainy Friday when the field turned too muddy for him to work it, he waited patiently in the downpour by the creek for a glimpse of her, only to discover that she was camped out in a tent under the tree house with a book, all nice and dry. Taking a huge risk, he crawled on his belly up the hill, slipped under the tarpaulin that made the tent, and in all his wet muddiness, traded entertainments with her. She read him part of a story about a boy on a raft in the river, and in return, he taught her to whistle on the grass as he had the year before.

It was the best summer he'd ever lived through, but it was not idyllic. He was getting older, understanding that things could happen, learning caution and worry and fear.

He could only come to the field after the tobacco was set, because Thorne himself supervised the hands as they set the tiny green plants, and he shuddered at the thought of Thorne seeing him near his little girl. It was Colley's job to maintain the crop in the circle field during the summer that followed, while the other field hands worked in other sections.

There were other people who intruded into their private little kingdom, too. On one occasion that July when he came to the tree platform to look for Lainie, he saw her but didn't whistle to get her attention the way he sometimes did nowadays—not on the grass but through his hands—because a tall, lanky boy was in the backyard visiting, and

Colley stayed hidden, stung by his first taste of jealousy. The bite of that emotion stayed with him even later, when she told him that the boy was only a relative, her cousin Way.

One more thing made him very, very uneasy: Devil came around more. That summer Charley brought a colt to the nearest barn, a satiny, coal black stallion, and said, "Colley, he says this animal is for you to break. I never saw his like on this farm, or any farm, before. I told Devil that you're young to be working with a horse this high-strung, but he says you're strong enough to handle things, to let you try it. Mind that you do it right and take care not to get hurt. This nag hit the ground worth more money than I'll ever see."

It was pure heaven to have the animal under his hands—so sleek, so perfect, so pampered. It reminded him of the little girl, and the thought made him gentle and patient.

"You gonna love that horse into obedience, boy?"

Colley jerked in surprise, turning from his hold on the bridle he'd finally coaxed the colt into wearing, and the horse pranced uneasily at his distress. Devil stood in the dark, cool corner of the big barn, sunlight sifting around him, making the tiny dust motes and the bits of swirling hay look golden in the air.

"I just don't want to hurt him," he answered.

"Sometimes that's a part of it," Devil said with a shrug. "You do what you gotta do to make this a good horse, or I'll take it away and put you back out in the fields all day long. Don't be soft. It'll cost you too much. I had one son, Brodie, who could have done anything. He died instead, because he was soft. There was a rock slide at the quarry one summer, and some of the men were trapped in there. He went in after 'em when nobody else would, mostly cause a girl who worked here on the farm had friends down in that hole. He did it for her as much as anything. Helped them get out, and in the process, he got hurt. They didn't try to drag him out, like he'd done them when they were trapped. Those old rocks started rumbling, and they ran, like a bunch of dogs. Left him right where he fell. I tried to get in and fetch him, but it was too late by the time I got there. Now he's dead. He died believin' a lie, believin' that they would come back and save him. Believin' that the girl would love him forever. She was gone before a year had passed."

Devil pulled off the wall, the barn as quiet as the boy in front of him. Even the colt was eerily still. "This horse'll kill you if you let him, Colley, and you'll ruin him if you keep on like this. Don't make the mistake that Brodie made of trusting blind in the good nature of a creature. Most of us got to be made to do our duties. It don't come natural."

Colley watched Devil leave the barn, and that night, he told Charley, "I aim to do it right, but surely there's some room for me to let that colt know I like him."

"There's room," Charley answered. "Devil's too hard. Life's been rough on him. Do what you have to do to break the colt and love him the rest of the time. You'll get a better horse for it, just like you'd get a better human." And he went off into one of his everlasting coughing fits.

So Colley broke the horse and spent the four days with the little girl, and another summer passed.

Come the second September of their acquaintance, she asked him anxiously, "Will you stop coming to the tree house?"

"It's hard for me to come now," he tried to explain. "The work in the circle field is almost done, and there's no reason for me to be on this side of the farm until next spring. I'm afraid that if I come too much, he—they'll catch me, and I can't ever come again. I don't want that to happen. And besides, pretty soon everybody else will be gone, and it'll just be me, and Charley, and Nadine for the winter, doing it all. You gotta go to school, and I have to go back for a while."

"But next spring?" she persisted.

"I'll be here," he promised, and added wryly, "Where do you think I'd be going, anyway?"

She looked at him a long time, as if she were soaking into her brain the sight of his face, his long, leggy body, his dark hair. Then she stepped right into him and put her lips on his cheek.

"I love you, Colley," she whispered, and turned and ran up the high hill toward home, never once looking back.

He couldn't speak for a while, maybe didn't even breathe.

But that night, lying in the hot little shack on his cot, right in front of the open door so that he could catch the breeze and watch the stars as they blazed above the hollow, he didn't hear Charley snoring on the bed across the room behind him.

He heard her words instead, and felt her touch.

He put his hand at last to the cheek where she had laid her lips.

Colley wasn't sure, but he thought it was the first time anybody had ever kissed him.

4

Colley flung the door open on the side of the house before Nadine could even get out of the way on the other side. She grunted as it swung back on her, and she had to grab at it with one hand and try to balance the big tray she was carrying with the other.

"Mercy, Colley, this ain't no train station," she grumbled.

"Sorry," he said shortly, and headed across the big kitchen to the bathroom in the hall. He was hot, sweaty, tired, and mad. A shower could take care of about three of those.

"You're gonna think 'sorry' if you don't get yourself out on the back patio," Nadine called after him. "Mr. Albert's been waitin' on you to show up for a good two hours."

Colley turned to stare at the old woman. "He knew I would be late tonight. I told him so."

"Well, maybe he didn't know that James was comin' down."

"James! Is he here? What for?" It was a pointless question;

he knew. James was there for the same reason he always was: to find fault with his nephew.

But Nadine tried to answer him. "How would I know? But your grandpa's been tellin' me to get you out there as soon as you got home."

Colley looked down at himself, at the blue jeans and the T-shirt he wore. There was a streak of grease across the once-white front of it where one of the tractors had jammed today, and he'd finally got tired of waiting for the hands to figure out what was wrong and just laid down under it and fixed it himself.

Nadine read his thoughts. "I believe it'd be healthier to worry about what Mr. Albert wants instead of how dirty you are."

"I don't feel like fussing with the two of them tonight," Colley muttered to himself, and turned away toward the back of the house.

One soft lantern burned on the patio. It revealed the white metal chairs with their round, smooth backs, and two or three flowerpots with Nadine's petunias and begonias in them. That was the only softening touch. Albert had no use for fancy furniture or stylish porch decor.

It was funny how this fading patio made Colley think of the crumbling porches of the Magnolia, but one was shabby because of poverty, and the other just because Albert chose to let it be. He'd never wasted one penny of his money on fancy trappings, no matter how his little wife had pleaded.

At the one table, a wrought-iron, uncomfortable affair that she had somehow managed to acquire at least twenty years earlier sat Albert's only surviving son, his eldest, James, but he wasn't his usual pristine self. Heat, humidity, and bugs had forced him to take off his coat and tie, open his collar, and roll up his sleeves. He looked wilted and aggravated.

"Nadine said you wanted me," Colley told the second figure, the old man in the faded overalls who sat smoking a cigarette over on the darkest side of the porch, the one overhung by one of the last big red oaks in the county.

James reacted immediately, coming up on the iron chair. "It's about time," he said sharply.

Albert didn't move. Probably, Colley thought in wry amusement, the old man had known the minute that he walked in Nadine's kitchen. He had hearing as keen as a woods animal. After another long drag on the cigarette, Albert turned to face his grandson. Under the brim of the old blue cap he wore, his hair was snowy white—but his eyes were as black as Colley's.

"I figured you'd be late," he said, his voice calm and even. "Did you get the tractor fixed?"

How Albert always knew everything before Colley could even tell him—that was another mystery about the old man. Colley figured that his grandfather kept some kind of stool pigeon on the farm, although he'd never been able to tell just who it was.

"It's up and running again," Colley answered.

"Good. Ain't no use in callin' in somebody when you can do it yourself," Albert said flatly, and dropped the butt of his cigarette in the tin can that sat beside the chair.

"Look, Colley, I'm on a tight schedule here," James interrupted brusquely. "I came to see my son, but Preston is being a stubborn ass."

"You seen your cousin today?" Albert asked Colley, rocking back in his old chair.

"Not today, no," Colley said warily.

"But you know where he is," James said without a flicker of doubt. "You've been home a week, and already, you know things. You're that much like your grandpa."

"I might."

"Well?" James demanded impatiently.

"He's mostly running with the crowd he brought with him," Colley answered slowly, and James's face lightened. "Their names are Jack and Mark."

"The twins?" he said in relief. "I didn't know they were staying in the Springs."

"They're not. They rented a cabin down on the lake. Preston goes there a lot. So does a man named Lloyd Tate. He's older. He has a big houseboat down there this summer. I don't know anything about him. He's new around here."

"Tate. I never heard of him. But the twins—they're all right," James answered.

Colley shrugged. "I wouldn't know."

"Preston golfs and boats with them when they're at home in Nashville. Maybe they drink a little when they fish. Nothing serious."

"Then they're acting pretty normal," Colley said brusquely.

There was a long pause, until James took two steps closer to his nephew. "You didn't say anything about women," he said quietly.

"I can't hardly believe that Preston's runnin' with 'em if they're not keen on whorin'," Albert commented sardonically from his chair.

Colley could feel a mosquito crawling along the side of his throat, and he slapped at it, then raked the damp hair off his neck by running his hand through it roughly. "There's women," he said at last, reluctantly. "I've seen a few of them on Tate's houseboat, but I didn't know them."

"Women?" James answered slowly. "Like in whoring, the way Daddy says it, Colley? Because if that's all it is, it's nothing to get excited about. But I don't want another situation like the one with the Langford girl."

"The boy ain't fool enough to do the same damn thing again," Albert told the other two, crossing his right leg over his left by lifting it into place. That right leg was completely straight, stiffened permanently by an accident at the old quarry before Colley was born. "Even if he was, he won't. He knows I'd send Colley again—"

"No," said Colley and his uncle simultaneously.

Colley cut off his own words, but James rushed on. "That whole thing was handled completely wrong. If I'd been told in time, I would have gone and stopped it. But sending Colley—he had no business telling Preston what to do, especially in front of that girl. Teresa's furious with me over the mess, especially over Colley's part in it, and so is Preston himself."

"It's a sorry day when a man lets a woman tell him how to run things," Albert returned implacably. "And I sent word to you once that things were gettin' out of hand with that Langford woman. I tried to tell you that her old man was lookin' to make his fortune off Preston, either as a son-in-law or as a defendant in a paternity suit. Hell, James, I sent the boy down there on my personal business, and if I'd left it to you and your fancy piece of a wife, we'd'a all been ruined. Don't he know nothin'?"

"Don't you start on me, Daddy," James returned angrily. "You've got no room to talk. You didn't do any better with Colley. Why, he ran around nearly naked until he was almost grown. And he's probably got the longest hair in the county even now."

Colley leaned back against the narrow porch post that was nearest and put in with amusement, "Not naked. I've been wearing a full set of clothes since I was at least twenty."

"Colley was raised hard, just like I was. He was brought up the way they're afraid to bring up men anymore, and he can do whatever he has to—break the rules, or break a horse, or break a man. I did better by him than I did with either you or Brodie, James, because there was no woman interferin' to make him soft or baby him. He don't need none, either."

"Maybe so . . . but how many houses around the county invite Colley for supper?" James retorted. "They're scared of him, at least all the decent folks are, and you've given them reason to be."

"Then he'll have to be satisfied with the indecent, and there's a lot more of them," Albert answered placidly. "Most people always put me in that category . . . and you, too, James, until you married the little Cooper debutante. But there's no point in squabblin' over it. Colley has his uses, and Preston has his. But Preston ain't gonna be available if there's another mess like the one in Atlanta."

"There won't be. And Colley's not to act his better, nor to push him around."

"I didn't tell him what to do," Colley said, angry at last. "He took one look at me and walked out. I was the one who had to break the news to the girl that he was through; I was the one helping her pack her bags while she cried all over me. I was the one who got her out of his apartment and put ten thousand dollars in her hand and took her to a—a goddamned clinic so she could"—He pushed himself off the post, his back to his uncle.

"It won't happen again," James told Albert in the long silence after Colley turned away. "Eventually Preston will get over his temper. He blames me for the way things came down, but he's more angry with Colley for interfering in something that wasn't any of his business."

Albert said unsympathetically, "It's time for him to think with his brain, not what's between his legs. And Colley was only doing what he was told."

James hesitated a minute, eyeing his silent nephew as he picked up his crumpled coat off the back of a porch chair. "All I'm asking you to do is let him calm down. He's young, that's all."

"I'm younger than he is," Colley protested.

"You're different. You never were . . ." James hesitated.

"Normal?" the younger man finally finished dryly.

James shrugged. "Whatever. What in the hell did you bring Colley home for, Daddy, when you knew Preston was going to be here? You know they can't get along."

"Then it's high time they learned to. Things can't work until they do," Albert answered.

James made a frustrated sound and flung the maltreated coat over one arm. He started off the porch, but halfway down the steps, he turned again. "I left the paperwork about the Lamberson deal in your study. Have Colley bring it to me if you want to go through with it. And I'll get to the blueprints for the stables next week."

"All you're doin' is approvin' the prints, James. Understand that. The deal's already made. There'll be a breeding stable built here on the farm." Albert's voice brooked no objections.

"Did I say I had a problem with it?" James answered testily. "As long as Colley keeps turning over the money with the stables, I've got no objections. What I do have objections to is the way you let him see everything before you make any decisions anymore. Hell, I'm your son. I want what's best for the company more than Colley does. He can't be understanding half of the stuff. He never set foot in one single school."

The two men on the dark porch watched him as he picked his way across the wet grass. "This is ruining my shoes," he was muttering. "Good Italian leather, too. Hey, Colley," James stopped to call back, "if you can do so damn much, why don't you build a sidewalk to the garage? There's a job you can do without a diploma."

When the lights of his Mercedes faded into the night, Albert slid his hands behind the bib of his overalls, one under each side. "Don't even tell me you don't want to go to Nashville, because you're goin' when I'm ready to send the papers back."

"Why? So he can tell me again that Preston's too good to be taking instructions from me? Or that I'm too dumb to understand his contracts? He's a son of a—"

"You watch your mouth, boy, before I watch it for you. You'll not talk about your uncle that way. This is the way I want it—you runnin' the tobacco barns and reportin' to me, and him doin' the investin' in Nashville and reportin' to me, too. It keeps ever'body honest. And if it's makin' him mad, well, maybe he has a need to be kept honest."

"And Preston?"

"You know where he fits in."

"Send him to Nashville instead of me," Colley said intently. "Let him do my job for once. This one's an easy one."

His grandfather stared at him.

"Why not?" Colley persisted. "That way he'd have to face his daddy."

"Don't be a fool," Albert said shortly. "I've got Preston right where I want him for now. I've got things for him to do, just like I have for you. I need to see what he's made of. Anyway, you know how it works. This is our end of things and that's theirs. James does the fancy work, the head work, and you do the sweat and back work. You're made strong for it, Colley, strong and tough."

Colley walked to the edge of the patio, staring but seeing nothing out toward the garage where his uncle had vanished moments earlier. He slid his hands into his pockets.

"And Preston's nice and shiny, just like his daddy, all dolled up to be the front man."

"I could always see it in him, just like I'd placed a special order for it. The looks, the way he can talk. There ain't one in a thousand can work their tongues around people like he can. They wouldn't have me or you, boy. We're too rough, too much of the hills in us. But they'll take anything he says and swallow it. With Preston, there might even be a Rawlins, one of those backward hillbillies that used to work dark West Virginia coal mines and get spit on and die young, a Rawlins, in the governor's seat one of these days. If I don't live to see it, you will," Albert vowed. "And you can bet I'll know it, even if I'm burnin' in hell or singin' in glory when it happens."

"Send him back home, where he belongs," Colley said fiercely. He had no time to hear the old man's ambitions again. "Now."

There was a long silence between the two of them, broken only when Colley wheeled to face Albert. The old man was watching him speculatively, being still as a mouse.

"So what's he got into?" he asked Colley at last. "I knew you wudn't straight with James. You better be straight with me."

"There's nothing yet."

How could he tell his grandfather the sight of Preston at the Magnolia the other night had made him sick? What right did his cousin have to go there, to look at Lainie Thorne?

That had to be the reason for any man like Preston to be in the old hotel.

His goddamned cousin had better stay away from the girl at the Magnolia . . . just like Colley himself had to.

"What do you mean, 'yet'?"

Colley ran both hands through his hair, and then over his

face. "I've just got this feeling, that's all. I've not seen him with a girl, but I know better. There's one somewhere. There always is with Preston."

Albert had the unlit cigarette already between his lips, about to tear a match off to strike, but at Colley's words, he let his hands drop, pulling the cigarette with them, and he laughed, a rusty sound of amusement. "Don't tell me he's learning to give you the slip," he drawled. "Must be gettin' smarter than I thought he was."

"The thing is," Colley said tightly, "if she's from here, she's probably not used to Preston and his friends. She's likely to take every word he says as the gospel truth, just like the one in Atlanta did, and if she gets in trouble, too—"

"I get the picture. So keep your eye on him, a little closer this time."

"And what if I find somebody?" Colley persisted. "It won't do any good to talk to him. Saying no to Preston is like waving a red flag at a mad bull."

Albert examined the dark face of his grandson speculatively for a minute. "I can't hardly see him holdin' on to a woman like that. That's more your style, ain't it?"

Colley came upright at the implied rebuke and turned his back on the old man, who went on imperturbably, as if he'd said nothing.

"Most men understand that there's always another warm body, Colley, but if he gets muleheaded in the case of another girl, we'll go right to her this time to begin with. If she plans to cause trouble, well, we'll have to stop her. Buy her off. Don't get so worried about it. We can do it."

"You can do it," Colley answered hotly. "Me, I'm sick of running after him. And I'm tired of being the mule for this plow and him riding high and free, getting everything he wants. I work and he plays."

He took two big steps toward the house before Albert's voice arrested his motion.

"You know what you're doin' here."

Colley considered the stark words, but he still didn't turn around.

"I told you when I took you out of that shack," Albert went on, his voice clear in the night. "One of you for the sun, one of you for the shadow. That's how you were made to be. Preston's the one who has to sit on the throne. The one that can put all of us in power. James is right. They don't invite me and you to their big parties or their fancy houses. A'course, you don't seem to have any worries on that score up in Kentucky, where they don't know much about your past. And me, well, I'll be damned if I'd go anyway. But sometimes you need somebody who can get in all the right places. That's your cousin."

"I don't care if he sits on a million thrones," Colley said angrily, and wheeled to face Albert. "I'm just sick of him."

"It appears that he feels the same about you. Be that as it may, you're the one who has to hold everythin' together while he climbs. You're the one to work the land. Somebody has to. A family can't leave it. They gotta have it to stay rooted. It was the land that gave me my start; it's the land that holds us steady now. You're the one that was raised to touch it. It's why I couldn't let you sink roots on Harding's ground in Danville. This is our land. Our stake. I told you eight years ago how it would be, and you begged me to let you stay, to let you do it. You swore you would."

"I was sixteen and scared to death," Colley protested.

"You knew what you were doin'. I saw it in your eyes. A man's word is his bond," Albert said stoically. "Even if he gives it for something weak and foolish, like hanging on to a girl, the way you gave yours so you could keep close to Thorne's daughter, for all the good it did you. You nearly ruined it all over a woman."

Colley looked at his grandfather for a long moment, then he turned and walked into the house.

What Albert said was true. But inside him, a little voice, the same little voice that had been with him ever since he came to live with Devil, was telling him that there were other bonds.

There had to be love somewhere, even if it hadn't held sway in his life. He didn't think Albert had ever loved him. He mostly just needed him, and used him, and in return gave him a place to live, a place to belong.

His mother hadn't particularly loved him, either, or nothing could have made her hand him over to Albert and walk out when he was a baby.

Without even conscious thought, his hand reached to his throat for the whistle. But it wasn't there. He'd put it away, all too aware of the strife it would cause if he wore it out in the open.

Surely the old man had heard about the ruckus at the Magnolia. But if he had, he was choosing to stay quiet, and that suited Colley just fine. The whistle was his, and he didn't mean to give it up, not for the old man, not even for Lainie herself.

Damn Preston for taking it. Another reason to despise him. How had he ever found it, ever picked up on its importance to Colley?

Maybe the whistle was worthless to everybody but him now, but it was proof, the only proof he still had, that once Lainie had cared, and her caring had made all the difference for three long, hot summers of his life.

*   *   *

When the third long, hot summer rolled around, everything changed.

The changes began the night that River Charley died despite Colley's best efforts to save him. When he realized what was happening, he ran all the way to the farmhouse without a single stop and stumbled up on the back porch to shove open the door. Accustomed to the dark, he was blinded by the yellow lights of the kitchen for a second. Nadine was at work; he heard her call his name as he shot across the room to the opposite door and raced into another, larger room where four people sat gathered around a table having supper.

One was a woman; her shriek was a little more piercing than Nadine's, and it rang over the man's deeper, "What in hell?"

Devil came to his feet, still in his own overalls, his only concession to the meal the fact that he'd removed his hat. His hair was a thick, coarse mane, and as white as snow. Colley registered that, and the fact that the last inhabitant of the room was a boy somewhat older than he who stared as if Colley were straight from the moon. Colley had seen him once in a while from a distance when he came rarely to visit. It was the old man's grandson.

"You gotta come, Mr.—" He didn't know what to call Devil, so he didn't finish his ragged sentence. "He didn't come home. I found him in one of the barns."

"It's Charley," Devil realized, looking over the boy in front of him. Colley didn't know until that moment how panic-stricken and wild he must have looked.

"Get this creature out of here," the woman gasped. "We're trying to have dinner."

"I'll be there in a minute," Devil interrupted her to tell Colley.

"That's not good enough. You come now," he demanded, not even aware of his own temerity. "He wants you now."

Devil for once was at a loss as he confronted the intense, demanding boy before him. "Is it that bad? Then we'll take the truck."

They left the gaping people right there in the dining room. Colley was used to the chugging of one of the heavy tractors on the farm, but not to a truck. The immense speed as they bounced across the shadowy fields would have scared him if he hadn't been so frightened already.

Charley was a darker bundle than the night as he lay between the walls of the stall while they bent over him. Devil's flashlight haloed him, making him blink, but nothing could turn him from the other man for long. His whole body was tuned in to receive Rawlins.

"I'm . . . dying. . . ." he greeted him.

"Hell, we're all dyin'," Devil said dryly, advancing to look down on him.

"I'm doin . . . it . . . faster than most," Charley rasped. "There's a time—" he stopped to cough, holding a towel to his mouth, "appointed man to die, and then to face the judgment." This time he stopped to breathe, his breathing shallow, as if it came only from his throat and not his chest—"I mean to tell you be . . . fore . . . die. I was a . . . teach . . . er once back in West Vir . . . Virginia. Killed a man . . . for taking my . . . my . . . wife. That's why I was running when we met all the years back . . . why I came with you and stayed here. Hiding. My own little . . . hell. But I tried. I . . . did right by . . . Colley. Now you . . . you keep your word, De . . . vil."

Devil straightened from his slightly bent posture. "I said I would, when the time was right."

"Now." The faint word demanded.

"When he's older. Eighteen. When the state can't tell me what to do with him."

"Old enough. It's wrong to keep . . . him . . . pinned like . . .

ani . . . mal. Not enough innocence . . . kills . . . so does too . . . much." The words came between the heaves of his breath.

Devil stood, stubborn and silent.

"Can't hold him much longer," Charley whispered. "Only love h-holds in the . . . end, any . . ." He tried to smother the cough before it rose in his throat.

"Don't talk. Please, Charley, don't talk," begged Colley frantically. Then he turned furiously on Devil. "Whatever it is he wants, just—just give it to him. You're the Man. He's dying."

"Nothin' I'm gonna say will stop it," Devil said shortly. "But I'll send for the doc—"

"Hell." Charley's word was unexpectedly strong, but it had an ominous, bubbling sound. "I'll be gone before he gets here. No doctor . . . could change it. . . . But . . . I've sent . . . my own let-ter. Knew you, too, Devil. This thing . . . with Colley . . . ends now, no matter what you—"

He rose upright suddenly, as if pulled by strings, sucking at the air, grasping at it with his hand. Colley stood transfixed and frozen as death reached out for Charley Rivers and the old man rose to meet it.

The release when it came was abrupt. Charley fell back on the hay beneath him, and with an anguished cry, Colley turned and ran for the door. "Wait—" Devil called after him, catching at him, but Colley gave him a hard, rough shove backward.

"You keep away from me," he panted, and slid into the misty night.

It was nearly two before Lainie got to the tree house that day. She didn't come all the time, and Colley hadn't gone to the creek down below very often lately, either.

She missed him, but she had learned: he came when he could.

"You're getting me all muddy," she informed the big dog as he leaped around her, trying to catch her jeans as she shot up the ladder on the tree into the bower of leaves as they bent down all around her. Looking back at him on the ground below, his tongue hanging out comically, she began to laugh. "You're the silliest"—and then gave a gasp as she bumped a warm body sitting just at the top of the steps.

It was Colley, Colley, who practically never crossed the creek, sitting huddled against the big trunk, just where the platform wrapped it.

She couldn't say a word.

He looked terrible, as if he hadn't slept in weeks. She thought that just maybe he'd been crying.

"Charley's dead."

Even his voice was different, old and tarnished sounding.

Down below, the dog, sensing something was wrong, began to bark.

"Shhh," she told him frantically. "It's only Colley."

The animal settled into a low whine, and then subsided.

"I'm sorry," she murmured at last, pulling herself up beside him and looking at him nervously.

"I won't cry anymore, if that's what you're worried about," he said brusquely. "I've cried so much there's not a drop of tears left in me."

"I wouldn't care," she whispered.

He pulled his knees up to his chest, wrapping them with his hands and letting his forehead rest on top of them. "Part of me's not even crying for Charley. I was crying for me. I've got—" Colley didn't finish, cutting off the words.

"Don't say it. I'll be your friend forever. And I won't die for a long time," Lainie told the top of his bent head.

He looked up and gave a husky laugh. "Forever's longer than a long time," he observed wryly.

"Whichever comes first," she returned solemnly.

"Is that a promise, Elaina Marie Thorne?"

"Yes . . . and I even have something to seal it with, too," she said in triumph. "Move over."

She pushed him out of the way and then stepped on him in her haste to climb to the tree limb that jutted sideways out of the trunk at his back. He tilted his head back to squint into the sun, watching her as she fumbled in an old squirrel hole and came out with a plastic bag.

"Here it is," she called down, just as she leaped and he rolled to avoid her feet.

"Look." Dangling the package right in front of his nose as she clambered up to her knees, bracing herself against his leg, she watched his face expectantly.

"It's a whistle," he said slowly, but he didn't reach for it.

"My aunt Olivia used to use it, when there were all sorts of maids and cooks at the Magnolia and she had to get everybody's attention. She gave it to me. It's solid silver. That's why it looks black, because it has to be polished. It has a magnolia engraved on it. Here, it's for you." Lainie pushed it into his still hand as it rested in his lap.

"I can't take it," he said shortly, shoving it away. "I've got nothing for you."

"That's the best kind of present, Mama says, when you give it not wanting anything back," Lainie said urgently. "Besides, if you're worried that somebody will see it, who is there to care anymore, Colley?"

Her innocent question hurt him so much that his face twisted, and he rose to his feet, letting her slide off his leg with a thump.

"I'm afraid," he said with a shiver. "Charley didn't tell me he was really dying until it was nearly over," he concluded in a panicky rush, swinging around to see the world. "And Devil, he didn't help at all. Reckon he's not as strong as I always thought he was. Maybe nothing's like I thought. See, I used to think I wanted to stand up this high and this free. Instead, I'm just scared. I don't even know who I am, and I want to know. Charley used to say that there was a place I belonged, and he was going to put me back there. Somebody tell me where it is. I want to go there—and I don't. It's safer here. But where was the place he was talking about? Where?"

"Don't go," she said, in her own fear. "Stay. Please, Colley."

He looked down at her kneeling at his feet, wide eyes turned up to him. "Someday you'll get too old to want to see me like this, Lainie," he said somberly.

"I won't. I never will," she gasped, beginning to cry.

"Well, don't worry about it," he advised roughly, reaching down a hand to smear the tears off her face. "I told you once before, I've got nowhere to go, except here, until you grow up." He swung out onto the ladder, and just as he lowered himself enough that they were nearly face to face, she pushed the silver whistle into the front bib pocket of his overalls.

"I brought it here the first Christmas," she said. "You never came and got it. If you don't take it, it won't be anybody else's. I'll just leave it here in the tree, like I have ever since then. I don't know what's wrong, but the whistle shows you that I'm telling the truth, that you can call me when you want to. We're friends, Colley. Forever."

He wasn't the adolescent she'd played with all this time; adulthood and bitter reality lay over the witch boy like she'd never seen it, but she couldn't say good-bye.

After a moment, he laughed and tried to tease. "Or a real long time, whichever comes first."

5

The little sign that hung in front of the office on the corner of Main and the highway that led to the county seat of Lafayette was small and unassuming. It said simply, Theo Matheson Jr., Agent.

Insurance, that was Theo's business, just as it had been Theo senior's. If a newcomer couldn't figure it out from his shingle, that wasn't his problem. Everybody in town who needed to know did.

But as furtively as Lainie Thorne entered the place late Friday afternoon, Theo could have been involved in some far more underhanded undertaking, and as apprehensive as she was about the upcoming conversation, he might as well have been.

"Good afternoon, Lainie." The middle-aged man rose from behind the oak desk. "I knew you'd be prompt. I sent the secretary home fifteen minutes early so our conversation could be in private."

She pulled in her breath shakily and sat down, unbidden,

in the blue leather chair in front of him. "I hope this is not going to be as bad as it already sounds," she said with an attempted smile.

Matheson cleared his throat nervously and adjusted the silver glasses that kept sliding down his thin nose. "If I could change what I'm about to tell you, my dear, I would."

Lainie made herself look away from his face and out the long window beside him while she considered his words and braced herself. "The company wouldn't reconsider," she said at last for him, facing the news that she'd been dreading for weeks now.

"I've been your family's agent for all my career. My father was Lansing's friend as well as his business associate," he reminded her, almost apologetically. "I would do almost anything to help."

"I know that," Lainie said slowly. The afternoon was bright and sunny outside; the rays of warmth spilled through the glass panes and sparkled off of the shiny black truck that sat across the road at the farm store.

But something dark had blossomed suddenly in her stomach.

"It's fairly unpleasant. You're awfully young to bear the weight of all this. Isn't there somebody . . ." he murmured more to himself than to her.

"No." Her voice was as steady as her blue gaze on him.

Matheson ran both hands up under his glasses, lifting them a little off his nose to rub his eyes in frustration. Then he settled the frames back in place, looked her in the eye, and delivered his news.

"The insurance on the Magnolia will be canceled. I have no more say-so in the matter. I've pointed out that the Blackburns have been insured with us for sixty years, that there has never been even one claim on the place, that you have struggled to make payments on the premiums. Nothing will change their minds."

Lainie felt her face go pale. "But why now ?" she whispered. "Why after all this time?"

"I did find out that much. It seems they sent an agent from out of the county to walk in and inspect the place without telling me about it," he said miserably. "Lord, Lainie, I don't know how I'll face your great-aunt and Deborah. I've gone to church with all of you for as long as I can remember. You know I wouldn't do this. I'd keep you on with the company from now on. But this man is new and ambitious. Doesn't give a fig about anything but money. And most of all, he can't understand that the Magnolia may be old, but it's an institution. He just says it's not up to modern safety standards."

The words sounded lost in the big room, and Matheson stood, pushing up his glasses over and over. "I've argued with him until I'm blue, and I've come up with only one solution: he's finally agreed that if you renovate the dining section, just that one, to make it more modern, he'll advise the company to reinstate insurance on it, alone. That would be much cheaper than trying to redo the entire establishment."

"What does he think that will cost?" Lainie managed to ask steadily, but she wanted to cry. If it had been two cents, they might have scraped it together. Not much more.

"Not as bad as you'd think," he answered eagerly. "Sixteen thousand dollars. Twenty, tops."

"Sixteen thousand!" she repeated dazedly. "Twenty? Mr. Matheson, you might as well ask us for the moon. We don't have sixteen hundred."

"I was afraid of that. You could maybe ask the bank for a loan?"

Normally Lainie would have cut her throat before she

revealed to anybody her desperation, but she was too distraught at the moment to stop her words. "Albert Rawlins's bank?" she said bitterly.

Matheson's face fell. "Yes, of course. I wasn't thinking. And that's another thing, Lainie, something that I would not want repeated. In fact, I would be forced to deny it if someone asked me if I'd told you about it. But. . . ." He twisted his hands in an agitated fervor and straightened his tie.

"What?"

"It may not be wise to reveal this," he murmured more to himself than to her.

Lainie stood, too, facing the man across the desk without a word. Something in her level blue gaze made him capitulate.

"The man whom the company sent out to inspect the Magnolia in secret is an acquaintance of the Rawlins family," Matheson burst out. "*Flunkey* seems to be a good word to apply to him, in fact."

She didn't flinch. She just stood a little straighter, and her face drained of color beneath its healthy summer tan.

"Lainie, I have other information, too, and you may not appreciate my knowing it. Understand, I wouldn't speak to you about it, except there's no man to help you, none but Way, of course, and he's not much older than you and certainly not interested in the Magnolia. I'm afraid he's no better off financially than the rest of the Blackburns currently are," the agent concluded hurriedly.

Embarrassment returned the color high to Lainie's cheeks.

"What else?" she asked, putting her chin up.

"The property taxes on the Magnolia and on Olivia's house haven't been paid in over twelve years," Matheson said on a sigh.

Lainie looked at him a long, blind moment, felt for the chair behind her, and sat down in it again abruptly. "Twelve?"

"That's right. Twelve years, plus penalties."

"But I've only been trying to handle the money for the last two," she said pleadingly. "I know the taxes weren't paid last year, and they haven't been paid yet for this one, but I had hoped we would have a better season. I have part of the money saved, and we were supposed to host several family reunions in July. I meant to manage two years' payment later this summer. It was my understanding that the county wouldn't take action for at least three."

Matheson said nothing.

"I was busy trying to pay the insurance," she whispered at last, with a tiny laugh that was pure panic. "How much?"

He made a gesture of protest. "Never mind that now, Lainie. There's nothing you can—"

"How much?"

"Taxes are fairly low in rural areas like this, and the hotel is older. About fifteen thousand."

Such huge numbers. So easy to say, so hard for her to hear.

"Altogether, I need nearly forty thousand dollars?" she asked numbly.

Matheson reached for his glasses again and finally gave up on them, pulling them off entirely. "As far as I'm concerned, Lainie, you can stay open without insurance. I'm not going to be telling anybody else. But it's dangerous. And if the right people make waves, the fat's going to be in the fire. There'll be trouble."

"Devil Rawlins."

The agent didn't flinch at the nickname. "He knows about all of it, Lainie. The tax assessor is the one who clued me in to your problem because Rawlins sent somebody right to the assessor's office last month to check up on you. If the old man forces the issue, the Magnolia and Olivia's house could be sold to whoever wants to pay the back taxes."

"She's eighty," Lainie cried, and her fingers dug into the arms of the leather on the chair beneath her. "I know he hates the Blackburns, and the Thornes, too. Can't he at least let her alone for the last few years of her life? Let him take it when she's gone. I'll survive. I'll understand what's happening. She won't. And what will Mama do?"

"I honestly don't know. I'm aware that there is tension between your families, but I'm not entirely sure why. Nobody seems to know anything for certain. I've heard rumors that it has something to do with you and his youngest grandson," Matheson answered, and he sounded as confused and helpless as Lainie felt. "Couldn't you two come to some kind of settlement and end this?"

He didn't understand. He didn't know the whole story, and she would never tell it. Matheson would never feel the same flaming, painful anger, either.

"No. Damn the Rawlinses."

The agent was a little on the prudish side. His cheeks reddened as the girl in front of him swore viciously, but he said nothing. He just watched as she picked up her handbag, swung it over her shoulder, and reached for the doorknob, all in one jerky, furious movement.

"At least now I know why he thinks it's safe for Colley to come back," she muttered to herself. "He doesn't plan for me to be here much longer."

Outside, she plunged down the broken sidewalk. The Magnolia lay on Main Street, too, a half mile from the insurance office, on the outskirts of town. It was a close enough distance to walk, and that was a good thing: she didn't have to buy gas.

Widow's Creek, the same bubbling stream that circled the hotel, met the road and ran beside it for a while. An old willow tree hung between the road and the creek just past Matheson's office, and Lainie ran right under its long, sheltering limbs to hide herself and her agitation.

She'd been bad-mannered enough to forget to thank Mr. Matheson, she thought with a sting of guilt. But she couldn't go back now, when she was this upset.

What was she going to do?

Her head hurt, her heart hurt, and her stomach had twisted into permanent knots of worry.

They were going to lose everything.

Just down the road, she could see the corner of the wooden bridge that crossed the creek and led into the front yard of the Magnolia. Massive trees hid the hotel itself from her view, but the very thought that it was there had been comfort enough over the years.

Maybe there was no other place in the whole world like it, at least not for her. It was home, work, family, way of life.

And it was a painful cross to bear.

It didn't do much in the way of a hotel anymore, but the Magnolia had long ago found a new way to survive, one that a hungry man might appreciate as soon as he stepped into the big, high-ceilinged parlor at mealtime. In the summer, the whirring blades of the overhead fans pushed the delicious smell of good cooking to all who came near the place.

The crowds during the week were mostly local, but on the weekends, they came from miles away to sample the fine, old-fashioned, down-home Southern cooking that the kitchen served up promptly at seven, at noon, and at six every day of the week.

They came, too, to celebrate the tradition of the place.

Aunt Olivia, or Deborah when the old lady was under the weather, ran things with a firm hand. At the three appointed times, one of them rang the huge silver dinner bell that sat in the side yard under the cherry tree.

Then, and only then, could the people who'd made reservations file into the dining room where the tables were already set with steaming bowls of food. The doors were shut, and somebody—Olivia herself, or a devout diner—said grace.

Anyone who came after the closing of the doors and the final "amen" did not get fed. It was that simple, just like most things in the Springs.

Did her aunt and her mother even know how to live without that daily ritual that was as normal as breathing to them? Lainie herself hated it, and she loved it.

The Blackburns and their descendants had always accepted the tremendous amount of work that was required to keep the Magnolia open and those three meals constantly supplied and prepared. Because now there was nobody else to do it, and precious little money to spend, the hotel claimed all of Deborah's life except the few hours that she took to go to church. It had taken all of Olivia's life, and it was trying to take over Lainie's existence, too.

They had to have it to live; how else might they survive in a little town that offered few if any jobs for women?

But it was a fight they couldn't win. The hotel was crumbling around them, and not one of them had the ability or most of all, the money to fight the war against time.

So far, Lainie had learned to do what Mama did: she kept on with the chores that she could do and tried not to think about the other problems until she had to.

Now she had to.

A truck engine roared into life somewhere behind

her, and she lifted her hot, aching head from the trunk of the tree and looked through the wispy willow limbs for it.

It was the shiny black one that had been at the farm store, and it was sliding out of its parking place effortlessly, humming with power as it pulled into the road and away in a cloud of summer dust.

Lainie knew exactly who the driver was; she'd seen the truck several times in the days since his return. Colley Rawlins was at the wheel.

Why couldn't she just plain hate him? She should.

Fancy, high-dollar truck to drive.

Fancy, high-dollar clothes to wear.

Fancy, high-dollar woman on his arm.

I've watched you go up, and we've gone down so far I can't even see the sun, she told him silently, her throat aching with unshed tears.

I won't give in—not to your grandfather, not to you.

Not to my own heart.

I'll find a way. I will survive. I might not win, but I will survive.

I'll sell something. The Magnolia is full of antiques. Preston knows about these things, and he says it is. There must be something there that Mama and Aunt wouldn't miss, that has value for somebody with money to burn. Somebody rich, like you, Colley. Maybe careless with his money, too—like your cousin.

Lainie was still watching the curving road, still staring at the empty stretch of highway where the black truck had vanished around the bend and into the trees, when she realized, all in an instant, what exactly it was that the Magnolia held which might interest one very rich man, and she sucked in her breath in a rush.

Me.

It was a crazy, horrible thought, born of desperation—
but she couldn't vanquish it.

Preston says he wants *me*.

"Abby Horner says she wants you, John," Deborah told her
husband uneasily as they sat down at the dinner table. "It's
about the letter she received."

Lainie heard her mother from her own seat and listened
in interest.

"I don't want anything to do with that letter, and I don't
have anything to say about it," said Papa in firm, distasteful
denial.

Even the secluded little parking lot on the far side of the
Magnolia was full at noon that Sunday. Every congregation
around had somebody present, apparently to find out more
of the latest gossip.

Today the scandal was about Albert Rawlins himself, and
like everything that concerned him, it was exotic news.

Abby Horner, the local director of the Department of
Human Services, had gotten a letter in the mail.

The letter claimed that there was a sixteen-year-old boy
out on Rawlins Farm who'd been born there in the shantytown and had never really been off the place. He had no
social security number, no public schooling, no existence as
far as the state of Tennessee was concerned. The letter
implied that he was nearly a prisoner out on the farm.

"Who in the world sent such a letter?" asked Way's
mother Eileen. "Why would they? And what in the world
makes this boy so special? If we only knew the truth of it,
probably every single one of those shantytown people is an
illegal alien. If they're not that, they're just pure trash."

Bella Foster was sharing the table with them that day,
along with her sister May. On Sundays, the Magnolia sat

tables for eight, and the two of them finished out the Thorne and Blackburn table on this particular Sabbath. "This is not a prank. I asked Abby myself right after church, and she told me in confidence, but I know she won't mind if I tell you, John, since you work so closely with Albert, that the letter came from an old man who'd been living on the farm for years. He claims to have raised the boy, and when he realized he was dying, he sent the letter."

"Is that so?" Papa asked politely, and it was as clear as day to everybody there that he truly had nothing more to say about the subject. Disappointed, Bella straightened from her confidential bend across the table and looked right into the round eyes of John's daughter. "Goodness, Elaina, what's wrong?"

Lainie shook her head and reached nervously for food, but the damage was done: Deborah had noticed. "You're not eating, Lainie. I don't think you've touched your chicken. Are you sick?"

"I'm just not hungry. Papa, what if there really is a boy out on the farm, like they say?"

John put down his fork and looked at her, his face closed. "What we'd best do is give Mr. Rawlins time to do what he wants. If it's true, let him handle it. I remember when Mrs. Horner once tried to make some of the shanty-town children attend school regularly. She couldn't. Nobody has much luck dealing with these kind of people. There's no difference now."

"Well, of course there is," Bella exclaimed. "This time one of them cared enough to write a letter to a concerned person. The letter writer knew that Abby was with DHS. This is a cry for help."

"It sounds to me more like a cry for money," Lainie's aunt Eileen said cynically. "Or just to stir up trouble. After all these years of those people living out on old man Rawlins's farm, one suddenly makes a fuss? No, I don't believe it."

Lainie looked at Papa again. She had long ago figured out that Colley was one of the kids from the shantytown. She didn't know when she had first realized it; the idea had just started small and gotten bigger and bigger inside her.

She understood, too, how much Papa hated them. "Poor white trash," that was what he called the people on the river. Once she had believed every word her respectable, well-educated father had uttered . . . until Colley proved that he was wrong.

He had to know, didn't he, that the boy in the letter was Colley? If she knew it instinctively, surely Papa did.

But the witch boy was nothing to John Thorne. To her, he was a beloved friend. She couldn't erase the memory of the way Colley had sounded the last time she saw him, how lost, how confused he had been. Papa didn't know that. "Do you think, " she asked her mama slowly, "that if there was a boy like that out there, that he would want to be found? What would happen to him?"

"It's an awfully far-fetched story," Deborah said, frowning. "I'm not even sure it's possible nowadays. But if it is, he deserves a chance, and he deserves a good home, with people who'll do right by him. Somebody could adopt him and love him."

"The letter claims he's sixteen," Eileen pointed out. "That's not a lovable age, is it, Way?" she added dryly.

"Maybe he's happy the way he is," Lainie persisted.

"If he is, it's because he's been kept so ignorant of the world that he doesn't know what he's missing," Deborah said pityingly.

"Like Aunt Olivia's chicken," Way put in with a grin, reaching for another piece from the platter.

"Just think about it, Lainie," Mama said. "Would you want to live in one of those shacks and never go to school and never have the love of a good family? It would be a crime against a child to let him grow up like that—if there really was such a child."

Bella took a sip from her tea and said ingratiatingly, "You know, John Thorne, if anybody could find out about this boy and could get old Albert to do something about it, it's you."

Papa knew exactly what Bella was up to. His lips twitched a little, but his face was as unreadable as always. "I don't like having any kind of dealings with the migrant workers other than what I have to. They're nothing but trouble," he said. "I just think we need to put a little faith in Albert Rawlins. He's a hard man, but he's fair. And I never saw him try to keep any one of those workers a prisoner. That's the most ridiculous part of this whole thing."

"Be that as it may, Abby told me," Bella leaned across the table again and dropped her voice to a low murmur, "that she has asked the sheriff for a search warrant. She means to go to the farm this very afternoon."

As it turned out, nobody had to go anywhere to see old Albert.

By two o'clock, most of the diners had departed, leaving only a few to linger on the front porches and have a second piece of strawberry shortcake.

Papa was out in the side yard with Uncle Neil and Way, playing horseshoes, and Lainie, Mama, and Aunt Eileen helped Olivia and Susan in the kitchen. They did it every Sunday afternoon, just like Lainie and Deborah came to the Magnolia every Saturday morning to work. Aunt Olivia was too old to do it all anymore, and they were the family members next in line.

"Lainie—"

Aunt Olivia stood in the door to the kitchen, her face as white as the layers of thin cotton that made up her Sunday dress under the apron she wore.

"Yes, ma'am?"

"There's someone here who says he needs to see you."

Whatever the odd note was in her voice, it made the hairs on Lainie's arms stand up, and it made the other three women also come to a standstill.

"He's out on the back porch. He won't come in. He doesn't like crowds much, I don't guess."

Looking back at Mama, Lainie wiped her hands off on her own apron and followed her aunt.

In the shadow of the trees, just where sunlight dappled through, stood Devil Rawlins.

Her feet wouldn't walk anymore; only Aunt Olivia's hand in her back pushed her closer to the man.

"This is my great-niece, Lainie," Olivia said, and her voice was breathy, as if she, too, were scared of his heavy presence.

Behind them, Lainie could hear her mother's footsteps, and heavier ones that had to belong to Susan. She took heart; they would protect her from whatever was about to happen.

"Sweet Lord!" For once, Susan didn't sound strong and gruff when she spoke behind Lainie. She sounded upset; her words were a little cracked. "What's he doing here?"

Devil Rawlins looked at the woman, but he questioned Olivia.

"Thorne's daughter? She's the one you gave this to?" the old man asked her, his voice gravelly and rough.

"Yes."

Devil frowned at Lainie from under the brim of his old cap, held out his hand, and opened it in front of her face. "Is this yours?"

It was the whistle.

Lainie stared at the way it glimmered against his rough palm—Colley had tried to polish it—and finally croaked, "Yes . . . no."

"Yes or no. Which is it?"

"It was mine, but I . . . I gave it to somebody." Where was Colley? How had the old man come to gain possession of it?

"Who?"

She looked from him to Aunt Olivia, twisting the dish towel in her hands.

"You gave it to Colley, didn't you?" His voice was so sure that Lainie could do nothing but swallow so hard it hurt and nod.

Devil let the hand with the whistle drop, and he relaxed a little. "Why?"

"I wanted to," she whispered.

"You wanted to give a silver whistle to a boy from the river? That don't make sense. How'd you know him? What did he do that you handed it to him? When?"

His questions were so sharp that she took a step back, right into Aunt Olivia. Her great-aunt was small; although Lainie was only thirteen, she was already taller, but Olivia caught her and put her arms around her waist protectively. "You're scaring her."

"Lainie." Deborah's voice was quiet and stern as she stepped up beside the two of them. "Tell Mr. Rawlins what he wants to know. And tell me what this is all about. Who is Colley?"

"He's . . . he's the witch boy, Mama," she confessed hurriedly.

Deborah stared at her. "Who?"

"What's she talkin' about?" Albert demanded, but Lainie couldn't see anything except her mother's shocked face.

"I tried to tell you about him, but you thought he was make-believe. He's not. He's real. I met him just by accident, and he made me promise not to tell. It was the first summer in the new house. You were asleep on the couch, and I went wading down the creek, wading so far that I was on Mr. Rawlins's property, and I fell in a blue hole. That's what Colley called it. Anyway, I nearly drowned, except this boy who'd been working in the circle field where he grows tobacco dragged me out of the water. I've known him ever since."

Her voice just trailed off, and Deborah's face paled in shock.

"What does that mean? How could you?"

"He comes sometimes to the creek below the tree house. We play in the water. He can skip a rock farther than even Way."

"Play in the water!" Albert echoed in angry incredulity. "How long? How long has he been doin' this?"

"I first met him when I was . . . I was eleven. For three summers."

Deborah took an unsteady step, grasping her daughter's shoulders with shaking hands. "All this time, Elaina, you've deceived us all this time?"

"No, Mama! It wasn't like that. You wouldn't believe me the first time. I tried to tell you. And how could it be wrong, me playing in the creek with Colley? It was more fun than I ever had. He'd never hurt me. Colley is good."

"All this time, I thought I was keepin' him away from the things that might make him weak, and he's been seein' you. Damn it to hell. If you've ruined him, girl, I'll—" Albert couldn't find words to express his anger, and the three women stared at him in blank confusion.

Aunt Olivia recovered enough to speak. "She's only a child." Her aunt's cheeks burned slightly. "How could Lainie hurt the boy?" she asked in distress.

He didn't answer; instead, he closed his fist over the whistle. "A Blackburn. By God, it ain't enough that there's a girl, but she had to be a Blackburn. One of Lansing's get."

Olivia made no move, but there were tears in her eyes.

Susan stepped up pugnaciously, right between the other woman and the old man. "You've got no reason to talk to Miss Livy that way. Her daddy—"

"Her daddy's where he should be, in the boneyard. But I hope he knows what's happenin'. I want him to know that I'm standin' on his precious hotel grounds today," Albert Rawlins said forcefully. His face held little or no emotion, but he looked up at the old walls and the peeling paint and the balconies leaning with age. "Ain't quite what it used to be. But then, maybe it never was."

Olivia was crying openly now, the tears sliding quietly down her cheeks. Susan pulled her to her side with her arm around Olivia's back.

It was so still in the backyard; nothing, not even a bird, made a sound.

Lainie herself was the one who broke the silence. "I don't know what's happening, but I'll tell whatever you want to know if it'll make you go away and leave Aunt alone. I gave Colley the whistle because that's how he . . . how he used to call me. He taught me to whistle for him. And the last time I saw him, that's when I gave it to him. I thought he was going to leave and I'd never be with him again. Charley had died. That's the man he lived with. Mama, he's smart. He can read. He's . . ."

The old man relaxed a little. "So." Albert made the word a sigh of sound. "He's kept quiet all this time. He is smart. Maybe too smart for his own good. And maybe some good can come out of this, because it seems to me that any boy that could claim such a friend as Miss Elaina Thorne ain't as deprived and backward as they're tellin' Colley is.

Seems to me, little girl, that you make Abby Horner's story a lie."

Lainie said nothing, and finally Devil opened his palm again and stared down at the whistle one more time. His face suddenly looked as though it might crumple. "I found this in the shack this mornin', and it was like a kick in the stomach. I didn't know how, I just knew it had to be Colley's."

"Where is he?" Lainie whispered in sudden fear.

"Now that's the question," Devil returned heavily. "I need to find him. He's been runnin' from me ever since Charley died. The fool kid acts like I'm to blame. He won't come for me . . . but he might for you."

Lainie knew in an instant what the old man wanted. "You want me to call him. But I can't always make him come. He has to be close enough to hear me. And he hasn't for days and days."

"If I take you somewhere close to where I think he is, will you try to make him come to you?"

"Why? What are you going to do to him?"

"I ain't gonna hurt him. I swear it. But he can't keep on runnin'. He can't hide forever."

Lainie was torn, afraid, just as she thought Devil was, too, that Colley was going to try to leave and never come back; afraid that if she did make him face Devil, he would be in trouble. But mostly, she wanted to see him for herself. And Devil had given his oath, after all.

"I'll try," she agreed at last, and she didn't look at Mama.

Lainie rode to Rawlins Farm in Devil's truck with the old man and his housekeeper Nadine, who drove. She sat between them stiffly, afraid that if she relaxed even a little, she'd touch Albert Rawlins and incite his anger again.

As if he weren't frightening enough, Papa had scared her senseless as well.

"You've been with the one they call Colley? My Lainie?

All these summers?" He looked at her as if he might hit her, and she moved a step away, her eyes terrified. "No. No, I won't have it."

"What's done is done," Albert said heavily. "Let her come with me and try to find him, and I'll take him with me. I'll keep him away from your girl, Thorne, and you keep her away from him."

"She'll be under lock and key from now on," he said tightly. "Lainie, do you know what you—"

"No," Deborah interrupted at last, pulling Lainie to her. "John, she's a child. Thirteen. He was somebody to play with. Don't."

"I reckon I understand a little of the way you feel," Albert said to his overseer. "But if you'll let her come with me, let her call the boy, I'll take him with me to the house. I can keep an eye on him there. I'll do what I can to see that he never gets the chance to meet your girl again."

"Papa, please, I have to," Lainie pleaded.

"Think about it this way," Devil advised dryly. "He's out there on the loose. He may come lookin' for her if she don't bring him to me first."

John Thorne's face was gray as he considered the idea. "If I agree," he said tightly, "if I let you use my only child like a helpless lamb to call your wolf cub in, you have to stay with her. And I'm going, too. In return, you give me your God's word that you'll take him and keep him away. Far away. I have to have your oath on it."

"You forget yourself, Thorne." Albert spoke sharply. "You're my overseer. A good worker, but you overstep your bounds."

"Not when it's my Lainie. Your oath, or she's going nowhere with you," John answered. He stood implacably before the old man, not moving an inch.

It was Albert who capitulated. "All right, then. You've got it." He didn't like Thorne's plan or his words, that was plain, but he had no alternative, so he gave in.

They were not the only ones interested. Abby Horner and a very reluctant sheriff waited for them at the Rawlins house, which they passed on the way to the farm and the creek. Albert took one look at them through the window of the old Ford truck and swore more in one sentence than Lainie had heard Colley swear in a whole summer. Then he jerked the truck to a jarring halt.

"Damnation, woman, what do you want now?" he exclaimed to the social worker, climbing out.

"I'm sorry about this, Mr. Rawlins," the sheriff began lamely, but Abby took over.

"If there is no boy being kept against his will out here, then you shouldn't object to a search of the place. Why, Deborah!" Abby broke off her words with a gasp as the other car pulled up behind them. "And John!" For the first time, Abby seemed to realize that Lainie was in the truck with Devil. "What's going on?"

"Everything's going to be all right, Abby," Mama said soothingly, although her own face gave lie to the words. "Mr. Rawlins means to try to find the boy you're looking for."

"There is one, then," Abby cried in triumph, then she said in puzzlement, "but what's Lainie—"

"He thinks she can help him," Mama said steadily.

Abby stared at first one of them and then the other in confusion. "I'll just stay awhile and see," she said at last, pugnaciously.

Albert swore again, but he turned his back on her. "You, girl," he said to Lainie, "come with me."

They rode part of the way in the old truck, bouncing and jouncing down a rutted trail heading inexorably toward the river, while Mama and Papa plowed along behind them in Papa's Jeep, and farther back, Abby and the sheriff ate dust in her white station wagon. Then Albert turned away from the river, heading back toward Martin Hollow Road, and even when the trail played out after a little way, the old man kept on, pushing the battered truck through the weeds and vines until they couldn't move anymore. Then he stopped and they climbed out.

"We're farther down than I reckon you've ever been. If you keep going straight, you'll find the creek. On this side of it is a clearing, and a path leadin' right down into the water and then out of it on the other side. It's hard to follow. Blackberry brambles, and honeysuckles, and trees. I reckon you don't need to try to. Just go to the edge of the creek and see if you can find him. If he's there, he'll come from the direction of the path. But don't call him until I get close. This damned leg. Well, go on, girl."

Her heart beat fast, and the brambles tore and yanked at her Sunday dress as she pushed her way toward Widow's Creek. A stick found its way between the sole of her foot and the open sandal she was wearing, and she had to stop to pull it out.

The clearing was there at last, just as he had said. It lay hot and sunny in the open, full of the noise of a summer afternoon. The creek bubbled, the katydids sang, the birds chirped, the jar flies rumbled.

She ran her hands down her dress nervously.

"Colley!"

The call was almost lost in the noisy air.

"Colley, please, where are you?"

This time her voice was louder and stronger, but there was still no answer.

Putting her fingers to her mouth, she took a deep breath

and blew. The sound was long and loud and it warbled just a little at the end—just like it was supposed to.

The birds fell silent, then twittered at the sound. She waited an eternity, her pulses racing.

Then something moved in front of her, and there he was, right in the middle of the path on the other side of the creek, his narrow brown ribcage above the ragged, cutoff pants heaving as he gasped for breath.

"What are you doing here?" he demanded in shock.

A movement over her shoulder caught his eye—Rawlins. Colley's face went from stunned to terrified, and he splashed across the creek to snatch Lainie's hand and pull her back into its ankle-deep water with him, behind him, holding her arm around his bare waist as if to make sure she stayed put against his back, her dress pure and white against his dark skin.

"Don't do anything to her," he said quickly to Rawlins, as the old man drew nearer. "I don't know how the hell she got here, but she's just a kid. She didn't know any better than to come."

"Oh, she knew," Albert said with harshly drawn breaths punctuating his words. He stepped right into the creek, too, and caught Colley hard by the arm, holding him tightly just above the elbow. Suddenly afraid for the boy, more afraid for him than she was of her father's wrath, Lainie wrapped her other arm, the one Colley wasn't already clasping, around his waist, too.

That was how the other people following found them when they struggled through the weeds to the clearing, the three in the creek tied together like a triangle, linked by the hold each had on the other.

"My God," John said hoarsely.

"John, wait," Deborah said involuntarily, catching at her husband.

Albert's voice was ominous as he finished, "Just like you knew to keep it a secret that you were meetin' her," he finished ominously.

Colley looked from Devil to those beyond, to the white-faced, angry overseer, to the tears that were sliding unchecked down the cheeks of the woman with Thorne.

Then he let Lainie's arm go abruptly. "You told," he accused.

"He found the whistle," she returned pleadingly, still clinging to him.

"Charley taught you more, maybe, than is good for you. More than I meant for you to know," Albert observed. "Like how to hide. You been slippin' away from me like a fox on the run since he died. I couldn't stop him dyin', Colley. It ain't my fault."

"You got her to call me because you thought I'd come for her," Colley accused.

"It worked, didn't it ? Like I said, you're full of surprises. You of all people, comin' when a girl calls. Maybe Charley was right. Maybe you ain't what I want. Maybe it's time to let you go after all."

"What are you talking about?" Colley asked slowly, pulling away from Lainie.

Albert dropped the boy's arm. "You got no need to keep runnin.' That woman up there"—he pointed up to where Abby stood with the other three—"she's here to take you away if that's what you want. See that big sheriff? He's here to help her."

Abby took a step nearer. "We don't want to hurt you. Don't let him scare you. We just want to take you with us, to find you a good home, that's all."

Colley pulled back two steps, his face wary and afraid.

"You're free to go with her, boy," Albert said casually. "She's with the state of Tennessee. They think you're bein' treated bad. They want to civilize you." His voice was heavy with irony. "They'll give you a new life, away from me and away from the farm."

Colley's eyes flew to Lainie as she stood forlornly in the middle of the creek in her girlish, innocent white frock.

"Away from her, too, maybe," the old man observed shrewdly.

Colley took a hard, deep breath. "I won't go," he said defiantly. "I'm . . . I'm not ready yet."

Albert straightened a little. "What's that, boy? I didn't hear you good. Say it again, real loud and clear."

"I said, I want to stay," he repeated, humble enough.

"Are you askin' or tellin'?"

Colley was heartbreakingly honest. "I'm begging."

"I've got some things to ask of you, too, so I reckon that it's fair enough." Then Albert raised his voice. "You, Miss Human Services, did you hear all that, or do you need Colley to say it again?"

Abby said angrily, "It doesn't make any difference what he says, Mr. Rawlins, because this boy is a ward of the state. You have no legal or family ties to hold him, so—"

"Yes, he does," Deborah interrupted unsteadily. She came across the clearing and stepped into the creek with them. But it wasn't Lainie she reached for. The tears she had cried earlier still made her face pink and glistening as she laid both hands on the boy's thin shoulders and turned him to face her.

"Deborah! Get back," John called, but she was deaf to his command.

Colley was startled, but he stood still under her touch.

Lainie hadn't realized how much he had grown lately. He was taller than Mama, a lot taller. Deborah looked from his silky black hair to his high cheeks, his dark eyes, his sharply defined mouth. "Looking at you is like looking in the face of a ghost."

"He don't know yet," Albert said warningly.

"But you'll tell him."

"After everybody else is gone, when it's just me and him. Charley was right; it's come the season for the truth."

Mama's hand stroked through his hair one time. "Then give me my daughter, and we'll go home." She let her fingers drop lingeringly, and her eyes fell on the social worker. "Abby, why don't you come with us?"

"But I can't leave this boy with—"

"Yes, you can. Colley belongs here. Tomorrow, when I've had time to calm down and think about things, I'll come to your office and tell you why he does."

The certainty of Deborah's voice worked on Abby. She finally walked away, a part of the strange, quiet group that headed back to the cars. Colley hung far behind them and behind Lainie, who was caught firmly in her father's grasp. She knew Papa was angry, but it was a deeper, darker anger than she had ever seen, and she didn't know why.

Up at Albert's truck, Colley hesitated while everybody else got in their cars. Lainie heard her father mutter something under his breath as he settled himself in the Jeep, and she followed his gaze. He was watching Colley.

Suddenly something weird happened to her vision. Out of the clear blue, she saw the witch boy as John did.

What had happened to the child who pulled her from the creek?

He was sixteen now, five eleven and still growing. His face had changed, too. He had the look of an adult. When had that occurred? The inborn leanness of his frame would stop him from ever being stockily muscular, but the hard summers in the fields had put well-defined, long tendons in his arms and chest and neck.

Maybe it was those hints of manhood visible in him, or

maybe it was the sheer untamed, bare-chested, long-legged wildness of his looks that was making John Thorne stiff with dislike.

"Get on in," Devil told Colley, and finally, the boy vaulted into the back of the truck and settled himself in place. When they pulled away, John trailed after them in his Jeep, his silence filling the whole world. Nobody talked at all until they got home.

"He's Brodie's son," Mama said suddenly, once the front door of the house was shut. "It's written all over him. There was talk that Brodie fell in love with one of the shantytown girls and got her pregnant."

"That's not love, Deborah. The Rawlinses don't fall in love," John said sharply. "They tell me that Albert once used those old cabins like they were cathouses, and that's about as close to love as I can see him ever coming. He has less use for women, less respect for them, than any man I know. He doesn't like them."

"Brodie could have loved her. You didn't know him. He was dead before you ever came to the Springs. You took over the job that he had once done on Rawlins Farm. Brodie was as different from Albert and James as night is from day. He would have counted the whole world well lost for love. I don't know what happened to the girl, but that boy today proves that some of the rumors at least were true."

"There's going to be a lot more rumors than those," Papa said harshly. "That's no boy, Deborah. He's halfway to being a man, and our daughter's handling him like he was her pet. She's been meeting him on the sly."

Lainie froze, her eyes wide, and Deborah protested, "John, no. She did wrong, and she needs to be punished for deceiving us. But she's a child. Please, don't shame her with something she doesn't even understand yet."

"She has to be told the truth."

"Don't," Deborah implored again, glancing at Lainie's scared face. "I've told you before, you don't see things clear where the river people are concerned."

"I've got reason to. Why are you defending him? You know what he is. I won't let her be hurt."

"This boy hasn't done anything, John. This boy tried to save Lainie when he thought Albert was after her. He once pulled her from the creek, where she could have drowned. He's Brodie's. Do you know what that means? I've got friends and family who are alive right this minute because of Brodie Rawlins, because he was there to get them out of that quarry. Surely this town owes something to his son."

Papa's face twisted in an amazed anger. "I can't believe my own ears. What are you saying? No matter what he did, Lainie won't be part of any payment to a savage like him."

"You're not going to let me see Colley again?" Lainie's voice shook with distress. "But why? I wish I'd never found him for that old man. Why can't I see him anymore?"

Papa turned on her. "Don't you understand? You can't because he—"

"John. No. She's too young. I won't let you pour your own grief out on a child." This time Mama's voice was harsh, so angry that Lainie fell silent in surprise. Deborah never lost her temper.

It had an effect on Papa, too. When he spoke to her again, Lainie knew it wasn't what he had meant to say.

"You think Colley's a kid to play in the creek with. I know a different side of him. I was there when he beat another boy into the ground in a fight. I've seen him work the tobacco crop like a man twice his age. I've watched while he handled a horse like he was half animal himself. I know what I'm talking about when I say he's no fit friend for you, Beth."

The name echoed in the tiny silence, and finally, Mama said in a calm, careful voice, "Our daughter is called Elaina, John. She's not Beth."

Part 2

Lonely Hearts

6

The smaller of the two downstairs parlors held a rosewood organ that Lansing Blackburn once played vigorously every Saturday night for friends and visitors. The elaborate scrollwork on it required minute attention to dusting, but today, Lainie kept stopping in her cleaning to look in the slightly warped mirror that hung above it.

Black hair with just a touch of brown, wavy about her face.

Bright blue eyes, huge and long lashed. Shockingly blue in the tan of her face, against the darkness of her hair and eyebrows.

Small nose, full mouth.

It was her mother's face, except where Deborah glowed, Lainie sparkled.

Less serenity and more vibrancy.

One more unfair fact of life, that was what her face had taught her: if a woman was beautiful, she was far more likely to get the things that she wanted. It wasn't right that simple genetics should affect a life so much, but it was the way it was.

What you're about to do is wrong, her conscience whispered sternly, somewhere behind that face.

But there were circumstances that made a conscience nothing but an encumbrance, she told herself. Enough bad had happened to her that surely God would let her get away with deliberately using her best asset to get what she needed.

"You must like what you see in that mirror," Mama's voice said humorously behind her. "You've been looking at it long enough."

Startled, Lainie found her mother's eyes in the glass, too, as Deborah walked up behind her. "Mama," she said slowly, looking back at herself, "am I pretty?"

Surprised, Deborah let her hand touch Lainie's hair. "I reckon you know the answer to that. You'll do fine."

"But you've never told me."

"There's no point in it. Pretty is only as pretty does. Make sure you do what's good."

Lainie made a frustrated gesture. She didn't need a sermon. "That's not what I meant."

She was going to seduce the only available rich and willing man in town, Preston Rawlins, away from some of his money. My God, a Rawlins. There was some kind of poetic justice in that.

Lainie's heart shivered, and she turned away from the mirror and her mother's eyes. What would this cost her? Too big a price, but she had to do it.

She had to hold on to the Magnolia. She owed Mama, and whether Deborah liked it or not, she would settle the debt.

"Where's the telephone?" Lainie asked abruptly. She wanted to make a call to a houseboat.

∘   ∘   ∘

Lloyd Tate's big boat was moored at Hurricane Mills Dock down on Center Hill Lake, several miles outside of Cookeville. The silver panels along its sides reflected the light of the hot Saturday afternoon so brilliantly that it nearly made the sun in the sky above them obsolete.

In the middle of the music blaring from a nearby CD player and the sound of voices and laughter, someone called to someone else down the length of the boat.

"Here, child, come to Papa," Mark Gregory implored a pretty blond from the front deck, and she obliged by strolling up to him and settling herself into his lap.

Lainie wasn't sure whether Mark wanted the girl or the bottle of Jim Beam that she was holding, but it didn't seem to matter. The blonde thrust the whiskey into one of his hands and dropped a kiss on his lips as he sat sprawled in one of the chairs in a pair of brown Dockers and worn-down loafers and very little else.

She turned away from the sight; it made her uncomfortable. Finding Preston in the small crowd wasn't hard. He stood out like a tall Viking as he talked to Tate and the other Gregory twin under the shade of the cool awning at the other end of the boat.

A curvaceous redhead was standing with them, one arm through Preston's and the other through Jack Gregory's.

Lainie looked at Preston Rawlins for a long moment. He wasn't even noticing what the other woman was doing, or the way she kept watching his face like a hungry barracuda.

His indifference might be because he was used to women fawning all over him. Or, if she was a real romantic, she might believe it was for the reason he said he'd stopped looking at other females: he only wanted Lainie.

In a minute, Preston's eyes slid away from Jack Gregory

and searched the boat before him, finally finding her.
"Lainie!" His voice went from cool to warm, so warm that a
dart of uneasiness shot through her as she moved forward.
"So there's where you wandered off to. Well, I've found
you now. Come on back over here where you belong, and
make it snappy, woman," he said teasingly, and he pulled
his arm from that of the redhead's. "You wouldn't believe
how I had to beg before this girl finally called me and said
she'd come to the party," he informed Jack with just the
right touch of rueful self-pity.

Lainie knew exactly what she needed to do. She walked
up to him, into his arms, and lifted her head to kiss him full
on the lips. He was damp from the swimming they'd been
doing most of the afternoon, and he smelled cool, like the
lake, not of sunshine and that woods scent that had always
clung to Colley. He had a taste, too, of expensive gin, the
kind Tate's bar had been serving steadily.

"So you got your little angel to wear her choir robes right
into sin, did you, Preston?" Lloyd Tate materialized out of
the cabin door at Preston's back, and his voice was amused
as he spoke over the other man's shoulder. He let his eyes
drift down over the simple white bathing suit Lainie wore,
over the way the halter top of it tied in a secure, perky bow
behind her neck.

Preston's eyes, blue like the sky at noon instead of black
as midnight, came back to her face, and he smiled down at
her, inviting her to share his amusement at the expense of
the other man. "What would you know about angels,
Lloyd?"

"Probably more than you," Tate said dryly.

"Maybe so. All I know is, I like them. I've been a good
boy lately. Are you my reward, little angel?" The palm of
his hand soothed over her arm, warm and insistent.

Lainie wanted to hide somewhere, but she knew

instinctively that she had to stay cool. She had known when she called him what she wanted and what she had to do. *Now, girl, play the part.*

"How good were you?" she teased, reaching out to trace his golden skin just inside the V of his shirt. Inside her, something squirmed uncomfortably. She had always been straightforward with men; never once had she deliberately flirted and manipulated and used sexuality the way she was today with Preston.

He knew exactly what she was doing, and he knew that something had changed Lainie. The knowledge was in his eyes when he looked at her. Surely he'd make his offer again.

"It depends on what you're asking him about," Jack Gregory interposed humorously. "He was a devil on the green early this morning. We had a little bet going, and I lost enough that I'll have to sell my car to pay him. So maybe you should be good to me instead of him. I'm the one in need of a little human warmth here."

Preston put a hand on Jack's chest. "Too bad," he said unsympathetically. "Because this"—and he ran his hand across Lainie's back and grasped her arm on the other side of her body—"is all mine. Find your own angel, buddy."

"I've never been accused of being an angel," the redhead interposed, sliding her arm more tightly through Gregory's and shooting a glance at Lainie, "but I'm very entertaining."

"I'll bet you are," he said with a laugh. "And I'm in the mood for it. Tell me exactly what you do for entertainment, Julie. That was your name, wasn't it?"

"If anybody's looking for someplace private, the cabin below is available," Tate said, tilting his glass up to his lips. He wiped his mouth off with the back of his hand—the movement had an earthy look to it, the way that he did it—

and looked straight into Lainie's eyes. His own were an odd, light-colored gray, hot and direct, and knowledge hit her like a blow: he was coming on to her, right here, deliberately, with Preston at her side. "Have you ever seen my boat up close and personal, Elaina? That's your name, isn't it?"

He looked from her to Preston at last, almost challenging him.

She stepped backward involuntarily.

"I'll show her if she needs a tour," Preston said, his voice full of a warning only slightly muffled under the laziness of his words. Lloyd looked back down into his glass. Then Preston laughed. "We're leaving you animals before you scare Lainie away. Don't you want something to drink, angel?"

"I'll bet her mama never lets her touch hard liquor," Lloyd drawled derisively.

Lainie hoped she hid her blush.

How had the older man seen through her enough today to know of her hesitation with the liquor they all consumed at an alarming rate?

Except for a wedding she'd attended when Mary Fran Dollar married a boy from Chicago whom she met while at the university in Bowling Green, where they actually served champagne at the reception, Lainie had never had anything at all to drink, unless she counted the communion wine. She hadn't even liked Mary Fran's champagne. She'd thought it would be more wonderful than 7UP, and instead, it had tasted dry and bitter, not worth the scandal it caused among the good hearts of the Springs.

"Champagne! That's what happens when a girl marries some Episcopalian from God knows where," Susan McAlester had snorted. "Why couldn't she settle for a good Church of Christ boy and lemonade?"

I don't think the bar on this boat has lemonade, Lainie

thought a little humorously. It was too uptown. So was the lifestyle of most of the people here. They indulged themselves, just as Preston did. Surely it wouldn't be hard to live with him in the middle of such luxury for a while. But the thought made her flinch, and she must have made a noise. Preston turned from his conversation with Mark Gregory.

"You like that idea?" he asked teasingly.

"I'm sorry. I was daydreaming. What idea?" She looked up, and wished she hadn't. Tate was still there, right beside them, and from somewhere, he'd picked up the redhead from Jack Gregory.

Something about the woman was vaguely, uncomfortably familiar. Who was she?

"Wake up, sleepyhead, and listen. Lloyd said we should go diving at the old quarry, maybe even take some scuba gear—"

Lainie pulled herself more upright against the rail of the deck, alarm zinging through her. "Are you talking about the old Lo-Joe Quarry? But you can't."

Preston's face immediately became more interested. "Why not?" he demanded. "It's on Grandfather's property. It belongs to him. Who's to stop us?"

"He would," Lainie said with certainty. "Nobody goes there anymore, not since all those men died there in the rock slide."

"That was thirty years ago," Preston protested with a deprecating laugh.

"Twenty-five," Lainie corrected, "and one of them is still there, buried under the rubble somewhere. They couldn't find him."

"You're talking about Brodie," Preston said. "Well, hell, why would he care? He'd probably like some company after all this time."

"Make it interesting," Lloyd said with a shrug. "The first to find Brodie Rawlins wins the game."

"Is the water deep?" Jack Gregory interposed, with a placatory look at Lainie.

"Deep as the bottomless pit and cold as ice, I've always heard," Preston returned.

"Why don't you just dive here?" Lainie demanded. "The lake is where everybody else scubas."

Tate considered Preston's face and then took a sip of his own drink. "She's right," he said carelessly. "It's a dumb idea. Risky."

Preston returned, "Which is why we all have a yen to do it, isn't it? So maybe we will."

"Colley Rawlins won't like it," Tate said steadily, looking into his glass.

There was a tiny little pause, and Preston said tightly, "Do you think I give a damn what that heathen thinks? I'm not afraid of him. I know what he is. I remember the first day I ever was around Colley at Grandfather's. He spent all his time in the barn because it was the only place he belonged. And the first time he ever came to Nashville on an errand for the old man, everybody there laughed."

"That must have been years ago," Lloyd noted. "Nobody's laughing now. Down in the shantytown they call him the Man."

"How do you know things like that?" Lainie burst out.

Lloyd's eyes narrowed to gray, intent slits. "I know everything, honey," he said smoothly. "I'm a good listener. You know what else I've heard? That the Man's got eyes for you."

The redhead took in a sudden, harsh breath and stared intently at Lainie's face as she stood in the shadows of the awning over the deck. "You're the girl from the hotel in Indian Springs," she said slowly. "Elaina Thorne. That's why you look so familiar. I remember all about you. It'd be hard not to."

"Do you think we could avoid rehashing all the past history?" Preston protested. "I've had about all I can take of it."

His words couldn't stop the woman; maybe she didn't even hear them. She turned to Lloyd and Jack as though she were about to impart the gospel instead of just old gossip. "Her family was always genteel and proper, until she got mixed up with Colley. He was living like an animal, half wild down on the creek. She was the only person from town who could get near him to bring him in. They say that she ran with him all over those woods."

"I was thirteen years old. A kid," Lainie said defensively, shocked by the openness of the other woman's attack.

"You weren't a kid when your father caused a scene in front of half the town when Colley came to the Magnolia after you. People say John Thorne had an accident awfully fast after that happened." The other woman's voice was careless and cruel.

Something sharp as a sword jabbed Lainie's throat. She wouldn't cry, not here.

"Since you're here, there was something I always wanted to know," the redhead asked lazily. "What's Colley Rawlins like in bed?"

Lainie took a deep breath. "Why don't you go to bed with him and find out for yourself? He's not too choosy about who he sleeps with."

Lloyd gave a tiny laugh and tipped his glass to her in amusement, but Lainie didn't even acknowledge him.

"I think I want to go home." She pushed her way past Tate and headed for the other end of the point. Behind her, she heard Preston's footsteps as he followed.

"Lainie!" Preston called her name once before he caught

her, but she pulled away from his hand. He stared at the unspilled tears shining in her eyes. "I'm the one who should be crying," he said harshly. "It's not an easy thing, hearing about you and Colley. But I'm not fool enough to give up something I want just because he wanted it, too. I think you owe me, Lainie."

"Me!"

"I had a hard enough job just getting you here," he said quietly. "It's the very first time I've not had to sneak around to meet you. Stay. We're going diving at Lo-Joe, I've decided. If Colley doesn't like it or anything else I do, he can go to hell. And when this afternoon's over, me and you, we have to talk about things. Lainie, please, come with us to the quarry. I need you to."

She needed things, as well. She couldn't let herself be distracted from that fact, not by her own fear of the quarry, by the redhead's spite, or by Colley himself.

"Then I'll come." She capitulated reluctantly, and then she gave a shiver at what she'd agreed to.

"Worried about something?" Preston asked silkily, letting his hands gently trace her cheek. "Colley, maybe?"

Lainie settled for a half-truth. "I can't help being worried, Preston. Lo-Joe is full of ghosts."

"Good. It's going to be fun. Don't be a spoilsport, angel." His face lightened with anticipation.

Lainie turned back to stare at the lake, biting her lip. Preston was an outsider; he didn't understand.

Colley didn't always understand the new way that he was living; he felt like an outsider in some new world that he didn't think he liked much.

In fact, if he had realized that he could ever hate anything as much as he hated those first months as Albert

Rawlins's grandson, he might have stayed hidden in the woods on the farm forever.

He had lost Lainie. Now Devil wouldn't let him slip away to the circle field, and even if he had, she wouldn't have been there.

"You know how to dig your own grave, boy," the old man said. "You managed to get hooked up with the one family that I won't let you go near. Anyway, Thorne ain't about to have you around that little girl of his anymore."

"But why?" Colley demanded in frustration. "Why can't I see her?"

"First off, because I told you you couldn't. And second, there ain't no need in givin' the gossips in this town more to talk about. They've got plenty to tell about you and her already, and she ain't nothin' but a kid. There's some mean mouths in the Springs."

"What are they saying?" he asked in confusion.

Devil shrugged. "Ask for the truth and I'll give it to you. One or two of those old fools say that maybe you were takin' liberties with her."

Colley stared, still not understanding.

"Maybe you were with her like the stallion was with that chestnut mare we put in with him last month," Albert said brusquely, looking away.

Colley's ears reddened, and he turned without another word and walked right out of the house toward the fields. The old man followed him to the door and called after him, "You didn't hear me say I believed it, did you?"

He tried not to think about it at all, tried not to miss Lainie's laughter. Devil did his part to keep him busy. To satisfy the state and the woman called Abby Horner, Colley had to get papers, things called birth certificates and social security cards, all to prove that he was a real person, just like they couldn't look at him and see it for themselves.

That was how he came to visit Nashville for the first time. It frightened him, closed in on him, made him sick.

"You got blood kin livin' in this town," Devil told him, and the thought intrigued Colley. When he looked at them, would he see answers about himself? Would he understand himself better? But on that day, he didn't get a chance to find out. "Ain't no need in gettin' them all up in the air about you until we have to," Devil said wryly. "You'll meet them soon enough."

One Saturday morning he had to go to school, the place he'd yearned to go years before, and let a woman give him a test. She stared at him and whispered to another lady there and finally told Devil in stiff, bewildered amazement that Colley was two years above the norms for his age, whatever that meant. He was glad to leave her and the school behind. Maybe he'd liked the idea of school just because it was where Lainie had spent time; it wasn't wonderful, after all.

But he banished the thought of the girl quickly; he couldn't remember her without the flush of embarrassed anger that always swept over him.

It wasn't just at the school that people stared at him; it happened in town, too, whenever he went with his grandfather. It got easier to look through and over people than to look at them.

Come the fall, when Devil shrewdly decided that Colley could study at home with a tutor who would come to the house three days a week, he agreed. He wasn't so sure he liked the world of the Springs, anyway. Maybe it would be better if he hid on the farm a while longer.

He spent his time at hard work, trying to ignore his own loneliness. There was no Charley to talk to, no Lainie coming the next summer to enliven the days, and he was still too wary of Albert Rawlins to say much to him except what he had to.

Christmas crept up on him like a benediction, a relief in the cold silence around him. It seemed that he had an uncle, an aunt, a cousin—all in Nashville. Maybe with one of them, he'd feel an instant connection, a recognition of blood like he'd never felt with anyone yet.

Colley was anxious to meet his relatives.

"This is your cousin," Devil said flatly on Christmas morning when the three of them arrived. He motioned Colley toward the boy who looked a year or two older than he himself was, the one standing silent in the living room when Nadine ushered Colley in. She'd taken time to warn him, too: "Use whatever you got that looks like manners, now," she'd said. "Mr. James's wife puts a big store by that kind of thing. I want 'em to like you, Colley. You need a friend or two."

So Colley did his best. "I'm glad to meet you," he mumbled.

And he realized suddenly that he'd seen the people here once before: they'd been the ones gathered around the supper table the night that Charley died, and he'd come rushing in. He didn't think they remembered him at all.

"He's not my real cousin, is he?" Preston asked his father dubiously.

James was Devil's oldest son, and Colley was more curious about him than he was any of the others. Was there any part of him like the mysterious Brodie? There didn't seem to be any similarity; James was blond, like the picture of Devil's wife. Colley swallowed his disappointment.

James didn't answer his son. "You should never have done this, Daddy," he said tightly. "Until three weeks ago, we didn't know this boy existed. You never said one word. How could you?"

"I wanted him raised my way," Devil responded, "and I wanted to know that he was really Brodie's son. Now that you've seen him, is there any room for doubt in your mind, James?"

James hesitated, then stepped forward, circling Colley slowly, examining him from every angle as if he'd been livestock that he was considering for purchase. Colley burned with embarrassment. Nadine was wrong. These people didn't have any manners.

"No." His uncle sighed reluctantly.

"Good. So you can accept the fact that he belongs here today, just as much as Preston does."

The woman in the corner made a sudden motion of protest. "You can't compare him to Preston. Even if Brodie did father him, there's still the mother to be considered."

"He had one. What more is there?" Albert said coolly.

Teresa Rawlins looked from her father-in-law to her husband. "Ask him, James," she said insistently.

James glanced at the three faces around him. "Send the two boys out, then. I need some privacy."

Devil motioned to Colley. "Go on. Go down to the barn. Take Preston with you."

Once outside in the cold December air, neither of them spoke. In the warm, smelly barn, Colley went instinctively to the stall with the big black horse, and it welcomed him with a velvet nose nudging at him inquiringly.

"My dad said that you were my uncle Brodie's son," Preston said suddenly.

"That's what they tell me."

"I guess you think because of that, you can have anything of Grandfather's that you want—like Captain." Preston was definitely not friendly. In fact, he was belligerent.

"Who's Captain?" Colley asked in puzzlement.

Preston laughed incredulously. "That's Captain," he said, pointing to the black. "His name is Captain of the Storm, and he's worth a fortune. Dad says that Grandfather should sell him now instead of putting him to stud. He says too much goes wrong when you start guaranteeing foals."

"Sell him! Devil didn't say anything to me about selling him. I'd have known it if he was planning to," Colley answered, his voice rich with distress.

"Devil! Is that what you call my grandfather?" Preston echoed with a hint of scorn. "And anyway, what would you know about the Captain? Mama says that Dad has to tell Grandfather everything about stocks and investments because he's not smart about them. This horse is an investment, that's all. If Dad told him to deed Captain over to me, I could have him."

Colley stroked the nose of the horse. He hadn't even known its name after all this time. To him, the animal was just Black Horse. But he did know that he didn't want Preston to get his hands on him. And he already had one more thing figured out: his cousin from the city didn't like him, and Colley returned the sentiment wholeheartedly.

Blood didn't make liking, it seemed.

"Here," Colley said on a sudden wicked impulse as he swung open the door of the stall. "Catch him and I'll get a saddle for you to ride him with."

Black Horse gave an amazed snort at his unexpected freedom and started with a lunge for the great outdoors.

Preston squawked and scrambled for the top of a nearby stall.

When the stallion realized that the barn was closed and his escape limited, he pulled up short and nosed around in a pile of hay.

Colley went after him, trying to choke down his amusement, and as he led the animal back, Preston exploded.

"You did that deliberately, trying to scare me."

"Maybe so. I reckon you'd better wait a while before you go buying any horses," he said gravely.

Preston came down from his perch. "So I don't know much about animals. But I know something about you."

"Yeah? Like what?" Colley latched the stall shut carefully.

"My father found out a lot about you in the last week or two, after he heard you were here. He found out why you don't have a mother."

Mother. The word struck a nerve. Colley finished the job he was doing and turned slowly, already dreading whatever Preston was about to say. "How could he find that out?" he demanded, avoiding the harder questions. How, when nobody on this farm seemed to know except Devil? He'd broached the subject just twice before with him, and the old man had made it abundantly clear that it was not something he was going to talk about.

"He knows because he found the paperwork."

Ask. Ask, he commanded himself. "What paperwork?"

"Your mother sold you." The words burst out of Preston, who was nearly giddy with the telling of his story. He waited dramatically for the atrocious nature of what he'd said to hit home.

"I don't know what you're talking about," Colley said slowly. "Nobody can sell another person."

"She did. When you were six months old, Grandfather bought you from her with money. I don't know how much, but I do know that she could only have the money if she would give you to him. She had to sign papers—and she chose the money."

Colley couldn't stay in the barn a second longer with the triumphant face of Preston Rawlins in front of him. It didn't matter whether his so-called cousin knew that he was hurting or not. What mattered was that he get out of there and find truth.

He went straight to the house, right to the room where

Albert and James had sequestered themselves, and broke into their conversation. "He told me—Preston—that you paid my mother money to leave me here with you. Is that true?"

Albert swore, and James flushed. "He must have heard me talking to Teresa. I swear, I didn't tell him, Daddy."

"Is it true?" Colley persisted.

"I ain't sure what you're askin'." For once, Devil evaded. "She was young and couldn't take care of you. She had to have money to live. We just came to a deal. I gave her the money, and she gave you a good home where you'd be safe."

But Colley heard all he needed. "You kept me here, waiting to see if I was Brodie's son. I heard you. Not because you wanted me. You didn't even come around. You handed me over to Charley. You only needed my sweat."

Albert leaned back in the big chair where he sat. "I never pretended that I didn't."

Colley didn't know what he'd expected from his grandfather. He got what Albert always dealt in: hard facts, and they hurt.

Without a word, he went back to the barn, and he did his best to stay there as much as possible. It was the only place where he could get away from the Rawlins family.

The holiday was long and miserable. Colley wasn't accustomed to celebrating it. The only concession Charley had ever made to it was to enjoy the pie that Nadine always sent to the shack at the head of the hollow. He remembered, and grieved, and stayed away from all of them.

The day after James and his family returned to Nashville, Albert came to the barn to find Colley.

"Say what you got to say, boy," he commanded Colley, leaning against the high wall of one of the horse stalls. "You been sulled up with it this whole time."

In a flash, Colley came up off the hay where he'd been sitting. "You never even gave me a chance. You didn't give a damn what happened to me. You just pulled out your god-almighty money and took away the only person in the world who was mine."

"Your mama didn't have to take it. Nobody put a gun to her head. She wanted it, needed it, more than she wanted and needed you. She was a woman. That's the way they are. You were the illegitimate son of a dead man. What was she goin' to do with you?"

"So she didn't want me, either."

"Don't expect me to feel sorry for you."

"I don't." Colley sat down again heavily. His voice and his soul were both empty of emotion.

Most of the summer after she led the old man to Colley, Lainie had been kept close to home, right under Mama's eye and Papa's stern quietness. She knew she was under lock and key, but she was too afraid of stirring up that strange, deep rage in Papa to make a fuss of it.

It was in Sunday school, of all places, that she heard what they were saying about Colley, and about her.

"Yesterday Mr. Rawlins brought that river boy to town with him," Tina Forbes, the daughter of the librarian, told two of the other girls in the teen class as they huddled together in a corner before the teacher stepped in the room. "You should see him. Hair to his shoulders, baggy overalls. Backward acting. He looked at the ground all of the time."

"My aunt tested him at the school, and she said he was too quiet. He wouldn't speak a word until Mr. Rawlins made him," another teen girl chimed in. "She said if she was poor Deborah Thorne, she'd be worried sick."

Lainie caught the words as she walked into the tiny Sunday school room, all in the cool of a summer frock. "Why?" she demanded without even stopping to greet them. All she felt was a flare of quick temper and frustration. She'd done nothing, but she was being treated like a prisoner.

More than that, she couldn't see Colley again, not ever, Papa said.

Tina turned to face the other girl, not one whit embarrassed at being caught. If anything, she was eaten up with curiosity.

"Because of you and him, that's why," she said bluntly.

Lainie looked from Tina to Tina's friend. "We didn't do anything to make Mama worry," she returned steadily, trying to keep the blush out of her face.

"My mother says he's got that look about him," Tina answered with utmost confidence in Alma Forbes's knowledge about the opposite sex. "He knows exactly what to do with a girl, and it's not good."

"And you think that's what we did?" Lainie demanded hotly.

Her direct question at last embarrassed the other girl. "I didn't say that," she hedged.

"But your mother did. Well, you can tell her for me that it's a lie. Colley might not talk to anybody around the Springs, but I wouldn't either if all of you were saying things about me like what you just said about him. There's nothing wrong with him."

"He's an uncivilized heathen," Tina protested, and she even managed to look like her mother when she pronounced the judgment.

"He is not. He's just Colley." Lainie looked from one to the other of them, trying to make them understand.

"You ought to know," Tina said at last, with a giggle.

The following autumn in school, Way was suspended for three days for fighting with Ernest Thayer. He wouldn't tell Lainie what for, but she knew: Ernest had said something about her and the witch boy.

Then, right as the bright hope of Christmas was fading into the white dawn of a fresh year, Papa brought home news: Colley was gone.

The shantytown boy had vanished from the farm. He'd left. Run away, Nadine told Lainie the next time the two of them saw each other in town, and Lainie had to blink away hot tears.

Indian Springs heard with satisfaction about his leaving: it was exactly what Albert should have expected from somebody like that kid.

Mama's face stayed lit up like one of the holiday candles; Papa laughed like he used to.

But at night, all alone in her room, Lainie held her hands against her heart to try and stop its aching.

Colley left the day after Albert and he had their conversation about his mother, after he lifted two hundred dollars from the desk in the room the old man called the study. Maybe it was stealing, or maybe Devil owed it to him for sixteen years of his life spent working the farm.

He knew that the Springs lay to the east, so he headed west instead, cutting across frosty fields and frozen creeks.

The first two nights he spent in barns, eating whatever he could find. The third day it snowed, and he headed for the highway at last. A roadside diner was open, its lights glowing warm and yellow in the white blizzard, and half-frozen, half-starved, he went inside its deserted dining room and asked for food.

The woman who owned the place was working all by

herself, and she took one look at him, blue with cold, his long dark hair covered with snow, and offered him supper free. That night she let him sleep in a back room, and in return, he pumped gas for her whenever somebody pulled off the icy interstate nearby for fuel.

The next morning, she offered him a job along with the room, and because he had nothing else to do, he took it. She needed the help—her husband had run the place until his death six months earlier.

Her name was Rose. She was fifteen years older than Colley.

When March came, she invited him to her house back at the end of a road that was a half a mile from the diner. He ate supper there with her, and for the first time, he didn't go back to his own bed.

When he tried to leave, she reached out and touched him, and he lost his breath first and his virginity next.

Colley lay awake long after she slept, watching the shadows on the ceiling in the unfamiliar house. He had found someone as lonely as he was. Part of him liked what she had taught him, liked it so much that he would do it again when he was offered the chance. He knew that as well as he knew his own name.

But inside his richly flushed body, his heart was still a crystal of coldness. This, then, wasn't what he was looking for.

Rose's own body was heavy at his side, her scent all around him, sleep close enough for him to feel, and that was when she came to him.

Laughing blue eyes, dusky curls, sweet mouth.

Lainie.

NO.

What was she doing in his head tonight, where he didn't want her? Here, where he was farther from her than he'd ever been—and it wasn't a distance of miles.

He had crossed the gulf between childhood and adulthood, innocence and knowledge. He had left Lainie on the other side.

He had betrayed her, and he didn't even know how.

Suddenly, Colley missed Lainie Thorne and the creek and the farm, missed them until he hurt. He couldn't assuage the pain; it was too strong and too late.

The Springs was behind him. He had to live in the present. He had a place to live, food to eat, this woman to sleep with.

All his needs were satisfied.

He couldn't help it that his heart wasn't.

He was Rose's lover through his seventeenth birthday, through the hot summer, right up until time for harvest.

At dawn one morning, just as the leaves were starting to turn and the smell of fall was in the air, he walked down the road from her house to open the business and found Devil waiting, sitting outside the building in his old truck. Nadine was with him.

Colley wasn't surprised except at himself, because his heart was shockingly glad to see them. To see Nadine, he told himself.

"So this is what you traded the farm for," the old man said with a snort after he lifted his stiff leg down.

"It wasn't the farm I was leaving," Colley said shortly.

"You left me? Well, you didn't get far. I've knowed where you were since the fourth day. You ran because you thought I'd done some great big wrong to you. What wrong was it? I didn't go in a hole full of rocks to save people I didn't share kin with, like Brodie did, when he knew he had a baby comin'. I wouldn't'a took money for my own flesh and blood, like your mother did. But then, she knew to give you up because I would'a hounded her to hell before I let her run with you. And for all of James's fussin' and Teresa's bitchin', I didn't let them talk me out of you. You're my heir as much as Preston is. So where's the wrong?"

Colley didn't know how to put into words what it was that was tearing him apart, and even if he had, it wasn't something he could have said to Albert, anyway.

Love should have had a place in the equation somewhere. That was what he kept trying to explain.

What he actually said was, "You did all of that because you needed my back for the farm."

Albert shrugged. "I never denied it. But the summer's over and we'll have the same harvest we had in years past. You being gone didn't stop anything. All you're doin' is hurtin' yourself, givin' up the things you could have had. And if we're gonna talk about need—the woman here, what do you think she's doin' with you? Satisfyin' the need she has. So what's the difference? Except my rewards for you are greater."

He stood stubborn and still, even when he heard Rose's car pull up in the lot behind him.

"Colley?" she called fearfully. "Who are these people?"

Albert straightened. "I won't come again, boy. I'll never beg you. But if you ever come to your senses, the farm's waitin'."

Nadine had not said a word, but as Devil got in the truck, she came to Colley, tears in her eyes. "I miss you. You was the only life that old farm had. And the little girl, she cried when I told her you was gone. I saw her in town with her mama. Her daddy wasn't with 'em, and I reckon she talked Miss Deborah into letting her ask me where you were. Come home, Colley."

He watched them pull away, and Rose stood at his back and watched him.

"That's your family," she said at last.

His family. Maybe it was, whether he wanted it to be or not. Whether they loved him or not. They were where he belonged, where he knew who he was.

Back there, Lainie Thorne had wept for him. She was crying.

A few days later, he ended the struggle inside himself. That night Rose held him. Nothing else, just an embrace full of sadness because she knew without words what he was about to do. He was gone the next morning before she ever awoke.

Devil met him on the porch when he made it home. He watched in silence as Colley climbed the steps.

"I'll work for you, old man," he said brusquely, "and I'll do the things you're asking of me. But it's for the same reason you came after me. Because I choose to. Because there's something in it for me. I'll never be your slave."

"That's fair enough."

That night, Devil brought a blurry picture to him and dropped it on his bed. It was of a dark-haired, dark-eyed man who had his arms wrapped around the waist of a laughing girl. They stood together in a field of green summer clover, happy and young.

"Her name was Colleen, or maybe it wasn't. Never can tell about the river people. She had a name for you, but I forget what it was. There wasn't no birth certificate, and Charley always called you Colley, for her, I reckon. I don't know where she came from or why. Maybe she was seventeen or eighteen. I know where she went when she left; she went to Texas. And I know she's dead."

Colley looked at the dim faces in the picture, and they were strangers to him. He put it on the table. "I'll make my own place," he said to himself, but Devil heard and understood.

"Begin now, then. Little towns have got a mean, contrary

streak in 'em, Colley. Lay down, and they'll kick you. Go your own way and never give a damn what they want, and they'll lick your feet. It's time you decided how you're gonna live and what you're gonna be."

"The people on the river call you the Man," he said steadily, gazing right into Albert's black eyes.

"Among other things," Albert said dryly.

"Someday, that's what they'll call me." It was a vow he was making to himself as much as to his grandfather.

"Takin' my place, are you, boy? Think you're big enough?" But Albert didn't sound angry. He was just wry, and if it was possible, pleased. "Do it, then . . . if you can."

7

"Going somewhere, darling?"

The voice in the doorway nearly made Colley jump as he twisted from the open travel bag at the foot of the bed to find its source. Rachel Harding leaned lazily against the doorframe, her legs long and sleek underneath the short, simple linen sheath she wore against the summer heat.

Damn, he said inside his head.

But outwardly, he was calmer. "What are you doing in Nashville, Rachel?" Maybe his greeting still wasn't too civil, but he'd just spent the better part of twenty-four hours in a boardroom with his uncle. One day in the vicinity of James was enough to put him in a hellish mood. He was always deadly serious, deadly certain that he was his nephew's superior; Colley was more used to his grandfather, who was just deadly.

"That's no way to say hello," she said silkily, moving out of the doorway with practiced grace. Right in front of him, she laid both hands on his cotton T-shirt, letting her hands stroke his ribcage and drop to his jeans at his waist. "I heard you were in the big city, so I drove here, too."

She glanced over his shoulder at the bag he was tossing clothes into. "Looks like I got here in the nick of time. Why didn't you call me and tell me you were staying at the Sheraton? We could have had all night here, just you and me. We haven't made love in too long, Colley."

She laid her head with its rich auburn hair against his chest, and unwillingly, he did the only thing he could do. He let his hands rest on her back, holding her lightly.

"I was with Uncle James," he finally offered lamely. "You wouldn't have wanted to see me in the mood that puts me in."

Lifting her head, Rachel let her finger find the tiny indention at the edge of his mouth, the closest thing to a dimple Colley had. "Let me put you in a better one," she suggested. "I have friends in Nashville. We're invited to Belle Meade tonight for a party. Go with me, and tell them at the front desk that you want the room another night. Then we'll have another party, a private one, here in this very nice room."

She looked around appreciatively at the pale blue decor. "You won't be sorry," she offered huskily, leaning up toward him.

He let his arms drop and stepped away from her invitation. "I need to get back to the Springs, Rachel. The old man's waiting for the news."

"So call him. You know, use the telephone. You've heard of Bell's new invention, haven't you?" she said, her voice too silky.

Colley never looked at her. He just finished zipping the lightweight nylon bag that held the clothes he'd worn to the office the day before.

"Or is there something besides your grandfather that you have to get back to in that little dumpy town?"

Her words were suddenly sharp, and they froze his movement a second or two as he reached for the bag. Then he pulled in a deep breath, picked up the bag, and turned to face her.

"Yeah. A farm to run, and a new stable to build, and a thousand chores. I'm not a city person. I hate this place."

"You forgot to mention the girl at the Magnolia Hotel."

Rachel's face was calm, but her voice was angry. Colley's own heart thumped one time, hard, and then settled again in his chest. Carefully, he set the bag back down at the foot of the big bed.

"Say what you want to say, Rachel."

"I've heard her name connected with yours, and I don't like it."

"Whatever you heard, it's got nothing to do with us," he returned shortly.

"Then tell me that you don't want her. That she's not the reason you're rushing back home."

He could lie when he had to; he was no saint. But something caught the breath in his throat, so that all he could mutter was, "I"—He stopped. "For God's sake, Rachel, I don't have to take an oath to you. I am what I am. You either want me or you don't."

She looked at him a long time, letting her eyes search his. "That's not the question, is it? Here I am, but you're somewhere else. I knew the first time I saw her at the hotel that she had been something to you. What about me, Colley? Do you want me? Tell me the truth about us, and about her, too."

How could he have told her that Lainie was a part of his life, that she'd been his in his mind ever since they were children, that living without her had been like living without

his right arm? He couldn't, any more than he could tell
Rachel that he'd tried to love her, herself, to please Albert,
and he couldn't, and the effort was making him sick.

"You don't know me, Rachel," he said at last. "Not what I
really am or where I came from. You only know what you
think I am."

Rachel threw back her head and gave a tiny laugh. "Do
you really believe that? My father is Paul Harding. He can
find out anything he wants to. I know enough. People
around the Springs call you Devil's savage. I've heard all
they say, but I'm still here."

"Knowing is a lot different from seeing. If you could
have seen me then, the way I lived, the way I was, you
wouldn't be here now."

"She's not, either, Colley." Rachel's face hardened.
"Now that you're back in the Springs, is she what you
want? Do you think if you hang around enough, you'll
make her notice you again? I don't think so. She was pretty
definite the night I met her."

Her cool words made him wince. It was a certainty that
Lainie didn't want him. She had made that very, very clear.
He wished he could quit craving her as easily.

Preston had been watching her that Wednesday night
when Colley had caught him at the Magnolia. A beautiful
girl was the only reason he would ever have gone to a place
like the old hotel.

He would kill Preston if he put his hands on Lainie.

"Colley." Rachel's insistent voice brought him back to
the present. "I don't like all that I've found out about you in
the Springs, but I still want you. Your grandfather has
made it very clear that he's happy enough for us to marry. I
can do a lot for you. She can't. But I'll be damned if I'll be
ignored and turned down by you anymore. So you run back
home. I'll stay in Nashville and go to Belle Meade. And

when you wake up and understand that I'm the best thing that's ever happened to you, come and get me."

She slammed the door behind her, leaving nothing but the trace of her perfume and the echo of her angry voice behind.

He couldn't blame Rachel. He had tried, but she'd been getting nothing but half of him all along, and it was the half without his heart. Now he couldn't even give that.

All he could think of was Lainie, and Preston watching her like a dog in heat.

He had to get home; he had to keep pushing away from the late afternoon sun that rode his back as he settled himself into his truck and headed out of Nashville toward the Springs.

Colley Rawlins was not about to leave Lainie Thorne alone in the vicinity of his slick, snake-charming cousin any longer than he had to.

To stay calm, he kept reminding himself of the facts: Preston was a Rawlins. That alone ought to keep them separated. Surely Albert would protest, or even Deborah.

Lainie wasn't going anywhere with his cousin, Colley reassured himself. She hated the Rawlinses too much.

The people in the Springs knew that Lo-Joe Quarry was not to be taken lightly; Devil wanted it that way, and he and his fences and Colley saw to it that it was.

When Brodie died in its rocky depths, the place closed in fear of lawsuits, and Albert Rawlins bought it. He turned it into forbidden ground, almost a shrine, and he made every effort to keep people away. He put a fence around the twenty acres of land that circled the water-filled excavation, and another one around the quarry itself, even across the top of the high bluffs at the back.

They had never found Brodie's body, not in any of their searches, and when Devil called a halt to the heartbreaking effort, he did it like he did everything else, with clear, cutting finality. Dynamiters came and set charges around the hole.

People got the message.

Only once had the gates to Lo-Joe been opened in the last twenty-five years. Three years ago, someone had picked the lock on the gate out on Martin Hollow Road and left it swinging wide.

Nobody ever knew who'd gone to such an effort to get to the eerie circle of stone and water, or why.

Albert had the gate chained and locked again immediately, while the more imaginative natives whispered that it was Brodie's spirit looking for his way home that had opened the place. It made a good ghost story for Susan when she was in one of her mischievous moods to tell on the front porch of the Magnolia while the night sifted down around a wide-eyed, uneasy, gullible guest, and that was about all.

Except for that one occurrence, the quarry remained a deserted, solitary corner of Rawlins Farm.

Lainie had seen the overgrown, shadowy gravel road that led back to Lo-Joe on the other side of the rusting gate every time she left the house with her parents when she was a little girl. They had had to drive right by it to get anywhere. But she had never been back to it before today.

There was fear in Lo-Joe.

It wasn't scary in the way it had been to her when she was a child, and all she could think of was the dead man buried somewhere under the tons of rock; instead, it was scary in a far more practical sense.

The dynamite had served to make a swimming hole of one side of the granite ravine, turning it into a deep basin full of huge, fallen rocks that gradually got more shallow on the end where the Lo-Joe trucks had once loaded.

The other side of the quarry, the right one, had only been made a hundred times more hazardous by the explosion. There was no sloping entrance to that abyss, in fact, no entrance at all short of diving, and no way out had someone even gotten in. It was completely shut off, turned into an angled tunnel of smooth rocks leading straight down to icy water at least a hundred feet deep.

"This place looks like something out of *Deliverance*," Preston said lazily as he and Lainie lay sunning on top of one of the smooth, square hot rocks at the quarry's edge, just where the grassy field that led up to Lo-Joe ended. The squeals of the three women who were with Tate and the Gregorys down near the water mixed with a shout of laughter from one of the men about something.

"Beware of men who jump out and tie you to trees," she said with a laugh, laying one arm over her eyes to shield herself from the blazing afternoon sun.

"There's a thought," he said drowsily. "Why don't you tie me down to this rock? You could have your way with me."

Lainie's skin jumped. Everything Preston said today seemed to have a sexual edge, or was it just her own uncertainty?

At any rate, she had to play the game. This man was her ticket out of her problems.

She rolled over on her side to eye him humorously. "And what way is that?"

"Any way you want, angel."

"While all of these people watch?"

"They could use the pointers. Besides, they're not paying any attention. They're crazy about this big hole. I'm disappointed, myself. No sign of Uncle Brodie. Wonder if he haunts the other side?"

"Preston."

He turned his head and opened his eyes. "What?"

"I don't like jokes about what happened here. I feel like I'm dancing on a grave."

All of a sudden, he wasn't sweet and kind as he'd been all the other times before. His face just looked annoyed. "Come on, Lainie, don't go stuffy on me. You sound old."

"I can't help it. " She took a deep breath and tried to lighten up. "Maybe wild-eyed children might like this kind of thing," she said teasingly.

"Don't call me names. Besides . . ." He pulled her close unexpectedly and put his nose nearly against hers. "I'm not a child."

His head shut out the sunlight and his face dropped to hers as she closed her eyes. Then she gave a muffled shriek against his mouth and pulled away hastily as he pushed the cold glass he held against her bare midriff.

She caught his hand with its chilly load and held it back from her heated skin while he gave a little laugh.

"Stop." She tried to pull away from his threatening hand, and then discovered that his other one, the one at her neck, had been busy, too. The wide straps to her white halter swimsuit slithered down her shoulders.

The shock of the realization sizzled through her.

"Preston!" She grabbed at the straps, glancing around to reassure herself that no one was watching, and he straightened quickly, putting down the glass and catching at her hands with both of his.

"No." There was no teasing in his voice now; it was husky and strained. "I want to see."

Lainie went still, staring into his eyes, so close to her own as they faced each other there on the top of the rock. It was quiet, but in the distance, she could hear the redhead, Julie, saying something.

"Not here," she whispered in frantic confusion.

"Here. Now." He was insistent and determined as he dropped a hand to find the straps and give them a jerk that made her whole body quiver, too. Then he deliberately let his eyes fall to her breasts. Lainie couldn't move; all she could feel was the heat of the sun and embarrassment suffusing her as she stared fixedly at his aroused face.

"God," he whispered, "you're beautiful everywhere." And he let his fingers rise to caress one of her exposed breasts.

"Preston!" She caught frantically at his face as he bent toward it, reading his intention in shock.

The movement of his hand on her breast stopped, but he looked at her intently. "Why? Why are you saying no?"

"We're out here," she gasped.

"Nobody gives a damn what we're doing. Don't pretend, Lainie. You've made up your mind about us, haven't you? You're going to tell me what I want to hear. I knew it when you called me." His face softened a little, and he reached up a hand to stroke her hair. "You won't be sorry. I can give you what you need."

Did I mention forty thousand dollars? Lainie wondered with a little twist of misery.

"You don't know yet what that is," she whispered tautly.

"Tell me tonight," he breathed into her mouth as he leaned closer, "when you finally do something about this problem that keeps cropping up when we're together." He caught her hand in his and pulled her fingers down between his own legs.

Lainie's fingers jerked; so did her heart. She'd never touched a man like this before, not even him.

And as if Preston had read her thoughts, he said quietly, "You've been with a man before, haven't you? With—"

No, don't say his name out loud, not here, not when I'm

about to offer myself to you like a whore, she thought in frantic pain.

She had to get away. Pulling from him, she slid from the rock. On the ground, with shaking fingers, she tied the straps behind her neck again in a wild rush, and because she couldn't think of what else to do, she broke into a run.

She wanted away from him and from herself, too.

"Lainie!" Preston called after her hurriedly.

It wasn't his shout that made her come to a blind halt. It was just the stone-cold realization that she had nowhere to go. No place to run.

Preston was right on her when she halted. "Where in the hell do you think you're going?" he said furiously, and his narrow tanned chest rose in ragged breaths above his blue swim trunks.

"Just away."

"Away to here?"

She looked around, and felt her heart thud once. She was too close, tricked by the way the brambles and the bushes grew all the way to the edge of this far side of the quarry, not six feet from the first sharp corner of the impossible drop-off.

The realization made her stumble, and Preston caught her and drew her close to him.

"Look, I'm sorry." He breathed sharply again. "Why did you leave me like that?"

She was beginning to calm again, to think clearly. This was Preston. This was inevitable. *Don't chicken out now, Lainie.*

"Because I might want more from you than you know," she whispered at last. Maybe a stab at honesty would make this more bearable.

"Like what?" he said, caught between desire and arrested wariness.

"What do you normally give your other women?" she tried to say flippantly.

His face sharpened a little. "I know I've been drinking too much today," he said slowly, "but I don't think I remember talking about any other women. Who put the notion that I had them in your head? Colley?"

"Preston, don't say any more about him." Stung with pain, Lainie closed her eyes.

"Why not? Ever since Colley showed up at the Magnolia, you've been different. But I can make you forget you ever laid eyes on"—He blinked suddenly, and shook his head in rue. "I think I am a little too drunk. Or dizzy. The world's spinning. That's why I can't keep my mouth shut."

He took a stumbling step backward to lean against the big trunk of an ancient sycamore tree that sprawled out over the edge of the quarry; it was the only tree standing around the gaping hole, and it had been there so long that one sagging section of fence seemed to have grown into its bark.

That tree was so near the edge that part of its roots were exposed over it, hanging like a woven net over the water below.

"You're too close. Come back!" Her last word was only a tiny scream as he tried to straighten and stumbled, grabbing at an overhanging limb as the water sparkled up at him in a wicked surprise.

"Lainie!" He twisted in a panic back toward her and flailed at the sky for balance.

Without thought, she ran two steps—just two little steps—and grabbed at his hand. She missed, but he made a sudden wild leap for safety, and the hard brush of his body as he hit hers knocked her off balance, too far gone ever to come back.

She skinned her knees on the sloping rock as she fell and

then slid right over the edge, down into the pit as it gaped below, plunging straight toward the cold waters in the deepest part of Lo-Joe Quarry.

It was Nadine who plunged him straight back into the most meaningful part of his life. She brought the little girl to him again a week after his return home. Funny how she was just that, the little girl, to him now. He was thousands of years older.

Nadine kept him from the fields that morning with an explanation to Albert that he didn't hear. It wasn't until the old man was long gone, riding one of the horses to the other side of the river on an errand, that she told the truth to Colley of what she had done.

"Devil's gone. That's good. There ain't no need in him being here this mornin', findin' out what's goin' on and fussin' about it. There's somebody comin' to see you. I got to thinkin' that if you'd'a had a friend or two who cared about you anywhere around last year, you'd never'a left, Colley. So this mornin' I called Deborah Thorne and told her she was needed out here. She nearly always has her daughter with her on Saturdays."

"What'd you do that for?" he exclaimed in shocked anger. "I don't want her to come. She won't, anyway."

"She will. Maybe I let her think her husband needed her. He's off with Albert."

"Nadine!"

"It's too late now. So here, sit down." She motioned him to a straight-backed chair on the side porch. "You look like a bear with all that mane of yours. Let me cut it, and get you cleaned up so that you look more like the kind of boy she'd let her little girl talk to."

How could he explain to Nadine? Lainie Thorne was a

part of that innocent, dreamy, half-awake, piercingly sweet existence down at the creek. He couldn't bear to look into her face again. She might see the signs of his initiation into passion and resignation, and he wanted to protect her from those demons, keep her safe a little longer.

He was no fit friend for an innocent child.

Even knowing all of that, he wanted to see her so much that he couldn't make himself leave the house. She was coming here; how could he go away?

"I don't know what's wrong," Mama was saying, her face creased with worry as she drove. "Mr. Rawlins's housekeeper just said to come to the farmhouse. It's the first time in all the years John has worked here that it's happened. I hope he's not hurt."

Lainie was quiet, frightened. What was going on? She had a lot of reasons for not wanting to see the Rawlins farmhouse, no matter why they were going. It would make her miss Colley more.

By the time they had crossed the concrete bridge and the Rawlins home had grown close, Lainie could see the housekeeper on the exposed side porch. Somebody else was with her, sitting in a chair.

Somebody else.

Lainie gave a strangled cry and came up ramrod straight in the seat. "Colley," she whispered.

There was no sign of Papa, not anywhere. Deborah said nothing, but her lips tightened.

"Mama, is it really Colley?"

"I don't know what's happening here, but John will be angry," Mama said with a touch of anger all her own, and slowed the car to a crawl.

"No! Don't stop. I want to see him," Lainie pleaded, her eyes blue and wide as she caught at her mother's arm.

Hesitating, Deborah looked from her daughter to the boy on the porch.

"I hope I'm doing the right thing," she murmured, and she edged the car toward the white farmhouse that sat against the blue-green shadows of the river bottom.

Colley stood from the chair as the car pulled closer, waiting for them, stiff with anxiety.

When Lainie stepped out of the car, her heart was beating like thunder.

She didn't go far in her journey toward him before she stopped and waited; it was up to him. He was the one who had run.

After a second's hesitation, he came slowly down the steps and across the grass. They met halfway across the yard, his hair blacker than hers in the October sun.

Why had he been afraid? he wondered suddenly. Why had he tried to avoid her? She was as pretty as a picture, her eyes big and anxious as they met his and she searched his face.

His fear fell away, and he realized that innocence was its own protector. She was only fourteen. She couldn't see yet what had happened to him because it was outside her own experience. She saw only the boy from the creek, and he mattered to her.

I'm not old, he thought, and the world's not gray. It's red and orange and golden.

He smiled at her, unable to contain his own relief.

When he smiled, that was when she loved him the most, Lainie thought painfully. His mouth lifted on one side, giving a rakish, tender warmth to the dark intensity of his features.

"You told me once," she said, and her voice sounded odd

on the still air, "the day that I gave you the whistle, that you'd never go away, not until I got tired of seeing you. But you did."

"I'm sorry," he whispered. "I just got messed up in my head. I came back, Lainie. And I'm not going away again."

She took a step toward him, and another, and he didn't remember whether he reached for her first or she reached for him, but he laughed, the first time he remembered doing it in months, and pulled her close to swing her in a big circle, her long thin legs in their blue shorts coming off the ground and flying through the air like a windmill.

"That ain't the way you treat a girl, Colley," called a flustered Nadine from the porch.

"This is no girl," Colley said teasingly. "This is Lainie."

"You take my word for it, she's a girl. Now you put her down before her mama regrets bringin' her."

He remembered Deborah then, just the way he remembered Thorne's fears and Rose, and he let Lainie slip away and ducked from her mother, his cheeks red.

"There's nothing wrong with John, is there? You tricked me," Deborah accused Nadine quietly. "You knew I'd never bring her here to him."

Colley felt the chill of her anger. "I told you how it'd be," he accused the housekeeper.

Nadine was defensive but unrepentant.

"I can't help Mr. Thorne's feelings," she answered stubbornly. "I'm sorry I let you believe a lie, but somebody's got to think of Colley once in a while. I don't want him to leave again, but he's got—"

"You had no right to do such a cruel thing," Deborah interrupted in agitation.

"I don't want Lainie here anyway, not like this," Colley burst out in embarrassed anger.

"He's never done nothin' bad to anybody," Nadine pressed on determinedly. "Why is it that you treat him like he has? Why does your husband? How can you hate Colley for nothin'?"

"You don't understand," Deborah said helplessly.

"Go home," Colley said. He shoved his hands down into his pockets. "I didn't want you here. I told her how it'd be."

"Colley, no." Lainie stepped in the middle of the three of them, her eyes begging Deborah. "I want to see him, even if it's just for a little while."

"And if I let you today, will you stay away from him? Not be meeting him in secret again? You either promise me, or we leave now."

Lainie could read the determination in her mother's voice, and she settled for half a loaf. "I promise."

Deborah looked from Lainie's upset face to Colley's stoic one. Slowly, she relaxed a little. "We've come at a bad time," she finally told Nadine, awkward in her attempt to change the tone of the encounter. She glanced at the scissors in the older woman's hand.

Lainie sucked in a breath of relief. Colley didn't move.

On the housekeeper's face, gratitude shone as she tried to follow Deborah's lead. "No, ma'am. I'm just slow. I was tryin' to cut his hair some, but I'm old and nervous, and he don't sit still too long."

"I don't want it cut," Colley said defensively.

Lainie laughed. "It's too late now," she observed. "You've got one side already up to here." Reaching out, she touched his face just below his jawline.

Colley reached, too, trying to pull his hair around to see it. "Nadine," he exclaimed in frustration, "what'd you do that for?"

"Mr. Albert said he didn't want you lookin' like no girl."

"Colley wouldn't ever, anyway." Lainie defended him, considering his strong shoulders under the white T-shirt and the overall straps.

"I guess I've made a mess of it," Nadine said ruefully. "I ain't done it in a while. He'll just have to get a barber to cut it off."

"No," said Colley.

"No," protested Lainie. "I like his hair." Then she looked at Deborah. "Mama, you do it. You cut mine and Way's," she coaxed.

Colley said, panic-stricken, "I don't want her to."

"Yes, you do. You'll like it," Lainie assured him. "Please, Mama?"

Deborah's gaze went from Lainie to Nadine, who was already handing her the scissors, and at last to Colley, who still wouldn't look directly at her.

"If he's willing," she gave in at last.

Deborah Thorne was only a little older than the woman he'd taken to bed all summer. He couldn't glance at her without a trace of shame, and he didn't want to sit under her hands and be reminded of Rose. But they were all watching him expectantly, so there was no escaping. With reluctance, he slid again into the chair, and Deborah ran her fingers back uncertainly through his hair, just as she had done that day at the creek. She was nervous, as nervous as he was.

Her touch was completely different from Rose's.

Deborah Thorne had a mother's touch.

He didn't know how he knew it, the one who'd never known a mother, but he did. Her hands held compassion and tenderness. There was comfort in the fingers that guided the scissors through his hair.

Nadine watched. "You don't squirm around with her like you do with me, Colley Rawlins."

"You've got a last name now," Lainie said in surprise. "A last name to go with a bad haircut."

She could see the flash of his smile even as her mother's firm hands forced his head over, and just as she was thinking in a satisfied smugness that it was perfectly wonderful to have Colley back, he let his hand shoot out and a tiny pebble that she hadn't known he was holding stung her leg. "Ouch!"

"No fightin'," Nadine said mildly.

"Lainie deserves it, maybe," Mama said. "Nothing bad about Colley's hair. It's as thick as hers, but it's got no curl at all. Glossy as a raven's wing, just like his daddy's was."

What had he been running from and looking for? Colley wondered.

Today might come close to whatever that vague thing was that he'd chased, and he'd take it and be satisfied. He sat like Samson and let the three women try to make something civilized out of him.

While those thoughts absorbed him, Lainie had her own to contend with. She settled against a porch post, her knees up under her chin in the cool of the morning, listening to the *snip-snip* of Mama's scissors and watching Colley's hair fall on the wooden boards around him.

Somewhere back on the other side of the screen door, a radio was playing.

She was watching Colley's face.

Lainie wasn't sure yet if he was handsome. She thought maybe he was too dark and strong featured. She'd never even considered the issue of his looks until now. Maybe she had thought of it today because Dana and some of her friends at school had begun noticing boys with a vengeance that year.

Or maybe she was seeing him in this new light because

there was something changed about him, something that went deeper than the changes of age.

There was the sadness in his face, but that was habitual, caused by the way his eyes tilted downward at the corners. He looked as if he was watching things, seeing the details that everyone else overlooked in their hurry.

His nose—well, his nose lacked a lot. It wasn't straight and strong at all. It wavered a little in places.

But his mouth was gorgeous. Even at a protected fourteen, Lainie understood it. Maybe Mama did, too, and that was the reason she was so uptight about Lainie being with him. Maybe all women did.

It wasn't the upper lip that really caused the trouble. It was more narrow than the bottom, and it curved distinctly, sweetly. Or that might be a problem, too, because it made a girl trust Colley, made her smile at him, made her believe in him.

The bottom lip, though, was pure danger. Fuller than the top, it was sulky and sexual. Lainie was scared herself when she considered it. She knew what it meant, that Colley would be a man who liked kisses, the kind who took them. His kisses would be the kind that led good girls far astray.

Mama pulled up his head one last time, and Lainie saw what her handiwork had wrought. His hair hung somewhere between chin and shoulder now, but it wisped around his face at the temples and brushed off it at the cheekbones, showing the daring bone structure beneath the skin, softening the starkness of his coloring.

"Colley," she whispered in involuntary awe, "you're beautiful."

"Lainie!" Deborah protested.

Her face flamed as she realized what she'd said. He came up from the chair in an awkward embarrassment and strode off the porch without a word.

"Still ain't got no manners," said Nadine regretfully.

"Colley, wait," Deborah called after him, catching at Lainie's arm as she tried to follow him to explain. "I want to talk to him," she said gently to her daughter.

Colley halted uneasily out in the yard, waiting as Deborah followed him, her dress swishing around her knees. "Walk a little with me. I have something to say."

So they walked out toward the river. Inside, he was sick with nerves. "What do you want?" he asked at last and couldn't help it that he was rough.

"I'm glad you're home."

"No, you're not," he returned flatly. "You'd be happier if I'd never come back."

She grimaced in guilt. "I don't want anything bad to happen to you, Colley. But I'm afraid of you," she confessed.

Colley stopped abruptly. "Afraid of me!"

"You have such a hold on Lainie," Deborah answered frankly.

Hot blood rose in his face. "I've never bothered her. Not in that way," he said defensively.

"That's not what I mean. It's just that you've been in her life for so long, a lot longer than we can realize, and she's too comfortable with you. I don't know how to say it. I've never seen her touch any man except maybe her father or Way, but it's nothing like the way she touches you. She just reaches for you."

"Say it plain what you want," he managed.

"I don't hate you, understand that first."

Colley looked down at the river that ran near them with blind eyes. "And Thorne?"

"You know how he feels. It's not up to me to tell you why, but it can't be changed. As far as that goes, Albert Rawlins appears to hate us. There's nothing I can do about any of that. But Colley, you can do something. You can protect Lainie for a while."

"Protect her!"

"That's right." Deborah reached out and caught the chin of the boy across from her, letting her gaze meet his squarely. "You're too old and too different right now. Protect her from yourself, Colley. I'm only asking you to wait about—about things until she's older."

"You're asking me to stay away from her," he said harshly.

"Is it so much? It's only for a while. Someday she'll be old enough that if she wants to be with you, she can be. I'll have no more say-so about it when she becomes an adult, and I swear to you, I'll live with her decisions then."

"What do you think I'm going to do to her? You know I wouldn't hurt her. You're really doing it because you hope she'll forget that she ever knew me."

"Whatever my reasons, I'm trusting you enough to ask. And what I'm asking is what any mother would."

He stepped closer to the river below the bridge. "I wouldn't know much about that."

"Give her a little time, Colley. That's all."

He thought about what she was asking for a long, quiet moment. "I'll do what you want," he told her finally, reluctantly. "I don't know for sure, but maybe a mother has a right to ask."

And still she pressed him. "You give me your word, Colley? On your honor?"

Was there no getting away from Deborah Thorne?

"I said it, didn't I?" he answered impatiently, caught between pleasure that she trusted him and dismay at what she was making him promise.

Deep inside, though, he knew why he was really doing it. It wasn't for Deborah at all. It was for the little girl from the creek who'd kissed him and given him a silver whistle. She deserved a childhood. She deserved safe years.

He knew what life was like without them, and if he was the one who could supply them for her, as her mother seemed to think, then she would have them.

Three months later, he was called on to keep his promise to Deborah, and the keeping of it was so painful that he began to avoid Lainie completely.

Colley went into town with Albert, hanging behind him in silence. He didn't like the town and was leery of the people. They returned the favor, taking his silence for sullen backwardness. He tried not to care.

But Lainie was a different matter. When he walked by her without speaking, he really hadn't seen her. He hadn't known she was anywhere about until she called his name.

"Colley."

He turned, startled, and she was right there on the sidewalk close to him. Albert kept moving, and on Colley's other side, up where the walk met the street, he could see Deborah. Lainie's mother had turned, watching the girl and him, remembering that promise, Colley hadn't a doubt.

"You weren't even going to stop," Lainie accused in shaky surprise.

"I didn't see you," he mumbled.

"Would you have stopped if you had?" she demanded.

How was he supposed to handle this? he wondered, hesitating. "You're only fourteen. I'm older than you."

"I'm almost fifteen. You're no more older now than you've ever been," she retorted in anger, the color high in her face. "But now you're Albert Rawlins's grandson.

You're his." Glancing down the street after the old man, she let her resentment show. "Is that why I never see you anymore? Because if it is, I wish I'd never whistled for you. I liked you better before."

"That's not it," he protested. "You're a kid, Lainie. What are we going to do? Play games? I have to work. It's no good."

"You really don't want to see me again," she whispered in distress, and he couldn't bear the hurt in her blue eyes. "That's why you haven't come around."

"I'm still your friend, if you ever need me," he said desperately.

She tossed back her hair, and in a voice rough with bravado answered, "Why would I need you?"

For a second, he saw exactly what she would be like when she was grown. Her face had the angles and planes of maturity as she fought for an adult dignity in front of him, and she was too beautiful to walk away from.

On your honor, Deborah had made him swear.

Colley hated honor.

"Please, Lainie, don't cry so," Mama pleaded as she caressed the soft curls of her daughter's head.

Lainie lifted her hot, wet face from the pillows of her bed. "I love him, Mama, and he doesn't love me."

Deborah hesitated before she went back to stroking her hair. "I know you do, Lainie. Give yourself time. Colley did the right thing. In a few years, you may find that you don't love him at all, at least not in the way you think you do right now. There are other boys. Anyway, if God means for you to be with this one, it will work out."

"I don't care what God does. I'm never going near Colley again," Lainie vowed in a flash of proud anger.

"He thinks I care. He'll see. I won't cry over him anymore."

"I certainly hope not." Deborah's words held a little humor and a lot of doubt.

8

It was funny how lonely a Saturday afternoon could be.

Colley came home from Nashville to an empty house and stood on the front porch for a while, letting the hot, still sun shine down on him until he couldn't bear his own solitude. Then he went impatiently to his room, donned his oldest pair of blue jeans and work boots, and headed back outdoors.

Over the past three years, he'd tried everything to forget her.

The only panacea that even came close to succeeding was hard work. He'd done enough of it since he lost Lainie to kill himself. He could do a little more today.

But he didn't have time to get to the barn before a car came across the concrete bridge and stopped near him. Startled, shading his eyes, he squinted into the sun. It was from the sheriff's office, and he knew the deputy behind the wheel.

Way Blackburn.

Now what did he want?

Colley was in no mood to accommodate, so he stood and waited until Way walked to him, sweat beading his forehead the same way it did Colley's face and bare torso.

"Guess you're wondering why I'm here," Way said at last, uncomfortably.

"You could say that," Colley returned, letting his hands rest on the gate between them.

"I was just checking."

"Checking what?"

"Oh, to make sure you were here and not off fooling around at some swimming hole."

Colley frowned. "I hope you know what you're talking about, because I don't."

"Maybe it'll get clearer when I tell you that Lainie left work this afternoon. She never does that. I put the screws on Dana, and she finally told me that Lainie's got a date for swimming. But she didn't know just where, and she wouldn't tell me with who. You know what? I kept thinking of you."

Colley got very still. "She's not with me."

Way pulled off his sunglasses and wiped his wet face with his hand. "Good." His voice was flat. "You've got another woman now. Finally. So I guess I want you to tell me that I don't need to worry about you and Lainie anymore."

"I couldn't help what happened to John Thorne," Colley said, the words forced out of him. Why was he bothering to say this again? He'd said it until he was hoarse years before, for all the good it did him.

"It still happened, and Lainie nearly cried herself to death."

"If she ever decides to come to me," Colley said

intensely, and the mere words made him burn, "you'd better let her come. But"— he gave the gate near him a shove and came through it to face the policeman directly—"it's not me today."

Not him. Somebody else.

She was with somebody else.

Way looked at him for a long moment. "If I thought she'd forget and be happy with—aw, I hear you."

Way interrupted himself with the muttered words, turning back toward the open door of his patrol car. "They're trying to call me."

He trudged up the field toward his car and picked up the mike as he got to the vehicle. Colley heard the crackle of sound, and then Way's response. "I'm out at Rawlins farm, that's where. Yeah. What? But the quarry's shut down. Who'd be dumb enough to go out there and fa—who? God! I'm coming—now."

"The quarry?" Colley said in surprise. "But nobody goes—"

"I've found Lainie." Way's face was white as he slid into his patrol car. "I've been talking to the wrong Rawlins. Your pretty-boy cousin took her there and let her fall in."

Lainie didn't die when she hit the water. She just went down and down and down until the water was like blue ice around her.

Then she began to push up and up and up against it, and suddenly, there was light and warmth on her face, and air to pull into her exploding lungs.

On the surface, she struggled to stay afloat.

But how long could she keep struggling?

How many eons had she been in this huge well of water, trapped like a goldfish in a freak bowl?

Long enough that she'd quit worrying about ghosts and had swum over to the only wall that wasn't sheer, smooth rock right up to the sky. One section swelled out and around from the water, like a fat belly. Thick green kudzu vines hung from it like a green curtain. It was scary and snaky, but those strong vines were the only refuge she could find. They gave her something to hang on to, making time for her to rest . . . and think.

She wouldn't wish drowning in this place on her worst enemy. Or maybe she would; maybe this was exactly what she'd want to happen to an enemy. It would be a horrible way to go.

"Lainie, are you still there?"

The shout came from the ledge high above her.

"Yes."

How many times had Preston or one of the others peered frantically over at her as if she were some kind of dying experiment, demanding to know the answer to that question? How many times had they tried rescuing her, only to run into a problem?

And most of all, why had God played this terrible trick on her? She had been scared witless of water for years after she fell in the blue hole; it had become a phobia with her. If this had happened earlier in her life, before she finally forced herself to learn to swim, the terror of the watery quarry alone would have killed her before she ever got a chance to drown.

"You can't fight with it, Lainie," Colley had once told her in exasperation. He'd never been afraid of water; he should have been a fish as much as he loved it. "It's not doing anything to you. Just lie back in it and float. See, my hands are under you. You're not going down. I won't let you."

If she could have Colley here with her for a while, she'd be all right. The plunge into the cold water had been a trip back into memory, into their world at the creek where they first met.

She was reliving it all. She could see him, feel him, remember him again. Helpless to stop it in this merciless pool of remembrance.

Just for a few minutes, suspended from reality, she could unlock the bars around her heart and tell the truth, the truth that she would never admit up there, the truth that she would deny if she ever got out of here.

It was simple: she'd give almost everything to go back to those summers, she thought, resting her forehead on the vines her hands pulled taut against, when Colley was just a boy from a sharecropper shack playing hooky from the tobacco fields for an hour or so, when he was all hers. It had been a long time since those days, the ones before Albert Rawlins took him and changed their lives, when she was the most important thing in Colley's world and she really could lean blindly back against his hard, youthful, callused hands and trust him completely.

Where are your hands now, Colley? Tell me you're not going to let me go down, and truly mean it. Keep me away from the shadows and the ghosts.

"Elaina Marie!"

She was concentrating so hard on the past and on just hanging on that she first thought the stern shout was years back in her memory, but she twisted anyway to squint up at the sycamore.

There he was, just as if she'd conjured him up from a genie bottle.

Except that genies didn't ride big black horses that pranced against the sky. Colley was on him bareback, without even a bridle, and the animal didn't like coming this close to the ledge. He kept trying frantically to swirl away, and Colley kept circling him back with his blue-jeaned knees and his brown hands, his own blue-black hair whipping around his face like the mane of the horse.

"Elaina, answer me," he shouted again.

"I'm here," she croaked back, and everything inside her went giddy. She wasn't going to drown or freeze to death or die of snakebite after all. Colley Rawlins would make sure of her survival.

An object slammed down in the water, right in front of her, splattering her vigorously.

A rectangular ice chest, made out of Styrofoam. It must have been somewhere up there all this time. Maybe it was what Preston had been keeping his drinks in, and no one had thought to toss it down.

"Grab that if you think you're going under." His roar reverberated off the stone walls. "Did you hear me?"

"I'm . . . not going . . . under," she called back, panting for breath, but she fumbled for it and it bobbed teasingly up and down, just out of her reach for a moment.

"Did you get it? Damn it, Elaina, do as I tell you."

"I did. Now, will you please stop screaming at me and pull me out?" she demanded huskily from the safety of her homemade life preserver.

She couldn't see him now because her position in the water had changed, but she could still hear.

"Of all the fool things to do, to come out here with idiots and then act like one yourself. If you're not dead when I drag you from this water, you will be by the time I get through with you, girl."

"Promises, promises," she muttered to herself lightheadedly.

He must have dismounted from the horse, because she could see only his head and shoulders when she looked up the next time. "Colley, I want out." Her words shivered. "I don't like water like this."

"I remember," he answered, and his voice was a forced calm, "but you'll be safe here in a minute."

He hoped he sounded reassuring, but the truth was, it made him sick to see how far she'd fallen. Lainie looked like a tiny, battered doll that somebody had tossed carelessly off the quarry's edge. She hadn't said a word about being afraid, but he knew she was. He knew exactly how she shook in deep water, and where the pulse was in her throat that would be beating like a wild thing when he got her up.

He turned back to the fools who hovered around helplessly. Jack Gregory, who'd nearly embraced him in his relief at the arrival of sober help; his twin, Mark, and the Tate man; three women with them that he didn't know at all, and Preston, who'd gone stiff and silent as soon as Colley flung himself off the wild-eyed horse.

Preston and Lainie.

Damn it, damn it, damn it.

"What are you doing here? Butt out of my business and go back to Nashville where you were supposed to be. What are you going to do that we can't?" Preston said tightly now as his cousin strode away from the ledge. "We called from the car phone to the police station, and they've sent for a rescue unit. She—"

Colley cut in, "Get the hell out of my face."

The big horse sensed the panic in the air; he sidled away with a snort as Colley grabbed up the rope he'd taken from one of the stalls and carried there by the simple expedient of wrapping it around his waist. Then he fumbled in his jeans pocket for the chain clevis that had hung innocently in its place on a nail in the barn until fifteen minutes ago.

Fifteen minutes. A quarter of an hour, even pushing the startled horse across the back fields at a breakneck speed.

Too long . . . but it would take Way longer, coming by the road. He swung back to the nearest ledge. Where was she?

"Lainie," he called out urgently, scanning the darkening water, the empty, darkening water, while his heart gave a choking lurch upward.

"Here," she answered, her voice only a small echo, and she floated into view from somewhere right under him. "I was pretty sure you'd come back to this side, so I came over here to wait."

"You stay right there. I'm fixing a line, and I'll drop it over to you," he bent to tell her intently, his hands busy all the time, twisting the rope around the metal ring.

Looking up at him, her eyes were dark in her white face. "I have to tell you something, Colley. It's about my foot."

"Your foot?" His dark fingers stilled a second and then resumed their chore.

"I must have hit it on something when I fell. It all happened too fast. It's not hurting so much because I think it's too cold too hurt, but it feels like I have a ten-ton weight where it should be. My knees are stiff, too, where I scraped them. So I don't think I can climb a line, if you mean for me to brace my feet on that wall to do it." Her voice was nearly apologetic, her upturned face pleading.

His own face calmed. "Don't worry about it. I'll tell you what to do when the time comes."

He'd vanished again before Lainie could say another word.

"You," he called to the twins, "drive one of those—"

"Look, Colley, you're not the damn cavalry," Preston began, but the sound of a police siren cut him off, and he twisted to look across the field to the distant road. The white car that was rushing toward them had its blue lights on, and they made the words on its side, Logan County Sheriff's Office, appear to flash as well.

"There's the cavalry," Lloyd Tate murmured, and he was the one who grabbed the end of the rope that Colley thrust at them.

"What in the name of God is going on out here?" shouted Way Blackburn, as he pulled his lanky body out of the driver's seat. "And where's Lainie?"

"Unless you've got some kind of big net to drag mermaids up out of this hole," Colley interrupted tersely, "you better pull your car over here so we can brace the rope on it. That tree might not hold. She can't help herself much on the way up."

The deputy's face was white as paste. "She's—"

"Her foot is hurt."

"Where's the rescue squad?"

"In the pit of hell, for all I know, " Colley interrupted roughly, "but she's not staying down there until they come. I'm going down after her. I'll get her up."

Way stared at the other man's set, sweaty face. "I believe you. All right. Tell me what you're doing and I'll do it, too."

They wrapped the rope around the car bumper for leverage, Colley stopping only to wipe sweat away as it dripped from his hair onto his hands and down his face, and to demand that somebody keep telling him how Lainie was faring.

He was only vaguely aware that Preston's friends, all but Tate and the rapidly sobering Jack, both of whom hovered near, were talking like a bunch of magpies in a watchful circle a few feet away.

He didn't think of them at all when everything was in readiness and he bent right where he stood to yank off his old brown boots.

"You're going down," one of the women cried, stepping forward to stare at his bare feet, letting her eyes travel back to his face.

"Let me down at least half the way," he told Way as he lowered the rope over his shoulders and settled himself into the loop swing he'd made under the metal ring. "If it's safe, I'll dive from there."

"I was hoping you knew what you were doing when you made this thing," Way answered.

"So was I," Colley returned.

Way looked at him a moment as he positioned himself on the edge of the quarry and finally laughed. "It's no wonder you got a rep, Colley. The scary thing is, you deserve it."

Lainie glimpsed him when he first came over the side, and then her eyes blurred from quick tears that she brushed away. Seeing Colley this way, rappelling barefooted and bare-chested down the wall as gracefully and free as a cat, his dark hair falling over his shoulders, clinging to his brown face, he might have been fourteen again, dropping into the past.

Maybe she was going to get her wish; maybe this really was their happy past, and she could do it all again and this time get it right. No mistakes.

Halfway down, he twisted to look at the water and her, and he was much, much closer.

"Deep?" he asked, and she nodded wordlessly. "Real deep? Good." Letting himself slip from the crude seat, using it to swing out over the water, he dropped like Tarzan might have from a jungle vine.

He went in the water as smooth as a flash of lightning, with little or no splash, and he came up the same way, sleek and shining.

"I think," Lainie said unsteadily, "that you're having entirely too good a time."

Colley moved quickly to her in the water without answering her comment. "Which foot is hurt?"

"The right one."

"Okay, I'll be careful with it."

"And what are you going to do?"

"Put you in the sling on the end of the rope and let them pull you up," he said as he tread water over to where the rope seat dangled in his reach.

He caught it and clung to it just before he turned back toward her, his movement sending ripples across the water. His high cheekbones glistened with moisture, and his eyes looked black and absorbed. Lainie swallowed.

"Here. It goes under your arms." He had at least ten hands, and they were everywhere on her as he pulled one of her own from its position on the Styrofoam cooler and laid it across his shoulder. "Hold on to me while I get it in place."

His skin beneath her fingertips was cool, but the muscles under it were bunched with tension.

The other night at the Magnolia when he had handled her like familiar property, a hundred little embers had fanned into life inside her, points of remembrance that she had tried to wash away with the years of abstinence from his touch. Those tiny embers were there again now, stirred by the way they were face-to-face, body to body, just as if they were lovers again.

The frightening realization made her clutch at whatever was under her hands. His shoulders. There was something she should have remembered about them, but she couldn't take her concentration off his face to think about what it was.

He swung the loop over her head. "Now put your arm through it," he instructed. When she did, she clutched him tightly with the other hand, and the movement pulled her so close that their faces brushed. She gasped a little, and he twisted her with one arm under the water so that she rolled around his body.

"Now, the other arm," he said huskily. This time she tried to keep her eyes away from his as she bumped him again, but there was no escaping. His arms about her, his face over hers—so close that one tiny movement of her lips would have touched his.

She was so absorbed in trying to stay calm that what he did next came as a total shock: he ran his hands down the sides of her breasts, and the cold water suddenly blazed around her.

"Colley!" she choked out, splashing both of them as she jerked, clutching at him again as she went under a little.

He was as upset as she was.

There was red blood running up under his skin; this close she could see it clearly. "I've got to make sure the rope is around you in the right place," he defended himself brusquely.

"Is it?" she asked flippantly, holding to his shoulders.

"I hope so. I can't stand to make sure again," he said desperately. "Take your hands"—he caught both of them in his—"and hold the rope up high, here, above the loop. Hold on tight and don't turn loose."

She couldn't; he fastened her fingers above their heads with his own, straining until they were pressed together, his wet body plastered against hers, their legs tangling under the water like their arms were above.

His movement stopped; he looked right into her eyes.

She was trapped; she couldn't move away.

Their lips were too close and his eyes too brown. She had to be too close if she was seeing the brown lights in them. He pulled in his breath at something he glimpsed in her face, and she gave up the fight.

It was just a kiss, a silly waste of time down here in this watery hole, an odd, calm break in his quick movements to get her out.

Just a kiss.

A taste . . . the bittersweet taste of yesterday, his mouth as it closed over hers.

A feeling. His face against hers, his breath, the rough honey of his lips. Heart pounding.

And that ever-present heat.

She had been so cold for the last three years, and here in this chilly water, she had found the warmth again.

His kiss burned. It burned like fire, and she felt it, sweet and hot and licking up right in the center of her stomach.

Touch him. She fought one hand free from his hold above their heads and let it drop to his cheek while she strained to hold his lips.

With it, she traced his throat, letting her fingers come to rest on his shoulder.

She felt the odd abrasion on the skin under her hand. It was rough, so different from the hard silk that covered the rest of him. Lainie was aware of it on the edges of her mind, but she had been so taken up with his lips, his face, that until now, she hadn't looked at it.

It was important that she see what was under her fingers, and she pulled away from his clinging mouth to stare at it.

"Colley," she whispered, and felt the sick shock all the way down to her toes.

The first scar was a jagged line across his shoulder running to a deeper, circular, ragged one just below his collar bone. They showed up white against his dark skin, startling and vicious.

She knew what they were. She knew how they got there. But she hadn't seen them since the day they were fresh, jagged, bleeding wounds.

He released his hold on her other hand and let his own drop with it.

"Don't," he said roughly, catching her chin to try and pull her face away. She resisted his force a minute before she looked into his eyes again. He was panting for breath. "If you look at it too long, you'll remember to hate me."

She recalled with vivid clarity the day of the wound. All of a sudden she remembered more: the sweetness of his kisses, the pleasure of his face pressed to hers. "Lie down, Lainie," he had asked so long ago, and she had obeyed willingly.

She remembered the blood, the way he'd fallen, white and still after the accident happened.

Just an accident.

And without another thought, she bent her head and put her lips to the worst part of the scar, the gouged-out hole.

"My—God." His words were so thick she could barely understand them. His heart thumped like a racing time bomb, and he moved his hand down to hold her face to his chest.

He had always protected her in water. This place was theirs for a second, a floating kingdom free of anything that might take her from him. Nobody up at the top could see them here, this close to the side of the quarry. Here, in the deep, clean, timeless water, here surely she could caress him and ease his pain for an eon or so.

She hadn't been there to do it three years ago.

They had each suffered alone.

And that was all she had time to think, because Way was shouting something from up above. Colley pulled back rapidly, breathing like a hard-run animal, the same sound she thought she was making, his wet hair brushing the tops of her shoulders. He tried twice before he shouted up at the men they couldn't see who were waiting on the overhanging ledge, "Take her up slow."

"Colley," she managed over her shoulder as the first tug on the rope brought her out of the water. "This hurts."

"I didn't have time to fix it better. I'm sorry, baby." The only sign he gave that he was still upset was in his harsh breathing that made the words sound ragged. "Pull yourself up a little, so that you're not lying back so much on the rope. That way it won't burn. And use your good foot to keep yourself off the wall."

She tried to do as he said, and it still hurt. The rope cut into her shoulders. But the hardest part was at the top, when Way had to lie on his stomach and she had to trust him enough to let go of the rope and let him pull her up by her arms, his face red from the strain.

When she thought that she couldn't take any more, that he'd pull her arms right off her body, she came over the edge, collapsing on her cousin's legs.

"Get away from here," he gasped roughly, and she stumbled forward across him and promptly fell, her right foot crumpling under her with a sharp pain.

"I think they'll have to drag me," she whispered, and then Preston stepped up. "Lainie, here, lean on me," he implored.

Preston Rawlins looked odd to her for a second, as if he were out of place. Maybe she'd even forgotten him momentarily somewhere in her watery trip back in time. He wrapped his arm around her waist, pressed his face against her hair. It felt strange.

"I'm sorry, angel. God, if something had happened to you, what would I have done?" he whispered.

With his help, she hobbled to the side of Way's patrol car and braced herself painfully on it as Tate loaded two towels around her to stop her shivering. It wasn't that she was really cold; it was more that she was safe, and the ground was solid beneath her feet, and there was a lot of space around her instead of stone walls.

And there was some kind of mental adjustment that she had to make, too. That time leap again.

I kissed his lips. His shoulder. I kissed his scars, knew how he got them, and wanted him, anyway.

No, that wasn't possible. Not up here.

"Colley's still down there," she reminded her cousin.

"Yeah," Lloyd Tate called, and Lainie looked to find the others in a tiny group over on the opposite side of the car. "You're not going to leave Rawlins down in the quarry with his old man, are you?"

"You know, you're not so much help but what you couldn't go on home if you wanted to," Way retorted. "Nothing else to see here, anyway. Come on, Gregory, and you, too," he said to Preston, who was still hovering around Lainie, "let's get him up. Last I noticed, he didn't have a halo and wings to fly out with."

"That'll be the day," Tate murmured, and then turned his attention to Lainie. "Are you okay?" A momentary trace of real concern was in his voice, and it made her as uncomfortable and surprised as his little flashes of amused sarcasm and sexual aggressiveness did.

She didn't answer, falling instead into the white vinyl seat on the passenger side of the car as soon as she got the door open. Then she twisted to frown into the sun, waiting for them to pull Colley Rawlins back up to the real world again, too.

Somewhere down here in this quarry, his father rested.

Colley's eyes searched the quiet walls as they rose cool and strong in the shadows, giving away nothing. Brodie had died before Colley's birth; he had belonged to Lo-Joe for a quarter of a century now.

Maybe he was at peace.

God knew that Colley wasn't. He let his fingers touch his shoulder where her lips had caressed him. What had she meant by that? After shunning him for years, she had kissed him. No, she'd done more than that.

She'd kissed his scars.

And she'd come out here with his cousin. With Preston.

He couldn't bear it.

"No man who ruins his life for love of a woman is worth bein' called a man," he could hear Devil say. "Believin' that a female will love you true is a lie. Don't be fooled into thinkin' things are pretty and good, like Brodie was."

But I'm your son, he wanted the man down here in the quarry to know. *They say you loved my mother; even Devil says it. What am I going to do about Lainie Thorne?*

Lo-Joe might hold Brodie, but it held no answers. The only sound was the *slap, slap* of the water against the walls.

Up above him, Way was throwing the rope sling down toward him.

"Come on, Colley, the party's over. Time to go home," he shouted.

His black head barely had time to show before he was pulling himself up onto the ground, coming upright to shake himself vigorously like a dog, his hair whipping about his cheeks. "You're getting my uniform wet," Way grumbled.

"Where is she?" Colley asked intently, scanning the gathered faces.

"I'm here," she said, coming up to one knee in the car seat so she could see him clearly over Preston, who stood close by.

He was at the car in two or three long strides, forcing all the others to retreat, and he bent to grasp Lainie by the shoulders. "You're really okay." Then his initial relief faded. "What do you think you're doing, coming out here and falling in like that?"

His sudden flash of anger surprised her. "I didn't mean to."

"No? And here I thought you were trying to break your neck."

"Nobody's neck got broken today, Colley," Preston said hotly from behind his cousin, and the words made the other man stiffen, but Colley didn't even look in his direction.

"Here." Colley dropped to a crouch before her. "Let me see your ankle." His hands lifted it gently to his wet pants leg. His shoulder was right at eye level, and she didn't want to see the huge white scar anymore. It was far more noticeable there in the direct sun. She tried to pull her foot from him, and he looked up at her, his face going still. He let her ankle slide out of his grasp to the ground.

"It's in bad shape. And your back . . . I'm sorry, Lainie. I should have had some better way. You need to see a doctor."

"Then I'll take her," Preston interposed, bending over to grasp her arm. "Come on, angel—

"Get your hand off her," Colley said quietly, suddenly speaking to his cousin at last, as if he'd been waiting deliberately for this moment. He came to his feet and let his own hands drop free.

The silence was deafening between them. Colley's words had not been loud, but it seemed as if the whole world heard and turned to listen. The handful of people who lingered all understood: there was going to be trouble between the two men.

"She likes my hand on her," Preston said tightly.

"Is that true?" Colley never took his eyes off of Preston, but his question was toward her. "And since when did you start running around with him, anyway? Did you forget who he was, or something?"

So much was at stake in his bitter, ironic words. Preston was waiting. Colley was waiting, too, and remembering the kiss.

I want to give up. I want to go back to all those summers ago. I want to forget what you did, Colley. I want to want you again, like I used to.

"Well, is it? Because if it is true, I want to know what you meant when we were down there in the water," Colley said hoarsely. "What was that all about? Or was it just because you knew I had to let you go, so you figured you could do whatever you wanted to me and then leave with him? Was it just to hurt me again?"

Preston's face darkened with what might have been jealousy, and he looked at Lainie for some kind of explanation.

"Leave me alone," she whispered. "I'm grateful for what you just did for me. But whatever I do, it's my life, Colley."

"She doesn't have to answer to anybody," Way said quickly, stepping up to try to stem the impending violence. "She's riding home with me, if she wants."

Lainie nearly collapsed with relief. "I want to," she said, her voice husky with strain.

"Well." Preston's voice was almost relieved. "That settles that, then."

But Colley wasn't through. "It settles nothing. She's not one of your women. You can't just come out to this quarry and nearly get her killed and expect it to be forgotten. She's scared to death of deep water. Hit me, you bastard, so I can return the favor."

"Why would I hit you?" Preston was trying hard to sound superior and amused, but mostly, he just sounded scared. "You may live like a brute, but I—"

Colley knocked him flat, blood splattering his own chest

from his cousin's shattered lips. The thudding, meaty sound of the blow was as loud as thunder.

Julie screamed, and the whole circle of people fell back in a buzz of reaction. "He really hit him," the redhead told everybody around her in shock. "Preston's bleeding."

"Colley!" Lainie pleaded.

But he was blind and deaf in his fury, and before Preston could even get up to his feet again, Colley was on him, shoving him. "Fight, damn you. Fight like a man," he panted, "instead of like a sneaking coward."

Preston came up in a rush, shaking off his cousin, and slapped at him in a wild reaction. "Fighting me won't make her come back to you," he gasped out furiously. His slap unexpectedly hit home and gave him time to regain his footing. He made a strong right hook toward Colley's chin and missed only because his cousin moved like lightning.

Colley laughed, a sound of pure joy. "Good. Good." This time his blow was to Preston's abdomen. Preston made a retching sound when he fell.

Way rushed wildly into the melee, grabbing Colley from the back to pin his arms to his sides, and there was a mad scuffle between them for a second.

"Stop it!" Way said in a choked shout. "You, Gregory, help me before he kills Preston!"

Jack hesitated and didn't move.

"Grab him!" Way roared, and Lloyd Tate finally closed in as Way struggled to hold him. After a second or two, Colley went still, captured between the two of them, breathing like a freight train.

"Now you listen," Way said in his ear. "Give it up. You're not fixing anything this way, and the old man's gonna be real unhappy if you two bruise up each other. Let it be done, Colley."

She could almost see the struggle going on in the man

they held; he had to force himself to breathe slow and steady. "Turn loose . . . of me."

Tate obeyed immediately. It took Way a little longer as he lingered just to make sure that Preston, whom Jack was helping to stand across from them, was safe from his cousin.

"One of these days, Preston," Colley said violently, "you'll push me too far. When you do, I'll kill you."

Then he strode away to the trees in the distance, where the big black horse had retreated, and they watched him go. The last rays of the evening sun struck his hair; they lit the long muscles in his back above the wet jeans as they molded his hips and legs.

He vaulted easily onto the back of the horse, letting his knees and his bare feet—where were his boots, anyway?—wrap the animal, and with his hands on its shiny neck, he nudged it closer to where they stood, looking up at him. "This place is posted. Can't you read? Get the hell off," he called harshly. "Now."

"This is my land as much as it is yours," Preston said, grunting.

"Get away from this quarry," Colley said fiercely, "all of you." The horse snorted, throwing up his head sharply as if to emphasize his rider's words.

"God," Julie whispered, her voice strange and breathless sounding. "I never saw anybody like him in my life."

"He's a piece of work," Lloyd muttered, in resentful, reluctant admiration.

One by one, they began to leave, moving with haste, while he sat the horse like the king of the jungle.

But it was Lainie whom Colley watched as she hopped and hobbled back toward Way's car, the one she'd come out of when the fight started, while her cousin unhooked the ropes that had pulled her to safety.

And it was Lainie toward whom he turned the horse just as she reached the vehicle and braced herself on it.

She backed against its hot metal side as the snorting animal pulled up in front of her. She had to frown to see Colley as he sat astraddle the horse, a black shadow against the setting sun.

"How long have you been meeting Preston, Lainie?"

"I don't have to tell you anything," she retorted, trying hard to be tough, wrapping her arms around her waist. She was aching all over.

"Play the game, then. But nothing will come of your running with Preston and this bunch of rich boys he hangs out with." Colley's words were cold, but she could hear his struggle to breathe beneath them. He was furious with her. "The old man's got plans for him, just like he does for everybody around him, and they don't include little country girls. Devil won't like this. He'll let it go just so far before he reels my cousin back in. I've seen it happen before. No matter what line Preston gives you, no matter how good you look, he knows what he wants, and he knows only Albert can give it to him."

"And what if I were what Preston wanted?" she asked in a blazing temper. How dare he of all people accuse her of being backward?

She couldn't see Colley's face clearly, but the horse under him snorted and jerked, as though his rider had pushed his knees into him too tightly.

"Don't be a little fool," Colley said flatly. "Even if Albert didn't stop it, I would."

"Who do you think you are?" she gasped. "You've got Rachel Harding hanging all over you, and then you tell me that I can't see anybody?"

There was a tiny pause. "What do you know about Rachel and me? Is she the reason you've decided to torment me with Preston?"

"No."

There was a long pause.

His voice was as cold as icicles when he spoke. "You're going to get hurt, whatever the reason you're flirting with Preston. Damn it, I'm trying to help you."

"You can help me by getting out of my life, Colley Rawlins. I said it when I was eighteen, and I meant it then. I mean it now, too."

"Leave him alone," he answered doggedly. "He's older than I was when you made up your mind to hate me forever, and he's not like me. I listened to you. I walked. He won't. He's too used to having anything he decides to reach for."

"I'm glad he's not like you," she cried furiously. "Don't you understand? That's what I want, somebody not like you."

She tried to slide away from him, down the length of the car, but the horse followed her, making her lean away. He was doing it deliberately.

"Stop it," she whispered.

The only good thing was that now she could see his face. He pulled the horse back from her, and for a minute, they confronted each other, him looking down on her, his eyes a blazing black flame.

"I reckon I'll just get in this thing all the way and say exactly what I mean." His voice was full of menace. "And you better hear me, Lainie. You ought to know by now that there's one way my cousin and me are alike—because I wanted you, too. I never got you, and I mean to see that Preston sure as hell never does, either. That's coming right from me. It's got nothing to do with the old man. There's too much between us for me to see you fall into Preston's slimy hands."

"Hey, you, Rawlins!" Way had come up from the edge of

the quarry and finally caught sight of the man on the horse and the girl so near him. "Leave her alone."

Colley obeyed; he wheeled the stallion away, the muscles in his bare shoulders flexing under the brown skin as he controlled the huge animal.

"Just remember, Lainie," he said quietly, "I've waited a long time for you. Keep the hell away from Preston, or pay the price with me."

Then he galloped off across the field, bent low over the shiny neck of the horse.

"Damn son of a bitch," Way swore furiously as he came striding toward her to help her in the car. "One minute I can't stop myself from liking him, and the next I want to punch his face in. What'd he say to you?"

"He's not happy about Preston," Lainie tried to say humorously. "I want to go home."

"I'm not too happy about Preston myself," the man opposite her muttered, "but I'll get you in the car before I complain. I thought somebody was helping you, or did Colley scare them all off?"

She didn't answer; she just slid into the car seat with shaky relief.

They passed the rescue squad as they turned out onto Martin Hollow Road.

"A day late and a dollar short," Way muttered. "They didn't expect Colley, I don't reckon. He beat them to their own job. Sometimes he's too big for life. Like now, on that horse. I swear, he's gonna wind up just like the old man. I can't believe it."

"I can," Lainie returned wearily.

"And just what do you think you're doing, hanging around with the Rawlinses again?" Way demanded in an outrage that he was finally giving vent to. "You swore after John died that you were done with that family."

"Preston didn't have anything to do with that. It was Colley." The rope burn along her shoulders was hurting again; she shifted sideways in the seat to get farther away from Way.

"I know what happened. I'm one of the few that knows the truth, so you can't put me off. But can't you see that Colley will never give in for you to be with Preston?"

"He's got Rachel Harding. Why would he care now if I'm with his cousin? Anyway, Preston's only in the Springs because Devil made him come for the summer. He hates it here. He'll never come back when he leaves at the end of this month, and"— she shut her eyes and forced herself to say the words before she could think about them again—"I mean to go with him."

She heard the slow, surprised breath that Way took, and the dismay in his voice when he spoke. "But this is your home. You always said you'd never leave the Springs."

"I will if staying means having to suffer."

"Suffer what? Things like seeing Colley with the Harding woman?"

She made an involuntary sound of protest, but Way ignored it. "Or is Preston what you're after because he's the best way to get to Colley?"

"I like him," she protested.

"You like that man I just met at the quarry?" Way asked in disbelief.

Lainie flushed. "I don't know what's wrong with him. He wasn't like this until he found out that I'd once been with Colley."

"He's just like all the rest of that crowd. Are those people today your new friends? You don't live like them. You've been raised a whole different way. You're a better person. A deeper, more decent person."

Lainie laid her head back on the seat and stared out at

the dusk that was slowly falling. Her foot was hurting, her heart was hurting. "And who in this wide world cares about that anymore?" she asked bitterly.

"Stop it, Lainie. What's got into you? Aunt Deborah would tell you that you're wrong."

"Oh, Mama. Everybody knows that she's a good woman. But nobody wants to live her life, do they? The life that I helped to give her."

Way was quiet for a moment. "So you're going to make it all up to her by going off with Preston. Lainie, have some sense."

"Don't sound so gloomy. I'm not exactly sacrificing myself. It's no hardship to be with a rich, handsome man."

"If you love him. Do you?"

Lainie rushed on feverishly. "He's the answer I've been looking for. It was my fault that Papa died. Mama lost everything, and that was my fault, too."

"Hell, Lainie, it just happened," Way interrupted harshly, but she didn't even stop to hear him.

"There was no money to save the house, no money for college, and Mama needed me. So did Aunt Olivia and the Magnolia. That was okay. It was my chance to do things right for once. But now it's all coming apart. Aunt Olivia gets older and Mama gets tired, and the hotel—I love it, but it's killing us."

"Let it go, then. It's a part of my past, too, but I won't live my life for it."

"I can't. Aunt and Mama, they don't fit anywhere else anymore. They couldn't be happy away from it. There's something I haven't told anybody yet, not even Mama. You can't tell her, either. The insurance has been cancelled, and we owe back taxes."

Way hesitated. "I've got a little money saved," he said carefully. "How much does the place need?"

"Forty thousand dollars," she said bluntly. "None of us

have it. So it will have to close, and that's the end of life as we know it."

"And you've decided that the answer is to marry Preston," Way said slowly. "That is what you're thinking of, isn't it?"

"It doesn't matter whether I marry him or not, as long as . . . as I get what I want. Money, and a way out of the mess I've made of things."

"Did your new friends teach you to think this way?" Way demanded furiously.

"Necessity did."

The dark silence between them was long and full of protest. His, and her own heart's. But she couldn't let him know that.

"Colley's rich," Way said at last. "He's always wanted you. He's bound to have as much as Preston does, whether he acts it or not."

Lainie laughed a little. "You know I can't marry Colley."

"It'd be a lesser crime to marry him, even with John Thorne between you, than to sleep with Preston like a cheap whore for money and a fast ticket out of here," Way said brutally. "What will Deborah and Olivia do when you leave?"

"I'll come back, often. You know I will. I'd never forget them. Anyway, they'll have enough money to—"

But Way was too angry to let her finish. "You might save the Magnolia and give them all they need. There aren't many women with faces like yours; I can believe that even Preston Rawlins would knuckle under and lay out the money for you. But will they want it at the price you're going to have to pay?"

"I'll see to it that they—"

"That they never know the lie you're going to live with him?"

She drew in a sobbing breath in the light evening shadows of the car, and there was silence. The dim yellow lights of the Magnolia had just been turned on; the hotel came into view, but Way didn't turn in to it or to the house beside it.

"You said you'd take me home," she said quickly.

"You can't go home until the doctor sees you." His voice was still a little angry. "You fell in the quarry. Your foot looks like you wear a man's size twenty shoe. Your back has a burn on it. Your knees are all skinned up. And you've been crying for the last five miles."

"I'm fine. I told you, insurance isn't our thing lately. We owe Dr. Maxwell already because Mama had to take Aunt Olivia to him twice last month. Besides, I just did something stupid. I blew the only hundred dollars I had saved on this swimsuit to"— this time Way couldn't tell whether she was laughing or crying—"to impress Preston, and I fell in the qu-quarry instead."

"You're seeing the doctor," he said, but his anger abated a little. "And if you're going to cry all over me, I might as well give you more reasons to. Lainie, honey, you think you're all grown up because you've learned that life is hard. But wait until you crawl in bed with a man you don't love and let him paw you just so you can have his money. You're not made that way. You'll hate yourself, girl, more than you ever hated your witch boy. For God's sake, listen to me. Don't do this thing."

"Listen to me and do the things I ask, that's all I want," Devil told Colley implacably.

The old man pushed him until he was ready to drop on his feet with exhaustion.

Colley still worked the massive tobacco crop like a field

hand, taking orders from Thorne like he was just another one of the people from the shantytown. The two of them kept their distance from each other, speaking little, holding back the tension between them.

Always, when some little thing happened that made Colley certain all over again that Thorne despised him, he remembered his private conversation with Deborah. She had asked, not ordered; she had trusted.

You have such a hold on her. She just reaches for you.

He was beginning to realize that Lainie Thorne was going to matter to him in a big way. Now if only he could figure out how to handle the situation between him and her father.

He was happiest away from the man, and that meant in the barns, where Colley and not Thorne ruled. He handled everything from the horses that Devil was acquiring to the money accounts. Devil checked the books for accuracy every week, questioning every move. Sometimes Colley wanted to put a fist through a wall with frustration after one of their sessions, and other times, he wanted to laugh at just how shrewd the old man was in his business dealings.

Most of all, he prided himself on the fact that his grandfather diligently hunted for mistakes, and more and more of late, he couldn't find them. The old man was pleased with his work; it was James Rawlins who couldn't be pacified.

"You're letting an eighteen-year-old kid who's never been to school handle a fortune in those horses," he accused Devil one bright Saturday morning. Colley heard the argument all the way out on the porch. He thought maybe he was supposed to. "At least let me get you an accountant who knows what he's doing."

"I don't want somebody who's never dirtied his shoes by

settin' foot in a barn. It's my business and my horses. Colley's mine, too. No skin off your nose. You've got all the rest of it. You're keepin' two dozen employees busy doin' things with my money at the office in Nashville."

"You'll have reason to regret this, Daddy."

For a while, it looked as if James might be right. Colley had trouble making the adjustment from field hand to stable manager, and the trouble sprang from an unlikely source: the shantytown people.

They couldn't come to grips with the news that the man who'd once lived like them, in a shack near the river, was suddenly in control of part of the farm. What confused them even more was the gradual way Devil was working him into the scheme of things, the way the old man still sent him to labor in the fields under Thorne side by side with them.

The climax of the uneasy situation came one hot day when the whole farm worked at spiking a field of tobacco.

It was hard, dangerous work. Long, silver, deadly sharp spikes shaped like inverted cones were slid over the end of waist-high wooden sticks. Those sticks were propped on the ground beside individual plants, and then the whole plant was bent sideways over the spike until the thick, sticky stalk was skewered and pushed down onto the stick.

When each stick was full, the spike at the top was removed for use somewhere else, and the tobacco plants were taken to the barns to be hung and dried, still impaled on the wooden poles.

The three people who worked the row over from Colley were all connected somehow, although he doubted that they were family members, as they claimed. Being family meant that the three of them could share one of the shacks; otherwise, the woman would have had to live alone, or with some other female.

The two men in the field spent most of their breath talking about women's anatomy in colorful, coarse terms. Colley heard them in his own row of tobacco and tried not to think about them at all.

The woman was a short, chunky, strong blonde, not as old as most of the women who spiked the tobacco, and she hummed a piece of a song as she worked, staying close to the dark-haired, dark-skinned, silent and shirtless man just across from her.

Three hours into the day, she gave a quick cry of terror.

It startled him into finding her as she stood between the tall tobacco plants, blood dripping from her arm. "What'd you do?" he demanded hurriedly, reaching for the arm that she extended toward him in panic.

"Reckon I hit that spike," she tried to explain, nodding toward the razor-sharp blade that pointed to the sky, protruding through the heavy tobacco. "Jesus, that hurts. And look at all the blood. . . ." Her eyes were scared in her grimacing face.

"You better go on over to the water barrel and wash it off," he advised. "Thorne can look at it and tell you if it needs more."

"It's a awful long way," she asked piteously. "I'm so hot, and I feel dizzy . . ."

He hesitated a moment, but it was clear that she was in pain. He'd been scratched enough times by the spikes that he could imagine what this deep a wound would feel like. Besides, the sticky residue from the plants could burn. So he helped her to the water barrel and pointed her to the overseer before he retreated from the man, back to the fields.

Aching and hot, so sweaty that salt had crusted on his skin, Colley could barely stand even the slight pressure of the straps of the overalls across his sunburned shoulders at the end of the day. His hands were so sore that he could hardly move his fingers.

Trudging out of the field after the others had gone on ahead, he walked past Thorne on his way to the big truck that waited to haul them back to the shantytown and then on to the white farmhouse where he lived now.

Trees grew at the end of the field. The woman surprised him by stepping out of their shadows as he drew near.

"My arm's gonna be okay," she offered, showing him the edges of a vicious red cut that had been cleaned and doctored with a red, antibiotic wash that gleamed around the extremes of the bandage. "But I ain't gonna be no good in the field the rest of the week."

"Won't be any hardship to stay away from here when it's as hot as this," he said in way of consolation.

She fell into step beside him. Up ahead, he could see the two men whom she called her relatives glancing back now and then.

"'Course, I got other ways of makin' the green," she said casually, and she let the hand between them, the one not attached to her injured arm, brush lingeringly down his hip and thigh as they walked.

Colley understood instantly, but her move was such a surprise that if his face had not already been blood rich with the heat of the day's work, he would have blushed. He'd never expected a proposition right here in the open daylight, not thirty feet from the other workers.

His shock made him blunt. "I'm not going to have much time. I'll be working. I didn't get hurt."

She caught him by the elbow, and when he stopped, they were right in the thicket of trees, sheltered a little from those up ahead. "I been watchin' you, mister, and I sure do like the way you move. You ain't too old, but you got a look about you that says mighty plain you could keep a woman happy. I bet you have before, too."

Her knowing eyes confused him, and instantly, he remembered Rose and how she'd made him feel. Something inside him wanted that feeling again, immediately.

She stepped into him, and she was as hot and sweaty as he was. Her eyes were brown; he saw that much before she ran her hand over the skin of his shoulder. "See? I was right. You want it. I don't charge so much when I like the man. But it ain't gonna be nothin' to you to pay, is it? They say that Devil Rawlins claims you. I could give you some fun, just what you need, and you could give me some of the old bastard's cash."

"Look," he began awkwardly, "I don't—"

"Get on to the truck, woman!" John Thorne called the harsh command to them as he came up the path from behind. He didn't admonish the other half of her embrace, and they both knew why: he was Albert's grandson. Colley stood still as she ran toward the others.

What Thorne thought should have been of no importance to him. But the truth was, it mattered. This was Lainie's father. Colley wanted his respect at least.

He tried to say something, but guilt kept his tongue glued to the roof of his mouth. Thorne never stopped when he passed Colley, but he reached out an arm and pushed the younger man out of his way.

He lay awake that night, torn between emotions. The next morning, he was delayed on his way out to the fields by a mare due to foal soon, but as soon as he determined that she had time to spare, he went on to work in the tobacco. Thorne looked through him when he took his place in the field, and Colley couldn't think of anything at all to say.

The woman was gone, but the two men had a new topic of conversation. They talked just loud enough for him to hear them.

"That one got Millie in trouble with Thorne. Guess he's too good for her. He ain't nothing but a bastard hisself."

The other one agreed.

"I tol' her, I wouldn't want Colley Rawlins. He lived with Charley, with all his words and big books, and the ol' coot was plumb crazy. This one ain't got no reason to think he's somebody."

He ignored them, and that night, they took their revenge.

They broke into the horse barn—his barn—and turned out the mare. He hunted most of the hours around midnight for her, and when he found her in a wet, swampy field close to the river, she was in the process of giving birth to a spindly legged colt.

Colley helped deliver the foal up to his knees in mud just at dawn.

When he finally got the two animals back in place, safe and sound, he went to the house, still caked with mud and blood. "I want money," he told Albert bluntly.

"Yeah? How much?" Albert squinted at him through the cigarette haze that hovered in the kitchen as he drank coffee.

"Enough to pay off three people for a week's work."

"If this has to do with that mare, hell, don't give them three nothin' except trouble."

But he grudgingly went at last to the safe and handed over the amount Colley had asked for.

Then Colley went to the barn and pulled the black whip that Devil had once used on Garner from the wall.

By the time he'd asked enough questions to figure out which of the shacks they lived in, the three had gotten wind of what was about to happen. They were gone, the dust still rolling from the wheels of their old truck.

He mounted Black Horse in the pasture and caught up with them at the gas pumps at the store Devil owned. It sat at the boundary of Rawlins Farm. They were trying to argue the attendant out of a gallon of gas.

Pulling back the reins of the horse, he slid right up to the open window of the truck where the woman sat, her face terrified. Then he threw the money in her lap.

"Take it and get out. Don't come back. The old man won't be needing you on the farm anymore."

He wheeled the snorting horse and trotted him right up to the two men and the attendant, all of whom backed off at his approach. Unfurling the vicious whip, he let it drag in the dirt like a languorous snake. "That mare and her colt nearly died because of what you did. I ought to stripe you bloody for that damn trick. But I'm letting you leave whole. Just make sure you don't ever come back."

He and the silent, wide-eyed attendant watched the truck as it rumbled into the distance.

Then he went home.

That night the story was told all over the Springs. The shantytown boy had grown up while they weren't looking. He'd unexpectedly become a fierce man with a big whip, Devil's true spawn.

Thorne raised hell. At last, Colley had gotten a reaction from the overseer.

"He ran off the three Burtons," he told Devil furiously. "It's the height of the season. How am I going to get the crop in when he gets rid of the workers, and I'm short-handed already?"

"He fired them, and he had reason," Devil said brusquely before Colley could speak.

His words didn't placate Thorne. "He fired them! He

doesn't have the authority. I hire and fire, not a shantytown brat."

Suddenly, Colley had had enough. "I've got a name," he said furiously to Thorne. "You can use it any way you like, use any part of it you want. But don't you call me anything else again. I'm as good as you are."

Devil stayed quiet, watching the confrontation through hooded eyes.

Thorne's face was white. "I know just how good you are, whatever your name. I saw you with that woman in the fields. You wanted whatever she offered you. Why didn't you take it? You might as well. You won't get it from Lainie."

He had said it, finally put into words what was wrong. They had come to the heart of the matter.

"That's what this is about," Colley accused. "You think I'd hurt Lainie. I never did. I never have. I never would."

"I know you would. It's in the blood of people like you."

"That's enough," Devil cut in shortly. "You forget yourself, Thorne. This is my grandson you're talkin' to."

Thorne forced himself back from Colley. "All I've got to say is, if you're going to hold up for him, if he wants my job and you mean for him to have it, then I'll quit today."

"He ain't after your job. He's got enough for now. I need you. As long as he's workin' the fields, he's yours to tell what to do. If the load is heavy for you because of him, then make him pick up the slack. Just remember, you have to come in from the tobacco. When you do, he'd better be in one piece. And in the horse barns, what he says, goes. The Burtons were fired for sound reasons, not for what they did in the fields, but for what they did in the barns. They'll stay fired."

That night Albert came to the door of Colley's room. "I been thinkin' about what Thorne was tellin'. Whatever happened between you and the field woman, that's a natural thing. Nothin' to be ashamed of. You're a man. You're at the age to crave a female, crave her bad. There's one down on the other side of the river who'll do right by you. You get to thinkin' about it, take yourself to her. But as for Thorne's girl, if you're still missin' her, you'll just have to miss on."

"Why do you hate her so?" Colley demanded in frustration.

"I've got my reasons."

"I want to hear them. I have a right to know. You tell me to stay away, but you don't tell me why."

"She's Olivia Blackburn's niece. That's enough reason."

Whatever Colley had expected Devil to say, it wasn't that. He stared at his grandfather in bewilderment. "Olivia! What's she got to do with it? She's helpless. She's as old as—as—"

"As I am?" Albert finished dryly, but a flash of some rare emotion passed over his face, and his hand shook a little as he reached to grasp the door frame beside him. "She wasn't always."

The old man was looking right at Colley, but Colley knew by instinct alone that he wasn't seeing him. Devil was watching a distant memory.

The truth burst upon Colley in a blaze of inward light that was as blinding as heat lightning. "You loved her," he whispered, shock making him bold. "You wanted a Blackburn, too, and she wouldn't have you."

Devil stared at him, and the memory that had trapped him was gone. The anger sparkling in his grandfather's eyes before he hid it made nerves sting in the back of Colley's neck.

"You think you know a lot, don't you, boy? Let me tell you something: You don't know a damn thing. It wadn't that Olivia didn't want me. It was that her father made her choose between me and that hotel. It was close to a palace then. I was nothin' but a dirt-poor coal miner who'd come to town, and she turned her back on me just to keep it and her family and her place in the Springs."

"But—"

Devil motioned sharply with his hand and cut off Colley's attempt to speak.

"Hear it all. I made up my mind the night that she let me down that I'd have more than any Blackburn ever did, and I've done it, ain't I? What's more, I've watched them fall. I had sons. What does she have? I've got a farm, and land, and money. The Magnolia's just a piece of the past. I'll live to see it fade to nothin'."

"But she couldn't help it if she didn't love you," Colley said slowly.

Devil made a sound that in another man would have been laughter. "That's the worst part of all. She did. She loved me with her whole heart. That's why she ain't never married. And she still gave me up. I quit lovin' her. I learned about women and people like hers. I mean to see that you don't make my mistakes. Keep away from Lainie Thorne. Keep away from the Magnolia. Stay where you belong, here, on the river."

Colley wound up doing exactly that. He spent two and a half long years on the farm beside the Timms Fork, rarely venturing into the Springs.

He saw Lainie now and again, distant glimpses in town with her mother or with John Thorne in the Jeep. She didn't come to the farm again, and she completely ignored Colley if they were ever close enough to acknowledge each other, which was rare.

But he always knew where she was.

In the Springs, Lainie kept reluctant track of him, too.

She couldn't help it; her heart clung to every bit of information it could discover about the witch boy.

Colley knew what she did on her sixteenth birthday, and she knew when Albert forced him to go to Nashville to stay with James for weeks on end so he could learn about the family business.

Lainie herself was in a minor car accident with Dana when she was seventeen. Colley heard about it immediately, and he lay awake that night scared, wondering what he would do if she was hurt.

The next year, the big black horse sired a foal by a mare Colley had added to the stables at Rawlins Farm, and the foal sold to a Kentucky racing stable for more money than any house in the Springs was worth. Lainie heard the news, just as she heard when the townspeople began to say in resentment that the silent, younger Rawlins was going to turn out meaner and richer than the old one.

She recognized their jealousy and wondered at it. All she could feel was pride in him.

Lainie worked hard to kill that pride, just as she struggled to forget Colley himself. He was twenty-one now, and she was too old to cling to childhood dreams. His aloofness made her furious. She should dislike him even more than the townspeople did.

The problem was, she didn't.

9

She had kissed Colley Rawlins again.

Lainie awoke the morning after her plunge into the Lo-Joe quarry with her foot throbbing, her shoulders burning, and her head full of the memory of his lips on hers.

Pressing her fingers to her lips, she tried to taste him again, and then scrubbed the back of her hand across her mouth to rub all trace of him away.

She couldn't have him, or his kisses.

She had dreamed most of the night after Way brought her home, dreams that she didn't want to remember. Maybe they had been the result of the two white tablets that Dr. Maxwell had insisted she take before she left his office, but she suspected she was remembering so much because of yesterday, when she had let her lips touch Colley's, just like years ago.

How could she have known that her first sight of the scar on his shoulder would affect her so much?

Rain was pouring down against the screen in her window, and the fan that sat there was flinging the drops in on her face, like the tears that she wanted to cry.

She could hear Deborah moving in the kitchen and smell bacon cooking. Somebody—she hoped it had been Mama and not Way—had undressed her the night before while she slept heavily under the medication, pulling her out of the bathing suit and towels and putting her in a cotton sleep shirt.

Looking down at herself, she saw more. Her bandaged foot was swollen, even beyond the wrap Dr. Maxwell had put on it, and a streak of purple bruising angled a third of the way above her ankle. She could hobble, and that was about all.

"Mercy, Lainie, what on earth happened to you?" Susan's voice was clear and shocked as she watched the girl hop into the kitchen.

"I fell into the quarry," she said ruefully.

Susan gasped. "Lo-Joe? My Lord, what were you doing all the way out there at that pile of rocks? How'd you get in the place?"

Lainie ignored the real meaning behind Susan's words and said with as much humor as she could muster, "Somebody took the fence down out at the road. But if you mean, how did I get in the water, I think you'd call it free falling. I just stepped over the edge. Easy. It was getting out that was murder."

If she kept it light, Deborah's stiff posture might relax a little. Over at the sink, her mother's back was ramrod straight.

Mama didn't turn until Lainie's stumbling footsteps halted at the kitchen table, then she twisted, watching her daughter as she slid into a chair gingerly. "The way of the transgressor is hard," she said with a touch of pointed humor. Deborah's face was dry and knowledgeable as her eyes met Lainie's over Susan's shoulder.

Lainie flushed and spoke directly to her. "I'm sorry that I didn't tell you about Preston Rawlins."

Susan glanced from daughter to mother in quick enlightenment. "Maybe I'd better go check on Miss Livy this morning. She's sleeping mighty late." Her blue cotton housecoat, made in an enormous size to accommodate her frame, brushed over Lainie's bare feet as she strode past on her way out of the kitchen.

Deborah concentrated on the bacon that she was turning, waiting until Susan was out of earshot. Then she pushed the skillet off the hot cap and faced Lainie, her fork still in her hand. The humor was gone. "Sorry or not, you've still been seeing him all this time. I don't like him. Sort of soft looking. But you know what really worries me about him? His cousin."

Lainie looked blindly at the African violet sitting in the middle of the table. "You've got nothing to worry about with Colley."

"I'll believe that the day they lay him six feet under," Deborah said in agitation.

"You once told me that you didn't hate Colley."

"I don't. Maybe for a while I did, right after it happened. I reckon I'm finally past that. But I hoped you were free from him. It'd be hard on me if . . . if you weren't."

"I've said I'll never go back to Colley, haven't I?"

"Then if that's true, why bring his attention to you with his cousin? The biggest wrong is in the trouble you're liable to stir up. It's clear that Preston and he can't get along. I blame Albert Rawlins for the problems between them, for letting them be raised so differently. Colley has to resent that Preston has an easier life, and Colley is so strong and so much a part of the old man that Preston wouldn't be human if he wasn't jealous."

"I don't see what that has to do with me."

"Don't you? I've already heard from Bella Foster this morning. She claims that Colley threatened to kill Preston yesterday at the quarry, and it was over you."

Lainie moved uneasily. "How would she have heard that?" she demanded evasively.

"Julie Jones was spreading it all over town. So the talk has started again. You and Colley, your names always paired together. Preston will wind up caught in the middle, like everybody else always has been with you two. What if he gets hurt, Lainie? Another man dead?"

Her daughter's face turned white. "Don't, Mama."

"I don't want to say such things, but somebody has got to make you think before it's too late."

"Colley was talking, that's all."

Deborah paused a moment and then said quietly, "Colley never has wasted much time saying things he didn't mean."

Lainie came to her feet, wincing as she forgot and tried to stand on the damaged one. "Surely you don't think that I should give up a man that I'm interested in just because Colley doesn't like it. That's crazy. You told me to find a life away from him."

"Preston won't take you away from Colley, Lainie, no matter where you might go with him. He's of the same blood. He'll only bring you closer. I'm not part of any feud between the families; as far as I'm concerned, there isn't one. But I do know one thing: the Rawlinses have brought sorrow to me. I can't stand the thought of losing you, too, because of them, like I might have yesterday." Deborah turned away quickly to the sink before her voice broke. "I've lost too much in the last few years."

"Nothing happened, Mama. Nothing will. I'm listening to my head these days, not my heart. I'm not going to make any more mistakes."

"There's a mighty fancy car pulling up in front of the house," Susan called from the hallway. "Big and silver."

Deborah bent forward to look out the kitchen window. "So there is," she said unsteadily. "I'm going to get dressed and go to church. And you, Lainie, I'll let you handle the company."

"It's Preston," Lainie realized with a little shiver of surprise. He was pressing his suit, hard, just like he had been yesterday. She should be pleased; he still wanted her, and he was making it public knowledge. Surely a man with anything but honorable intentions wouldn't step right up to her mother's door.

"That's not who I see coming up our walk. I see one of those mistakes you're never going to make anymore," Deborah said flatly.

"Mama . . ." Lainie hesitated. She should be glad that Preston was there, right out in the open. Instead, sight of him scared her. What was she doing with him? She kept remembering how little and petty and vicious he'd been yesterday in front of Colley. Or was it just that every man paled beside the witch boy? "I can't see him today. Stop him. Just tell him I'm sick, or not here."

"Lainie Thorne, you're going to regret ever getting mixed up with him," Deborah said flatly. "I'll send him away. With any luck, he won't come back."

Out on Rawlins Farm, Colley had a few regrets of his own about the day before.

He should have left her in the quarry, he thought bitterly. Going down there after her had been nothing but foolish. Letting himself down into the big hole in the ground had been letting himself down into every pain he'd suffered over her.

He'd give almost anything to do it again, to pull her so close that her body was almost part of his, to have her help-less under his hands, to lay his soul bare under her kiss.

Even today, his shoulder felt the press of her lips.

Why had she been gentle, so much like the girl he'd known from childhood, for those few minutes? He wished she hadn't; now he wanted that girl back, aching for her as he had for all the years before he had forced himself into numbness.

And then he heard it, the sound he'd been waiting for all day, the low humming of the silver Jaguar that Preston drove. He came to the open doors of the big barn to watch it pull off the distant highway and cross the wide concrete bridge that looked like a pale bar of white sand under the light drizzle of rain that had been falling off and on all day.

Preston hadn't come home the previous night.

Maybe he'd gone to Lainie.

Colley was nearly sick with the thought. The girl had been so defiant about it, so determined for him to under-stand that she was keeping company with his son-of-a-bitch cousin. Her words—"I want somebody not like you"—kept circling in his head. Some monster kept whispering to him all last night, all this morning, that she might be with the other man.

He doubted it; she'd been beat half to death from the fall, and then he himself hadn't helped matters when he turned Black Horse on her, he thought guiltily.

But Colley couldn't concentrate on anything much when that voice talked in his ear. He just kept waiting.

But now his waiting was over: Preston was back.

His cousin carefully angled the Jag into the white garage that stood on the side of the house opposite the barn.

"He's a fool for that car," Devil always remarked when Preston came home, and Colley had to stop himself from telling the old man that Preston was a fool for anything that he thought somebody else wanted.

Like Elaina.

He saw Preston step slowly up to the porch of the house in the distance, right where Devil sat in a chair that he'd pulled into the shade to smoke.

There was a brief conversation between the two of them.

"Colley!"

His grandfather's roar shook the foundation of the barn, even over the sound of the rain, and he stepped outside into the late evening downpour.

"What's wrong?" he demanded of the old man, who stood like a bristling porcupine on the side porch as he shook the rain off himself.

"Look at your cousin," Devil commanded furiously.

Colley looked, and his heart felt savagely glad at what he saw. One of Preston's eyes was swelled shut, his bottom lip was split, and a blue bruise marred his left cheekbone. Not so pretty now.

"Did the little boy come running home to tattle?" Colley drawled, stepping slowly back.

It was Devil who spoke. "You told me last night that you two had an argument about his swimmin' in the quarry. I agreed with you. You don't party where your own blood has died. But you didn't tell me you'd beat him like this. What in the hell is wrong with you?"

"My big ol' watchdog cousin got mad because I was partying with a lady he knows." Preston tried to speak coolly, but his sore jaw made his words sound blurred. "I'm getting tired of his attitude. I told him in Atlanta, butt out of my business with the women."

"I didn't ask to get involved. I got sent where I didn't

want to go because you were messy and careless and she wound up pregnant. I don't want to have to pick up the pieces again," Colley said tightly, his hand finding the porch post beside him to hold on to. "Especially not with her." He couldn't help that he was letting his emotions show, right there in front of the two he couldn't afford to be vulnerable around.

"She is a fine piece, isn't she?" Preston said consideringly. "A little naive and innocent, but I'm finding out firsthand how sweet that kind of woman is when she finally gives in. She's as good as she looks." He challenged Colley with his words, and Colley couldn't control himself any longer.

He made a sudden lunge, catching Preston's upper arm in a bone-crushing hold. "Son of a bitch!"

"Stop it!" Devil thrust himself between them, his hard, wiry arms separating them, his angry face close to their hot ones.

"It's Lainie Thorne he's chasing after this time," Colley burst out passionately.

Devil went still.

"Tell him to stay the hell away. Make him, or I will," Colley demanded, yanking himself back from the old man's restraint. "You made me."

"She made you," Devil flared. "I would to God I could have. If I'd had my druthers, you'd have forgot she ever existed."

"Why should I stay away?" taunted Preston. "She's old enough to know what she wants. She knows how to say no, but she's not saying it."

"I know why you're doing this. To get back at me. You want to hurt me, go ahead. But leave Lainie out of what's between us." He twisted toward his grandfather. "You raised hell when I wanted her. What's different with him?"

Albert turned from Colley, then leaned upon one of the porch posts. "Preston, do you think you love the girl?"

Preston looked from his grandfather to his cousin. When he laughed at last, it became a wince, and he reached to touch his battered cheek. "I love the thoughts of what I'm going to do with her in bed. Is that enough?"

The rain increased suddenly; it pounded with a quick ferocity on the roof above them.

Colley didn't move, but Devil put a hand against his chest anyway. "There's the difference," he said heavily to his younger grandson. "He's not like you. He'll forget her the day after he has her. You'd let love make you weak. You'd forget what I've raised you to do with your life."

Colley's throat worked. He had to speak; he had to plead for Lainie, right here in front of Preston. "He still can't have her. You owe me, old man. I've worked for you all these years when he was gone. Now I'm asking you to send him off and get him away from Lainie."

"Afraid she's going to say yes to me? You've got reason to be, boy," Preston said harshly.

Colley winced. "He's going to hurt her. He's right; she's innocent. She's never even been out of the Springs to anywhere much. She'll think he means every damn word he says, and she's lonely enough to fall for him. She's got nothing but her family and that old hotel that she's killing herself trying to keep open."

"Then maybe she'd better think about leavin' it, and soon," Albert said flatly. "The place is falling apart, and they owe more taxes on it than it's worth. I could pay them, and quick as a flash, the Magnolia would be mine by law. As of a month ago, it's not even insured. One little accident there, and they'd be ruined forever."

Colley looked at him, and the truth blinded him.

"You mean to take the hotel from them."

Albert shook his head. "No. I just wanted you to know I could. But I won't, because you're gonna do what you have to do. You're gonna leave the Thorne girl alone. I'm agreeable to you marryin' Rachel Harding if you've just got to have a woman. Settle down to making something out of my money and my life."

Colley could barely speak. "And what of him?" he said hoarsely, jerking his head in Preston's direction.

"I'm goin' to talk to him alone about her. I won't have you two fightin' like a pack of wolves over a Blackburn, do you hear me, Colley?"

"I hear."

"Stop playin' the fool. Be like your cousin here. Get over her."

"She couldn't help what happened, old man. Nobody could have."

"Maybe not, but there's some things that can't be changed in life, and the fact is that you can never have Elaina Thorne. She's accepted the truth. What do I have to do to make you see it? I've warned you what I'll do if you don't let go of her. I'll ruin what's left of her family and force them out of this town. I'm talkin' right to you, Colley. Leave her be."

Leave her be, that was what Colley tried to do where Lainie Thorne was concerned.

He tried for more than three years, from the day that he gave his word to her mother. But when she turned eighteen, all his good intentions came apart.

It began one fine spring morning when Thorne collapsed in the tobacco field.

"Hey, Thorne's down!" came a sudden shout from one of the hands across from Colley, and he straightened in surprise to look for the overseer, who'd been standing in the back of his Jeep surveying the planting. No one stood there now, but when he shaded his eyes, Colley could see the heap of khaki on the ground behind the vehicle where Thorne really had fallen.

Joining the rush of the hands, he got to the man just as several of the workers made a cautious circle around his limp body.

Thorne's eyes were closed, his face white and wet.

"He ain't dead, is he?" asked somebody fearfully, and every eye turned to Colley, as if they expected him to have all the answers.

Reluctantly, he dropped to his knees beside Thorne and reached out a hand to touch him. The overseer was burning up with a fever, and he moaned and twisted away from Colley.

"Help me lift him into the Jeep," he implored the men. "We'll have to get him to the doctor."

When they had Thorne in place, the workers stood expectantly looking at Colley. "Go on with the planting," he told them at last. "I'll be back to see that we get it finished just as soon as I take care of him. You, Jackson, you're in charge until I get here again."

Thorne's eyes opened at Colley's words, and he tried to pull himself up. "This is my job," he panted. "I'm the one in charge. Not you, Rawlins. You don't tell anybody what—"

Unable to finish, he slid back down, his breathing so loud it rattled in Colley's ears, his eyes closed. The men looked from Thorne to Colley, and he said harshly, "I gave you orders, didn't I? Damn it, get busy doing them."

They scattered back to the fields, and Colley faced the unpleasant truth that Thorne wasn't going to like the fact that he was the one driving the Jeep, but that was just too bad. For Lainie, he had to make sure the overseer got to the hospital.

Pneumonia, that was what Flavius Maxwell diagnosed almost instantly, and called Deborah Thorne. Colley heard it from her when she left her husband's room. She came to find him as he waited in a visitation area of the hospital in Lafayette.

"He's not been feeling well for two weeks, but he kept going. He was worried that . . ." Deborah didn't finish the sentence, but she looked up into Colley's face and he read the truth. Thorne was afraid to be sick, afraid that Colley would wind up with his job.

"You'd better not tell him that I was the one who drove him in," Colley advised harshly.

"No, I won't. But I'll remember," she said quietly.

He was on his way out of the hospital before he realized that he had no way back to the farm unless he took Thorne's Jeep, which he wasn't about to do. Maybe he'd catch Nadine or Devil if he called the house. As he stood hesitating, footsteps approached from behind him.

"Uhh . . . Mrs. Thorne said you might need somebody to take you back," a male voice said cautiously.

It belonged to a tall, thin boy in a baseball cap and a shirt that said "No Fear." Colley didn't have a clue where he'd come from, but he knew him vaguely. He sometimes came with his father to sell tobacco at the Rawlins warehouse. Willis, that was his name.

"I can—" he began, but he never finished. Lainie Thorne stepped from behind the boy's lanky frame.

It was the first time in years he'd been close enough to her to note details, and he forgot to talk, staring at her in shock. What had happened to the little girl? She was taller, and she had a shape. Still slender, still girlish, but definitely a shape.

He realized all of a sudden, watching her as she leaned up against the brown-haired boy as they stood in the middle of a spill of afternoon sun, that the little girl from the creek had become more than pretty. Breathtaking was a better word for her. It was something about her eyes, the way they sparkled, and about the curve of her cheek, so clean and delicate.

"C.K. will drive you home," she said coolly, not looking at him at all, her face flushed a little.

C.K.—were the two initials the best the damned kid could do for a name? Colley wondered in an irrational flash of anger—smiled down at Lainie and reached out to catch her hand in his. "It won't take me long," he promised happily, and he hugged her up against him so that the side of her breast pressed him.

"No, thanks," Colley interrupted. He glanced from him to her. "I'd rather walk."

All of a sudden, he was angry enough that he meant it. Striding away from them, he didn't even hear her calling his name until he was halfway across the parking lot.

"Don't be silly," she was admonishing, her breath coming in little short pants as she ran after him.

He stopped abruptly, and she banged into his back. A split-second contact, and he felt it all the way down to his toes.

Lainie jerked away from him instantly, and he turned to look down at her. He didn't say a word. Finally, she flung into the silence, "It's miles back to the farm. You can't walk all the way."

"I'm not about to let that kid drive me," Colley said flatly, glancing up over her head to find Willis watching them from a distance.

"He's not a kid," she flared. "You're only three years older than he is."

Colley said nothing, but for a second, he forgot to be angry. It felt good just to look at her, to be so close that he could see every little detail. It took a second for him to realize that they were alone together—almost, anyway—that they were talking, they were out of the stillness they'd been forced into for the last years.

Finally she looked at him, really looked at him, blue eyes into black.

The world was silent for a long moment.

"You take me home."

His husky command made her eyes widen and she jerked a little.

"C.K. is—"

"I don't give a damn what C.K. is. Are you afraid?" he demanded.

"No. Yes. Colley." The last word held a plea.

"That's my name," he said flippantly, ignoring her confusion. "I'm glad you remember it. Now, are you going to drive me home or not? I brought your father here. You could say you owe me a favor."

She wasn't so cool now. In fact, Miss Lainie Thorne looked as if she were as angry as he was.

"You've made your point. Get in the Jeep," she managed, her cheeks flushed.

"Get in the Jeep, please," he retorted, but he started walking in a quick rush of anticipation. He was about to be alone with Lainie for the first time since he was a teenager.

"What's going on?" C.K. demanded in confusion, looking from Colley to Lainie.

Colley glanced again at his shirt. No Fear? He would very much like to put a little fear in Willis, and the way the boy suddenly backed away, maybe he was doing just that.

"I'll take him," she told C.K.

"But your mother said—"

"Don't worry. It'll be all right," Lainie interrupted, climbing into the driver's seat of the open vehicle.

"I won't eat her for supper," Colley drawled ironically.

"Well . . ." C.K. capitulated with poor grace. "Maybe I'll see you at the Magnolia, Lainie. The folk medicine festival is due in town soon. We could go to it." In a burst of boldness, C.K. leaned in between Lainie and the steering wheel and kissed her square on the lips.

Lainie jerked in surprise, and C.K. let her go, shooting one satisfied look at Colley.

The engine roared, and Lainie backed out of the parking space. Colley never took his gaze off her. She had on a pale pink top and white shorts. Her hands on the wheel as they shot down the highway weren't quite steady.

"What'd you let him do that for?" he asked quietly, a little surprised at the intensity of his own reaction.

She didn't pretend that she didn't know exactly what he was talking about. "Because I wanted to," she said flippantly, her cheeks red. "Who are you, anyway? I wouldn't know. So what's it to you?"

"A damn lot," he answered honestly, without even thinking.

Her hands tightened on the wheel. "Stop swearing. It was just a kiss. People do it all the time. I'm sure you don't. You're only a big, bad farmer in his overalls."

He'd never, never, known Lainie Thorne could act this way. "How old are you?" he demanded unexpectedly.

"The last time we talked, we had this same conversation," she retorted. "Just before you told me that you didn't mean for us to be friends anymore. Lord, Colley, you really don't get off the farm much, do you?" She dropped a hand from the wheel to brush nonexistent dust off the front of her sleeveless shirt. He couldn't stop himself: everywhere that her hands brushed, his eyes touched, too. He didn't know how to explain why he'd left her alone since she was fifteen.

"John Thorne really must be sick if he's giving in to let you run wild with all the boys," he finally said flatly.

"I'm not doing anything wrong," she snapped. "I'm just having fun. But you wouldn't know about that. You're old, Colley. Too old for me and everybody else."

The words stung.

"I can't help it if I have to work."

"We all work. But you do it all the time. You know what I think? I think it's just your excuse to stay by yourself and never say a word to anybody. Not that anybody ever wants to talk to Devil Rawlins's stuck-up grandson, anyway," she flashed back.

"At least I'm not sneaking kisses from girls."

Lainie's eyes found his and then fell to his lips before she looked back at the road sliding by, and almost involuntarily, she answered, "Colley—" She stopped short.

"What?" he demanded impatiently.

"Nothing. You wouldn't understand. You don't need any friends, and you don't know anything about girls. I don't know a one of them who'd let you catch her."

He didn't know what to do, or what to say. Where was his Lainie? The little girl who brought him whistles and wrapped her arms around him when she thought he was in trouble? He stared hard at her, his eyes serious, confused, and she swallowed as she felt his gaze. Her smooth brown throat revealed the tiny, nervous motion.

They rode in a silence that wasn't a silence at all. It hummed with emotion and unasked questions.

Colley didn't know what to say, unsure of how to handle the resentment he could feel in her. His dealings with women had been strictly perfunctory and physical.

She pulled up to the wide concrete bridge that spanned the river at the edge of the farm. "I won't go farther. I might get shot for trespassing."

"I couldn't keep hanging around back then, Lainie," he finally burst out in the stillness left by the halting of the Jeep. "They were saying things about me and you."

A pink wash of embarrassment crept up her throat, but her voice was nearly steady. "I heard them. I didn't know that you did."

Silence again.

"What in the hell was I supposed to do, then?" he demanded.

The girl opposite didn't answer for a minute, staring fixedly out over the wheel of the Jeep toward the bridge, and his frustration made him bold. He reached out a hand and caught her chin in his fingers. She jerked violently, his very fingertips tingled, but he didn't let go, forcing her face to turn toward his, her eyes to meet his.

"You could have at least told me what was wrong," she burst out, and she reached up to shove his hand away.

He let her. "You were what? Fifteen? What was I supposed to say? Hey, Lainie, they're saying that we—" Even now, he didn't know how to finish it. He didn't know what to do, so he got mad. Swearing under his breath, he flung himself out of the Jeep. "Never mind."

Three long strides toward the bridge, he heard her when she called him.

"Wait."

Turning, he looked back at her as she sat, tense and flushed, in the vehicle. "C.K. is mostly a friend," she offered hurriedly.

Colley snorted a little. "Yeah, sure."

"He comes to the Magnolia a lot."

"To see you."

She acknowledged the fact with a tiny little twist of her lips, a near smile. "It's where I am most weekends." Her words hung suggestively between them.

It dawned on him suddenly what she was trying to do, and he sucked in his breath in a hiss.

"Lainie . . ."

"I was eighteen last month, Colley." She answered his one word of protest steadily, looking right at him. Jesus, she was beautiful. "How old do I have to be?"

Barely able to speak, he could only croak out, "Thorne hates me."

"I don't." She wouldn't look at him anymore as she reached down to shift the gears in the Jeep. "But it's the last time I'll ever tell you so if you don't do something about it. . . ."

"No, Lainie, wait—"

If she heard his shout, she didn't respond. Swinging the Jeep in a big circle, she pulled away and left him alone, there by the edge of the road.

That night and the next one and the next one, he couldn't sleep. Not even the grueling work in the field could tire him enough to stop his thoughts. He could still see her, leaning against that boy, the long line of her throat exposed, her breasts soft against Willis's arm.

Willis couldn't know what danger he had been in when he held Lainie against him. It shouldn't have been the other man pulling her up close; it should have been him, Colley. *Me,* he thought. And she wouldn't turn away. She would offer herself, throat, breasts, lips, all, to him. To him.

He'd kept his promise to her mother. But Deborah had said "someday." If Lainie could hang out with other men, why couldn't she be with him? Had someday come?

Every moment, he thought about going in to town to see her. Two things held him captive on the farm: his own uncertainty about the situation, and the crops. After all these years, he had stepped right into the role that Devil had been grooming him for. Because of Thorne's illness, Colley was carrying the full weight of the farm on his back, in charge of planting and overseeing the fields, and it kept him busy from daylight until dark while the tobacco was being set.

But the idea was always hovering: Lainie and him, together, finally.

It was too crazy. She was the protected daughter of John Thorne. She belonged in Sunday school dresses and at fair, tender places like the Magnolia.

He was the abandoned son of a river woman, grandson of the meanest bastard in the county. Nothing tender about him.

But he couldn't forget the vision: Lainie, putting her lips to his.

And her words beat in his ears like the sound of his own blood pounding: "If you don't do something about it . . ."

"Is that you, Lainie?"

"Yes, Papa." She answered John only reluctantly as he stepped out on the porch. He was pale from the past ten days of pneumonia, and the gray at his temples seemed more pronounced than before. "Are you feeling better?"

"I'm fine. The doctor said I could get out of the house any day now. I might even call Albert and tell him I'm ready to go back to work next week. Much as I love Deborah, if she sticks a thermometer in my mouth one more time, I'll bite," he said wryly, with a tiny smile. "I need to smell the dirt, and sweat a little."

He leaned against the banisters, looking out over the yard of the house. Martin Hollow Road dead-ended just past them; there wasn't much to see except the trees with their new green leaves. "Way called. He asked if you wanted to go with him to the carnival this afternoon. I told him that you stayed home from church this morning with me, so it'd be a good idea for you to get out. He'll come and get you."

Lainie didn't answer for an instant. "All right," she said at last.

"What's the matter? Don't you want to go?" Papa asked in surprise.

"I was just thinking."

"About?"

She pulled herself up and laughed. "Nothing much. Are you really going back to work?"

"He thinks he's as hearty as ever," Mama said. She had walked up to the screen door behind them. "I don't know what the rush is. Rawlins isn't going to roll up that farm and haul it off somewhere. It'll be there."

Papa's face darkened. "You'd be surprised at what could happen."

Mama started to turn away, to ignore the ominous tone in his voice, but she changed her mind and spoke with determination. "If Albert wanted Colley to run that place for good, he'd let him. But he knows, just like you do, that it's too much for him right now. Maybe it's always going to be too much for one man."

"I know how people think," Papa said somberly. "They want their own blood to work their own land. Besides, I'm getting older. He's young. Strong as an ox."

"You're still smarter about tobacco farming. You've got years of experience, and Colley is wrapped up in those horses. He might not even want the work involved with the rest of the farm."

"He wants it. He's the kind with an appetite, for a lot of

things," Papa said. "I mean to hold him off a little longer if I can."

He took a step down the porch. "I need to walk a little. Lainie, girl, you want to go with the old man? I'll pull a fast one on those boys who come to see you and take a stroll with you myself."

She hesitated, then smiled. "Sure, Papa." What else could she have told him? That she was nearly sick inside because she'd practically thrown herself at the witch boy and he hadn't responded? Because she was wondering if he really wanted her after all? Had she just been deluding herself the past few years with the idea that he was watching her and waiting for her with the same secret longing that she'd felt for him, and that she tried to quench?

No, those weren't things Papa would understand right now.

Colley Rawlins did not do Sunday afternoons with girls. Everybody else in the Springs who was male, single, and under thirty might cruise the one main road up and down town or hang out around the Magnolia looking for the feminine set, but not Colley. He'd never even known that such was the pastime until this particular Sunday afternoon.

The yearly folk medicine show, the pride of the Indian Springs Civic Club, was still in progress, and nobody much noticed him or commented on his appearance in the unusual crowd of people in the streets.

He didn't want to think about why he was there. He was just looking, just being quiet in secluded corners and under old trees. After a while, he talked himself into strolling casually farther down the road toward the Magnolia, where the sound of music filled the air.

He couldn't go there, but he could get close.

"If you don't do something about it," she'd said. What in the hell was he supposed to do?

At the hotel, Lainie stood in the cool shade. The lawn was full of people. A bluegrass band was sawing away on "Uncle Pen," and long tables set with tubs of watermelon and pitchers of lemonade stretched under the trees. It was a perfect summer afternoon, the carnival atmosphere of the medicine show was at its peak, and she was so lonely she wanted to cry.

That was when she turned and saw him walking toward her down the old sidewalk. His black hair glistened under the sun, but his steps were slower, not long and free as they had been when he was a wild kid on the creek. She had to look twice to make sure he really was the right man.

Colley never came to town if he could help it, and he wouldn't set foot anywhere near the Magnolia, but there he was—just as she had invited him to be, his eyes scanning the crowd, looking for someone.

He had responded to her at last.

"Colley," she whispered, and took a step. "Colley Rawlins!"

He heard her voice, even across the music and the noisy people on the lawn beyond her, and he forgot all his anxiety in the light of her happy face. She was glad to see him. Some hotter, deeper emotion bubbled suddenly: he wanted to kiss her, right there in front of all creation. That was what came of thinking about it forever. Kiss her. It was the only crazy thought in his head, and he might have been fool enough to act on it, except for the innocent intervention of a middle-aged stranger.

When Lainie called him, she had been standing close, using a cane to support herself. The girl's cry must have startled her. She turned and took two quick, awkward steps toward Lainie and fell, cane and all.

It stopped everything. Lainie's progress toward him halted as she bent over the woman.

"Are you hurt?" she asked, tearing her eyes from Colley.

The woman smiled a little, her face flushed. "I'm sorry," she said ruefully. "I thought you were calling for me. I fall if I'm not careful. I don't think I can get up, either." A spasm of embarrassment crossed her face.

Colley hesitated. He stayed away from strangers, and he rarely offered anything of himself. The years had taught him that most people regarded him with suspicion when he did. But Lainie looked at him, her face beseeching, and he said finally, "If you want, I'll help you."

"Please," the lady asked, biting her lip.

By the time he got her up, Lainie had recognized her. "You're the woman in the room off the downstairs porch. You're here to meet your family at a reunion, was that it?"

"I met them," the lady said with a tiny laugh, and she sounded as if she were about to break out in tears. "But they're distant. They don't even really know me. I'm alone."

"Here, Colley, we'd better help her to the room," Lainie said anxiously, looking up into his face.

She was so close, right there, and she was asking him to walk into the Magnolia.

Just stroll into the place with its cool columns and fading glory.

He couldn't. Suddenly, he knew why he never came here. He was afraid, scared to death to enter the kingdom. It was Lainie's castle, the fortress where his grandfather had been forbidden.

Where kings guarded princesses against the beasts.

Thinking he could step into that realm was as foolish an

idea as thinking that the two of them might somehow fit together.

"Lainie . . . I . . . your father won't like it," he said at last desperately, over the head of the thin woman at his side.

"He's not here. We can't leave her alone," she pointed out, and she never gave him a chance to protest again. "I'll bring your cane, ma'am, and he can help you."

The rest of the Springs might be wary of him, but this one, this girl from the creek, didn't mind at all telling him what to do.

And that was how he came to walk into the Magnolia for the first time.

They cut through the backyard of the hotel, deep with late afternoon shade, and avoided most of the crowd. The lady's room was just off the main porch. Colley tried very hard not to think about his surroundings, and the woman kept up a stream of questions about everything from who he was to where he lived while they got her settled on the old-fashioned high-backed bed.

Just as they got ready to leave, she spoke again. "Thank you for the help. You're a . . . a very kind young couple."

A couple.

The word rushed through his head. Surely this woman, stranger though she was, could tell that they weren't one.

He looked around himself to get his mind off Lainie beside him. The room was graceful, with high ceilings, but it was old. Outside, the porch was inviting and full of peace, but it was crumbling. This world really was deteriorating to nothing, just as Albert had once told him, he registered in slow surprise. There was gentility and beauty here, but it had none of the raw power and strength that the Rawlins money bought. His barns were stronger and sturdier.

Maybe this kingdom, for all its charm, needed the beast.

Did Lainie really want him there?

She hesitated outside on the porch. "Colley, I—"

"What in the hell is he doing at the Magnolia?" The words were belligerent; so was the face that came with them. Way Blackburn advanced from the corner of the building across the yard with every intention of dragging Lainie away from the man beside her if he had to.

"I asked him to come," she retorted, taking a step back against Colley as if to save him from her cousin's wrath.

"Rawlins? You asked him to—"

"Way, who is this with Lainie?" Aunt Olivia's voice behind her nephew shook nearly as much as it had on the Sunday afternoon that Albert Rawlins had scared the life out of her, when he had come after Lainie, and both of her relatives jumped in guilty surprise when she spoke. Olivia stepped on the back porch out of the door that led to the kitchen, and she grasped one of the columns. Her whole attention was given to the dark-haired man behind Lainie.

Colley could feel it, the way she focused on him, and he took an involuntary step back, off the porch onto the grassy yard. At least he wasn't touching the hotel. God, what was he doing there, anyway?

Way shot Lainie a look that said, "Now see what you've done," but he left the talking to her.

On an impulse, she stepped down on the grass with Colley, catching his hand up from his side.

Nerves tingled in her own palm. How long had it been since she'd touched him in all his graceful strength? His hard fingers stilled and then slowly wrapped hers. Lainie tugged him closer to Olivia.

"This is Colley Rawlins, Aunt," she said in reassurance. "Haven't you ever seen him before?"

"Rawlins?"

"He's Albert Rawlins's grandson," Lainie explained. "Mama said he looks so much like Brodie—that was his father—that it made her jump the first time she ever looked at him." Was that the reason for Aunt's strange behavior? The old woman's soft cheeks were flushed with pink.

"No," Olivia said unsteadily, "it's not Brodie he reminds me of. He's—he's so young. What—what year is this, Lainie?"

But there was no time to answer her aunt.

"Why, you have my whistle," Olivia exclaimed suddenly, and her hand reached down toward Colley as he stood below her.

His face turned bloodred, and his free hand, the one Lainie wasn't clasping, covered the tiny silver object. "I wore it because . . . because it was the first time I ever came here and—"

And because he hadn't had the words to let Lainie know what he wanted, and he'd meant the whistle to speak for him.

"Don't you remember, Aunt? I gave it to him a long time ago," she put in hurriedly, trying to ease his awkwardness.

Olivia's fingers hovered, and at last, Colley moved his hand so she could touch the whistle, lifting it on its leather string from its place just at the top of the bib of his overalls. Handling it carefully, she looked from it to his face.

"I reckon this means that you finally belong to the Magnolia," she said at last. "I've waited. You've been so long, so long in the coming. All my life. I thought I'd die without seeing you like this again." There were huge, unexplained tears in her eyes, and under the sparkle, they were bluer and more brilliant than Lainie had ever seen. For a flash in time, she glimpsed what Olivia must have looked like in her youth, her beautiful youth, lost in the walls and the rooms behind her.

Those walls, those rooms, they seemed to understand

what Olivia was saying; Lainie didn't, nor Way, nor Colley himself. But the old hotel waited just as Olivia did for his answer.

"If you think it's all right for me to be here, I'd be happy." Colley's dark voice was rich with emotion.

The music was slow and quiet somewhere beyond them, just a fiddle crying into the depths of a Dobro.

Olivia laid the whistle against his white T-shirt, and then she let her fingers touch his upturned face briefly, in her own kind of blessing. "You're welcome at the Magnolia. Now. Forever."

When she moved her hand away, that odd spell was broken. "Lainie, you need to get your friend some of my tea. Colley, is that his name? And would you find Susan for me? I think I want to walk over to the house and lie down a little while."

"Yes, ma'am," she answered hurriedly, with a pleading look at Way. Let him alone, that's what she was asking, and Way understood. His face was different, too, when he looked at Colley. The other man had somehow known what to say to Aunt; he hadn't laughed or acted as if she were crazy.

Colley Rawlins had done what nobody else in town would have believed him capable of: he'd been a gentleman. No, a gentle man.

Lainie doubted that she'd ever have to defend Devil's grandson to Way again.

She went after Susan, her heart in a jumble, and when she finally got back to the yard, Colley was standing alone, hidden under the circle of trees around the old stone cellar, watching her. As she drew near him, he stepped out right in her path.

"Oh! Colley." Lainie was hot all over now that he was near, his keen dark eyes on her. "I'm sorry about Aunt," she said belatedly. "She's fine usually, but once in a while, she gets confused about time. I don't know who she thought you were."

"It doesn't matter," he said easily. "I liked what she said. I was pretty scared of this place. Maybe I needed her to say it."

Lainie stared at him in amazement. "Why would you be scared of the Magnolia?"

He shrugged, looking up at the long, quiet facade of the hotel, its giant columns gleaming like alabaster in the twilight. "It's not exactly the shack on the creek," he said humorously. "It makes me feel like I'm not very big."

"When I was a little girl," she said with sudden confidentiality, "I thought there was no time here. Aunt had this old clock that hung in the hall, and it was stuck. Seventeen minutes after two for always. Sometimes I couldn't stand it, the peace and the stillness, and the way all the people who'd ever been here were just waiting around the corners. I'd take my bicycle and peddle to town just to fight with Way. But I always came back. It let me go and come just like I needed to."

"You fit with it."

Lainie found him beside her, close, and he looked away. The silence between them was so thick that she had to struggle to break it.

"I'll show you the rest of the place," she offered hurriedly.

He didn't respond while he considered her face—what was he looking for?—and then, as if he'd made up his mind, he reached out his hand and caught hers, just as she had done moments earlier.

The contact was electric and sizzling; she loved touching

him. Colley's movements, his hands, his skin, his warmth had been part of his magic. She couldn't turn loose now. Instead, she tightened her grip. "It's been a long time, Colley," she whispered painfully.

"Feels like I got lost somewhere," he returned huskily, "but not anymore. You wanted me to come."

She flushed at the implied question in his words, but she answered honestly, "Yes."

"The boy you were with that day at the hospital, Lainie. . . ."

"What? Oh, C.K." Colley would mention him; she should have known.

"Do you want to be with him?"

She looked at the whistle to avoid his eyes. "I like him well enough."

"Well enough that you let him kiss you."

"A kiss doesn't mean much, Colley."

"I don't believe you." His voice was husky and slow as he put out a hand to brush her cheek. He knew what his tongue was about to say, but he was helpless to stop it. "If it's such an easy thing, then kiss me."

"I can't," she whispered painfully.

"You can't? Because I'm a big, dumb farmer in overalls?" he remembered with a twist of his mouth.

"I didn't mean what I said. You know I didn't."

"Then why can't you kiss me?" he demanded insistently, letting his hands slide to her shoulders and tug her gently closer.

"A kiss with somebody else is nothing," she clarified raggedly, trying to pull away a little. "But with you—I'm—it's too important. I've thought about it too long. I'm not ready. You just got here." What was she saying? She pushed back the words that kept tumbling out, helter-skelter. Around him, she couldn't think.

He was so still that she finally looked up from her confused embarrassment. Another person might have thought
he was frowning; she knew what he was really doing. He
was standing still and quiet, concentrating on her with all
the power in him. Just watching. Thinking.

Thinking about what she had said.

"Lainie."

She knew as soon as he spoke her name what he meant
to do; the threat of danger was palpable.

Lainie took a step back, and he followed, and then they
stepped back a second time.

"Let me."

She wasn't old enough, after all. Still too young. Fear
leaped like an oil slick fire inside her. He wasn't playing
around, like C.K. did. He didn't know how.

Papa was right; she shouldn't be with Colley. A kiss with
the witch boy might burn her alive.

But he had her right where he wanted her, because
without even knowing it, she had let him back her up
into the circle of maples that hung over the old stone
cellar. She bumped its low wooden door with the calves
of her legs and came away from it instantly to stand
upright.

"Do it, then." The desperate words were a surrender.
There was nothing else to do, anyway. "But it's our first
time, Colley."

Determination and desire made his dark face sharp as he
bent over her, and his arms, the hardest arms she'd ever
felt, wrapped her and pulled her to him so tightly that his
overall front cut into her breasts. His eyes clung to her
mouth. He never looked away from their trembling curve,
and he never said a word.

He just kissed her.

His lips held the same grace that his movements always

did. Her arms wrapped him, her hands searched frantically for his skin.

A first kiss between two people should be a brief thing, but she couldn't turn loose to make it that. She couldn't, because under that grace was the darkness, the danger, and it was making every pulse in her sing, every nerve beat with a primitive wildness.

He moved his mouth on hers, made a strangled sound in his throat, and instinctively slid an arm under her hips to pull her up tighter to him.

Her feet in their white tennis shoes hit the wooden door of the cellar, and the loud sound and his motion dragged her awake.

She pulled her mouth away from his, and it took every ounce of her will to make her body follow suit. "E-nough," she gasped out, shoving his shoulders back.

He opened his eyes in a daze and let her go so quickly that she fell right out of his arms, back onto the waist-high, grassy mound that was the top of the old cellar. She scrambled off the other side of it, facing him from under the largest of the maples.

Birds were singing cheerfully in the tree above her, and the smell of frying chicken wafted from the kitchen window just around the corner of the building where somebody had begun fixing the supper for that day's crowd.

The world was just the same, comfortable and known.

But she wasn't. She had never been where he had just taken her.

"You ruined it," she said on a hard, nearly hysterical sob. "It wasn't supposed to be like that. You made it—" She couldn't find words to tell him what devastation he had left.

His heart was slamming, his breath rasping. He couldn't defend himself. What did the beast say to the princess when all he'd done was to act out what he felt with her?

"Just go away."

Colley hesitated. "Lainie—I—"

She turned her back on him.

So he did what she asked. He twisted, ducked under the limbs of the trees as smoothly as a cat, and walked into the afternoon.

He walked right into John Thorne, whom he'd hoped and prayed was still too sick to leave his bed, but who must have arrived while he and Lainie had been with the woman in her room.

If Colley hadn't been deaf, dumb, and blind with emotion, he might have seen the other man standing on the front porch of the Magnolia with several others. But he had his head set on one thing, escaping, and he skirted the edge of the yard without a look on either side of him.

"YOU!"

Everything and everybody seemed to grind to a halt. First the conversation slowed, breaking up into little scattered words and bits of laughter that couldn't be caught back in time.

Colley kept walking, not heeding anything.

"I'm talking to you, boy. Rawlins. Can't you hear?"

The name brought him up short, and even before he turned, he knew what he had done. He'd let John Thorne catch him, and he was on Thorne's territory.

Easy, he told himself, as he found the man, standing on the steps in front of the hotel, maybe twenty feet from him as he had tried to skirt the corner of the place.

"I hear you," Colley said slowly, his voice cool and calm.

"You've got no business here. Your grandfather would tell you so. So what are you doing at the Magnolia?"

Think, he told himself. "Everybody's here. I was just looking."

"At what?"

Thorne showed the effects of his bout with pneumonia; he was pale and shaking a little. Or maybe those were the natural reactions of a man when he faced another one that he hated, Colley thought quietly.

"Colley, wait. I don't—" Lainie's words preceded her.

No, no, no. But he couldn't say it out loud to the girl who came running around the side of the hotel after him, trying to tell him before he got away that she was sorry.

That was when the music halted, when the fiddle player and the guitar man out under another tree realized that something was happening.

Thorne looked from his daughter, who'd stopped short, understanding too late, to the tall, dark man in the overalls who'd dropped his hands loose to his sides, ready to defend himself. There was no point in denying anything. It was as plain as the leaves on the trees.

Rage darkened Thorne's cheeks.

"You came in after her," he said, his voice loud and clear. "You could stay out on the farm and live with the rest of the savages until it came to her."

"Papa, leave him alone. Why can't he come to see me if he wants to?" Lainie pleaded, edging closer to Colley, her eyes wide.

"Get away from him, Elaina Marie, before I have to make you," Thorne said harshly. He came off the steps, moving toward them.

"Don't hurt her." Colley spoke fast, trying to stop him.

"I never have. She's my baby girl. I love her. That's why I won't let a man like you near." Thorne's face had settled into a grim, still mask. "Elaina, obey me."

She looked from Colley to Thorne.

"Go on. Do what he says," Colley said, his voice low and urgent.

Lainie hesitated, then stepped back. Thorne stopped, too, just a few feet away now.

"Stay with your mother on the porch," he said.

People had moved in silently, until there was a wide, broken ring of faces around them, all watching, waiting.

"You go home to the farm where shantytown trash belongs, Colley," Thorne said hoarsely. "That's what you still are, no matter what last name you call yourself by. I know it's what you are, because I know what you're here for. You're looking for a woman to ride, like one savage rides another. You tried to mark her as yours a long time ago, but I stopped it. It won't ever be Lainie. Find somebody else, or I'll take a knife to you the same way you geld horses. Do you understand?"

The crowd took a long, deep, horrified breath as if they were one body.

"Papa!"

Colley's hands wanted to curl around Thorne's throat; his vision blurred with his own anger. "You shame her as much as you do me. If you weren't old and sick, and her father," he said tightly, "I'd slap you all the way down to your knees."

Thorne stepped closer. "I'm not that old, or that sick. Try it."

A film of sweat shone on his forehead; the gray in his hair was wet with it.

And then Lainie pleaded for Thorne. "Colley, don't."

For her, Colley did no more than reach out and shove the older man out of his way. Thorne stumbled and caught himself on the tree nearby. Colley plowed on, pushing his way between the people who couldn't move fast enough to get out of his furious path.

He only knew one face in the crowd—Deborah's. She appeared in front of him out of nowhere.

"Please—" she said, but she didn't finish.

Colley was through with her, too. "I kept my word," he said hoarsely, panting for breath. "But you said someday. Why didn't you keep yours?"

"How could you, Papa? In front of the whole town, just because Colley talked to me," Lainie cried, backed up from her father across her bedroom.

His face was lined and sick looking. "You don't understand. I should have told you long ago, but Deborah thought you were too young. Maybe you still are. Maybe everybody's always too young to have to hear my story. But I have to tell you."

"You hate Colley. What could you tell me to make me understand why you'd hate a man so much when he's not done anything?" Lainie accused, taking another step down the wall when Papa came around the end of her bed closer to her.

"John, don't do it this way," Deborah protested faintly at the door. "Colley is right. You shamed her today at the Magnolia by acting as if they'd done something terrible. She's eighteen. She'll be out of school in another month or two. Why can't she—"

"I, shame her? If I did, if it makes her lose this fascination with him, then it was worth it." Papa looked from one to the other of them, his face twisted with pain. "I understand his kind, Lainie. I'm not from around here, you know that. I was born in Arkansas, to a rich family. They had a farm bigger and better than even the Rawlins place, and they hired people like the migrant workers, just like Albert does. I learned the business from the ground up. I brought my wife there when I married."

Lainie looked from him to Deborah, a mute, shocked question on her face.

"Your father was married before, Lainie," Mama said gently. "Long before we ever met."

"Didn't you ever wonder why I was so much older than she is?" Papa asked tiredly, raking his fingers back through his graying hair. "It's because I had another life . . . another daughter . . . before you."

It took a minute to think about his words. Her father—hers—belonged to someone else. Somewhere, another woman had his blood. Hers, too.

"I have a sister?" She stumbled a little, and for an instant, she felt betrayed. John Thorne had loved another woman before Mama, and another child before her.

"No. She's . . . she's dead." He struggled to say the word. "And it was my fault."

Mama stepped forward involuntarily. "Don't, John."

But Lainie was remembering. "Beth," she said slowly. "Her name was Beth, wasn't it?"

Papa didn't answer, just gripped the bedpost with white-knuckled fingers. "She was almost as pretty as you, Lainie," he whispered. "I never dreamed that someone could ever hurt her. The summer that she was twelve, I hired three drifters to work for me. One of them . . ." He had to stop, running a hand over his face, hard and rough. "Oh, God."

Total silence blanketed the room. Mama had quit protesting, standing like a statue in the door, willing him to say it, to get it over with. Lainie knew what he would tell before he said it, but she had to hear.

"He was nothing but a boy himself. I didn't know somebody so young could be so evil. She treated him like a playmate all summer. He knew the games she played, a child's games, because he sometimes played with her in a corner of the hayloft. Just at the end of the season, when I was out in the field, not long before he was due to leave the farm . . . he asked me where she was. He wanted to tell her good-bye. I sent him right to her."

Papa turned loose of the bedpost, letting his hands drop to his sides, staring at the walls, at nothing. "He raped Beth."

"Oh, oh . . ." The sound was Lainie's expectant breath as she released it in a whimper of hurt.

"And he strangled her." Papa said it without any emotion at all, his voice as flat as the heart line on the monitor of a dead man. "I found her in the hayloft, her doll beside her, her eyes open. Blood everywh–"

Breaking down suddenly, he grunted as if he'd been hit in the stomach, bending over the foot of the bed in agony.

Deborah moved so fast that Lainie, wide-eyed and frozen against the wall, didn't even see her until she had both her arms around Papa, holding him hard against the memories. "Finish, John," she whispered urgently. "Tell it to her one time, and get it over with. Then there will be nobody else you'll ever have to tell again. It'll be over."

"It'll never be over," he groaned, turning his face into her neck. "How can you bear to live with me, Deborah? I've tried to be a good man, but I'll never be whole. You've always deserved more."

"I've got what I want. Tell her the rest."

Papa straightened at last, turning again to face Lainie, but he held on to the woman beside him as if she were his lifeline, the one thing that kept him from drowning in sorrow.

"They caught him. He was so dirty . . . so . . . I couldn't bear to look at him, to think of that animal touching—" He took a deep breath. "He went to prison, for all the good that did my little Beth. Me, I've been in prison all my life. My wife blamed me. I blamed me. She left. I knew she would. It was the only way she could survive. I began to drift. I don't know why I didn't kill myself. Maybe I thought living was my punishment, because every day was hell. Then I came here."

He wrapped his arm tighter around Deborah. "She was my salvation. And then you were born, Lainie."

Papa turned loose of Mama finally and reached out for the girl at the wall. His hands grasped her shoulders, and he pulled her toward him a little. "I've got a second chance. I won't let anything happen to you, baby. I know what Colley Rawlins is. I knew him before Devil ever claimed him. There are a hundred other men in this town you can have, but as God is my witness, Lainie, I won't let what happened to Beth happen to you. I love you too much. I can't bear to see you hurt."

Sickness lay just at the bottom of Lainie's stomach. She couldn't defend Colley to Papa now. She saw too plainly how her father ached for the unknown Beth. The tears on his face made it impossible for her to do anything except reach out for him and hug him against her. He was the man who'd raised her and loved her and tried to protect her.

He was never going to understand about Colley Rawlins.

What was she going to do? How could she tell him that she loved the very one he hated?

Devil caught Colley before he could get out the kitchen door the next morning. "You can just stay here for a minute. I got somethin' to tell you."

"You found out that I went to the Magnolia yesterday. So what? The whole world knows it. You're going to raise hell over me seeing Lainie Thorne. Well, I don't want to hear it anymore, old man," Colley said passionately. He'd had enough of people pushing him around, whether it was his grandfather, or her crazy father.

"This is about Thorne."

"He doesn't like me. He can be damned."

"He'll be the one to damn you before he lets you touch her. Do you hear me?" Devil roared suddenly, letting his hard hand slap the table. The silverware jingled against the plates.

But Colley's own temper was up, and he knew the old man better now. He wasn't as easy to intimidate as he had once been. "He's going to have to let her go sometime. He can't shoot every man who looks at her. I'd gamble he'd have half the men in the Springs in the graveyard. She's free enough with Willis, and there are no bullet holes in him," Colley argued furiously. "What's wrong with me talking to her?"

"I said he'd kill *you*. Not them. No, don't get up. I'm gonna tell you a story about Mr. John Thorne, and you're gonna listen. I did some heavy checkin' up on him over the years. It took awhile to run his past to ground. I just got all of it lately, that's how hard it was to trace him. He had another wife before this one. He had another little girl."

Colley went very still. "So he's got another family. What's that got to do—"

"A young boy, a migrant worker on his family's farm, raped and killed his first daughter." Devil's voice was harsh.

What he was telling was so stark that for a moment, Colley couldn't take it all in. "He killed her?"

"That's right. No man ought to have to bury his own children, especially not like that. Deborah Blackburn got a man in mortal agony when she got him. He ain't in his right mind about the farm workers. And he ain't in his right mind," Albert said slowly, " about you and his second girl."

"I'm no rapist or murderer," Colley said hotly, coming out of the chair and shoving past his grandfather, understanding in a flash what Albert was trying to say. "I'm not. Damn it,

I'm not." Sick from the story Devil had told, frustrated from his own need to make the Springs understand that he was something different from what they thought, Colley took a long stride to the door. It wasn't fair, it wasn't fair. He hadn't done anything.

"Colley! Thorne can't think clear where you're concerned." Albert followed him to the door and shoved open the screen to call one more warning after him. "I'm gonna fire him."

That halted him. "Fire him! But he'd have to leave. There's no work around here for a man like him," Colley said slowly.

"Then he'll go, and take his family with him. If he don't, he'll kill you, or one of us will have to kill him."

Lainie would leave, too. She would leave him. The thoughts danced wildly in Colley's head.

"The Blackburns belong in the Springs," he protested. "Deborah's never lived anywhere else."

"That's none of my concern. When Thorne shows up for work, I'll tell him he's got two weeks to find a new job, and I'm gonna stick with him like glue those weeks to keep him away from you. Don't give me any back talk about it, Colley. It's time for you to take over the farm, anyway. And while Thorne winds things up, you stay the hell out of his sight and away from his girl."

"He gave me my notice," Papa said stoically, standing in the kitchen of the house on Martin Hollow Road. Deborah had both hands at her mouth, her face pasty white. "Two weeks. When I finish them out, I get a full month's pay. And then I have to leave."

"Leave?" Lainie said blankly.

"In the end, Colley got his way. He got the farm," Papa

said, trying hard to control his resentful anger. "I knew it was coming. What happened at the hotel last Sunday just speeded things up."

"But what will we do? Where will you work?" Mama whispered in dismay.

"Albert knows I can't get work here. He means for me to leave town." Papa grasped the back of the chair at the table. "The only thing is, I'm fifty-five. It'll be hard to find a job. But he'll give me a good recommendation, and he says he'll help me find a place, maybe somewhere in West Virginia. He has ties there."

"West Virginia! But the hotel. Aunt Livy. My whole life, John—it's here."

Papa straightened and looked her in the eye. "Ruth told Naomi, 'Whither thou goest.' You married me, Deborah. Will you go with me?"

"This is about Colley and me," Lainie burst out. "Just because of us."

"It's for the best, Lainie," Papa said shortly. "Surely you can see that. Don't you see that I love you so much I couldn't do anything that I didn't feel was right for you? I'm willing to give up everything I've worked for to save you from him. Can you do any less for me?"

Lainie stared out at the falling rain and didn't see it. The Saturday afternoon shower was hard and sweet with the fragrance of just-bloomed lilacs and new grass.

Spring was here, but she was as cold as ice.

She was leaving Colley Rawlins.

Maybe he thought she was glad to be going.

If only she could tell him what had happened inside her when he kissed her. If she could just explain why she had run scared for a few minutes.

When Colley had put his mouth against hers, he had gone straight to the reason for kissing—sex. No flirting, no teasing. None of the easy charm of the town boys. He didn't even understand that.

He was no rapist, but he knew exactly what he wanted. He hadn't left any doubts in her mind, either. He was a predator that she had instinctively tried to protect herself from.

He had made her sick with knowledge.

He had nearly mesmerized her, fatally tempted her.

Now Lainie had to decide: did she want to leave him, and be safe from the demands he had made on her with that one kiss, or did she just want him?

Lainie didn't have much time to figure out the answers. The only thing she knew for sure was that she had to see Colley. He wouldn't come to the Magnolia again, so the only thing to do was to get Way to help her. He would let her have his car to drive to Rawlins Farm. That afternoon, Papa and Albert were going to tour the fields one last time so that Papa could point out things that still needed to be done after he was gone.

Colley Rawlins was famous around the town for the way he worked in the barns, the way he spent his weekends cleaning them and grooming the animals until they were as spotless as anything in a woman's kitchen. He was there now.

If she meant to see the witch boy one final time before they left, it would have to be today.

Colley couldn't concentrate at all on what he was doing. The rain had poured all week long, and today, the water was beating holes in the muddy ground.

He wanted to see Lainie, but she'd sent him away.

Colley turned from the storage area where he had been putting up supplies, and even over the sound of the rain, he thought he heard a car outside. Devil was gone. Nadine had told him so just before she herself left the house at noon. He was there alone. Who had just pulled up?

Outside, Lainie drew a deep breath. Her stomach was shaking so much she was nearly sick. Where was Colley? How would she ever find him?

And then out of nowhere, he just showed up. The tall, lean figure that materialized in the open door of the stables had shining black hair and slanting dark eyes—she knew it by heart, the way he stood.

Lainie, he thought. Lainie was there, right in front of him.

The shock waves were rippling over him. The girl coming toward him in the rain was the girl from the creek. He needed to touch her. But she stopped him cold in his tracks. Her face was tentative, and she looked so sophisticated that he was nearly afraid.

She was a woman. There was not a single hint of the skinny little girl. And this woman hadn't liked his kisses.

Why had she come, when she'd told him to go away? What did she want?

"Colley," she said quietly, the single word cutting across the misty rain.

He didn't answer; instead he just leaned up against the door and stared at her.

Her face turned pink. "Aren't you going to let me come in the barn, out of the rain?" she asked, flustered by his rudeness.

The black hair was a little ruffled around his face, as though he'd run his hand through it. His decided jawline was firmer than ever, and his body had filled out, until the bare, bronze shoulders under the overalls were heavy with muscles. Even his hands had the lean, sinewy look of strength as he fumbled for his pockets to slide his thumbs in them.

"I reckon I'll let you in," Colley said at last, and he added defiantly, "unless you're afraid I might kiss you and ruin everything again."

Lainie ignored his belligerence. "No," she managed. He still didn't move, so she had to slide past him into the dry, shadowy barn, and he let his eyes follow her. She did it quickly, hoping that she didn't give away just how much the silent man rattled her.

Then he turned to face her, letting his hands slide out of his pockets and reach behind him to find the facing of the door that he'd propped himself up on. "Well?" In his head, he could still hear her rebuff after that kiss. He could still remember her father's attack on him in front of the whole town.

He'd be damned if he'd make things easy for her, but this might be the last time. The last time. He was trapped between pride and longing.

She looked around herself, and slowly, she said at last, "Rawlins Farm must—"

He didn't even let her finish the polite sentence. To hell with it. "Why did I ruin the kiss?" he asked roughly, looking right down into her face.

She jerked, gasped, and then laughed, the sound husky and embarrassed. "Colley, I just got here."

"What difference does that make? John Thorne's leaving the Springs, and he's taking you with him. I don't have time to be civilized."

She didn't, either. They could hold a nice, mannerly conversation that neither one of them wanted, or they could forget the rules and tell the truth. She knew exactly what he was talking about, and there was no point in pretending that she didn't, or that it wasn't why she had come. Not with Colley.

"I ruined it because I went too fast and too far." He answered his own question.

"So far that I didn't even have a chance to get started," she blurted out, looking anywhere but at him.

He frowned, concentrating on what she was saying, and he looked so much like the boy from the creek that she relaxed and let herself lean back against the door opposite him in an imitation of his own casual stance. "You didn't have any right to kiss me like that, Colley. It should have been different."

"If I did it wrong, it was because you make it hard for me to think. I can't help that I wanted you, Lainie," he said harshly. "It seemed right to kiss you. I've thought about doing it a lot."

Her cheeks on fire, she kept her eyes on the distant highway that she could see from the barn's entrance. "You can't. Not like that. I want sweet kisses, the kind that go slow."

"I don't have time to go slow. Damn it, Lainie, I've waited all my life. I promised your mother I would, and I kept my word, didn't I?"

"Mama!"

He ignored her surprise and continued desperately, "You knew I'd come for you someday, didn't you? You've been mine all along. I don't know how else to do it, or say it."

Her eyes were a brilliant purply blue, just like they had been all those summers ago when he pulled her from the creek.

"If I'm yours, it's only because I choose to be. I'm not going to be just a body, Colley, somebody you can have and never talk to. Somebody you can use and never think about. I don't want that."

He looked down at his hands. They were gripping the edges of the overall bib because if he turned loose, he'd do just what she'd said—reach and take, grab her, and pull her to him, and find a place to hide her, and yank the clothes off her, and—"You make things pretty damn clear. Then so will I. I've left you alone since the day your mama begged me to. Why come to tell me all this? I already knew I didn't kiss you the way I was supposed to. You can get the hell out of my barn if that's all you've got to say." Hurt and disappointment made him mean.

"Where are you going?" she asked quickly as he came up out of his stance where he'd been leaning on the wall and pushed his fingers back through his hair.

"I've got work to do, and I might as well get it over with before dark. You know your own way back home." Why was he saying this? He really wanted to beg her to stay. Stay, Lainie.

"Colley, I could show you the way I want to be kissed."

Where here on this green earth had that come from? Lainie clapped her hand to her mouth the instant it got uttered, but it froze him right where he stood, his hand caught in midair, the taut tendons visible all the way up to his neck.

His black eyes were wide, not slanted, as they met her blue ones above her hand. "Go ahead, then," he whispered. "Show me."

Her hand dropped and she tried to back out someway, somehow. "I didn't mean—"

"Yes, you did," he said intently. "You did mean." Then he caught her hands. "Show me," he said roughly.

Lainie's fingers shook in his rough palms. "You do act like a savage," she whispered in a flash of rebellion.

He didn't have time to take offense, not now, not with so much at stake. "Then show me how to act different."

A muscle in her smoothly tanned cheek flinched just a little. She wanted to kiss him. "Let me kiss you, then," she whispered. She twisted her fingers until she was the one holding his hands. "And don't pull loose from me. Keep your hands right here." She took a deep breath. "Close your eyes."

He obeyed without a whimper, and as she gazed at him standing there, his eyes shut, his face full of concentration, she felt a sudden rush of warmth. She wet her lips, looking at his tender, sullen mouth. It would be easy to kiss him.

Her own eyes closed as she leaned into him, his hands firmly in hers between their bodies. She touched his mouth with hers, a delicate, tentative brush of the lips, just enough to remind herself how sweet Colley Rawlins really was.

He couldn't know how much that kiss meant, that she needed it to prove to herself that he wasn't what Papa said, that even after all the time he'd spent with Devil, he could be gentle, that he was still the witch boy who'd cried over Charley.

Lainie found her answer in the kiss he let her take from him, and happiness and joy and something she hadn't felt before, something close to plain old lust, swamped her.

If she could just go on kissing him—but before she could yield to temptation, she pulled away.

When his eyes opened, he was expectant and confused. "Is that the kiss you wanted from me?" he asked, puzzled.

She nodded, not able to speak at all. She felt as light as spun sugar.

His eyes a black flame in his face, he protested, "Hell, Lainie, I want more than that. Any man would."

"I know you do, but—"

"But part of you is scared to death that I'm really what your father says I am," he finished in pained anger. "Shantytown trash. A savage."

She hadn't hid it from him, after all, what she'd been up to.

"I've heard all about it, Lainie. Devil says Thorne's not sane about me because of his first daughter. But you know me better than anyone else does. Don't you see that I can be with you, and not hurt you? That I could love you, and it wouldn't be bad? You don't have to test me with these baby kisses to know the truth."

"All I can see is that I'm going away." Lainie broke down suddenly, putting her hands to her cheeks. "What if I don't come back, Colley? What if I never find you again?"

He didn't think at all; he just reacted. Reaching out for her, he urged her to him, pulling her right between his legs. When she was tight against his body, he let his lips touch her throat and her cheek before he settled on her mouth with a groan of sound.

She might never have been separated from him. He was right: she had always known where she belonged. She wanted Colley, just like she always had. She didn't think she'd ever want anybody else. His touch, his kiss—he made the few other males she knew fade into inconsequence. He didn't know any boundaries, didn't seem to realize that he was showing every emotion while he slid his hands all over her with a fierce possession.

Her shoulders.

Her back.

Her hips and thighs.

He caressed them all. Branded himself on her, and she found nothing but pleasure in it.

Except for their breathing and the rain pattering down on the roof, it was quiet there.

"Lainie," he whispered from above her, the word soft against her face. "Don't go away with Thorne. Stay with me."

She froze a moment in surprise, then tried to pull from

him, but he caught her and held her tight. "Shhh. Listen. I know a place where we can be by ourselves. Let me take you there now. Today. Let me make love to you. If you like what you find when we do, then marry me tonight. You're old enough. That way, nobody can tell me to leave you alone anymore."

This time he let her go when she pulled back. "Colley, listen to what you're saying," she implored shakily. "You don't have to put yourself on trial for me."

"Maybe not, but I want to make love to you. I want you to know what I am. And if you don't want me when it's over, it'd be better for me to find it out than to keep on loving you, and you thinking I'm what your father said."

His face was white. He really meant it, Lainie thought in a pounding wave of pity and passion.

"I've only kissed a boy or two," she confessed, dropping her head to look at his throat, warm and brown.

He pulled in his breath, slow and steady. "I told you, I'll be careful. Please, Lainie, come with me. Then you'll never believe Thorne again. And if you marry me, it'll be too late for him to do anything. He'll see that I mean right by you— that I love you." He stumbled over the words. It was the first time in his entire life that he'd ever said them.

I love you.

He twisted toward her, his mouth found hers.

Sweet, persuasive, and bold.

"I'll . . ." she whispered breathlessly when the kiss ended, and something crazy and wild broke inside her, "I'll do it."

She could feel the change in him immediately, the way he gasped for breath. "Lainie."

"I have to take Way's car back, and get some things."

"No," he protested quickly. "What if you don't come back?"

She pulled away to look up into his flushed face. "I will. I love you, too, Colley."

He cupped her upturned face in his hands, brushing her hair back over and over. "Then listen. You say you have to go home. I'll be at the creek down below your house in two hours, just like I used to be. We'll hide until dark. Then we'll cut across by the quarry and leave that way. Nobody will ever see us." His hands found her again, this time caressing her arms, the sides of her breasts. "I'll make things good. You'll see. We don't have to be lonely any-more, Lainie."

Part 3

Rain

10

The rain that had begun so gently on Sunday got harder and heavier the next morning, and it refused to quit. By Monday night, Widow's Creek was raging and swollen in front of the Magnolia, and the wind was whipping trees into wild dances in the yard.

Lainie awoke before dawn on Tuesday, as the wind howled around the corner of the house, and saw lights already on somewhere down the hall. She got up carefully, pulling her bandaged foot behind her as she went to the kitchen. Raising her voice over the wind, she called to Mama, "What's wrong?"

The kitchen was lit warmly, like a lighthouse in the middle of a gusty sea. Not only was Mama up, but so were Aunt Olivia and Susan, all of them sitting in a huddle around the table. "Nothing," Mama reassured her. "The storm woke all of us, that's all."

"I'm so silly," Olivia said with a little laugh. "I was so frightened by this wind that I got up, and I think I've waked everybody else up, too. It's just that it feels like something bad is going to happen. It reminds me of when the tornado hit. Don't you remember?"

"No," Lainie answered gently.

"I'll get you some coffee," Mama said.

"You don't remember the tornado? But it was just a few days ago," Olivia said in amazement. "I can recall it so well. The summer was miserably hot. That July, Dawson Anderson's boy got run over by his own tractor. I thought my heart would break for his poor mother, she cried so in the cemetery. The sun kept blazing down through it all. I had to take off my gloves to fan myself. When was that, Susan?"

"Longer than you think, Miss Livy," Susan murmured. "I believe it was 1954."

"You remember, don't you, how the sky was yellow and strange, just like—oh!"

The "oh!" was Deborah's reaction, too, as she stood near the window and a loud crack of thunder rolled over the house. The lights flickered and went off. As they sat in the deep gray of the early morning, the rain burst upon them again, so heavily that Lainie could barely hear Mama.

"The outside lights just went off at the Magnolia just like they are here," she called. "I reckon that means that the power lines are down. I doubt that the electric company is coming out in all this downpour. It looks like we're going to have a holiday today."

Nobody in the family had ever been accused of having empty hands, so they polished and cleaned while the storm beat around them. At noon, the rain lightened a little, and out of boredom, the four of them went down the path and through the gate to the Magnolia next door. The long windows let in enough light for them to clean a little there, too.

Just before three, Olivia fell asleep on a couch in the front parlor.

"Thank goodness," Susan said in relief. "She was up half the night. My poor Miss Livy can't abide storms."

Lainie went to the kitchen to look out over the rainy, wet yard. Sometimes the rain was hard for her to bear, too, especially when she was lonely, like today. She didn't really know what she was lonely for. All she knew was that when the loneliness came, she always remembered another day when it had been raining like this.

On that afternoon, Colley had been with her. She could almost see his callused hands as he ran them back over his wet face and hair. His teeth had flashed white in the downpour as he turned to laugh at her. That had been the last perfect afternoon.

Crack!

The noise shattered the earth and split her eardrums. It deafened her.

A white light shot across the sky, blinding her completely.

And under her feet, she felt the earth move, or maybe it was only the foundation of the Magnolia.

When Lainie could hear again, Susan was shouting something behind her and Aunt Olivia was sobbing. When sight returned, the whole screen in front of her was filled with green—the soft, wet leaves of a giant maple.

"Lightning! It was lightning. But it's over now." She tried to calm the other two who had come to the kitchen behind her. "It knocked down one of the trees."

The back door wouldn't open, jammed in place by the fallen maple, so she had to circle to the side porch to get out. Even in the downpour, what Lainie saw pulled her up sharp and made her sick.

It was one of the maples that shaded the old stone cellar, and when it fell, its roots had torn open the ancient door, right where Colley had once backed her up.

But the tree's upper branches had done far more damage than that. They had crashed right into one of the three wings that extended off the back of the Magnolia. The whole roof was caved in over the center arm, the one where the dining room was. The second floor rested now just where it had collapsed, right in the middle of the first.

Once that second floor had housed the office where Olivia's father, Lansing Blackburn, had managed the hotel. The heavy desk that he had used hung half in, half out of the torn, slanting walls, dangling with other debris like doll furniture against the limbs of the tree.

"Oh." Sight of the wreckage hurt Lainie as much as if somebody had stabbed her. "No. No." She was crying too much to distinguish between what was rain and what was tears.

It was gone, the whole wing. The most important wing, where they had served the meals.

Deborah struggled through the gray sheet to stand beside her daughter, finally putting her arm around her as she cried, too.

When they could hear better over the thunder, she said close to Lainie's ear, "Aunt Olivia will be upset. But we have to make the best of it. Maybe it's not so bad. The dining room needed work. We'll call the insurance as soon as we get to a working phone."

There is no insurance, she wanted to scream. None. The Magnolia is finished. Our little world is gone, washed away by the rain.

She couldn't find a way to tell her mother the bad news, not that day, and not the next, either. But at least they didn't have to fumble their way through a conversation. The whole town made it impossible for them to have privacy. They came to see the devastation at the hotel the day after the storm.

"What a shame. Just think, the hotel stood a century, and all it took was one bolt of lightning to shut it down," Bella Foster said pityingly as she surveyed the damage. "How long before you can hope to reopen, Deborah?"

Deborah avoided her daughter's eyes. "I really don't know, Bella. We have to figure out some things."

"Well, honey, you know the Benevolence Committee at church will want to help. Charity work, that's what Christianity is all about."

Lainie couldn't stand it anymore. Charity. They had become the church's newest charity. Pushing open the screen door, she went outside to the porch, where at least three other people sat, exclaiming over the damage to the back part of the Magnolia.

And it was still raining, a tiny gray drizzle that dampened clothes and hearts.

"Oh, Lainie, look what I've found," Aunt Olivia called from the side of the hotel. Her silver hair had curled into tiny ringlets about her face in the moist air, and the soft white of her gauzy cotton dress clung to her diminutive figure, making her look like an aging porcelain doll. Even her hands were too translucent and thin to be holding the big black metal box that she clasped tightly against herself.

"What is it, Aunt?" From the tremulous look of Olivia's face, her find was not a particularly pleasant one, but to Lainie, there was nothing special about the box except maybe the silver lock that sealed it closed.

"It's my father's strongbox. He never trusted anybody with it. He always kept it hidden so that none of us could find it, but today, there it was, lying under the rubble."

Susan strode forward from the porch. "It must have been somewhere in that upstairs room that collapsed. Here, Miss Livy, let me take that heavy thing."

"No, I want to carry it. You know, Susan, I was almost

afraid of this box when I was young," Olivia said with a shivering laugh. "Father was always very stern about it."

"Lansing Blackburn was stern about everything," Susan said dryly. "For goodness' sakes, let's at least carry it to the house. You can sit and hug it over there, where it's dry."

"Yes, I want to take it home. Father will be happy to get it back."

Lainie watched them go, and Bella, who'd joined the ladies on the porch in time to hear most of what Olivia said, murmured piously, "At least some good came out of this destruction. Miss Livy found a piece of her past."

"Poor little thing, she lives there most of the time," whispered another of the women, and Lainie wondered if she could get the broom and run all of them off, just as she did the cat when she didn't want him lying in front of the doors.

But her temper calmed when she caught a glimpse of the big silver Jaguar that was pulling into the lot. The curious ladies on the porch fell silent, examining the blond young man in an immaculate white shirt and pants who came gingerly through the wet grass toward Lainie.

"Good Lord," Preston said as he came up the porch steps. "I just saw a glimpse of the wreckage. That lightning bolt sure had the Magnolia's name on it."

She bit her lip, trying not to cry, and he turned from the contemplation of the yard, strewn with broken limbs and leaves. "Pretty bad."

"Oh, Preston, it's terrible."

Her voice didn't make it through the words, and he realized that she was on the verge of tears. "Are you talking about my face or this hotel?" he said teasingly.

For the first time, she really looked at him. A bruise was fading on one cheek, and his left eye was bloodshot in the corner.

"The fight," she whispered in quick remembrance, and she let her hands touch his cheek carefully.

"Don't worry. I'm healing. So will the Magnolia. We can put it back," he said soothingly, pulling her up against him, regardless of their audience. "Here, angel, don't take it this hard."

She sucked in her breath. "I hate to cry in front of everybody."

"Then let's go inside, so you can cry in front of me," he returned promptly. He held the door as she hobbled through. "Still got a bum leg from the quarry, I see."

"I can take the bandages off tomorrow."

They found a quiet refuge on a Victorian love seat under the stairs, and he pulled her up against him.

"Now, tell Dr. Preston what's wrong," he teased.

"My house blew away, and I don't think I landed in Oz," she answered. Lainie didn't want to tease and joke; she wanted somebody that she could pour her troubles out to. But she understood now what she was going to have to do, and this was the way to do it. She needed him to come through for her. She had had enough.

Almost as if on cue, he responded. "Well, maybe I've got something to make you feel better," he said quietly, fumbling in his pocket. He held out a tiny white velvet box. She looked from it to him, and with trembling hands, finally reached out and took it.

Inside it was a diamond, square and big and brilliant even in these shadows.

"What does this mean?" she asked painfully, too afraid to play the game now.

"Exactly what you think it does." Preston reached to lift her chin. "Do you like it?"

"Any girl would. I've never had one before."

He said, "Ahhh" with satisfaction. "So at long last I've managed one thing that Colley didn't do."

She didn't answer, just held the box tightly in her hand.

"I want to give this to you, Lainie. I knew how I felt about you the day we went to the quarry and I got afraid you'd die down in the water. What would I have done without you? I meant to ask you Sunday, but you wouldn't see me. Then I got really scared. I know we hadn't talked about a ring, but I hope there's enough between us that you'll consider it. Do you think you can?"

She couldn't look at him, but she could still speak. "Yes . . . I can . . . I want to think about marriage. That is what this is about?"

"That's what it's about. The only problem is, this ring and this engagement come with some strings."

Lainie frowned. "What?"

Preston bent and kissed the frown line tenderly, lifting his hands to soothe them over her slender shoulders. "The old man is raising hell with me because I dared to touch you and set Colley's black temper off."

"Why is Colley always in every conversation we have?" she burst out.

"I guess because you haven't taken enough steps to get him out of your life. Anyway, Grandfather's sending me back to Nashville this Sunday. I want this ring on your finger, Lainie, so that when I leave here, I can set about getting us an apartment and telling my parents about you. I want people to know about us so that Colley will keep his damn hands off for a week or two until I can come and get you and take you with me."

Lainie looked at his lips and watched them form all the right words, and tried, tried—dug down to the bottom of her soul and tried—to find joy.

She had accomplished her goal, with not a moment to spare. She could have all she'd wanted.

A new life.

Money. There would be so much money.

A name, Preston Rawlins's respectable one.

She'd be out of the Springs and the crumbling Magnolia.

Her children, when she had them, would never have to know poverty and its worries. They wouldn't know the beauty of the fading hotel.

They would be Preston's children. Not Colley's.

She was going away, leaving Colley.

"Yes," she whispered with numb lips.

"There's just one problem," he said regretfully. "I'm scared, Lainie."

"You, scared? You've got everything. What could scare you?"

"The thought that I'm giving everything to a beautiful woman, and she might not ever love me."

Lainie nearly jumped out of her skin with guilt. "But that's crazy. Why wouldn't I? Why would I marry you if I— I didn't love you?"

"Because you still have feelings for somebody else. No, I won't call his name again. But if you marry me, we'll have to see him sometimes. Not often. God, I hadn't been to this place for more than two years until this summer, and I hope never to come here again. But I know that somewhere down the road, I will. You will, as my wife. Can I trust you?"

"If you can't, then don't marry me." And for a flash of time, she thought, *Please, don't. Take the ring back, and I'll pretend you never asked. I'll tell myself that I can't help it that I never escaped that other love; I'll say that I couldn't make Preston want me, so I had to stay here, and keep remembering the witch boy.*

But the man with her had something else to say.

"All I want is for you to give me proof. I'm offering you

everything, Lainie, and my everything is considerably more than most men's. Will you give me proof that you're mine?"

Ah. She understood. "You want me to go to bed with you," she said steadily.

"Is that so much to ask? Most women do it with everybody they date. Or maybe it is a lot, and that's why I'm asking. Like you said, I can tell you're not a woman who gives herself easily, Lainie. I'm not a man that offers his name to just anybody, either." He bent his head, touched her lips with his cool ones, let his hands slide down her arms in a gentle caress. "I swear that you'll never know it's not your real wedding night. I'll treat you like the precious virgin that I suspect you are. Please, Lainie. Do this for me."

She looked around herself for a moment. The pictures on the wall, the old rose carpet, that feeling that time was waiting here in the Magnolia, holding back the hurry and rush of the outside world—those would be gone soon.

Colley, you asked the same thing that Preston has, and I was willing to give it to you without even the slightest hesitation.

But that was another rendezvous, another time. This one was very different.

Why did she have to try with Preston? Why couldn't it feel unstoppable, inevitable, joyful with him, as it had with Colley? Even when the whole world said no, it had been right with him.

This was going to be her future—Preston and his kind of life.

Her "forever."

Not Colley.

She couldn't put this off anymore; she might as well let it start now. Because it hurt to move quickly, she was a little clumsy when she rose, trying not to hobble as she pulled from Preston's hands.

"Lainie, where—"

Laying one finger over his lips, she whispered, "Shhh."

He waited, puzzled, as she crossed the hall and went to the big front desk. Her fingers hesitated for a moment as she considered the board on the wall under the cash register.

Not one of those. Those were the rooms that had been wrecked by the storm.

One of these.

When she came back to him, she said quietly, her cheeks flushed, "Open your hand."

When he did, she laid a key across his palm. It was old-fashioned, long and ornate, and it had a misty blue-and-white crocheted tassel hanging from it. "It's the key to the princess's castle," she said teasingly. "The last room on the farthest end, at the top of the outside stairs. It'll be our own private hon-honeymoon suite."

His fingers closed over it convulsively. There was leaping relief in his face. "You won't be sorry, Lainie. God. God. When, angel? I have to leave Sunday."

"We'll make it your going-away party, then. This Saturday night."

He hesitated. "The ring," he said at last. "Maybe I'm sentimental, but I want to keep it until our night together. Let me put it on your hand before we make love. It'll be our own vow to each other," he suggested urgently.

In Lainie's palm, the ring box burned. With thinly disguised relief, she pushed it toward him. It might be easier to wear the heavy diamond after she had sealed her fate.

He dropped the box into his pocket and pulled her up to him for a hard kiss. "You really are an angel. You've taken me straight to heaven this afternoon."

°   °   °

Heaven was about to begin that afternoon. Lainie didn't know where Papa was exactly, off somewhere with Albert Rawlins, but she couldn't leave without saying something to Mama, so she went by the Magnolia one last time.

"Are you feeling better?" Mama asked in surprise as Lainie stood in the kitchen door, and she remembered too late that she'd claimed illness as an excuse for not going with Deborah to the hotel earlier that day.

"Yes. I borrowed Way's car to come here. I guess I just wanted to see if everything was okay."

"It's fine." Deborah smiled at her from the bread dough she was kneading.

"Mama, did you tell Colley Rawlins to leave me alone?" Lainie burst out.

Deborah stilled a second, then faced her daughter. "I did. You were too young. He gave his word of honor, and he kept it, as much as any man should ever have to."

"You know he's not what Papa says."

Deborah looked away and shifted the dough on the floured board where she worked. "You'll never make John see it, Lainie."

"Then what will I do if I can't forget Colley?"

"That's a decision I had hoped you'd never have to make. But if you do, you'll have to decide between your witch boy and your father. John will never get over it. We'd have to keep them apart. We'd more than likely have to stay apart, too."

"And you, Mama?" Lainie whispered. "Will you stop loving me?"

Deborah glanced at her. "A mother loves her children more than they ever love her, Lainie. I guess I'll love you on and on, even if you make up your mind you've got to have Colley." Her hands stilled a little. "Is that what you've decided?" she asked carefully.

"I don't know. I just know that I want to be like you," Lainie said, the words quiet in the fragrant room. She went to the counter where Deborah stood and pressed a quick kiss on her cheek. "I'm happy, Mama. Remember that."

She left her mother standing still as a statue in the kitchen; maybe Deborah was crying.

It was sprinkling again when Lainie pulled out of the Magnolia. She loved her mother and her father, but she was grown. She wanted her own life, and she wanted Colley.

He was waiting for her in the increasingly heavy rain at the bottom of the hill. She ran right into his arms, and he smothered her face with kisses. "I didn't believe you were really coming to me until I saw you," he said hoarsely.

The water beat down against her face, and her hair stuck to her cheeks; he was soaked through and through as he tugged her along after him through the creek, and the clinging wet forest, and the dripping trees.

"Colley, I'm cold and wet," she called to him at last.

He turned, shoving the wet hair off his face, flashed a smile at her, and kissed her lips roughly and quickly. "I'll dry you off and warm you up. The rain feels good to me. This whole day feels like a dream, the best one I ever had."

They had to splash through the creek one more time, and then she realized where she was—in the clearing where she had whistled for him.

They were going to the shack where he had lived with Charley.

A crack of thunder reverberated across the sky, and he shouted something at her, but she couldn't hear him. Then there was a shadowy outline in front of them in the mist, and they climbed up on an old porch where the rain had not yet fallen. It was dry and musty smelling there, and the water pattered down upon the tin roof over their heads.

He pushed open the old door—the knob rattled loosely in the fitting—and stood aside for her to come in.

The place was one big room, with a fireplace in one corner, and an old wooden stove in the other. There were two chairs overturned in the corner, and there was a bed.

Lainie pushed her wet hair out of her face and sucked in her breath. "Did you really live here?" She hadn't realized how primitive it was, and the way he moved so naturally in it made him seem primitive, too.

"Yeah. I told you. I guess it's pretty dusty now, but I tried to clean it up a little after I got here this afternoon," he said huskily. "Besides, we won't be here long. Just until dark."

"Colley, I'm not—"

"No, don't say it. You're scared again. Don't be. Let me hold you, and touch you, and kiss you for a while. And if you don't want to do anything else, then we'll wait until you do."

She looked up into his face. Here in the dusky cabin, he was strange to her, but not frightening. If he'd just sweep her off her feet, maybe the feelings of doubt and worry would go away.

But instead, he seemed unsure of what to do or say. At last he turned to the old fireplace. "I'll build a fire. It's cold enough and rainy enough that a little one will do us both some good. You sit there," he added, pointing to the bed.

She did as she was told, sinking gingerly into the puffy mattress, expecting dust and mice. Instead, the fresh, clean smell of sage drifted up to her, and the sheet was white and fragrant, too. "This bed," she began, and Colley looked up from the tiny little fire he was coaxing into a flame, blowing gently on it as he cupped his lean hands around the flickering flame.

"I made a fresh bed for us," he said at last, his face

flushed from the fire or the thought, she couldn't tell which. "Soon as I left the barn, I came here. Swept it out. I got soft sage and grass, and filled a cotton ticking from the house. Clean sheets. I want it to be right, Lainie. I want you to like it."

The little blaze crackled into life and he stood slowly.

"Are we doing the right thing?" she asked painfully, and he came over to the bed to sit beside her on it and pull her up against him.

"For who? Not if you ask your papa. But there'll never be anybody else in my life like you, Lainie. It seems to me that this is the only way I don't know you yet. The only part of you that's not mine and of me that's not yours."

She put out her hands and framed his face, looking for the traces of brown in his eyes, stroking his hair.

"Do you trust me enough to know that I'm not about to hurt you?" he whispered.

A tiny nerve moved in her cheek. The pulse of fear beat in her throat. "I do."

"No, you don't. Not yet. But you will. Lie down, Lainie. I made this bed for you."

He didn't touch her with anything but his gaze, and from somewhere she found the courage to slide back, her face against the sweet-smelling bed. Above them was the low, dark ceiling, where the shadow of the flames danced in the same rhythm as the heavy rain that pattered against the tin roof.

"I won't touch you until you tell me to. And when I do, if you don't like it," he said so quietly that she could barely hear him, "tell me to stop. I will, I swear it." He made himself lie down beside her, forced his hands to let go of her.

No touch that she didn't will.

Suddenly, her heart was free. She twisted on the bed until she was close to his warm body. Her hands found him, her lips brushed the corner of his mouth, and the side of his cheek, and his ear that she exposed when her lips brushed back his hair as he lay rigidly, panting for breath.

He still didn't have on a shirt.

That one fact was about to kill her. Too many years, she had been fascinated with the quick play of his body. Nearly bare-chested before her, he offered her a hundred tiny enticements. The side of his throat, where the muscles of his shoulder began, tasted wet and salty.

His shoulder was unexpectedly cool. She ran her lips down it, right to the strap that held his overalls in place, and nudged it aside, letting her tongue trace down its length, down to where the muscles that held his rib cage began. Her hand wanted to touch him, too, and she let her fingers slide under the dropped side of the old bib.

A pulse pounded just above where his heart was, and when she kissed it, another one at the base of his neck beckoned, and she kissed it as well.

He had told the truth. He would let her control him—but could she control herself?

He was swearing, a slow, steady, frustrated stream of profanity as her hair brushed his chin, and suddenly, he caught her chin and pulled her mouth up to his.

"Please, Lainie, please," he was begging in between frantic kisses.

Twisting his hand from her face, she laid his palm against her own pounding heart. He sucked in his breath as he felt the tiny buttons under his fingers and realized what she was saying.

"Colley, go slow. You promised," she pleaded, catching his hand when he would have torn the garment.

"Slow. I'm trying, girl. Slow."

He could barely speak at all. His hands stroked her from her face to her throat, and he was breathing as raggedly as the wind was blowing around the corner of the shack when he put his hands to her buttons again, carefully peeling her wet blouse back from her skin, tanned a lighter shade than his by the sun.

Suddenly, Lainie wasn't afraid at all. She didn't need the fire for warmth, either. Fumbling, she loosed one of the latches of the overalls to let a side fall down his chest. Then she pulled herself up to open her mouth on his, finding his beating heart and his probing tongue simultaneously.

For a long, beautiful, painful moment, there was just the rain, and the fire, and her hands and mouth learning him, his body fitting close to hers.

Then everything went wrong.

Forever wrong.

With a whining screech of warning, the door opened. Someone released a harsh, loud gust of breath that she heard dimly, over the rain and the beating of her heart.

"Whose—Elaina! My God, no!"

Papa.

John Thorne stood framed in the doorway, his face aghast. Lainie's throat closed up in shock and her body froze before she whimpered like a child and tried to hide against Colley's frame as he lifted himself off of her, his face wary and stiff.

"You. In this shack. With—her. My little girl—"

"Papa, please . . ."

Colley tried to disentangle himself from her, trying to get ready for whatever was coming, reading the murder in the other man's eyes. "We only—"

"I'll kill you!"

Thorne lifted his hand. He had a silver spike in it, one of those that they used working the tobacco.

The firelight hit it at the same moment that another roll

of thunder struck. The sound hid Lainie's cry. "No, Papa, no. Don't hurt him!"

John Thorne's face twisted and he made a lunge toward them. Colley met him in midair, in a pantherish leap as he jumped for Papa's arm to deflect the blow.

Instead, the spike scraped along the top of his shoulder, threw him off balance, and found another target somewhere under his collar bone. She saw his spasmodic jerk, heard his hard grunt of pain as Papa pulled from him, still clutching the spike, bloodred now.

The same red blood spattered across the white sheets and ran like a river down his left arm. Colley twisted in a hot, unbearable ache toward her as he clutched at the gaping wound.

"Colley—Colley!"

If he heard, he didn't respond. His hands were slippery with his own blood, and when he fell, catching at the bed as he slid to the floor, he marked the sheets with his hands.

"No!" She tried to untangle herself to get to him, sobbing in her own misery.

"Get back. I mean for him to die for hurting you!" Thorne grabbed at his daughter, kicking Colley away from the bed.

He groaned in agony, and she cried, "He didn't hurt me! I love him! I want to be with him!"

John Thorne stared at the open front of her blouse in sick shock, and then his eyes rose to her face, confused and wild. "You—you—" His hand came up, shaking, and he slapped her hard across the face.

The heavy blow might have been meant for Colley. It would have dazed a man his size or larger. It sent Lainie reeling completely across the bed. She slammed into the wall behind her.

A red haze covered everything in the room, but not

before she saw Colley pull himself up with the sheets and throw himself at her father. Somebody shouted, somebody screamed. Maybe she did, but she couldn't tell whose voice it was, her ears were ringing so.

Then the world went black.

When she could see again, the cabin was full of shadows that seemed to wash across everything in front of her.

Her ears still roared like a train was rushing by.

Lainie knew where she was immediately, but she was too sick to sit up. The sheet was still binding her, but now there was a weight on its dragging length, pulling it taut across her body.

Colley. Where was he?

Clasping the rough headboard of the bed, she clawed her way upright, looked around the room in scared apprehension—and screamed.

This time she knew it was herself screaming, on and on, and she couldn't seem to stop.

It was Papa who weighted the sheet down now, not Colley.

The silver spike had been driven right through his chest.

Impaled, John Thorne stared with open sightless eyes at his own hand beside his face. Blood stained his side, and the sheet, and made the floor wet beneath him.

"Papa, Papa . . . Oh, God, oh, God—"

The refrain meant everything: *I'm sorry. I didn't know this morning that the day would end like this. I only wanted to be happy. Live. Breathe again. Make this really a dream. I'm sorry.*

She stumbled off the bed clumsily, frantically, trying without real thought to lift John Thorne into her lap.

"Leave him be."

The command was so loud and so harsh that it got to her even through the nightmare. It was Albert Rawlins, in the far corner of the shack, on his knees beside another body.

"Colley," she whispered, and her hands went limp against her father's blood-soaked chest as she began to shake.

"Don't you go the hell crazy on me, girl," he said hoarsely, wiping sweat and rain from his forehead with the back of his hand and leaving a smear of blood.

More blood. Blood everywhere. Papa's, cold, cold now—and Colley's.

Her eyes felt as big as dark wells as she made herself look at the one Albert knelt beside. The old man had his hand on his grandson's shoulder, riding it with all his weight, trying to staunch the blood bubbling from Colley's shoulder.

She sucked tears and hurt into herself, gagging with her own panic.

This was only a dream. Nothing this bad would ever happen to her.

This is a dream.

"Lai . . ."

Colley. He was alive beneath Albert's hands. He was struggling to speak, blood frothing at the corner of his mouth.

"Come on, boy, come on," the old man was commanding over and over. It was a mindless chant to stop death.

"Dea—dead—"

She understood that word.

"Don't talk," Devil Rawlins rasped to his grandson, and Colley gave up his struggle, going limp against the floor.

She didn't make a sound for a long, long moment, and Albert Rawlins finally looked for her.

"You can't help John Thorne anymore," he said. "But

you can help my boy. Go find the Jeep. It's in the circle field, where we left it. Drive it to the house and call Flavius Maxwell. Tell him that there's been a bad accident. Say that . . . that I'm the one who's hurt, and I need him here, now. Don't tell more than that to anybody."

"I can't leave Papa," she whispered in blank shock, clutching again at John's hand.

Albert freed one bloody hand to shake it at her. "There's one dead here already today. I'm not gonna let Colley die, too. Now you get the hell out of here and do what I say," he roared.

The sheer force of his will tore her out of her numbness, and she began to sob, moving to obey the old man. Her head pounded sickeningly from her fall against the wall, and she stumbled, grabbing at air to try to stand upright.

"Don't faint again. Don't think. Don't stop. Just hurry."

"I'll try," she managed as she fumbled with the buttons on her shirt.

Dreams end. This will be over soon, and I'll wake up back at the Magnolia.

She didn't remember much about the Jeep ride or calling the doctor or waiting for him.

There were just bits and pieces of scenes.

Dr. Maxwell's horrified face when he walked to the door of the shack was one of her clearest memories.

She couldn't go in again; instead, she was sick on the edge of the porch.

The way the soft old mattress—sage and sweet grass, he said he'd put into it—closed around Colley's body when his grandfather and the doctor managed to carry him on it out the door.

He was completely unconscious, his face as pale as she had ever seen it.

My witch boy, how did we ever come to this?

She couldn't stop herself. She reached for him, and then grabbed the mattress to help as they carried him to the Jeep and laid him on the floor.

The rain had stopped, but everything she touched was wet. The wetness felt red to her.

But mostly she remembered the moment when the doctor went back into the cabin to cover her father's body with a tarpaulin.

Colley moaned and tried to move, and Devil clutched at him to force him into lassitude again.

"Will he . . . he won't die, too, will he?" She couldn't bear the thought that the witch boy might prove his mortality. *Please, Colley, no.*

Albert turned fiercely on her. His white hair stood up, and in the gray outside light, the blood that streaked him looked brown, just as the stains on her own hands did. "He's not gonna die. I won't let him. I knew it was your doings when I finally got to the shack and found the two of them. Stay away from Colley. And if you ever think of coming after my grandson again, you just remember that it was a Rawlins who sent John Thorne to hell today."

For the first time, the truth dawned on Lainie. She remembered Colley leaping for her father, the way he'd gone at him with one intent—to kill.

Colley, her Colley, had been the one who had driven the spike through Papa's chest. He had pushed it between his ribs.

She took a hysterical step back from the Jeep. "Colley killed him," she said to no one in particular.

Albert Rawlins turned from the accusation, and Dr.

Maxwell came out of the shack beyond them, shutting the old creaky door firmly.

She understood what he was doing, and she ran to it, clutching the doorknob. "I'm staying here," she told him frantically.

"No, you're not. You're in shock, Lainie," he said gently, taking her by the arm. "You can't wait here until the ambulance comes. Let's go to the house. It won't be long. Then you can ride back with them and help your father. Somebody will have to help Deborah, too. You want to be the one, don't you? Come on, Lainie, come with us." His voice soothed her, his arms held her as he led her away.

It was the rain that caused it. For a while, she tried to tell herself that it wasn't her fault, or Colley's, that Papa was dead.

The rain had changed her afternoon of heaven into years of hell.

John Thorne and Albert Rawlins had gone unexpectedly to the circle field in the middle of a lull in the storm, just to see how the tobacco was faring in the downpour. Thorne saw smoke coming from the direction of the shack, picked up one of the spikes as a last-minute precaution, and went to see what vagrants were using the place.

They told that much of the truth to the shocked people of the Springs. But the rest of the story was pure fabrication. John, they said, had found the place empty. Whoever was there must have heard him coming. In his hurry to leave, he slipped in his wet boots and fell.

It was one of those ghastly tricks of fate that he fell on the spike that he'd dropped.

Nobody really explained how Lainie came to be at

Rawlins Farm when the ambulance got there; there were rumors and whispers, but no answers, not ever.

John Thorne died awfully fast after he threatened the man from the shantytown, they said, and Colley, in some terrible way, gained from the rumors.

He was more powerful now because they thought he was ruthless, and more dangerous because he was powerful.

But nobody knew anything for sure, and that made speculation worse. All that was a certainty was that Colley didn't go into town for a long time.

The town never suspected once how near he himself came to death; they never even knew that he was ill.

It was Dr. Maxwell's idea to keep Colley's injuries a secret. It was Dr. Maxwell who worked over him in an upstairs room at Albert's, and Dr. Maxwell who told the fictional story of John's death.

It was best for everybody, he said, and Mama finally agreed. The truth about what Lainie was doing in the shack would have come out if she pressed the issue, so she didn't.

Like the town, the sheriff suspected a whole lot more, but he agreed to accept the doctor's version of events, too, since there was no one filing any charges and everybody was agreed on the facts.

Lainie suffered as much as if her part in Papa's death had been made public. Every night, she cried in one room and Mama in another. Sometimes she thought she was losing her mind.

She still loved Colley, and she prayed every night to a god who had forsaken her to make him live. But she hated him more, hated the thing he had done.

How could she love a man who had killed her father?

But more important, how could she love herself for her own share in it?

It was easier to stay away from Colley Rawlins. If she

never saw him again, it would be better. She made her vow: she would destroy her love for him if it was the last thing she ever did.

She would never know her witch boy as a husband or a lover.

Colley tried to talk to her one last time.

John Thorne had been dead for three long months, and he had spent most of the interval fighting to live and then struggling to get his strength back. Thorne had very nearly done what he set out to do, destroy the man from the shantytown.

Even when he was able to get out and around, Colley avoided the Springs and everybody in it.

Lainie had not come to see him or called once.

He didn't even remember how he finally discovered the fact that Deborah had sold the house on Martin Hollow Road and gone to live with Olivia at the house in the field beside the Magnolia, but the news broke through his fear and reserve, even through his own burden of guilt.

He had killed a man. Finally done exactly what most of the town thought he was capable of all along. More than that, he had killed Lainie's father. Even when he reminded himself that it had been self-defense, he understood that he'd destroyed more than Thorne's life.

Colley was beginning to see that Lainie's love had died, too.

But he had to fight for it one time before he let her go.

He tried to look like any other normal man when he finally headed to town that day. He didn't want her thinking that he was the monster that Thorne's death hinted that he was. Besides, it was physically impossible for him to wear the overalls he'd spent his whole life in up until that point: the straps pulled too tight over the just-healed wounds of his shoulder. That Sunday, he had on jeans and a white shirt, and he could see for himself that he looked different in other ways as well. He was paler, thinner, older.

The Magnolia didn't open until noon on Sundays, so he went early in the day, trying to avoid everybody else but her and Deborah. As soon as he stepped up on the front porch and glanced through the open screen, his pulse throbbing in his temples, he knew he'd made a mistake.

What he had not known was that Deborah had a prayer group that was meeting there that morning on their way to church, or that Lainie, at the front desk, would react so violently at sight of him.

She saw him through the screen, just as he reached to open it. "No!"

Her tiny cry alerted the women who sat just beyond, heads bowed in reverent silence as they prayed.

Lainie backed away from his shadow at the door, unable to look from him, her face twisted with pain. "I don't want to see you again," she said jaggedly, her voice choked and low.

One or two of the shadow figures stood.

He didn't even try to open the door again. "I came to talk to you."

Turning blindly away, Lainie found Mama there behind her. "I can't. Tell him. You tell him, Mama." And she pushed past Deborah and ran down the wide hall, past the stairs, out of his sight. Her sobs died hard in the still air behind her.

Deborah hesitated, then stepped to the door, opened the screen, and stood beside him on the porch. He wasn't the only one who had aged in the hell of the past three months.

"Please, Colley," she pleaded, "don't do this. Lainie's told me everything."

"I want to see her," he said in desperate determination. "I love her. I couldn't help what happened."

"None of that makes any difference now. John is gone, and so is her heart and soul. What have you done? You can't come here to the Magnolia anymore. Not ever. Please, just go away."

For a long, heartbreaking moment, he looked at the curious listeners just beyond them, straining to catch their conversation, at the misery in Deborah's face, at the rich red and purple of the petunias spilling without a care from their hanging baskets down the length of the cool porch.

How had he not known that Lainie would never forgive him for Thorne's death?

Colley turned from the Magnolia and went back to the river. In the Springs over the course of the next week, the whispers grew into a muffled roar.

That fall, as soon as the tobacco was hung, the old man made plans to send Colley to Paul Harding's famous horse farm just south of Danville, Kentucky, and this time, Albert was willing for him to go away and stay.

Colley himself didn't give a damn.

Part 4

Memories
and Gin

11

Two days after the *Magnolia* was demolished by the storm, a sort of quietness settled over the Springs, as though the fury of the Earth were spent.

Lainie went to the garden late in the cool of the day, turning her face away from the damaged middle arm of the hotel. The oddest things had survived the wind and rain, things such as Aunt Olivia's garden, just beyond the mutilated stone cellar. The corn rose verdant and green, as if refreshed by the wet madness on Tuesday. It gave off a sweet pungency as she broke it from the stalks and stripped the damp shucks from the kernels beneath.

When she had filled a bucket with the white-gold ears, enough to fix at lunch the next day, she turned back to the shadowy yard and the hotel.

She was restless, but she tried not to think about why.

Just as she got even with the cellar, something moved beside it. She shivered a little, but she wasn't surprised when Colley stepped from the side of the last maple still remaining and stood watching her, his face quiet.

"You knew I'd come." His words were low but clear. They held no emotion except certainty. "You've known it ever since last Saturday, when I found you at the quarry with Preston."

"I knew," she whispered.

"I told myself I wouldn't fight for you anymore," he said in the throbbing stillness, his voice suddenly rich and husky, the sound of the hills so thick it made it nearly hard to understand.

But maybe she didn't have to comprehend his tongue; she thought that tonight was about two hearts saying good-bye.

The twilight was as beautiful as the first day of the world must have been. The dusky air was heavy with the scent of the old roses near the back door, and a bird was beginning a sleepy lullaby over their heads.

"But I remembered that for a long time you loved me." He said it without moving a muscle.

"Sometimes I forget and think I still do," she answered unsteadily. "Somewhere mixed in with the way I hurt every time I look at you."

He considered her in silence before he moved again. So close now. Close enough that she could see the way the silver whistle lay like a shard of cool starlight at the base of his throat.

He bent a little, reaching for one of the ears of corn that protruded from the bucket. "You once accused me of working all the time. Here you are, with it falling dark all around us, and you're still working. Do you know why I stay so busy, Lainie?"

Dumbly, she shook her head.

"You haven't guessed? To keep myself from thinking about you and what I did that afternoon in the cabin."

She turned away without even realizing she was doing it. It was just habit to remove herself from anything that might remind her of Papa's death.

But Colley caught her arm with one hand and with his other, pulled the bucket from her. "No, not this time. Please, not this time. Set your work down, Elaina. For me, just tonight."

"You'll make me remember," she whispered.

He stood the bucket beside the gaping hole where the cellar door had been ripped off. Then he turned and reached for her other arm, so that she faced him.

"Once I thought if I gave you time, you'd forget, and that it would be the best thing. But you didn't, and it's not." His hand slid gently from her arm up her shoulder to her neck, where he nudged her chin up so that blue eyes looked into black. "Tonight, when time is running out for me and you, we have to remember. Even if it makes you hate me more. I have to take the chance."

Everything about him was quiet, but beneath the calm, there was pulsing life. She could feel his want, his pain.

"Speak, then." She said it raggedly. "One time I'll let myself look back. Then never again, Colley. It hurts me too much to think of all I lost. Not just Papa, but you."

Her truthfulness broke the hold he had on himself; she felt his sudden shiver as if it were her own.

"I killed John Thorne," he said in agony, and when she uttered a little cry at his bluntness, he clutched her shoulders again, so tightly that she couldn't get away. "See? I've said it out loud. I've been trying to get the words out to you for three years. It's finally done."

She could still raise her hands; she put them over her face as he held her before him.

"I didn't mean to. I never would have. But it happened. One day I was just living, and the next, I had blood on my hands. Charley used to tell me that life had been hard on Devil and that it was what made him so mean. Back then, when I had the creek and you, I didn't understand. But, Lord, I've had some hard living since."

"Colley, stop," Lainie moaned, letting her forehead rest on his warm shoulder. "What do you want from me?"

He waited until she looked up at last. "I want you to do the greatest thing one human can do for another," he said huskily, and his eyes were pleading. "Forgive me."

"And if I say that I'll try, that I might, will it be all you want?"

He hesitated.

"Or is it that you want to hear me say that I still love you?"

The words were too clear in the fragrant cool air. His chest heaved. "If it's the truth," he managed.

"What difference would that make? Even if I did say those things, we'd still be just as far apart as we are now. Don't you understand, witch boy? I can't have you. It would be betraying my mother, my home, myself, if I lived with the man who took my father's life."

He turned loose of her too fast, and his anger rose as swiftly as the dew had fallen around them.

"But he meant to kill me, and maybe you, too."

"Papa wouldn't have hurt me."

"You don't know that. He was somewhere in his past. With another daughter, and with another man. One who truly did deserve to die."

"I know all about Beth. Mama told me. But I don't believe he meant to—"

"To kill me?"

She couldn't answer for a long moment.

"Would you have grieved for me so long, or punished him so much?" he demanded in frustration.

"I never got the chance to find out. You killed him. You didn't injure him, or hurt him, or try to slow him down. How much did you hate him, Colley?"

He didn't speak at all for a long moment, letting what she said burn over his skin and scald all the way to his heart.

"I didn't. You probably don't believe that, but it's true. There was a time when I even wanted him to like me, just because of you."

He rubbed his hand over his face in pain. "I let you say these things and I don't defend myself too well because the truth is that I can't remember much after he stabbed me. I fell. I heard you cry. I heard him hit you. I know that I tried to stop him. No, don't ask me. I'll tell you without questions. Yes, I probably meant to kill him after I saw him hit you. I don't remember anything else until I saw Devil over me, swearing. There was blood. I wondered, Is that my blood? Then I saw you, trying to slide off the bed, and I thought, she's not dead. She's coming to me."

Lainie let her fingers dig into the bark of the tree that she'd slowly backed into. "You want to talk about your grandfather? That night I began to call him Devil, too, I saw what the rest of the town saw. He wished Papa in hell. He told me he was glad you had been the one to ki-kill him. He knows how to hate, that old man, and you're his blood."

Colley winced. "I don't know about that. I didn't know anything at all for a week, and I couldn't leave the house for a month more because somebody might figure things out if I did. Devil told me it was what you wanted. I had to listen to him. You sure didn't come around to see if I was dead or alive. Don't you think that I needed to tell you that I would have cut off my arm for that day not to have happened? I would change it if I could, but I don't see what else there was for me to do. God, Lainie, I didn't want his death between us."

He wasn't supposed to be the one who was hurt; she was the person who'd been wronged, she thought in surprise.

She put her hand up to her throat; it was harder and harder to speak. "Mama and I lost on every count. Papa, and the house, and the very lives we were living. Every time we lost another piece of ourselves, I hated you a little more." She would tell it all if it killed her, so she added painfully, "You don't belong with me. Stay with the woman who came with you to the Magnolia."

"I don't want Rachel."

And I don't want Preston, she said silently, but I don't have much choice. I've done some hard living, too.

Colley stepped even closer, his face pleading. "I can't keep on this way much longer. Let's try, Lainie. Everything I've got is yours. It always was. It is now."

He took an unsteady step toward her, so close her arm brushed his, rough and warm and electrifying. Even her skin throbbed with nerves, and she had to force her eyes to stay wide open, her arms to keep away from him, her lips to speak instead of reaching for his.

"I can put things right for you, Lainie," he pleaded hoarsely. "I've got money. All of it you can ever want. I know there are problems with the Magnolia. I'll fix all of them. Give me a chance. Forgive me. Love me again."

"No."

He sucked in his breath and his temper rose. She wanted him angry; it was easier when he was angry. "My money's as good as Preston's," he said forcefully.

"But the memories don't come with his," she answered steadily, not even attempting to deny that Preston's money was a factor.

"I'd do better by you than he ever could."

"Where? In bed?"

"Everywhere. Yes, in bed, too," he said, his voice choked. "One time, the two of us making love, and this gap between us won't be worth thinking about again." His hands reached out for her, and she backed away too fast. His control broke completely. "Don't run from me. I'm sick of you always running. Running from me, running straight to him. I'm—" He couldn't finish. Instead, he grabbed her by the arms to pull her up against him, his mouth finding hers in frantic roughness.

She should have fought, she should have locked her lips against him.

She didn't.

He was strong, and his anger and grief added to his strength. Not gentle. He'd been gentle before, at the quarry, and in her dreams. Not now. His mouth bruised hers as it slanted over her lips, and he never even gave her a chance to refuse his tongue. It pushed between her teeth, parted her mouth as harshly as his arms locked her to him. His mouth, his tongue, his body—they scalded her.

Lainie couldn't have told even where she was. She was just there, with Colley, at the center of a cavorting universe.

Couldn't get enough, couldn't touch enough, couldn't feel her enough. Take her lips, take her breath, take anything you can get, he thought wildly, when he could think at all.

He let her lips go, but nearly cracked her ribs as he pulled her closer, closer, his mouth finding her eyes, her cheeks, her neck, as he pushed her head back. She was whimpering, making funny little sounds in her throat, struggling against his chest.

He wouldn't turn loose.

It didn't feel like she hated him. She was touching him, pulling his head closer to her face instead of pushing him away.

He felt her hand on the back of his head, tangling in his hair, and he lifted his face until his cheek just brushed her chin—faces together, one still minute in the raging fire, his darkness all around her. Their eyes met, so close, so close, and his breath was hot on her lips. Just a tiny movement to meet him, mouth to mouth, and she made it.

"Colley . . . Colley."

The grassy mound that was the top of the cellar, where he'd first kissed her three years before, was hard against her back now, his body living and beating and thrusting against hers. He slid his hard hands down her back, pushing them over her hips.

Lifting her, pulling one of her legs up, his hand under the bend in her knee, pushing his own knee into the very center of her, throwing her off balance until she clutched his back and his neck just to stay alive.

He had to find a place where he could cover her, skin to skin. Push into her and feel her around him.

Surely in that sweet oblivion he'd find peace and love again. He'd get her back.

Dropping her leg, one arm behind her back, he let the hand that he'd pulled her knee up with slide between them as he found the bend of her other knee. Kissing her breasts beneath the cotton shirt, nuzzling her stomach, Colley stooped to lift her up against him.

Rooms. Places to lay her down and lie down with her. They were all about him.

He didn't know how he crossed the yard, dark with night now, and found the steps that led up on the back porch to the dark, deserted hotel, but he did. Kissing her open mouth, he carried her like a lion looking for his den, for a refuge to hide her.

He dimly remembered that this was the Magnolia. He didn't like to come here anymore; the very walls might fall on him. But he hesitated for only for a second.

She caught at his head again, pulling him down to her. This time it was her tongue finding his, her hands that tangled in his shirt as she clutched it in her spread fingers, pulling them in again and again to crumple the cotton against him.

"Jesus," he panted, breaking away long enough to fumble for the knob of the door near his hand that he was still trying to hold her with. It opened suddenly onto the room beyond, before he even realized that he had it, and the way he stumbled in surprise aroused her out of her trance.

She winced and jerked herself out of his arms, tumbling away . . . and it was over, the two of them watching each other on the tiny, lonely porch.

Colley's face was blind with passion as he looked down at her.

Lainie had wanted him in this way for so long that it cut like a knife to hear her own voice.

"No more."

He didn't even seem to comprehend her choked refusal. His eyes were wild as he stared down at her.

"I can't, Colley. I won't," she whispered painfully. "Let it end."

"No," he said in harsh pain, reaching for her again.

Stop him. She had to stop him.

"I'm going away with Preston," she said in a rush. "Do you understand me? I'm sleeping with him, Colley."

The sound he made was a hard grunt of pain, like a man makes when he takes a punch that doubles him over. "I knew he wouldn't leave you alone," he gasped. "I told Devil, tell him no, and it makes him worse. But you don't love him. You love me. Me."

He pushed her away from him so fast she fell and had to catch herself on the post. Taking two steps away from her, he sucked in air and his eyes glittered in the night. His voice was so full of anger that she shivered. "You're spending your life blaming me for things I can't help. Can't you see that what's between us is more important than a hundred fathers? That you're killing yourself on the inside as sure as you're killing me?"

"I can't forget, Colley. He was my father. He'll always be between us. I couldn't be with you without knowing he wouldn't want it to be so."

His hands came out to brace his weight on the wall behind her as he drew deep, harsh breaths. His shoulders heaved with the effort he made to pull himself under control.

"He's dead, Lainie."

"I helped kill him," she burst out, and suddenly she was crying. Crying the same way she had cried that day long ago. "I knew I wasn't supposed to be with you. I knew I was disobeying him, and I did it anyway."

"So if you can just hurt yourself enough, and me, too, then maybe you can make it right? Is that it?" Colley straightened, rubbing his hands over his face in weary acceptance. "My way's better. I'd take you to bed and love you until you forgot the pain, until you understood that we're just two people who can't get by in this world too well unless we have each other. It was an accident. If he'd never found us that afternoon, I'd have made love to you. We'd be together."

"But that's not the way it happened," she whispered. "And now everything is changed. Colley, look. Do you see the room there?"

She pointed to the far east corner of the hotel. "In that room, I mean to sleep with Preston."

He bent a little, his hand going to his heart involuntarily, and his voice was rusty. "You take him into your world, when you won't let me in the doors, and give him yourself, when you don't love him. Why, Lainie?"

"Whatever I'm doing it for, they're my reasons. They don't have anything to do with us. I can go to bed with him if I want." The words sounded good, defiant and strong, but she didn't mean them. She was as guilty in front of him as if he were her husband confronting her about an illicit lover.

It took him a long time to speak in the aching silence.

"Is it because of the money? Or because you need a man? Or just to hurt me?" he said at last, defeated. "Goddamn it, then, do it, whatever the reason. Do it. Get it over with. When you see me bleeding to death, maybe then it'll be enough. Maybe then you can stop this and forgive me, and forgive yourself, because Thorne died. When it's over, you might need me then. You can come to me like I've wanted to come to you when I'd finished with another woman. I wanted to beg you to make me forget that somebody else ever tou—" He cut the word off sharp.

"It can't be that way. I won't be here. I'm going away with him, Colley."

More than anything else, that shocked him into facing the truth. "You'll hate life out there, where it's cold and mean, away from the Magnolia. You're too much like Olivia and Deborah."

"I know," she admitted in a pained harshness. "I've faced that, and I'm still going. I can learn to live out there; I'm young. I won't come back anymore, except to visit or if they need me. It would be too much for my heart to take. Don't you think it's hard to go? But one of us has to leave, Colley. When you came back, I knew I couldn't go on like I did three years ago, seeing and wanting what I'll never have. It answers all my other needs, too, to go away with Preston."

The man opposite her was deathly silent for a moment. Then he laid his head on the wall that he leaned against and laughed. The sound was bitter. "I should have killed him at the quarry. He won't take you with him, Lainie, not once he gets what he wants. Do you know how many women he's had? I can't count them. He won't be here when the sun comes up the next morning. You'll have to face yourself alone. Yourself, and me. The two of us, dying together."

"Get out of here, Colley," she lashed out at him. "You don't understand. He asked me to marry him. Tell me how many women he's asked that?"

He hadn't expected her news. She registered his shock as if it had been her own, but she had to drive him away somehow.

"It'll never happen," he said flatly, but he wasn't sure anymore. Preston was headstrong and stubborn. He really might go this far to get at Colley. Anyway, it was easy to want Lainie. Colley knew just how easy.

"You're afraid it will," she realized slowly.

Sucking in a deep breath, Colley capitulated. "Maybe I

am. You know why? Even if some of those names that this town likes to call me—savage, animal—are true, and they might be, you'd still be a damned sight better off with me than you ever will be with him."

12

"*You're not going anywhere* just yet."

Preston halted at the door of the kitchen, turning to find the one whose voice had startled him into stopping.

"Colley." He let his gaze drift down over the man who'd risen from the metal lawn chair that stood in the corner of the back porch of the Rawlins house. The T-shirt he wore was stained with sweat and the jeans were marked with dirt from the fields. A sparkle of amused contempt lit Preston's eyes. "And how are things on Tobacco Row, cousin?"

Colley ignored the words. "I meant to work myself into the ground and try to forget, but I reckon I've changed my mind," he said steadily. His eyes were so black and determined that they looked like bits of hard coal in his face.

Preston took one judicious step away. "What is it exactly you're trying to forget?"

His voice made a light echo in the isolated, ominously still kitchen that Nadine had cleaned before she left for the weekend.

"I hear that you've got plans. Some that involve Lainie."

When he registered what Colley was saying, Preston laughed. The sound of his self-satisfied mirth made his cousin want to break his jaw, but he'd learned control. He wasn't the same naive river boy he'd once been, too quick to show emotion, yanked around by the older, slicker Preston. This time he would do his best to play the game the same way James and his son might have.

"Yeah, I've got plans for your little girlfriend. I mean to take her to bed tomorrow night."

An invisible hand clutched Colley's throat.

"Maybe you could help me out, old man. I could use some pointers on what the lady likes. Oh"—Preston snapped his fingers in a mockery of remembrance—"I forgot. You wouldn't know. You never got this far with her, did you?"

Stay calm, Colley told his clenching heart and fists. "I'm not going to let you do this," he managed in spite of the tightness around his windpipe. "You're not going to hurt her, or even touch her."

"You're a fool, Colley, fighting for a woman who doesn't want you."

"I know all about Lainie and what she wants. And it doesn't matter much to me how foolish I seem to you, Preston. I don't expect you to do what's right just out of decency. You don't appear to have much of it. I'm going to give you some encouragement to help you leave Lainie alone. When I went to Georgia, I found out more about you than I ever wanted to know. I met a bookie who knew you real well. Devil was hellfired up over the girl at the time, so I didn't see any reason to tell him about your gambling. But the bookie was another one that I paid off; he cost more than getting rid of the baby did, which probably says something about you in general."

Preston's face twisted into a sneer of unpleasant surprise. "You stayed busy those two weeks in Atlanta, didn't you? Always minding my business."

"I don't give a rat's ass about your business. But Lainie is different. I care about her. You don't love her. I can see that. So you're going to get the hell out of the Springs. Don't touch her, and don't come back. The instant you try to, I'll tell Devil just a little of what I learned about you."

"Damn it, you can't prove it, so tell him anything you want," Preston said hoarsely, but the words were full of shaky bravado.

"Just get out of town. Look at it this way: I'm doing you a favor," Colley said with an effort at control. "Devil hates the Blackburns. He won't stand for you messing with one of them. And no matter what you claim, you and James want to stay in good with him. You don't want me to have all that money of his, do you? Take my advice and keep away from her."

Preston put both hands on the kitchen countertop beside him, as if he were bracing himself against his own rage. When he spoke, he tried to sound amused but didn't quite make the grade. "You're so sure that you're the Man now. Wake up, Colley, you idiot. Don't you know yet? The old man's got no more use for you than he does for me, or anybody else. Listen to me: *he wanted me to do it.* Do you understand? Grandfather told me to take the girl."

Colley felt the words right down to his feet, little sharp swords in his skin. "You lie," he said in hoarse disbelief.

Preston had struck home. He eased upright, his face calming in the light of Colley's shock. "Ask the old man yourself. I'm telling the truth. It's the reason he wanted me to stay here after I left Atlanta. 'Knock her off that pedestal,' he said, 'and Colley won't want her anymore.' I did it just to make us even, but I got more than I bargained for. You actually love her. I won it all from you, Colley."

"Then let that be enough. Let her go," he said, fighting sickness in his throat. Devil hadn't, had he?

Preston slid both hands in the pockets of his tailored summer slacks and leaned nonchalantly on the counter behind him. "There's one thing I care about more than beating you in the game. I want to collect what the little lady promised. She's the reward, and you're not going to blackmail me into giving her up. I'm just doing what my dear grandfather ordered. Besides, she's too easy to have. I don't want to walk away from all she's offering now."

"Shut up. There's nothing easy about Lainie. You had to promise her a wedding ring to touch her."

"She told you that, too? Well, maybe she has been a challenge in some ways, but Lainie is a little naive. She thinks that a gold band means a lifetime with one man. That's why I offered the ring. I knew it would get her. She'll just have to learn that life doesn't always work like a fairy tale, won't she? There's no stopping what's going to happen, Colley, so I guess you'll just have to bear it," Preston finished mockingly.

What was swelling inside of Colley was an emotion so big and dark that he couldn't think past it any longer. His hands curled into claws as he reached violently for his cousin's throat, and he quit listening to the little voice in his head that whispered, *No, stop, don't.*

Saturday was a busy time at the Magnolia.

"This place looks like cotton-picking day on the plantation," Dana said with a laugh. "I never saw so many people here."

The bright-haired girl clutched her big purse as she

edged her way across the back porch, past the stacks of short logs that the men from the church's Benevolence Committee had sawed that morning from the fallen maple tree. Just as she got around them and straightened, she tripped over a heavy, dusty sack.

Dana grabbed at the bag as she fell with a cry, and Lainie and Hargis Lowe, who'd been loading broken limbs into the back of a pickup truck that had been parked at the edge of the porch, grabbed for her.

"What is that?" Dana demanded indignantly, as the older man hauled her up. "It's as heavy as rock."

"That's pretty close to what it is," he returned. "Ready-mix concrete. I'll get it outta your way if you'll step aside."

Dana hastily obliged, pulling the purse in to her body protectively as Hargis bent and, with a grunt and a tiny explosion of dust, slung the bag over his shoulder. "Reckon I'll take this on over to the cellar, Lainie. Somebody had set the door back in place when we got here this morning, but it's in bad shape. Susan said we should probably go ahead and seal it for good with the concrete."

"Go ahead. There's nothing in there except an old pump that the Magnolia once used when people came to try the mineral water. We checked yesterday."

Hargis swung perilously close to Dana again as he shifted to go down the steps. "Young lady," he said with a frown, "the way you hang on to that big pocketbook of yours, it ought to be in a bank vault somewhere."

Startled, Dana relaxed her hold on the purse again and laughed as he strode across the yard. "Hargis is smarter than he looks."

Then she glanced around. Deborah was on the other side of the Magnolia, trying to sort out anything that could be saved from the ruins. "This bag is for you, Lainie," she said in a hushed voice as she pulled it from her shoulder.

"Me!" Lainie reached for it in surprise, and it was unexpectedly heavy.

"What is it?"

A pale blush suffused Dana's throat and headed for her cheeks. "It's a present from Preston. No, don't!" She caught urgently at Lainie's hand as she tried to tug the zip open. "I peeped," she confessed. "I know I shouldn't have, but I couldn't resist. He brought it yesterday while you were gone to take Miss Olivia to the doctor and I was sorting out things in the front parlor. I was supposed to keep it a secret until I saw you, and I did, I swear. But you can't open it here."

"What's in it?" Lainie demanded in confusion.

Dana leaned close to Lainie's ear and murmured, "Some chocolates, and a bottle of gin, and a—a pair of satin pajamas."

Lainie looked right into Dana's wide brown eyes and felt heat pouring into her face.

"Well, this is sweet." The voice came from the yard behind them; it belonged to Lloyd Tate, who had both hands on his hips and was looking at them through his sunglasses. "The two of you, whispering to each other. I'd bet money you're talking about men."

"Speaking of which, most of them are mixing concrete on the other side of the place," Dana informed him. "Maybe you could help stir or something."

"Maybe I could. I like stirring up things for people," he drawled, and turned away.

"He's always watching and listening," Lainie confided slowly as the two women watched Tate saunter off. "He's not what he seems, I can tell."

"Oh, forget him," advised Dana. "Considering the gift that Preston just sent you, you've got better things to think about."

*   *   *

Colley was sitting quietly at the kitchen table when Albert finally came in just as dusk fell on Saturday. Devil was muddy from the fields by the river, and his bad leg dragged painfully behind him. His grandson didn't let himself feel pity.

"I've been waiting for you, old man," he said harshly.

Albert halted a minute, startled, before he spoke. "Have you? Where's your cousin?"

"He's gone. That's all I care about."

Devil went to the stove and found the coffeepot. He pulled a cup from the shelf and carefully poured himself a drink before he spoke. "You and him been at it again? I hope it wasn't over the same thing you fought about the last time." He sat down across from Colley at the kitchen table.

"Once I made a vow to you, Devil," Colley said abruptly. "I tried to keep it. But I can't anymore."

The old man lifted his cap from his head and hung it carefully over the high back of the walnut chair where he sat. Then he reached for the steaming cup of coffee he'd just poured himself and took a long draught of it. After he wiped his mouth with the back of his hand, he leaned back in the chair and looked over the man in front of him.

"You look like you've been to hell and back." Squinting at his grandson through the haze above the coffee, he observed the tight face, the stiff posture. "Where were you all last night? Down at the river lettin' the whore rough you up?" Rawlins drawled ironically, reaching for the coffee the second time. "That might explain things."

Quick and violent in his movement, Colley reached out and knocked the cup off the table. It flew into the wall, where it crashed and shattered, and the dark brown liquid dripped to the floor as the two of them sat in silence.

Albert found his tongue fast enough. "You better have a—"

"I'm through. Did you hear me?"

"The whole world can. You're goin' off like some half-baked lunatic. What's wrong with you?"

"Preston's gone, Devil. Gone. Now it's just you and me, like you knew it'd be once he found a way to get his hands on Lainie Thorne." Colley could barely speak her name. It was killing him.

Albert stood slowly. "I see. This temper fit is over the girl again. Damn, Colley, if Preston's had her, that's between the two of them. It ain't my doin'."

"You lie. You lie to me now, you lie to me all the time. You sent him after her."

"Preston knows how to pick up his own—"

"You singled her out and pointed him straight to her. You meant for him to take her. It's the reason you brought him here this summer. It's the real reason you sent for me to come home, so I'd be here to see her fall into his hands. That's the truth, isn't it? I know, old man."

Albert gazed into Colley's furious face. He saw the way the muscles were tensed in his neck and shoulders. "So I told Preston to see if the little angel really flew or if she'd fall, right down into the mud. But whatever happened, she did it herself."

"You knew she was no match for him. You might as well have sent him after a baby. And you put pressure on her. You let it get out about the money the Magnolia needed."

"She didn't have to go with him. She wanted to," Albert exploded. "I'm tired of you moonin' over her and ruinin' your life. So she's going to bed with Preston. She's just like every other woman. Whatever man waves the most money at her, she'll go to him. Maybe you've finally learned that lesson."

"This was for me? For me to learn a lesson, you hurt her?"

"All I wanted was for you to get your head on the things I've got planned for—"

"You missed the point, Devil. I'm finished with your plan. I'm not like you. You live for the farm. You can't love anybody. I already knew that. But she once could. When I was seventeen, I came back for her. I used to be afraid to tell you that, but now I just don't care. I came back to this farm for Lainie, because I love her."

"Don't be soft—"

"Like Brodie? I wish to God I was more like my father. You should wish it, too. He might forgive you and keep on hanging around. I can't. The only reason I'm here talking to you now is to tell you that our deal is done."

The old man seemed to understand at last. His face whitened. "Think, Colley, what you're doin'. You'll want it all back if you give it up. You did before."

"Not this time. Your money never got me anything but misery. You spent all these years not loving anybody, not hurting because nobody loved you. Not me. I want the love. I want to know when I die that somebody's going to grieve for me. I want a woman to hold me and need me in her bed every night. I want her heart along with her body. I guess that means I'm soft. I'll go ahead and say it so that you don't have to again."

"Wait!" Albert took a step after him as he turned to the door. "What about what you promised me six years ago?"

"I kept my end of the deal. You didn't. As far as I'm concerned, you and your farm and your money can all burn together. I sold you my soul, Devil, but tonight I'm taking it back."

"I'm going to keep on working a while," Lainie said when her exhausted mother got ready to go home at seven. "I won't be home. I'll sleep here tonight so I can get an early start tomorrow morning."

"I know you're worrying over the insurance, Lainie," Deborah told her slowly. "Is that what's keeping you so late, going over the papers? Haven't we heard from them yet? It's four days now since the storm."

"I think I've got it all worked out, Mama," she answered and tried not to wince. "By the time the weekend's over, I ought to know for sure."

"Well, lock your door if you're staying. Normally, I wouldn't even worry about it, but all these people here today, staring and poking around, make me nervous. I would stay with you, but Susan is worried about Livy again. She just sits and thinks and doesn't hear a word that Susan asks her."

"Aunt has been a lot worse since the storm," Lainie said. "That box she found has got her upset."

Deborah agreed. "She located the key to the lock the same afternoon she found it, and opened it and took all the things out. Then she hid them. We don't even know what they were, but how important could they be? They had been hidden for fifty years. I halfway think she's acting so strange because she's afraid that her father will show up and punish her."

"He really was a terror, wasn't he?"

"I always heard he was. He's terrorizing Olivia right now. She's as restless as wind before water. I even took the phone off the hook last night. Bella was calling every few minutes, and Olivia kept being startled by the ringing. Poor Susan must have been up with her until all hours. She looked like death walking this morning."

"The two of you should have come and got me," Lainie protested.

"You'd already spent half a day with her at the clinic

yesterday, and you cleaned all afternoon. Besides, Susan wouldn't leave Olivia to somebody else at night unless she had to." Deborah turned tiredly to leave, but she called back one warning. "If you're really going to stay at the Magnolia, be careful."

Lainie remembered those two words, *be careful*, as she quietly stole across the darkened backyard two hours later. She was taking care, all right, care not to be seen by Deborah.

There was only a piece of a moon that night, bright but more distant than the one that had shone before when Colley had waited for her at the creek. Lainie looked away from the sky as she stole across the darkened yard, piled in places with stacks of tree limbs that the men had gathered but which hadn't yet been hauled away. The stone cellar glimmered as she edged past it, strangely bare on one side now that the maple was gone, and the smell of new concrete was still strong around the entrance.

It was a good thing that the place was changed so that she didn't look at it and remember anymore.

She didn't know why she was hiding. There was no one to see her, and Aunt Olivia's house in the distance was black and silent.

Maybe Livy was finally resting peacefully.

The room Lainie had chosen was far from everything, off the most isolated arm of the Magnolia, the side close to the hedges and sheltered by an elm.

There was a warped old black screen that she pulled open first, just so she could reach beyond and rattle the knob in the door. The key was almost a formality; one good, hard shove would have done the same thing, and the long, open window beside the door came almost to the floor. It would be an easy matter to push through its screen and step into the room beyond.

Lainie's heart was pounding as though Preston was already here.

But there was nothing except a turn-of-the-century room with a four-poster spindle bed, a matching bed stand with an antique globe lamp on it, and a dresser against a wallpapered wall.

She could see only the shadows of those things, but she knew what they looked like.

Not a single room had an air conditioner, but she'd left the fan in the second window, the open one at the back, on all afternoon, and between it and the shadowing elm, the place was close to cool. The fragrant wild roses that she'd cut off of the side fence made the air sweet from their glass vase by the lamp.

Not much time to do what she wanted. Not much time to think, either.

She didn't want any lamps tonight, just a candle. In its flickering glow, the room looked nearly romantic, especially after she pulled back the fresh, clean, snowy sheets and fluffed the pillows.

Which side should be his?

She wanted to laugh. There had to be a write-up that she had missed in one of the glossy magazines down at the drugstore, "Territorial Behavior to be Considered When One Is in Bed with a Man for the First Time."

Fumbling in the big bag Dana had brought her, she found the bottle of one of Preston's favorites, gin, as it lay cocooned against the short, silky sleep shirt that had been folded under it.

It was pale pink with a pencil-thin navy stripe down it at intervals and a deep navy collar and cuffs on the short sleeves. Navy bikinis.

Not bridal, and that was good.

Tonight, she couldn't have stood something bridal.

Instead, it was sexy and luscious and enticing, exactly the kind of thing that Preston would choose.

Lainie looked at the two pieces lying on the wide white bed and listed the things she had to do as if they were dutiful chores.

Had to have a shower.

Had to pull her hair from the braid she'd worn all day and comb it out.

She shivered, and at the other open window, the one without the fan in it, a hard-shelled bug slammed into the screen and buzzed off dizzily.

Where was the romance in this? Where was the hazy glow of love? Where was the joy she'd felt with Co—no, no, no.

This was all wrong. It was just real and gritty and far too clear.

There was one more thing she was going to have to do, she decided, and she was going to put it at the top of her list. Carefully, she unscrewed the lid of the clear glass bottle and turned it up like a man to take a long, deep pull of the gin.

It smelled like cheap aftershave and tasted worse. She had to force herself to swallow, gagging as the liquid burned its way to her stomach, but when her eyes stopped watering, she was shivering and cold still. So she turned it up again.

She had a whole bottle to find romance with.

Here was to the Magnolia. Long may it live, after tonight.

Here was to Papa, his death paid for, after tonight.

To Mama, and Aunt Olivia, she wished life here in peace, the only life they could live and be happy, theirs again, after tonight.

And . . . to you. Oh, to you, Colley.

For making me love you before I was old enough to know that I couldn't.

For the death and the pain we never meant to cause.

For the way I've had to watch you from afar, the way I've wanted to reach out and pull you right into me, and couldn't, for the way I hurt more with every passing day I didn't have you.

Tonight's for you.

$\overline{13}$

Something was happening to her.

Something was pulling her from the hazy cloud that encompassed her.

Couldn't think what it was. No need to think, though, because whatever was happening required no thought. It was lusciously carnal, of the heady dark pleasure of the body and the flesh.

A man was touching her.

She knew it was a man because his hands were rough and possessive and sexual in their contact with her skin. They cupped her face, pushing away the tears.

Why was she crying?

And why was she in this place? She puzzled over it, trying to remember. He was supposed to be here, she knew that. She was waiting for him.

To do what?

He moved. She felt it behind her closed lids. With the movement, he took whatever had covered her and left her naked.

The cool air of the hot fan was on her skin; she heard his breathing; she put out her hands to protest.

Her arms were featherweight, so light, that they tried to float back down, but before they got a chance, he had them in his tight grasp.

Too tight. Too hard.

He pushed them up, above her head, hurting her with his force before he loosed his grasp.

No, it wasn't supposed to be like this.

She tried to protest, but all she could do was make a whimpering sound.

Was he angry with her?

Colley.

Colley was the one who had been angry, but she didn't think he was supposed to be here. How had it happened? Why? Where had he come from?

She tried to buck, to struggle, to throw off his weight. She couldn't even see. Everything was black, black.

"No . . . no," she tried to say, but the words came out like tiny, unintelligible whimpers.

He pulled her arms back down to her sides, and everything stilled a moment until she could hear herself breathing, loud and hard.

Under her hands, she felt smooth cotton sheets. A bed. She floated on a cool bed of clouds and mist. The sensation distracted her and made her feel like laughing.

Then he struck out of the drifting darkness. His mouth suddenly found her breast, its warm wetness as his lips settled on her so shockingly unexpected that she cried out.

The tiny sound rang in the room like a crystal bell.

Its ringing cleared her thoughts a moment. This was Colley at her breast, Colley between her legs, Colley holding her arms down.

It had to be. She wouldn't let it be anybody else.

Please, God, I want it to be Colley.

She wanted to laugh again. How had he gotten here? But the answer didn't matter. Maybe she had dreamed him here, right out of a bottle of expensive gin. She would ask no more questions; she would just accept the wondrous miracle.

I tried, Papa.

Mama, Aunt Olivia.

My heart, I tried.

But she was only human. He was here. She'd been waiting for him ever since that day in the cabin.

Maybe that day never happened. Maybe that really was a dream, and this was reality.

It had to be.

Nothing had ever felt like this before.

And then she couldn't think. His lips on her breasts were too much, too much delight, too much passion. Their point of contact in a floating miasma.

He moved to slide away, and she fought the hand on her wrist to try and pull him back.

"Sta-stay." One word, and it took every effort to get it out.

"I will," he was whispering, his voice rolling around her. "I don't want . . . you to wake up . . . yet . . . baby."

Listening anxiously, she thought she understood, but she thrust up at him, searching again for the pleasures of his mouth, the lips that he wasted on talk.

"Want," she managed to say, the word clear. Want what? What could she say to make him understand? "Want."

"Shhh." His fingers found her lips, quieting them, rubbing over them, and something wild bloomed inside her.

She wanted to taste Colley's skin.

Opening her mouth against his hand, she bit him, and

before he could do more than register the pain with a
moan and a jerk, she kissed his fingers, and kissed them
again, pulling them deep into her mouth.

He took a hard breath. The sound wrapped around them
like an invisible veil. "Lainie," he said painfully, and he
stood, pulling his hand from her lips.

She felt the bed spring up at his movement, and then she
moved, too, trying to open her eyes and sit up.

Dizzy darkness was everywhere. She had to put her head
back down fast.

But she'd remembered something. It wasn't right, the
name. Not Colley. It was—

"Colley?"

The man in the room with her made a fierce sound;
maybe he cursed. Then his hand, not gentle at all, slid
under her head and lifted it, his fingers tangling in her hair.

She relaxed slowly. No time to consider what he was
doing, the way his hands stroked the curls away from her
cheeks, the way his face nuzzled her throat.

His hands were on her breasts again, caressing, cupping.

He knew how to pleasure a woman. More than Colley
ever should have.

She held to that thought only a second before she gave
an inarticulate sound of pleasure and arched toward him
again, blindly seeking his mouth.

He bent to give it to her.

Her hands slid free of his, finding his neck, straining him
to her body.

His arms lifted her from the bed, wrapping her to him,
his face against her beating heart.

The bare skin against hers was wringing wet with sweat,
taut with tension. Under her fingers the muscles of his
shoulders twitched as she raked her fingers down them.

Something was wrong.

But she couldn't stop to think about it now.

She had him at last. Time to finish that heady embrace of so long ago.

I didn't know, she thought suddenly, and the thought was a clear, calm hiatus in the middle of the frantic whirlwind inside her.

I didn't know that it was so sweet, or that a man's mouth could take me outside myself.

I want him to kiss me. Why won't he? Colley loves to kiss.

He let her down to the bed again, his hands dragging hers from his shoulders, pinning them again to the sheets as he kissed his way from breast to navel while she writhed and twisted under him.

I didn't know I couldn't bear to be still when his hands ran down me, that I would cry like a baby.

Why am I crying if I'm happy?

I didn't know that he could be so hard against me, so dead-set determined to have his way that I couldn't break his hold on my hands.

Too hard. Too strong. Where was the gentleness of Colley's touch?

But his fingers laced between hers, and she didn't want gentleness.

I want him.

Kiss me.

But he denied the need he had created in her and refused her movements and her silent pleas for a touch of his lips.

Instead, he released her hands again and let his slide down over her stomach, let his fingers slip between her legs, searching, finding . . . and some of her haziness abruptly slid away.

"No." Her one word cut through the night, sharp and

panic-stricken, and she tried to clamp her legs shut, to push him off her.

But he was single-minded and determined, frightening in his passion. His hard expulsion of breath was mixed with exultant laughter. "Just tonight . . . for all these nights . . ."

This time she didn't fight him when his hand searched for her. She gave in to him, moaning beneath his touch.

Hard to be still. She couldn't be. Pleasure, pleasure. There was too much pleasure in what he was doing.

Somebody was pleading with him, begging. Was it her?

"Colley, no. Yes. Pl . . . please."

He was the tree she twined around, the sun she centered her body upon, mindless except for what she sensed of him.

That was when the earth shook.

The sun was inside her, exploding in a giant, white-hot burst of sweet, sweet power.

It kept exploding in smaller and smaller swirls of heat and color.

She was crying his name, over and over, somewhere in her head. Or was she chanting it out loud?

"Lainie, angel. Lainie, girl."

She heard the husky voice through the haze enveloping her, but a reverent silence had settled inside her body. There was rest and peace in the blanket of release.

Movement was impossible for her, but not for him.

When he took away his hand, his legs dropped between hers. She forgot his puzzle and her own pleasure, everything except the hard pressure of him.

Colley. She would do this for Colley. The thought made her drag her arms up and wrap them about his shoulders.

His body covered hers. He stilled for a tiny space, gathered himself, and thrust.

She made herself hold back the tiny cry that sprang from her throat. Then the pain eased and she could breathe again, taking in a hard impulsion of air. The man above her broke his own lunge forward, stopping short, and she felt the sides of the bed near her shoulders dip as he tried to hold himself up off of her a little on his elbows. His hands cupped her face again roughly, caressing hurriedly behind her ears, sliding down her neck, smoothing back to her temples.

Saying something. What was he whispering as his hands ran through her hair at her throat, as the sharp pain subsided with his stillness?

For a century or so, the two of them lay motionless in the four-poster bed. Just her tears, his pants for breath, the beating of two hearts.

He seemed passive . . . but he didn't pull from her body.

She could still feel it in him, the dark, all-consuming drive for satisfaction that he was trying to control.

"I can't . . . let you go . . ."

And then he did what she had been aching for him to do: he tangled his hands in the hair at the sides of her neck, and kissed her.

Just the pressure of his mouth pleading with her.

Redemption was in that kiss.

She couldn't stop now. A shivering, full of delight, had started deep inside her stomach.

She couldn't stop her body, either. It just reached out for him, melting against his frame. Arms and legs wrapping him, she lifted her head to press her lips to his shoulder. It was her silent yielding.

"Lainie?"

Don't ask, she thought. You know already. Finish it. Let it be done.

For that pleading kiss, she gave him this.

He moved into her with a burst of relief, hurtling toward a mindless plateau.

Lainie dug her fingers into his slippery back, raking his sides. It was her only way to hold him as he rode the night, as she let him find the same pleasure he had given her. He was fast and desperate, uttering one hoarse cry as his body arched for an eon above hers.

Then he tumbled back to earth, collapsing half on, half off her. Her face pressed his thick wet hair and hot cheek as he burrowed into the pillow, and her arms clasped him while he shook as though he had a hard chill.

The world was somewhere out there, still waiting to reclaim them from the mad darkness.

She could hear it approaching: the blood beating in her ears, his harsh breaths, the rotating blades of the fan.

The sound of reality was like a laser beam of knowledge that cut through her foggy thoughts for just one split second.

It wasn't Colley.

She wanted it to be him . . . but it wasn't.

She was shivering everywhere, her skin goose-bumping.

What was his name?

PRESTON.

That was the name her mind had refused to release earlier.

She didn't think it was him, either.

But it had to be. It was supposed to be.

"Pres . . . Preston." She got it out at last, and it was only a little blurred.

The man against her moved in recognition of the name. It was his, and her heart nearly broke. It seemed to take him an eternity to answer. "Sleep," he whispered, and the whisper was jagged from the act he had completed. "Sleep."

His hands were covering her eyes again, but there was no need: a darkness greater than the night was all around her, and spreading fast to her soul.

It really was Preston, just like it was supposed to be.

That was what was wrong.

14

The morning light hurt.

Everything hurt.

Lainie's head, her stomach, her legs, her eyes.

She lay quietly in the bed for a long moment, afraid to move. If she moved, she would have to think.

But the sickness in her was too strong, churning away, and she came up in a terrified flash, held by the sheets until she fought herself free. The whole room swung as she stumbled to the bathroom, and her weak ankle nearly crashed under her.

Clinging to the sink basin, she heaved until her ribs hurt. Then she twisted on the water faucet with trembling hands and washed her mouth out, over and over.

She had gotten drunk, so drunk she could barely remember the night before.

She remembered enough, though, to know that he had come. He had lain in the bed with her, taken what he was after, and left before she was even awake.

Clinging to the sink in front of her, Lainie finally forced herself to look in the mirror. The girl in it had a mussed cloud of dark hair about her face, eyes too big, smudges above her cheeks, swollen lips, and tiny bruises on her breasts.

"Oh!" She put her hands up to try to hide them, to try to push away the memories of his lips as they marked her. But they flooded back in a grueling wave: he held down her hands, he kissed her breasts, he touched her in the most intimate spot, he pushed himself into—

She had to get out.

Stumbling into the bedroom, head pounding and spinning, she sat down on the bed before she realized that it was another proof of the night. It was stained and crumpled. Beside her on the table was a half-empty glass bottle.

The tears spilled down her face.

God's watching, Lainie.

I want to go home. Mama, what have I done? Forgive me. Make me into the girl I used to be.

I hate what I am this morning.

The tears kept falling—she didn't know how to stop them—while she dragged herself to the shower and let the water burn over her, so dizzy she had to cling to the wall to keep upright.

The fan blew across her cold, wet skin as she stood in front of it on the old hardwood floor, but it couldn't blow away the truth.

She just kept on hurting as she pulled on clothes.

You were right, Way. I can't do this. I can't go to bed with a man without love.

Straightening the room, stripping the bed, hiding the bottle.

Those simple, everyday things soothed her a little.

Elaina Thorne had lost two possessions the night before: her virginity and her self-respect.

The first was gone for good; she would live without it.

But the second was a different matter. She had to regain it somehow. It was essential to her existence.

Without it, she couldn't look Colley in the eye again.

"If you can just hurt yourself enough, and me, too, maybe you can make it right . . ."

The tears began again. Her punishment was just starting.

Lainie made herself face the worst truth of all: she had willfully lied to herself last night.

She had let Preston use her, but she had been using him, too. She had been pretending he was his cousin, making love to Colley's memory. Even in bed with another man, she hadn't rid herself of her craving for the witch boy.

If it had really been Colley . . .

The unbidden thought made her ache with longing. With him, she could have remembered the touches, the kisses, the intimacies with nothing but delicious delight.

There would not have been this overriding sense of shame.

Lainie faced the truth: she couldn't save the Magnolia, and she couldn't save herself.

They were both lost.

Preston was the wronged one in all of this, she supposed, but she doubted that he was hurt. Colley had been right about him. The ring he'd promised was nowhere in sight, and Lainie was glad.

She'd been out to prove that she didn't need Colley Rawlins. That she could hurt him the way she herself hurt. That she could make him pay for her own guilt at Papa's death. For being Devil's grandson instead of the witch boy.

Instead, she'd proved that she loved him, no matter what he was.

Lainie wondered in panic if Mama would be able to look

into her eyes that bright Sunday morning and instinctively know what she had done the night before, but it didn't seem to work that way.

For one thing, Deborah got too upset over the news that Lainie finally told her—the truth that she'd been hiding from her mother for too long: there was no insurance to pay for the damage. For another, the entire household was worried about Olivia. She didn't get out of bed at all, but instead, lay staring at nothing, weeping and shivering at an unnamed fear.

Susan was the only person in the whole house whom she would have in the room with her for any length of time, and the big woman turned so protective that she wouldn't leave Olivia alone for a minute until Dr. Maxwell finally arrived and administered a sedative. Olivia herself didn't want Susan out of her sight, clinging to her hands after Flavius Maxwell had gone.

"Father was right," she said drowsily, her eyes still shimmering with tears. "I should never have opened it. But I . . . I couldn't let him hur-hurt . . ."

"Shush, now. Go to sleep. Your father loves you, Livy," Susan said firmly.

"I'm throwing away that horrible old box," Deborah finally decided after Aunt had drifted into a restless sleep.

"It'd be for the best," Susan agreed without even a flicker of questioning. "Don't ever let her see it again. Out of sight, out of mind."

I wish I could throw away last night, Lainie thought wistfully as she tried to sleep on the tiny cot in the room with Aunt late Sunday, taking her turn to watch over the little lady.

On Monday everybody seemed to have a better grip. Olivia was calmer, and Lainie had quit worrying so much about Mama seeing something different in her.

Now she only hoped that she could be strong whenever Colley next came around. He would know what she had done.

She knew he would. From somewhere, she had to find the pride to face him. Never, ever would she let Colley know that she had lain with Preston and dreamed it was him instead.

He killed my father.

She kept reminding herself of his great crime, but somehow, she couldn't seem to dredge up the old hate and grief any longer.

Her own heart had deserted her. It was busy pleading Colley's case. Why do you have to give up the love you have for the witch boy, it whispered, just because you loved Papa? Would Mama understand that her daughter wanted a life with the one man who was the most forbidden?

Part of her wanted Colley to come to her, and soon. She had to find a way to talk to him. She had to know if he hated her for what she had done with Preston. She admitted that much to herself: she couldn't bear for him to hate her the way she had claimed to hate him for the past three years.

But he stayed away. What if he never came back? She'd get just what she'd said she wanted, and it would serve her right.

By Tuesday, the pressure of just living forced her to think of other things. She came to a painful decision: they would have to sell something to make ends meet for the next few weeks. The one fact that she'd considered earlier was still true. The antiques in the Magnolia were their only hope of earning any substantial money.

With that thought in mind, Lainie chose the best ones and cleaned them, preparing to take them to some of the shops in nearby Gainesboro, hoping they would bring a good price.

She herself was going farther than that. Cookeville, sixty miles away, was a growing college town. It had jobs, and she needed one immediately.

But Tuesday brought more than decisiveness. A little after noon, Devil Rawlins climbed the front porch steps, opened the screen, and walked into the parlor. Lainie was on her knees dusting a turn-of-the-century cherry tea table with claw feet when she saw the baggy blue overalls under the edge of the counter.

Her silly heart turned over and spilled thumping hope into her chest.

It took a minute for her to make herself stand, still holding the dustcloth, and see who waited on the other side of the Magnolia's check-out desk.

Devil.

It was only Devil.

Of course it was. Hadn't she known that? Colley hadn't worn overalls in a long time, not since the accident.

What did the old man want? He really was old, much more so than she remembered. He was still formidable in size, but there was something weirdly delicate about him, something that had to do with age. She had seen it in Olivia lately, too.

Then he spoke, and she almost laughed out loud at herself. What an illusion; there was nothing except iron in the man.

"If you know where Preston is, you'd better tell me, girl," he said without even a greeting.

Lainie let her hand with the cloth in it drop to the counter between them. "I haven't seen him lately," she managed. Whatever she'd thought Devil was doing there, she hadn't been expecting questions about

Preston. "And you're not welcome here," she threw in for good measure.

He ignored her challenge. "Don't lie to me. I know he was coming here Saturday night."

Her cheeks flushed as she answered with a sting of anger, "I'm not lying. He was here. He left. What's the matter? Did he run away from your happy home?"

Disregarding her flippancy, Devil reached up a hand and removed the red cap he wore. His hair sprung white and thick, at odd variance with his black eyes. The old man was strangely indecisive as he let his eyes search her face.

"I'm busy," Lainie said in abrupt discomfort. "We're not open for business, anyway."

"And Colley?"

Her lips opened, but she couldn't make a sound.

"I said, did you see Colley Saturday night?"

"No."

She turned back to her table so that he couldn't see her face, and she heard him when he walked away. But he didn't go outside. Instead, his heavy steps went down the hall beside the stairs, right to the swinging door that led to the ruined dining area.

"You can't go in there," Lainie called after him, hastily coming out from behind the counter to follow him.

The old man pushed open the door, regardless of her warning, and stood there looking at the destruction.

"I told you, the dining room is closed," Lainie said angrily. Who did Albert Rawlins think he was?

"I been waitin' for this day," he said to nobody in particular, and his voice was a little surprised. "I knew the place had to fall sometime. It just didn't happen like I expected it would. I thought I'd feel different."

"All of our problems make you happy," Lainie accused.

"Just as happy as the day Papa died. You always get what you want, Devil."

He didn't seem to hear the name. Releasing the door to let it swing shut on the rubble beyond, he twisted to look around himself at the long hall. "Once I wanted a woman," he said roughly.

"What?"

"I wanted Olivia," he answered.

"Aunt Livy? My Aunt Olivia?" Lainie faltered. Surely she hadn't heard him right.

"I thought she loved me in spite of her father. I wrote her, asked her to meet me one night. I meant to take her and leave. Run away with her." Devil walked back down the hall, pausing for a second to let his hand brush the curve of the bannister at the end of the stairs.

Lainie wondered, had she been dropped into a new dimension? This couldn't be her, standing here placidly letting Albert Rawlins stroll through her hotel, and it couldn't be him, telling this painful story. He couldn't love anybody.

"But she never came," he finished, and his voice echoed quietly against the high ceilings. "She couldn't leave this place. I waited and I waited that last night, for all the good it did. Her father and the Magnolia—they held her. Is it any wonder that I hate these walls? These porches? The Blackburns?"

"You didn't have to stay here and let your hate grow." Lainie finally found a choked version of her voice and spoke in the gaping silence. "Why didn't you just go away and make a new life somewhere else?"

"Why didn't you, three years ago?" Rawlins looked at her, and she realized suddenly that the old man's eyes were really brown, like Colley's. She had never looked at him before, always too afraid.

"I—I couldn't."

"See? Neither could Colley. I had to make him, and even then, he kept comin' back to you. Nothin' ever really changes. Some folks' hearts just want what they want, and they'll bear any kind of torture to be near the thing they crave. One way or another, that kind of blind heart ruins most of the Rawlinses. From the cradle to the grave, it rules them."

"I don't understand," she said in slow wonder and growing belief. The old man really had loved Olivia.

"The Springs is wrong. They say we don't love. The truth is, we don't dare. We love too much. Look at me. I married. I had children. But today, standing here, all I can see is how Livy Blackburn looked comin' down these stairs the first day I ever set foot in the Magnolia. Sixty years of wantin.' My son had the same fault. Brodie gave his life to satisfy a shantytown girl. And then there's Colley."

Devil considered Lainie keenly. "I only meant to protect him."

"From me?"

"He's spent nearly all of his first quarter of a century watchin' you. He's goin' to keep on doin' it, and it's God's own joke on us that not one single woman has ever been worth it. Livy left me waitin'. Colley's mother took money for him. And you brought death right to my door."

"I never meant to," Lainie protested, clutching the edge of the counter until her fingers ached.

"No woman ever means anything, does she? Preston's got the right idea. He ain't gonna stick to me unless there's money, and he ain't gonna stick to you, leastways not for love. Near as I can figure it, there ain't much Rawlins in him. He's his mother made over. Maybe his way don't sound right, but it's best in the end. It didn't come as much surprise to me to find Preston gone. The only thing is, I don't know where he went."

The old man's sudden shift back to their initial topic made it hard for Lainie to answer for a minute. "I don't know, either."

"I didn't really think you did. I wouldn't be askin', but I got this bad feelin' about things."

In the ominous stillness, somebody stepped on the porch outside. The creaking planks gave evidence of an approaching visitor only a moment before Way pulled open the screen and stuck his head around it. "Hey, Lainie," he called into the shadowy parlor, squinting from the outside sunlight, "the housekeeper at Rawlins Farm told me that old man Rawlins came here. What in—"

Way's words broke off sharply and his mouth dropped when his vision cleared and he realized that Devil himself was standing beside Lainie.

"Oh," he muttered, stepping all the way inside. "At least I found you."

"What do you want?" Devil demanded roughly.

Way hesitated, glancing from him to Lainie. She knew her cousin; he was upset about something.

"Remember a few days ago when you went to the quarry?" Way asked, talking right to Lainie as if he could avoid the old man. "Preston didn't have a key to open the gate to Lo-Joe Road, so he tore the whole thing down."

"I sent for a fencin' company out of Cookeville to come and run new chain-link fences, not just out at the road, but all around the quarry itself," Devil interrupted. "That's who's out there now, if that's what you're wantin' to know. They came yesterday, and they won't be finished until tomorrow sometime."

Way cleared his throat. "One of the crew thinks he's a regular Superman. He heard all about your dive into the place, Lainie, and today he came on the job with rappelling equipment and scuba gear. He went off in the same big hole that you did. Except he got more than he bargained for."

Something was wrong. What?

Way let his hand fumble with the belt that held his gun. Lainie couldn't ask her questions. Her eyes felt too big for her face. Devil was stiff, braced for some kind of blow.

"The sheriff asked for a retrieval unit out of Nashville. They're on their way. And he had me call your . . . call your son James. He's on his way, too. Because you see"—Way's words finally came in a rush—"there was a car in the quarry this morning. A brand-new, top-of-the-line, silver Jaguar."

The old man's breath hissed in her ear, but Lainie couldn't make a sound. Her throat was too tight.

This time Way managed to look right at Devil. "It's Preston's."

Lainie thought that Devil and Way talked a little longer. She couldn't hear very much over the ringing in her ears. She felt sick, and she knew that the old man did, too. His face was gray, and when he lifted his hand to wipe sweat from his cheek, he moved like he had weights tied to him.

She watched the two of them walk across the green lawn into the sunny day, and suddenly she noticed how sweet the odor of honeysuckle was. From somewhere drifted the thick, spicy scent of sassafras. Here was smell and sight, and here was breath and the feel of blood strumming gently through her veins.

A dead man knew none of those.

Lainie found one of the chairs and sat huddled in a little ball in it on the front porch with the clapboard walls of the

Magnolia looming like a comforting fortress at her back. Way's car had become just a dim speck off down the hot ribbon of the highway. Devil stood watching her cousin go, his hands hidden in the pockets of the heavy overalls.

Was he wondering if his grandson was really dead?

He couldn't be. The word wasn't even real, not for people like the golden-haired playboy that Preston was.

Why would he be at the bottom of the quarry?

"I should have killed him. . . ."

Lainie flinched. The words were so clear that Colley might have been standing before her, saying them again. They were as real as the roaring of the jar flies out over the creek.

Shivering all over even sitting here in the blazing sunlight, she watched Devil walk back to the porch. The cat, its fur gleaming, climbed the steps with him.

"The deputy said he thinks it's for the best if I don't go to Lo-Joe while they're pullin' the car up," the old man said abruptly. "But he can go to hell. He wouldn't want you there, either, I don't reckon."

"No."

"I've got somethin' else to tell you before I leave."

His voice was calm, but something in his face alerted her and made the hair rise on her arms.

"Me and Colley had a discussion, you might call it, Saturday night. He walked out. I ain't seen him since. His truck, his things, they're all right where they're supposed to be. He's not."

All of an instant, she understood the hard misery that rode him. It wasn't only Preston he was worried about.

"No," she said on the knife edge of realization. "No."

"I've made some mistakes. I need time to talk to him. I'm hopin' I've still got that time. I'm goin' to the quarry. Ain't much on drivin' myself, and I ain't too good at it anymore, but I got this far. I'll get there, too. I come here today hopin' you could whistle him up again for me, but it could be he's—he's where he can't hear you."

Lainie wanted to put her hands over her ears, but she didn't. She knew what she had to do. "I'm going with you."

The word got out somehow, all over town, that there was a car at the bottom of the quarry, and maybe even a body in it. By the time the retrieval unit had gotten to the turnoff into Lo-Joe, the sheriff's office had been forced to block-ade the road, stopping the cars that were trying to turn in, forcing them to park in lines up and down the edge of Martin Hollow Road.

The people milled about, waiting with avid interest for whatever disaster was about to strike.

Heat was soaring as the afternoon drew on.

When Devil finally pulled the truck over, they were still a distance from the quarry, but the route was blocked by several vehicles. Lainie made herself climb out into the sunshine and step over a section of fence that someone had conveniently lowered. One of Albert's cows grazed in this field; another was up to her neck in a pond that was brown with mud she'd stirred up. Up ahead of her, as near as they could get without the sheriff running them off, stood several more people watching. One of them—an older, bulky woman in a flowered house dress—held an umbrella over her head to guard against the rays of the sun, and another lady shared it with her.

"You two don't need to be this close to what's happenin' here." Devil broke into their conversation harshly as he and Lainie came close to the women.

The umbrella woman was Bella, and she jumped a foot into the air in her surprise, flushing to the roots of her henna-rinsed hair at sight of the man. The umbrella rattled in her hand.

She gasped, avoiding the old man's gaze. "Lord, De-Albert, you gave me a start."

At that moment a distant shout cracked across the air from the field above them. Then a muffled, crashing sound echoed.

"I'm going closer," Lainie said abruptly.

The two women watched her and the old man go in silence, and that silence grew more strained and awkward as they got closer. Jerry Byrne, the only other member of the police force in the Springs besides Way and the sheriff, stood at his car, and he let them pass without a word, his attention focused entirely on what lay ahead of them.

Lainie stopped sharply just as they got near enough to the quarry to see exactly what was happening. The water was visible now, brighter, deeper, colder than ever. It shimmered like a hard blue stone as it reflected both the cool gray of the sheer rock walls around it and the bright blue of the sky above. Only the hazy reflection of an unexpectedly white, fluffy cloud marred the smooth tones of its surface.

She shivered suddenly, wondering if the Jaguar had shot like a star over the edge into the pool below, or if it had hung and tumbled its way down, a rough flint striking fire from stone.

Standing there between sky and water, Lainie went a little insane. If they found Colley here, she thought quietly, she was close enough to the edge that she could just slip over it, too. It wasn't a difficult feat. She had done it before, only this time, they couldn't bring her back in time. He wouldn't be there to drag her out with every ounce of strength he possessed.

"Get back, Lainie." Way's voice right behind her was

deliberately calm as he reached out for her arm and pulled her away. "I don't have to ask why you came. I've already heard from Nadine that Colley's gone. All I can tell you is, he has better sense than to end up in Lo-Joe."

Looking awkwardly from her pale features, he motioned across the quarry to the huge pile of rocks at its back. "Look. Seems like everybody came to the party. How'd he get up there?"

A strong, square figure stood silhouetted against the blue sky as tall and stiff as a windmill.

"Lloyd Tate," Lainie said in recognition.

"One hell of a nosy man," Way finished.

The sheriff was right at the center of the activity, in the field beside a big black wrecker. Its operator had stabilized it with two outriggers, and the boom had been extended to the farthest length, as though the man inside the cab was afraid to get near the edge.

Back out at the gate to Lo-Joe Road, an ambulance, the rescue squad van, and a big black Oldsmobile, unmarked but ominous, made up another clump of traffic.

The operator in the wrecker suddenly squalled out the window in the general direction of the sheriff, "The diver just radioed from one of the ledges down there. He's got it hooked and I'm ready to pull up."

The sheriff waved his hand in understanding and headed down the road to where the big Oldsmobile waited. Lainie watched him go, watched him tap the dark window of the car, watched while he spoke to the man at the wheel, a red-haired man in dark sunglasses.

Both doors of the car opened. The man who climbed out on the other side came closer with visible dread. His face was drawn and his steps halting.

It was James Rawlins. Lainie knew it instinctively and felt a surge of pity.

James, the sheriff, and the official-looking stranger drew close, so close that Lainie heard what the sheriff was saying. "I don't know yet if you want to get so near. There's no tellin' what shape . . . things . . . are in."

The motor of the salvage truck gave a deep roar and the wrecker cable attached to the boom snapped sharply.

Way spoke for the first time, his words right in Lainie's ear. "There she comes," he murmured as the thick, heavy wire began to roll jerkily over the edge of the quarry. The car rose unwillingly from its watery resting place, the cable cracking every few seconds.

"Must be hanging on somethin'," Way muttered.

Nobody else spoke.

They just waited.

When the Jaguar appeared suddenly over the horizon, it took them all unaware, its ascension sudden and quick.

As silver in the sun as the quarry below it, the car streamed water like cold, clear blood from its broken windows, its bent grills, its flattened tires. The sound of that rushing flood poured down Lainie's back.

Beside her, Way was rigid with expectation as the huge metal shape rose up and up, a gray sea monster stirring from the depths. When the cable creaked up as far as it would go, the vehicle hung suspended in midair, swaying like a huge, bloated corpse at the end of a rope.

Devil didn't move, didn't seem even to breathe, but James made a harsh choking noise, one so full of grief that it seemed to sweep the open field. "That's his," he rasped.

The sheriff, who'd stepped close to the wrecker to have a consultation with the operator, turned now and called back, "The diver's coming up. He says nobody's in that car."

Way moved in relief, but the sheriff continued, "There's nobody in the car, but . . . there is a body in the quarry."

"A body!" Devil exclaimed harshly.

The sheriff plunged on. "Not your grandson. The Jag must have moved some rocks where it settled. That's where the diver found the—the person. Somebody we didn't count on. This one's been there awhile, he says."

Devil moved forward in a lunge, his hands grasping at the air in front of him. "Brodie."

Hope blazed from his face, and the sheriff looked away. "No, Mr. Rawlins, I'm sorry to say it's not. I don't know yet how he can tell, but the diver thinks it's a woman."

Silence hung as thick and pungent as smoke.

"A woman!" Way murmured at last. "Who in the world is she?"

15

"*I'm scared to death,*" Abby Horner said with a shiver. "One man missing and a body that nobody knew about at the bottom of the quarry. I won't sleep a wink tonight."

"We've got some kind of mass murderer on our hands, that's what. Who knows what else we'll find before this is over." Ben Sanders's voice was loud enough that it could be heard above the excited babble that filled the entire room.

Everybody seemed to have forgotten that the Magnolia had been in a storm and was at least partially closed. Out of sheer force of habit, because the Springs had no courthouse or other common meeting place big enough to hold all the people who'd collected, they'd come to its parlor to talk just as if it were Wednesday night after church instead of Tuesday after a grizzly find.

"It was really Preston's car?" Deborah asked Lainie in horror.

"Yes," she said with a twist of pain.

"So he has to be—"

She didn't finish and Lainie didn't answer.

"That woman didn't just roll off into the quarry of her own free will. When they finish the autopsy, they'll find she was murdered." Bella's opinion for once coincided with Ben's, but that was no great accomplishment. Everybody in town seemed to agree with him. "That poor Rawlins boy loved his Jaguar. If he wasn't dead, it'd never be in Lo-Joe."

"The diver said," Alma, the librarian, offered in a moment of silence, "that the woman had been there a while. What does that mean? Nobody's missing around these parts."

The air was fraught with what they all wanted to say but were too afraid to.

Finally, Ben said cautiously, "A lot of stray people come to Rawlins Farm."

"Are you suggesting that this woman is one of them?" Bella demanded.

"Why not? It makes sense. That would explain why none of us know about her."

Bella bit her finger, an oddly youthful gesture for a woman well past middle age. "And just how do you think she came to be at the bottom of Lo-Joe?"

Her question dropped silence over them like a blanket. Only Ben seemed willing to verbalize what they were all thinking.

"Not a soul can tell for sure who drifts onto the farm. Nobody knows or cares what happens to them, either, nobody except the Man. He's the only one who can go to Lo-Joe any time he wants without Devil questioning him."

Colley. They were talking about Colley.

"I should have killed him at the quarry. . . ."

"No. You're wrong," Lainie burst out, talking to her own heart and the roomful of people as well.

"You've always been blind where the river boy was concerned," Bella accused.

"What do you get," Abby interrupted suddenly, "when you take somebody raised like a beast in the wild and give him to a devil to raise? You get worse than you ever had."

Bella agreed. "Colley Rawlins has got money and power. Albert has set him to be lord over all the town. Maybe he thinks he can get away with murder."

Loud murmurs of assent went up from the gathered throng. "You're speaking the gospel now!" called a big farmer from near Lafayette, one of Ben's neighbors.

"Who are they talking about, Susan?" Olivia's quiet voice came unexpectedly from the open door, where she and the other woman had halted. "We saw the crowd from the rose garden, Lainie. I thought I might help. Why are they all standing here in the front parlor? Shouldn't we take them in to supper?"

"There's no supper at the Magnolia tonight, Aunt," Deborah answered.

"Miss Livy, let's go back to the house," Susan said urgently, tugging at the old woman's arm. "We don't have to listen to evil gossip."

"Evil gossip!" Abby and Bella spoke simultaneously, but Bella persevered. "How dare you speak to me like that, Susan McAlester! It's not gossip. If anybody knows that Colley is entirely capable of murdering Preston, it should be Olivia. She was here the very night he threatened his cousin over that silly whistle, if she can only remember. I certainly can. And you, Way." She called to the man who loomed suddenly behind Olivia in the door. "I hear that he did worse out at Lo-Joe itself just a few days ago."

"Your sources never fail, do they, Bella?" Way asked in exasperation.

"Is it true that he and Preston had a terrible fight?"

"It's true," Way returned reluctantly.

"The best thing we could do would be to hunt him down and have an old-fashioned hanging like they used to have before we got afraid of law and order," Ben declared, bolder in Way's lawful presence. "We all know what's going on here."

"And we won't let him get away with it," Abby put in fiercely. "Not even Devil can save him now, not when he's a killer, plain and simple."

"Maybe it's up to us to stop him!" The Lafayette farmer took a step forward.

Lainie couldn't bear it any longer. With a whimper of sound, she shoved away from the counter and ran to the door.

"Lainie, why are they so angry with Colley?" Aunt Olivia asked, half in fright as Lainie tried to push past her, her hands catching at her great-niece's arm.

"Because they don't know him."

"But we do. We won't let anything happen to him," Olivia said firmly.

"Justice can't be stopped," Bella answered, and Lainie ran.

Down the steps, away from the voices, across the cool lawn. She ran until she reached the silence of the shadowy kitchen in Olivia's empty house.

How dare they talk about Colley as if he were little better than a crazed animal? The witch boy who'd pulled her from the creek, who'd cried over Charley, who'd kept a promise of honor to her mother—the man that he had become couldn't have committed the crimes they were accusing him of. He had gentleness in him, more than any other man she'd ever known.

Colley was no killer.

The truth was blinding her with its brilliance.

"Lainie." Mama had followed her and now stood hesitantly at the door.

"I need to talk to him," she told Deborah in agitation.

"Colley. That's who, isn't it?"

"Devil thinks he's dead. What will I do if he is, if I never get a chance to see him again? Will it make everybody happy if he is?" Lainie demanded hysterically.

"I never wished him dead, no matter what."

"Mama, I can't go on hating him," Lainie whispered pleadingly. "I've tried."

"I never asked you to hate him," Deborah protested, crossing her arms over herself protectively.

"You don't want me with him."

Deborah's sad, wry face admitted the truth in Lainie's accusation. "It would be easier for me if you weren't. I'm afraid of him."

"Not you, too. Not of Colley." Lainie's eyes were wide with amazement. Out of all of her emotions, fear of the witch boy didn't even come into play. She might fear him a little in a sexual sense, in the way a woman feared a man whom she knew had singled her out and meant to have her, but that kind of fear had an edge of pleasure in it when the man was Colley. "He did a terrible thing. But he's not what Bella and Abby say. He really didn't mean to kill Papa. It was self-defense."

At last she had said it out loud. The bitter irony was that she hadn't faced the truth until she heard others actually say the same thing that she'd been accusing him of for three years, and it had been ludicrous on their lips.

Deborah took a step toward her daughter. "No matter what, John is still dead. You're able to forgive Colley, but can you forget?"

Lainie winced. "I don't know. Will I ever be able to look

at the witch boy and not see my father in his blood on the floor? But I can't want anybody else. What will I do?"

"I can't answer that for you. But I don't intend anymore to stop the inevitable. Whatever was between you and Colley was so explosive that I could feel it from the very first. I was afraid of it from the moment I saw you together in the creek. That's what scares me. I hoped you'd find somebody else that John could accept, but it was all to no avail."

"I tried, Mama."

Deborah lifted a hand to brush the dark hair off Lainie's hot cheek. "I know. You made yourself believe that Colley murdered John because that way, you could hate him. The hate took up all your energy, just like your loving him did. Then you didn't have time to blame yourself so much. But nobody's to blame. Nobody. I loved John, but I saw what he could turn into when he remembered Beth too much."

"I can't stand to hear all of the town call Colley the same names that I called him. It's funny how hearing them made me sure he's not a murderer." She hesitated. "Will you understand, Mama, if I tell you that Colley could have killed Preston? It's in him to do it if he had to."

"Oh, Devil should be happy," Deborah agreed quietly. "He got what he wanted when he raised Colley wild. I know, and this town knows, exactly what he might do if he had to. He'd never hurt you, but what he'd do to somebody that he thought might, or to somebody who was trying to take you away from him . . . that's why they say he's uncivilized. Why they're so full of fear, too."

"But he didn't kill his cousin," Lainie said with stubborn certainty. "If he had, he'd have done it out in the open and then dared the world to come and get him. He wouldn't sneak and hide and drop the body in Lo-Joe." Her voice cracked. "Where is he? I won't believe he's dead. I don't know where Preston is, or who the woman is. All I know is that if the town finds Colley, there's no telling what they'll do to him."

No one would ever think to look for him here, especially not Devil. That was the very reason that Colley had chosen this place to hide.

He needed time to think, time to decide what to do, time to face the thing that he had done.

The night was hot and still. There was no movement of wind in the trees, only the calling of a whippoorwill and the chirruping of a cricket somewhere in the wall of the house. In the three days since he had come here, those were the only sounds he'd heard.

Colley thought it might be cooler outside, and the ground couldn't be much harder than the floor where he lay, willing sleep, but the house gave him a sense of shelter. It was a refuge while he struggled with himself.

There was another reason for coming here, too. In this house at the dead end of Martin Hollow Road, Lainie had lived and played. He had chosen to hide in the one place nobody would ever think to look: the old Thorne house. If he couldn't find answers here, he didn't know what he was going to do.

Lainie, he begged her memory as he stared at the shadowy walls, forgive me.

How had he let himself get so out of control? He had been the kind of man she'd accused him of being. The kind of man that Devil had created. He had committed the worst offense of his life, giving in to the dark passions that drive men—anger, lust, jealousy.

But he kept remembering the love, that he loved Lainie,

that once she had loved him. It didn't make anything right, but it kept him from killing himself.

I have to confess. I can't live this way. Forgive me of this terrible sin. I don't give a damn what Devil does, and the rest of the world can go to hell along with me. But you, Lainie Thorne—I've got to make my peace with you.

"What is it? They've found Colley, haven't they? Haven't they?" The frantic question spilled out of Lainie as soon as she saw Way standing at the door of the kitchen the next morning.

"Don't get all hysterical on me. I have to ask you something, that's all." Way opened the door and reached in, pulling her out on the porch with him in the morning sunlight. "You don't have to answer any of what I'm about to ask, but if you don't, you'll wind up answering to James Rawlins and the private investigator he brought with him from Nashville. I got here early to warn you."

"About what?"

"They searched the Jaguar. Nothing much. Preston's suitcases in the back. I guess he was getting ready to move on. A key in the glove compartment. It was on a blue-and-white tassel."

Lainie went hot from head to toe. Way already knew, she could tell.

"You gave it to him, didn't you?"

She nodded wordlessly.

"I know what for." He turned loose of her. "I'm not asking for explanations. I just need to know when."

"Saturday night."

Way flinched. "That's—not good."

"Why not?"

"Because it makes you the last person to see him so far."

Lainie tucked her hair behind her ear nervously. "Does that make me guilty of something?"

"Not if he was alive and well when he walked out of the Magnolia."

She couldn't tell him. Shame alone would choke her before she got the words out.

"Lainie. Tell me that he was alive and well." Way's eyes searched her face, reading the guilt.

"I think he was. I was asleep."

"He didn't even wake you up to tell you he was leaving?" His face hardened.

Too late now for anything but the bald truth. "I had liquor, gin that he'd sent. I was nervous. I got drunk. Way, I can't even remember most of the night."

Shock turned her cousin's face bleak. "I see."

"Just go ahead and say it," she burst out. "You told me how I would feel when it was over, and you were right."

Way looked away and finally asked, "Wonder where Colley was while you were in bed with Preston?"

"In my heart," she whispered. "In my heart."

"Lainie, honey, what am I going to do with you?" he said in despair, dropping into a nearby porch chair. "And what am I going to do about them finding that key?"

"It's my problem."

"Yeah, sure." He came out of the chair as quickly as he'd fallen into it. "You'll have to show me the room. Quick, before the PI gets hold of the sheriff's news about it. It's no big deal as long as there's nothing else. Preston could have had the key for a dozen reasons. We'll think of something. But we have to make sure there's no other evidence to lead them to you. Aunt Deborah would never get over it if the story leaked out."

Mama. No, Lainie didn't want her to know.

She capitulated reluctantly. "I'll take you to the room."

*   *   *

The corner room had always been one of her favorites, but today Lainie hated pushing open its door. Sight of the dead bouquet that she had left on the table beside the bed made her turn her head.

Way felt no such hesitation. He went past her quickly, glancing from the newly made bed to the bedside table to the carpet at their feet. "Is this the way you left it?"

Lainie nodded.

"He didn't take anything out of it?"

"No."

The morning sunshine did its job too well as Way jerked open the drawer of the chest and the rays glinted off the bottle of liquor. "How drunk were you? Tell me you didn't down all of this while you were waiting for Preston to show. Can you remember anything at all?"

"Not much about Preston," she answered truthfully, but a flush of heat crept through her.

Way tried to hide the bottle by cradling it under his arm. "Let's get out of here," he said roughly, and held the door open. Just as he pulled it shut again behind them, the bottle slid sideways and tumbled to the porch. He managed to cushion its fall on the top of his soft leather shoe, but as he bent to pick it up, his attention was caught by an unfamiliar stain just beside the door to the room.

"Now what is it?" Lainie demanded apprehensively.

"I don't know. It looks like part of a shoe print, but it's not mud." Way's fingers rubbed over the spot again. "It's concrete," he realized suddenly.

Lainie's face cleared. "Oh, I know. There was fresh concrete poured Saturday. They used it to fix the back porch where the tree fell, and they put it around the door to the stone cellar. Maybe Preston stepped—"

"No. You had him park in the side lot, didn't you? It's where I'd have somebody park if I wanted to keep their coming a secret. There was no reason for him to go near the porch or the cellar. So who did?"

Lainie saw the man instantly, as clearly as she had yesterday when he was silhouetted against the sky. "Lloyd Tate was here Saturday."

Her heart tripped.

Why had she remembered him out of all those who came to the Magnolia that weekend?

"Well, that's odd," Way said slowly. "I ran a check on him. I don't even know why I did. But I can't find any record of a man by that name. He told the people at the marina that he was from Memphis, but there's no trace of him there. Nobody outside of the Springs has ever heard of Tate before. He's gone without a trace."

After Way left, Lainie hid in one of the massive rockers on the end of the front porch under the massing of the honeysuckle vines. She had to try to recall that Saturday night.

Preston had come. She had lain with him. That part of the memory was not pleasant.

But unwillingly, she kept being lured to another part, one far more mesmerizing. When she thought it was Colley touching her, she had wanted to wrap her whole body around him and hold on tight.

I can pretend. Just pretend for a minute that it really was the witch boy.

With her eyes closed, she let herself remember the dark enticement that she'd felt. She had bitten his fingers, and he had laid his hand—

Lainie dropped her face from the sun, trying to push the memory of it away. It was a whiskey memory, anyway;

Colley hadn't been with her. And it was not anything to help Way.

They had to find Preston and Colley alive, both of them, so she could sort out her own head when she looked at them, so she could—

"Keep dreaming, Lainie."

It was Aunt Olivia's soft voice above her head, and it was her hand that Lainie felt light as a robin's wing on the top of her head. Those two things brought her out of her reverie, and she sat upright in the rocker to look at the old lady who'd walked up silently beside her.

"I'm awake, Aunt, not asleep."

Livy's hand was cool and smelled of roses as she let it brush down the side of Lainie's face. "Does that matter?" she asked with a whimsical smile. "I dream some of my best dreams when I'm wide awake, sitting right here on the front porch."

The other rocker beside Lainie held nothing but the cat, and Olivia picked him up with both hands and took his place, letting him settle with a satisfied purr back into her lap. "I don't know all that goes on anymore. Some days are mostly clear, like good crystal. Then again, some of my days seem like clouds, soft and fuzzy and without any substance at all. Today is pure Waterford. At least it has been so far. Today, I know that you're hurting somewhere inside," she said to her great-niece, stroking the cat while she talked.

With Aunt Olivia, Lainie could be honest. The little lady might not even remember the conversation again, caught up in her clouds. "Colley's gone. He's missing. But how can he be? He has nowhere else to go."

"He belongs with you. You gave him the whistle. Why won't he come to you?"

Lainie looked from her clenched hands to her aunt's eyes. "I thought I didn't want him here. Because of Papa."

"Papa. Yours? Or Father? You didn't know him, did you? Lansing Blackburn was a good, good man, but he hated the one person I loved. So I grew almost to hate Father."

Olivia wasn't listening at all to Lainie. She was thinking about her own life.

"I didn't know how much until I found the box." She fumbled with the tiny buttons on the front of the soft white dress, the thin blue veins of her hands showing like delicate vines through her skin. "I wouldn't ever show Susan. She wouldn't understand. But you, Lainie, you might. You need to see."

Lainie watched in surprise as Olivia opened the last of the top three buttons, revealing the cotton lace of the camisole beneath. From her bosom, she brought a thin paper. It had been folded into a square until it was only an inch across.

"Read it," Olivia whispered as she refastened the buttons.

Hesitantly, Lainie unfolded the missive. The paper was yellow and dry. She had to open it carefully.

It was a note, and the handwriting was strong, the ink so black even after sixty years that it looked out of place on the ancient paper.

I know what this is, she thought with a tiny ache. Even before I begin reading, I know.

> *My dear Livy,*
> *Your father says he'll kill me if I come near you again, but I know living without you would be worse. If you love me enough to give up him and the Magnolia the same as I love you enough to risk dying for you, meet me at the stone cellar Friday night at midnight.*

> *We'll leave the Springs. I'll try my best to*
> *make you happy. Be my wife.*
>
> *Yours,*
> *Albert*

The old man whom the Springs called Devil, whom she'd hated for the way he'd let Colley live, the man without a heart or a soul.

He was the writer of this letter.

More than half a century ago, he'd stood at the cellar in the darkness and waited for a woman who never came.

"You gave him up for your father, just like I gave up Colley. Is that what you're trying to tell me?" she asked the old lady whose blue eyes watched her so anxiously.

But Olivia shook her head. "No. I never gave him up at all. Father made it impossible for me to see him. He wouldn't let me near. I kept waiting, thinking, if Albert really loves me, he'll find a way." She bent her face to the cat's soft black fur for a moment, and there were tears on her cheeks when she lifted it again.

"I was on the front porch of the Magnolia the day that Albert drove by on his way to be married," she said slowly, "and I stood out on the steps, straight and tall, because I meant for him to see me there. I wanted him to remember that he loved me. He stood up in the buggy and stared right back at me. Right on down the road, he kept watching, turned around in the buggy, the sun shining off his hair until it looked shiny and almost blue." She closed her eyes and more tears seeped from under her lids. "I wondered how he could marry her."

"But you didn't answer his letter, Aunt. You didn't go to meet him," Lainie tried to explain.

Olivia reached for the fragile note and took it back from

her niece. "I never saw this note until the wind blew my father's strongbox right to me."

"Oh. Oh," Lainie whispered in sudden understanding.

"Father must have found it first. I never saw it." Olivia let the cat slide from her lap, and her hands soothed the note just as she had the fur of the animal. "All this time, this wasted time."

"You would have gone with Albert Rawlins."

"And never looked back. I would rather have been his wife than my father's daughter. It didn't matter that he was nothing but a coal miner from the hills, or that he didn't talk or eat like a gentleman."

Lainie could almost taste the pain in her own throat. "What if his family had hurt your father? Would you have still loved him?"

"Father had a big gun. A . . . pearl-handled revol-revolver." Olivia frowned and stood slowly, the rocker swaying gently as her light weight left it. "I don't know why I remember it so well." She shivered. "He swore to kill Albert with it if he ever caught him at the Magnolia again. He would have, too. He even hired a man to watch for him." Gasping a little, the woman took two agitated steps.

"Be careful." Lainie rose quickly, catching Olivia's elbow to stop her from tumbling off the edge of the porch.

Olivia turned toward her niece and touched Lainie's face jerkily, still holding the note with the other. "That one who tried to hurt Albert, he was a bad one."

"Who was he, Aunt?"

"You know. You talked to him. He came to the Magnolia. Remember the one who had my whistle and wouldn't give it back until Albert made him?"

"Preston? But Aunt, it was Colley . . ." Lainie let the sentence trail off into nothing. The clouds were back again.

Olivia had confused the old man and the grandson, and there was no point in confusing her more.

"Keep a watch out for that one, Lainie. He's bad. I can feel it. I don't care if Father has hired him. Father is not always a good judge of character."

"I'll remember."

"Good. I want you to be safe." Olivia laughed a little. "How awful of me. A daughter shouldn't criticize her father. But she has to leave him if she wants to be a woman. It's not wrong to grow up. It's not wrong to love a man. The wrong comes when you close your heart. Then there's nothing left but a desert of years in front of you. They make a sorry excuse for life."

Lainie wrapped her arms around her aunt, hurting for her and for the young man who'd loved her, for herself and Colley, wherever he was. Olivia let her head drop against Lainie's heart, and they stood together in the sweet, hot summer day with the Magnolia at their backs, looking at the past.

16

"*I hate to take you away from* the house and your visitors, Deborah, but I've got a search warrant," the sheriff said apologetically, wiping sweat from his forehead with the back of his hand. "James Rawlins and his private detective are bound and determined to go through the Magnolia on account of the key we found in the Jaguar."

He twisted to glance back at the two men who waited in the parking lot of the hotel, watching him and the woman who was unlocking the front doors of the place.

Deborah pushed them open, her face confused. "Our visitors are only Bella and Alma, so don't worry about that. But I don't know how Preston came to have one of our keys. Maybe he found it the day he came to see the storm damage. The whole town was in the hotel, it seemed like, and a lot of little things are still missing."

Lainie stayed quiet near one of the rockers, not daring to look at Way, who hovered behind Sheriff Daryl Roberson.

Her cousin had been right that morning; the key had led the investigation straight to the Magnolia before the day was out.

"Hey! You two come on if you expect to get this place searched any time soon," the sheriff shouted in the direction of the waiting men. "And you, Way, tell—"

A truck rattled into the lot off the road, coming far faster than its worn old body seemed to want to, and it came to an abrupt halt near the shiny Oldsmobile that had carried James to the Magnolia.

"What in the hell do they want?" Roberson exclaimed irritably as Ben Sanders and two others climbed out of its cab. Except for the difference in age—Ben was old and the two with him much younger—they looked nearly identical in their caps and boots.

"What are you boys doing here?" Way raised his voice to shout at them.

They kept coming, falling in right behind James and the detective, and Ben answered with his own question. "Somebody said you're huntin' through the Magnolia. Are you?"

"You go on home," the sheriff retorted. "This is none of your business."

"I reckon it is," drawled the big farmer who'd been with Ben at the Magnolia the day before. "I got a wife and three kids, and I live in these parts. I ain't lettin' Colley Rawlins near them."

"That's right," echoed the third one, whom Lainie didn't know at all. "We heard that the woman in the quarry had been raped. What kind of animal would do that?"

"That's a damn lie," Way said furiously. "Nobody knows yet what happened to her."

"Take your tall tales and get, Boles," Sheriff Roberson answered the younger farmer, his voice quiet now that the men had arrived at the steps. "This search is routine police procedure. Nothing to get excited about."

"You better tell the whole town that. The way we've got it figured, it's high time you came to the hotel to ask some questions. Preston ain't the first one that Colley's got rid of, nor the woman, either. What really happened to John Thorne three years ago? You just tell me that," Ben demanded, and his gaze shot to Deborah and Lainie.

Lainie heard the tiny little whimper of surprise that broke from her mother's throat, and her own face paled.

"This has nothing to do with Papa," she said sharply.

Ben saw her then. "Elaina Thorne. You're right smart to keep her handy, Sheriff. She's the best bait I know of to get Rawlins in. He'll come after her, sooner or later. She's another woman he always did like, but maybe she didn't put up a fight. Maybe that's why John's dead, why she ain't in the quarry, too."

"Shut up!" Way took a violent step toward Ben, only to have the sheriff catch his arm.

The detective's face was full of sudden sharp interest as his attention focused on Lainie. "Has she been questioned?" he demanded of Roberson.

"Why in the hell would she have been?" Way answered furiously instead. "She's got nothing to do with this."

James frowned. "Just see that the room that matches the key gets searched," he told his detective.

"We're all going to help," the sheriff told Rawlins. "Way and me, both." Then he turned back to Ben. "When we get back outside, you'd best be gone."

"I'm speakin' for the Springs when I say that you'd best be catching that murderin' son of a bitch and lettin' decent people like us alone," the one called Boles returned in anger.

Lainie stepped into the Magnolia more slowly than the

others, hesitating on the heels of everybody else. They would hurt Colley if they had the chance, she knew it as she turned for one last worried look back at the trio of men.

"Hey, girlie," the third, youngest one called to her, "I got my rifle right out there in the truck, and a bullet that's got Rawlins's name on it. I hope he kissed you real good the last time he seen you, 'cause he ain't gonna get no more chances if I see him comin'."

Lainie slammed the screen behind her in fear. She believed him. "Way!" she cried, and ran to find her cousin.

Colley had finally made up his mind. It was now or never. He couldn't keep waiting. He had to see Elaina.

Since he'd left the truck behind at the farm, along with almost everything else except a few clothes, he'd just have to walk to get to her. It was the same way he'd gotten away three days before.

How did a man go about confessing his worst sin to the woman he loved? He'd thought about all of that, and especially about all that he might lose when he finally told the truth, and he still didn't have any real answers.

It was something he'd just have to do and let the consequences fall.

At the gate that led to Lo-Joe, he turned across the field, but not toward the quarry. Colley avoided it studiously. Instead, he clung to the trees that ran along the edge of the road until he got to the boundary line that separated Blackburn land from Rawlins.

Lo-Joe lay almost directly behind the Magnolia, but the distance was too great and the trees too big for one place to catch a glimpse of the other.

When he got close enough to see the high green corn in

Miss Olivia's garden and the back porches of the hotel on the other side, Colley stopped.

Sweat was pouring off him, partly from the heat of the day and his long walk in it, but mostly from nerves.

He had to find the right words to tell her. He had to have the guts.

If only she would forgive.

Taking a deep breath, he plunged down the nearest row of corn and headed straight to the Magnolia and to Lainie.

"They're just full of hot air," the sheriff said dismissively to Lainie. "I've known all three of them for years. Right now the town is scared to death, but it will calm down."

"Scared people are the most dangerous kind," the private investigator pointed out as he searched the corner room with smooth, quick, expert movements.

Lainie spared him barely a glance. The search that had made her so nervous earlier wasn't important now. "But he said he had a gun."

"Most farmers in these parts carry guns in their trucks," the sheriff said soothingly. "So what? Even if they are on the lookout for Colley, they'd have to find him first to shoot at him, and if they can do that—"

There was a man's shout from outside, and a scream broke through the air, clear and piercing. For a split second, it immobilized the five people in the room.

Lainie shoved past James Rawlins and ran outside to the second-story porch.

Bella Foster was at the corner of the hotel, right below them. Looking at her, Lainie didn't see the man near the tree, close to the garden, until a sudden crack of sound exploded like dynamite, cutting off Bella's second cry.

Gunfire!

The one called Boles had fired the rifle he held from his stance behind the tree. He was not much more than a shadow under the draping limbs, but Lainie saw him as he raised the gun to his eye a second time, the sight toward the garden.

He was drawing a bead on someone in the tall corn, someone whose hair flashed dark and shiny as a raven's wing for an instant in the blaze of merciless sun.

Terror. There was terror running like hot ice in her blood.

"Colley! No! No!"

The rustling of the corn and his own hard breathing obscured the yell that cut through the air, but Colley knew it was a man's voice shouting something. It startled him as he stepped out of the garden into the backyard of the Magnolia, and he looked for the source, squinting into the lowering sun. Its rays glinted off metal.

A gun barrel.

Some fool was pointing a gun right at him.

Pure instinct took over. Colley dived backward, back into the sheltering corn. There was a roar, and a bullet zinged into the ground near him, throwing up dirt. He threw himself flat on the ground, totally confused.

Why were there guns? What was happening? What?

"I saw him! He's there!"

Colley didn't know the squalling male voice, but he recognized instantly the high sweet sound of Lainie Thorne's cry against the wind.

She was there, near the man with the gun.

Daring to lift his head, his heart driving into the earth beneath him until he could only gasp for breath, Colley looked up just in time to see her run heedlessly around the side of the hotel.

She was running right into the path of the gunman.

The barrel glinted again to his right. A woman, not Lainie, screamed.

God. Was he going to shoot her?

"Colley! Colley!"

She was calling for him; he could make out the words now.

Another glint. Didn't she see?

"Get down! Lainie! Get out of here!" Coming to his feet in a rush, shoving his way to the edge of the corn, he shouted like a wild thing at her. "He's got a gun!"

She stopped instead—was she crazy?

Colley was there. He was alive. That was all she could think for a second, then she remembered.

"Run!" she screamed. "They're here to get you, not me! Run!"

What? What was she saying? He couldn't run and leave her.

"Put the gun down, Boles!" Way shouted, but instead Lainie saw the man crouch forward. To shoot again?

With only that thought, she made a rushing leap toward Colley as he hovered at the edge of the garden. He caught at her without even thinking as she knocked him to the ground and covered his body with her own, wrapping her arms and legs about him as tight as she could.

She wouldn't let them kill her witch boy.

"No, no, no," she was sobbing into his ear.

One more deafening gun blast shattered the air, louder and closer than the other, and in the wake of it, a new voice spoke.

"You touch him and I'll blow you to kingdom come."

Devil Rawlins. He had fired a big rifle of his own into the air.

Where had he come from?

Lainie saw his old boots, his baggy overalls, and relief washed down her. However Devil had gotten there, he would protect his grandson.

Colley lay beneath her.

She felt his heart as it slammed again and again into her own. His skin was hot, his eyes wide and black and dazed. He really was alive.

Colley couldn't make sense of anything. All he knew was that she had run to him and was clinging with every ounce of her strength.

"Drop that gun, you damn fool." That was Way's voice, and Colley sensed rather than saw the lowering of the first rifle. There was the sound of a slight scuffle as the deputy forced it out of Boles's hand. "You're under arrest."

"The hell he is! Arrest the real criminal, Blackburn," Boles said hoarsely. "Arrest Rawlins."

"You better be damn glad that I heard what was goin' on and got here in time." Devil's raspy voice shook as he stepped up into Boles's face, separating him from the man on the ground. "If you'd a shot him, you'd have been at the undertaker's before the sun set." Devil gave the man a shove and reached a hand down. "Here, boy."

Colley's hard fingers lifted Lainie off him. He sat upright, holding her with one hand and bracing himself against the ground with the other, and he completely ignored Devil.

Who were all these people, he wondered in bewilderment, and why was James there?

Colley heaved himself to his feet, pulling Lainie up with him as he did.

"Somebody tell me how this happened," Sheriff Roberson said in frustration, sliding his own gun back in his holster.

"I saw it all!"

Bella Foster called out the excited words. She stood quivering with nerves and excitement at the same corner where Lainie had located her just moments earlier.

"Alma and I were visiting Olivia, and we saw someone coming across the back field. When he cut through the corn, we came to tell Deborah, but we met Davis Boles and told him first. He ran and got that horrible gun and just went berserk." Bella wrung her hands together.

"Berserk," echoed Alma faintly from behind the other woman.

"I hollered at him to stop," Boles protested. "All he had to do was give himself up. I knew it was Rawlins. I could see his hair."

Every eye turned to Colley.

"Is this your doing?" he demanded of Devil, still struggling for understanding. "Did you send him after me?"

The old man stiffened, lowering the huge rifle that he'd fired. "I ain't never pulled a gun on any of my kin yet. I don't reckon I'll start now."

"I'm the one looking for you, Colley. Me and the law." James stepped forward.

"You?" he asked his uncle slowly, confused.

"Didn't I tell you that Colley Rawlins would come here?" Ben Sanders demanded of James triumphantly.

"Shut up," Way commanded.

James ignored the whole exchange. "Where's Preston?"

Colley looked from his uncle to the other faces. Lainie's hand tightened around his. "Preston! How should I know?"

"He's gone, Colley. Nobody can find him. Where have you been?" The girl's words spilled out as she clutched at his T-shirt. He caught her fingers with his so that he held both her hands in his.

"I don't know what you're talking about."

"Did you kill my son, you bastard?"

Colley got very still, but Devil exploded in rage.

"You're lettin' grief turn your brain, James. Colley didn't kill his own blood."

"He's no blood of mine." James stepped close to his father in a quick rage. "You dragged him out of the shantytown. You made him equal to my son when he was nothing but the brat that Brodie fathered on river trash. Do you think I give a damn about him, or him about me? But you'd do anything to save him. Well, what about Preston? What about my son? The real Rawlins? Where is he?"

"He killed him, that's what!" Boles raised a shaking hand to point it at Colley. "Just like he killed that woman! And John Thorne, too, if the truth was known."

The entire circle of men—the farmers, James, the detective, even the sheriff—tightened around Lainie and Colley.

They were suffocating her, pressing the life out of the two of them, she thought, and burst out, "Stop it! Leave him alone!"

Ben shouted in outrage, "What kind of woman are you to be clingin' to the likes of Rawlins? Don't you have any shame? You think just because you and your mama kept quiet about John, we can't figure out most of what happened? Deborah"—he turned to find the white-faced woman at the edge of the circle—"they've got Rawlins now. You can tell the truth. Did he kill your husband? Don't stay silent out of fear anymore. Speak!"

The pounding silence lingered over the word—*speak, speak, speak*—as if it loved it.

"Leave Mama out of it. I'm the one she's protecting, not Colley. I'll tell you."

Elaina's voice was so clear it cut like a diamond through the glassy air, and she broke free of Colley's hands before he could drag her back. Joan of Arc might have stood as straight before the fire as she did inside the ring of accusers.

"Lainie," Deborah whispered on a sob.

Colley took a stunned step toward her before the sheriff caught him back. "You don't owe them anything, girl," he pleaded.

"I want them to know." Her face was white and proud as she gazed at the ones about her. "There have been enough whispers. Three years ago, I tried to run away with Colley. We went to one of Devil's old cabins down close to the river to wait for dark. Papa caught us there." Her throat closed down for a minute, and in the throbbing silence, Boles spoke.

"I reckon we all know what he caught you doin'."

This time Colley broke free of the sheriff to lunge for her. His hand found her mouth and covered it so that she couldn't speak anymore, and his other forced her back against the strength of his chest. "Don't. Don't."

But she pushed his hand away. "Papa went crazy. He hit me, knocked me nearly unconscious into a wall. Then he tried to kill Colley with a tobacco spike—"

"I don't believe you," Ben interrupted in contempt. "I knew John. He didn't have it in him. How long will you lie for Rawlins, Elaina?"

She shook a little, as if a wind had blown her.

"Show them, Colley."

For a second, he didn't realize what Lainie was asking. She never looked away from the faces about them. "No," he protested in surprise.

"They're saying you're a cold-blooded murderer. Don't you care?"

He pushed her off him, twisting her body around until she had to face him, holding her with his hands on her shoulders. "What's it to me what they think? All I want is for you to know."

Her eyes were dark with determination. "Then do it for me. I'm tired of staying quiet. I'm tired of the names they call you."

He looked at her in confusion, and then beyond at Deborah, whose body was drawn in anguish. "Tell her to stop. You're her mother. She means to ruin herself and her father, too, when there's no need. It's three years past."

But Deborah shook her head. "She's right. Let the thing be told."

Lainie reached up, as quick as a cat, and caught the neck of his shirt in her two hands, yanking at it in frantic impatience. "Show them."

Colley caught her fingers and pulled them down. "All right. All right, Lainie." But he hesitated a second longer before he gave the neckline one hard, vicious jerk.

It ripped jaggedly, hanging off his shoulder.

"My Lord," Bella whispered into the stillness, putting her hands to her mouth.

The white marks were as long and deep and distinct as they had been days ago at the quarry, but today, they seemed worse, a hundred times worse. Now they were more than scars. They were the marks of Thorne's intent to kill.

Deborah whimpered in her throat, but Lainie looked right into Colley's eyes and never looked away.

"This is what Papa did to Colley," she said huskily, and she let her right hand brush the marks lightly for a second. "They fought. Papa wound up dead. Whatever it was, it wasn't murder."

She had confessed it right to him. It wasn't murder.

Nobody moved or spoke or breathed while he thought about what she had said.

"How many years have I waited to hear you say that, Lainie?" he asked huskily at last. "Why couldn't you say it before now? What if it's too late? You don't know what I've done."

The words broke the spell over the spectators.

James flinched. "What?" he demanded hoarsely. "What have you done?"

"Thorne is still dead, ain't he?" Boles asked. "And there's the woman and Preston to be considered."

"What woman?" Colley asked in puzzlement.

"Don't say more," Way put in quickly. "Not here. You have to be read your rights."

"Damn it, he ain't confessin' to murder," Devil said roughly. "He ain't never killed anybody. He didn't even kill Thorne."

"Then who did? Lainie?" Ben said ironically.

"I did."

The old man's voice had a whistling sound to it as he tried to breathe normally, but his chest rose and fell in agitation.

Lainie's heart stopped.

"I got to the cabin just as Colley passed out. Thorne dropped on him and raised that silver death, meanin' to kill what was mine. I threw myself on Thorne. We went backwards together. He slipped in blood—Colley's blood—and when he fell under me, I grabbed his hand. He still had the spike, and I pushed it into—"

"Stop!" Deborah cried, half strangled. "I don't want to hear more."

"You?" Colley took a step toward his grandfather.

"I killed him, defendin' my own. Just like John was defendin' her. The thing was, only one of us could win. It had to be me if you were goin' to live. It was done before I knew."

Lainie's voice was ragged. "Why didn't you tell it before?"

Devil's eyes were wry. "You oughta be able to figure that one out."

"You wanted her to hate me." Colley had the answer so fast that Lainie didn't have time to think about it.

"Is that possible?" The old man didn't wait for an answer. He just turned toward the sheriff and let the rifle slide to the ground at the man's feet. "I reckon you'll want me to come with you."

The sheriff nodded slowly. "You, and Colley, too, Mr. Rawlins. There's too many questions I don't have any answers to. I still don't know Preston's whereabouts."

"You'd better call your lawyer," the private investigator advised Devil unexpectedly.

The old man shook his head. "I got no use for one. But you, Colley. . . ." He reached out as if to catch his grandson's arm, but he didn't quite do it.

"I don't need anything from you." Colley faced Way. "Where's your car?" he asked the deputy.

Albert followed the two of them, moving slowly on his stiff leg. When he caught up with them at Way's vehicle, he said bluntly, "Colley."

His grandson went stiff. He didn't turn to look at the old man, but it didn't stop Devil from speaking. "I'm old. I don't matter. But you don't know what you're in for if they find Preston dead, boy. They'll be looking to crucify you. They don't understand you."

"What do you care?" Colley's face was hard. "Take me to the jail, Blackburn, or wherever in the hell it is you want me to go."

"It's mostly for questioning," Way began, but the old man ignored the deputy.

"Tell me what it is you want, Colley. I can get it for you. Anything."

Colley swung around at last to confront Devil, and

the emotion he couldn't hide any longer twisted his mouth.

"Can you give me back Lainie and me the way we could have been if you and Thorne and everybody else had just left us alone?"

"You know I can't."

"Then what is it that you have that I would want?"

Devil hesitated. "Nothin'," he said at last in defeat. "Nothin' at all."

Part 5

Love's Wages

17

Colley really hadn't killed Papa.

Lainie could barely think to answer the thousand questions that Roberson put to her again and again that night, questions about Colley and Albert and Papa.

While the barrage went on and on, the refrain echoed in her head: Colley didn't kill Papa.

Those four little words made life worth living.

Mama cried endlessly while she talked to the sheriff, and Dr. Maxwell finally got called to Olivia's front parlor as well. He fidgeted with his glasses while they questioned him. His answers finished off what Devil had told. No, said the doctor, he had never thought Colley had stabbed Thorne to death. He had lost so much blood so fast that it was a miracle he had survived himself.

The sheriff finished his questions just before midnight as they all sat in a circle of exhausted memory.

"The state could bring charges against Albert Rawlins,"

he concluded reluctantly. "I'd be acting as the state and I'd be the one to do it if you want."

"No." Deborah was sharp in her refusal. "What more could be gained? I won't testify, and I won't ruin another minute of Lainie's life by making her relive it. Please, can't it just end right here?"

Roberson rubbed the back of his neck. "I reckon we can call it finished," he finally conceded. "Unless something new comes up." He picked up his hat from a nearby chair and said to Susan as she opened the door for him, "That's one down. Tomorrow, I just have to figure out who that woman is, what she's doing in the quarry, and where Preston is. Maybe I'll get lucky and find him holed up in some big ol' country club with a mixed drink and a golf club, partying so hard he just forgot the time."

He laughed tiredly, but Susan didn't respond at all.

Colley answered his own set of questions down at the jail.

No, he didn't kill Preston.

Yes, he had threatened him.

And then there were the questions he stubbornly refused to answer at all: where was he last Saturday night? Why had he disappeared from the Springs for three days?

Jerry Byrne demanded at last, "What's it going to take to make you answer, Rawlins?"

"Let me talk to Lainie," Colley said to Way, ignoring Byrne.

"Why?"

"I've got to tell her something."

"Will what you're going to say hurt her?"

Colley flushed. "I hope not. I've got to say it before I answer any more questions."

Way and he eyed each other a long moment. Then Way

turned. "It's gone midnight," he observed slowly. "Sheriff Roberson just left Olivia's. I doubt Lainie's in any condition to come here to talk to you. But I could bring her tomorrow morning . . . if she'll come."

"Then I'll wait," Colley said insistently.

At last, as Way nodded and turned to leave, the words burst from Colley. "Devil? What's going to happen to him?"

"We got told not long ago to send him home. I might could let you go home, too, if—"

"No. I'm not going back to the farm," Colley said with a wry twist of his mouth. "I don't reckon there's any place left for me in this town to spend the night except the jail."

Bella Foster dumbfounded the Springs.

She defended Colley Rawlins.

"Lainie, honey," she told the girl bright and early the next morning, "I'm not saying he's a saint, but when I saw those awful marks on his shoulder, I felt such a wave of pity pass over me. I told the Ladies' Auxillary last night that I believe we have misjudged him somewhat. He's more innocent than guilty of John's death. The old man, now, I'm not so sure he shouldn't be punished."

"I think he has been," Lainie managed, remembering the look on Devil's face when Colley had turned away from him yesterday. "We want to forget."

"I quite understand. We'll say no more about it. I got up early to come by Olivia's and tell you the news. They've fined Davis Boles for that wild shooting spree yesterday, and have you heard what they've decided at the forensic lab in Nashville? I happened to be talking to Jerry Byrne a few minutes ago, and he said they'd just gotten word that it definitely was a woman. How do they know, I wonder?" Bella mused, fanning herself with her handkerchief.

"What else do they know?" Lainie asked unwillingly, remembering Boles's claim.

"Lord, what all did Jerry tell me? She's been in the quarry two—or did he say three?—years, and she was middle-aged when she died. Oh, yes, she had a necklace with a gold heart on it. Once there was a picture inside it, but it had been destroyed by the water. Pity. It might have told us her identity."

Lainie shivered. "Or how she got in Lo-Joe."

"Don't you worry. Colley Rawlins didn't put her there. I feel it in my bones." Bella paused and, much to Lainie's shock, added with an earthy sigh, "I never realized until yesterday just how fine his bones are, but I could suddenly see quite clearly why you are fond of him. Yes, indeed."

Way arrived as Bella was leaving. "What'd that old gossip have to say?" he demanded, frowning.

Lainie choked on nervous laughter. "You wouldn't believe it if I told you."

"Maybe not. Come on outside, Lainie. It's a fine morning. Walk with me."

They stepped together off the porch of Olivia's house and turned by mutual consent toward the distant Magnolia.

"Colley denies that he killed Preston," Way said abruptly. "But he won't answer any more questions until he talks to you and tells you whatever it is that's eating him. He agreed to stay last night at the jail and talk today if you'd see him this morning."

Lainie stopped at the fence. "I don't know what's happening to me. I think I'm having one of Aunt Olivia's crystal days after years of clouds. I want a life. I don't want to wind up like Devil or Aunt. This is me, Way. My time. Papa hated the witch boy, but I love him."

She shivered.

Opening the gate in the fence that separated the yard of the house from the hotel grounds, Way let her step through before he did. "Am I supposed to be surprised? All I can say is, you pick your moments, Lainie. You've decided to love him after the whole town calls him a murderer. But I'm not complaining. What you're saying makes what I came for easier. I want you to go with me to the jail where Colley is."

Her hand went to her throat. "If I do, I have to tell him the truth, and I'm not sure I can."

"What truth?"

"About what happened with Preston. What will I do if Colley hates me?"

"You're afraid he won't forgive you? He's not going to like it, that's sure. He may brood over it a long time. But Lainie, I wish I was as sure of heaven as I am that Colley's going to want you, anyway."

They had circled the side of the Magnolia without either of them really noticing where they were. The stone cellar sat bare in front of them. Way stopped to lean on it, propping his boots on a pile of rocks that promptly rolled away, and the morning sun struck brightly all around them.

"If you two—"

"What?" Lainie demanded of her suddenly still cousin.

Way stood abruptly, looking down at his feet, at a bare patch of ground where the heavy shade of the maple that once sheltered the cellar had vanquished the grass. "What's this?" he asked slowly, bending to get a closer look.

A dark, rusty stain had been hidden by the pile of rocks. It spread over the exposed flat layer of limestone near the cellar door.

"I don't know," Laine answered in surprise, "but there's Jerry. I think he's looking for you."

The other deputy was huffing as he hurried toward them, and Way straightened.

"You ain't believing this, son," Jerry called.

"What's happened?"

"I think you were right. That Tate guy that you kept looking for is back. He's down at the station now, acting like a man about to confess. Sheriff said to get you there fast."

Lainie's heart gave a thump. "I want to go," she told Way.

He made a wry grimace. "Roberson might not let you stay, but come on."

Colley Rawlins was one of the people in the small conference room at the police station. Lainie knew it the second she stepped across the threshold, and she stopped short.

He came to his feet instantly.

"Lainie!'

One quick look at him was all she dared. He still wore the shirt he'd had on the day before, but he'd tried to pull the torn shoulder together with a safety pin. His hair was thick and tangled, and her fingers twitched to comb through its black weight.

Please, love me, Colley, in spite of what I did with Preston.

Had he heard her silent plea? He stepped toward her involuntarily before Way intervened. "There's no time now for you and her. Wait."

Lainie was right there, close enough for him to see the pulse trembling in her tanned throat, and he couldn't touch her? Rebellion flashed over Colley.

"What in the hell is go—?"

The sight of Lloyd Tate as he appeared in the doorway cut off Colley's sentence.

"Don't ask me," Way murmured, answering anyway.

"Everybody sit," the sheriff commanded, before his eye fell on Lainie.

"What's she doing here?"

"I brought her," Way answered.

"It's all right," Tate interrupted. "I think she'll be interested in my story. But I'm telling it for him."

It was Colley he motioned toward, and Colley's face registered surprise.

"Don't do me any favors," he said warily.

"I never meant to," Tate retorted, "but I don't think I can help myself. Besides, somebody in this office is trying to track me down. I've already heard that you're looking for information about me." He directed the comment straight at Way.

"How would you know that?" Way demanded. "I went through the right channels."

"Because I've got connections. I worked with the Georgia Bureau of Investigation for several years."

"Georgia!" Jerry Byrne exclaimed.

"That's right. Until my wife disappeared and they decided I was a prime suspect."

Tate's voice was so matter-of-fact that Lainie could only stare at him.

"The woman in the quarry," Way guessed.

This time Tate's face twisted involuntarily. "Yes," he agreed. "She's Karen McKinley. Mrs. Douglas McKinley. That's my real name, not Tate."

The man found a nearby chair and pulled it up to sit in it heavily.

"So you've come back of your own free will to confess?" the sheriff asked dubiously.

A tiny muscle twitched beside Tate's mouth. "Confess to what?"

"You killed her. And Preston Rawlins—where is he?" With every question, Jerry took a step nearer the man.

"God keep me from rube cops," Tate said ironically, and his gray eyes glittered. "I didn't kill anybody."

This time Way intervened. "You knew both of the victims. You were in all the right places. Jerry's asking legitimate questions. You're not going to say that Colley did it, like the rest of the town, are you?"

Tate twisted a moment to look at the still man in the corner. "So they've really got you taking the rap, have they, Rawlins?" he asked, amused. "It's what I figured would happen. I'll tell my story once, and then I'm out of here. I only came back because Karen would want me to, for him."

"Who? Colley?" the sheriff asked in amazement.

"My wife's real name was Colleen Brown. She was his mother."

The entire room broke out in an uproar. Lainie heard it through the echo in her own head: his mother. Colley's mother.

Across from her, he came up out of the little corner chair. Hurt and incredulity made his words hard. "You're lying. Devil said she died years ago."

Tate—or McKinley—looked at him with ironic sympathy. "I think you know by now that Devil Rawlins would do anything to hold on to you. But what would be my reason to lie?"

His mother. His mother had lain at the bottom of the quarry. And suddenly, Colley knew why. He didn't really need to ask. "She came back because—"

"Because of you and Brodie." Tate's face darkened. "We met seventeen years ago, when I was stationed in Texas. I was twenty-seven then, already started on a career with the air force, in intelligence. She called herself Karen, not Colleen. I never heard that name for her until I traced her here a few months ago. When I asked her to marry me, she said no. When I kept asking, she told me why.

"She was from a broken home, and she'd grown up in foster care. When she was sixteen, she ran away, and to live, wound up working on a big farm. The rest of her story was so wild, I didn't half believe it. She fell in love with the rich farm owner's son, she got pregnant by him, he died in a quarry accident, she had the baby, the rich owner took him, gave her money to forget, and put her off the farm with a warning not to come back after the baby.

Tate paused for breath and shook his head. "I heard all that and still wanted to marry her. We traveled the world while I was in the service. She was happy except for one thing: we couldn't have a baby, no matter what we tried. Karen said it was God's judgment on her for giving up that first child.

"After I did twenty years, I retired from the air force, and we moved to Atlanta. I was still young enough that I wanted to work. I took on a job with the Bureau. I liked the work and the place where we lived. I thought we'd have a good life, but everything went wrong. She got to the point she couldn't stand up. She fell constantly. At Emory, they ran tests. Lou Gehrig's disease, they said."

Tate rose stiffly and crossed to the window. Lainie could hear the floor creaking under his feet.

"Have you ever seen anybody who has Lou Gehrig's disease?" He turned to face the people around him in the room. "No? Then you're lucky. They told her, three to five years. They said she'd get to where she couldn't walk, or talk, or even swallow. Chances were good she'd choke to death. Then they gave her a cane and sent her home to die. She worried all the time about the baby she'd left. At night, she'd dream of his father and call out for Brodie. My life was nearly as big a hell as hers.

"One day she just disappeared. Our bank account had been emptied. I never found out how she managed to leave. There was no trail. She just never came back. I knew what she'd done. She'd gone back to try to find that old life somewhere in Tennessee. I didn't know exactly where, or even who. She was too afraid to speak Brodie's last name, even in her sleep."

Tate fumbled in his back pocket for a moment, finally bringing out a leather wallet. He flipped it open and looked down at the picture. "This was Karen. Colleen."

His tread was light as he walked across the room, his gray eyes looking straight at Colley. "Here."

Colley hesitated, then reached for the extended wallet to look down in it.

Lainie's heart twisted for him.

"I don't—I'm sorry, but I don't know—"

"You've seen her before." This time Tate was talking to Lainie.

"Me?"

"She came to the Springs and stayed at the Magnolia. You keep all your registers. I told your mother that I'd heard you had them dating back a hundred years and asked her to let me see them. She took me to the room where you store them, and I found her name—Karen McKinley—in the one you used three summers ago. Surely you noticed her. She would have had the cane with her."

Colley made a strangled sound. "I remember her," he said in quick, stunned surprise. "Lainie, she was the woman who fell. You wanted me to take her to her room."

Now Lainie knew, too. "The one who wanted the room in the back. It was the day—" She broke off. The rest of the memory had nothing to do with this jail and these people.

Tate nodded, satisfied. "I thought she would find you somehow. She had to know if her son was all right before . . ."

"Before she went to the quarry and committed suicide," Way concluded slowly.

"As near as I can put it together," Tate said huskily, running his hands over his face. "She managed to walk across the field behind the Magnolia. I don't want to think about how long it took her to get that short distance. It's why she left me when she did, as soon as the diagnosis was confirmed. She meant to come here and end it before she got so sick that she couldn't. I imagine she's the one who picked the lock and left the gate open. I thought of her as soon as I heard the story."

Tate reached for the wallet in Colley's hand and looked down at the woman in the picture, letting his thumb caress the snapshot face. "I don't blame Karen as much as I used to. But it hurt Tuesday when I heard that there was a woman in the quarry. I knew who it was. The necklace she was wearing was my first gift to her. It was her way of remembering me even when she went back to him."

Colley stood, his movements jerky. "How did you find out where she was if she never told you who we were?"

We. He meant Devil and himself. Did Colley even know what he'd just said? Lainie wondered. He had made himself a Rawlins, a part of the *we*.

"Don't you know yet? Preston led me right to you."

"If he did, it was to cause trouble."

"Your grandfather finally got wind of the fact that Ka-Colleen was missing. He traced us everywhere, all these years, and I didn't even know it until she was dead, damn him. When nobody could find her, he sent Preston as a last resort to get to the bottom of it all. When I realized somebody was tracking me, I decided to turn the tables. Like I said, I had worked with intelligence awhile, and Preston wasn't good at what he'd been sent to do. He was no Devil Rawlins. The only mistake I made was, at first, I thought Preston was you. Karen's boy."

Lainie bit back her protest, her "no, no, not ever."

Tate laughed. "Talk about being sick. Then your grandfather sent you to bring Preston home. He wasn't expecting the mess Preston had gotten into, was he? You couldn't just yank him back. It took you two weeks to get him out of his troubles. I'd have given money to see the old bastard squirm, knowing you were down there so close to me. But Devil thought he was safe: he didn't know that I knew. And the second I laid eyes on you, Colley Rawlins, I knew everything. You don't look like her, but you've got the same high-powered soul."

"Why didn't you tell me?"

"Because I hated you. You were Brodie's. You'd ruined a good part of my life. And because you show your raisings. Rough as hell. I wanted to know all of it, and know what made you that way. I made up my mind when you took Preston back with you that I'd go, too. I'd follow you right to Karen."

Tate slid the wallet carefully into his pocket. "I did that much at least," he said in a painful whimsy. "You didn't know me from Adam when you looked at me here in the Springs, and I was careful to stay out of Albert's way, but Preston knew me from the beginning. He was scared out of his wits for about a minute, and then it was funny to him, especially when he found out that I wasn't interested in facing the old man. Preston thought I was a coward, but having me here gave him a secret that you two didn't have. Preston's the kind to enjoy secrets. I'm the kind who likes to goad jackasses like him. It was easy to pull his

strings. It was why I made up to Elaina Thorne. It was
how I got him to go out to the quarry so I could see it
firsthand."

I believe him, Lainie thought, all of what he's saying.
She didn't know why his story rang so true; she just knew
it was.

"Where is Preston now?" the sheriff demanded.

Tate twisted to look at Roberson. "Ask her," he advised,
pointing at Lainie.

"Who, Elaina?" the sheriff answered in mild surprise.

"He was coming to get her the last time I saw him. It was
last Friday night."

"No," Lainie protested, a flush rising to her cheeks.
Colley sat up straighter.

"He wasn't coming to get you?" Tate asked dubiously.
"He said he was."

"Not Friday night. It was Saturday that I was supposed
to—to meet him," she stumbled.

But Tate shook his head emphatically. "I saw him
Friday night. He'd had a row with Colley, and Colley had
ordered him to stay away from her. He was trying to stop
a—a date Preston had arranged with Elaina for Saturday
night." He looked from Colley to the sheriff. "He meant to
spite Colley and come and get her right then. Before the
night was over, he said he'd . . . well, never mind what he
said he and Elaina Thorne were going to do. He kept trying to call her from the phone on my boat. When he
couldn't get her, he left and said he was coming to the
hotel, anyway."

Lainie sat up straighter, her cheeks blazed, but she
wrapped some of her aunt's dignity about herself. "Preston
didn't come to the Magnolia Friday."

"Yes, he did," Tate contradicted. "I came on Saturday,
and his tire tracks were all over the parking lot. I couldn't

help feeling that I should have stopped Preston, but on Saturday morning when I saw you, you were fine. I was a fool to worry. It was nothing to you to spend the night with him."

"But I didn't. It was—" Lainie broke off. What could she say in front of Colley?

"So we know that Preston definitely drove to the Magnolia Friday night," Way puzzled slowly. "And nobody has seen him since."

"But that's not true, Way," Lainie said insistently, trying to remind him without words.

"I want to talk to you, alone." Colley's face was determined and he stepped closer to her.

"Colley."

The hard demand in Way's voice made the other man swing to face him.

"The boots that you're wearing . . . did you wear them last Saturday night?"

"What?"

The entire room stared at Way in the same bewilderment that Colley did.

"Did you wear them Saturday night?"

"Yeah. So what?"

"Because when you were sitting in the chair, you had them out in front of you. There's what looks to be concrete on the bottom of the right one, and there's a trace of it along the side of the heel." Way indicated Colley's right foot. "Wonder where you got it?"

Blankly, Colley considered the question, inspecting his own boot. Then he pulled in a sharp breath. "I—" There was nothing he could say. He looked from Way.

"That's what I thought." Way spoke to the sheriff, but his gaze stayed locked on Colley's guilty face. "We have to go back to the Magnolia."

"Not again! Why? We searched it, every inch, just yesterday," Jerry protested. "Hell, there's not a spider in the place that I don't know."

"We didn't search the stone cellar. We'll have to pry open the door. It's been concreted shut."

Colley got even more still, but the sheriff and Jerry spoke simultaneously. "The stone cellar!"

"I think he's having a hunch," said Tate with rough humor.

"No hunch. I know." Way shot another hard look at Colley. "This morning I saw a big stain under some rocks close to the door. It couldn't have been there long. Rain would wash most of it away. You know what it looked like? Like blood."

"He's in the cellar?" Jerry asked with a gasp.

Way was completely wrong, but all Lainie could manage to point out in front of the others was, "The place is flooded from a leaking pump. The water must be three feet deep inside."

"All the more reason to hide a body there," Way said implacably. "If I've made a mistake, it's not a big deal. But if I'm right . . ."

"Who would have put him in the cellar, though?"

Way's eyes flickered to Colley again at Jerry's question, but all he said was, "I don't know yet."

The sheriff grunted in irritation and stood. "One of you go get some shovels and a pick."

"Lainie can come with me," Way decided. "Aunt Deb and Aunt Olivia will want to know what's going on. She can help me explain."

But Colley moved suddenly, reaching out to catch Lainie's arm and tug her from Way. "Lainie, let me talk to you. I've got to."

Lainie backed away from him, afraid of what was happening around her. "Not now."

Way looked from one to the other, but he spoke to Colley. "I don't understand it all, but I've got a real good idea of what you're trying to tell her. If we find what I think we're going to find in the cellar, and if you got that concrete on your boot and on the porch of the Magnolia the way I think you did, I'm going to finish the job Boles started on you yesterday."

"Go ahead," Colley challenged, suddenly angry. "Do it, quick. If it'll get her to listen, I'll stand here and let you beat the hell out of me."

No, no, no.

The little words floated like quiet ghosts in Lainie's head.

She could hear the sound of hammers as the men chipped away at the door in the yard behind the Magnolia. Standing there on the long side porch, she kept her gaze fastened on Aunt Olivia's house. Deborah stood on that porch, a carbon copy of her daughter, watching as the heavy wood of the door cracked at the top.

The sheriff had called James and his detective and Devil Rawlins.

Colley was there, too, quiet and restrained, waiting to get to her. Roberson had ordered him to wait in the shade under a dogwood tree over by Olivia's fence. Colley was choosing to do as he was told for the time being, but he meant to corner Lainie at his first opportunity. She knew it, just like she knew that she wasn't going to let him.

He was going to ask her who she'd been with Saturday night, and she didn't know the answer anymore.

Why were they all acting as if they were really going to find something? Lainie thought in quiet horror. She felt numb, removed from everything, as if she were wrapped in insulation.

There's nobody there. There can't be.

I know that much. Way should know, too. Doesn't he remember?

Nobody is in the cellar.

It was like a child's song, spinning around and around in her head. Mary had a little lamb—nobody's in the cellar dead—London Bridge is falling down—nobody's in the cellar dead.

A busy butterfly landed on a stalk of spirea nearby, its wings glimmering like jewels in the sunlight.

Way went past her in a blind hurry, and she caught his arm, holding him tightly.

"I'll explain things later," he tossed at her impatiently, but she refused to release him.

"You know he can't be in the cellar," she said insistently. "They sealed it on Saturday morning."

It was getting funnier and funnier. Worse, it was scary. She couldn't stop to give him time to speak.

"Preston came to me in the room above us on Saturday *night*. Don't you see?" Lainie caught her breath, tried to stop laughing, and said on a sob, "Way, if he was dead—who did I go to bed with?"

18

ME.

You went to bed with me. Why can't you feel that? Why don't you know it?

Colley's body was strung as tightly as a whipcord as he made himself stay still at the edge of the yard. He knew by Lainie's face what she was saying to Way. If he had to, he would confess right there in front of everybody. He had done everything but that.

It was the only thing he could think of, waking or sleeping, what had happened in the corner room just opposite them.

It replayed in his mind every instant, what he had done to her last Saturday night. . . .

On that night, the bright moon had been working its way inexorably through the heavy-laden tree branches. Glowing sparks of hot moon rays glittered even on the clapboard wall that was deepest in the nightshade cast by the nearby elm.

He looked up at the balcony and the room on the corner, and the breath felt heavy in his chest. She was going to hate him for this.

And as if that alone weren't enough to deter him from the course of action that he was about to take, there was another consideration: Lainie's life was her own. She had made it clear that he had nothing to do with her anymore.

He thought about those two facts, but he kept walking toward the hotel looming in the night before him. He had left his truck parked at the deserted swimming pool down the road.

Colley stopped just at the old stone cellar. It looked odd; there was a tree missing, the one that had blown over.

But he found a deep, dark corner beside the cellar and hid himself in it, trying to keep his feet from the concrete that was still damp from the day's work.

Now all he had to do was wait and make sure that her would-be lover had understood that Colley meant what he had said the previous night, after he finally got a grip on himself and forced his hands down, to keep from choking his damned cousin.

Get out, Preston. Don't go near her ever again.

Colley was through with Preston's games and with Elaina's, too. She didn't love his cousin. She wasn't going to crawl in bed with him, either, no matter what. The thought left him growling like an animal, the sound vibrating in the back of his throat.

And you, Miss Elaina Thorne, will just have to get over it. For once this summer, you can't have your stubborn little way.

She was up there in that room alone. He was the only

man around now who knew she was there, and what she was waiting for.

Nerves stung in the back of his neck and down his spine.

God Almighty, he'd stood enough the last four weeks. What did she think he was made of, that she could just go to bed with Preston right under his nose? She wasn't going to stay up in that room, either, hoping and wishing for something he wasn't going to let happen. He was going to go up there and drag her out, march her across the yard to her aunt's house, and make her stay there, even if he had to tie her to the place. She couldn't sleep at the Magnolia tonight.

Just the thought of what she had planned for up there was making him bleed to death.

Self-survival, that's what this was, he thought wryly as he climbed the stairs. With each step, his heart pounded a little harder, beating like a tom-tom against his ribs.

Opening the black screen and wincing at its painful screak, he knocked on the door with his bare knuckles.

Silence.

Again he knocked.

"Lainie." Surely she could hear him as he bent near the screen on her opened window. He made his low voice insistent, and the only other sounds that were distinguishable were the rattling of a truck passing out on the highway and the whirring of the fan in the window on the opposite side.

He pressed close to the screen to see into the dark room. It was pitch-black except for two lights: the same moon that was setting the backyard on fire was streaming through the fan, making the beams dance like magic in an enchanted circle on the floor, four feet from the shadowy bulwark of the bed.

The second light was so very tiny . . . and so very important.

It was a candle guttering low beside the bed on a table, and what it caught in its tiny flickers of light made him stop breathing.

Her breast.

Naked, impudent, perfect.

The little flame lingered on the smooth, pert roundness, warming it with a yellow halo of light as she lay motionless on the bed beside it. That tiny ring of illumination, what it held, turned him hot from his head to his groin.

Breath came back into him with a gasping whoosh, and he straightened with a vicious upward thrust of his body, throwing his head back against the peeling paint of the wall, his hands clutching at his shirt.

Don't look.

But the image of her creamy breast and the way it began a gentle slope into her shoulder was already burned into his brain. It was behind his eyelids when he closed them.

She was asleep, he realized suddenly. Asleep. He had no business staring at her like some lowlife Peeping Tom.

Don't look.

How in the hell could a woman go to sleep when she was expecting a man?

Where in damnation did she get this idea, to wait for Preston as naked as the day she was born? His sweet, innocent Lainie, sleeping like a baby—without a stitch.

Blood was pounding in his temples, and pooling fast and heavy between his legs.

"No."

He spoke the one word out loud forcefully. What was he denying? Her? Himself? His own body?

Or what he was about to do?

He moved without even meaning to, in a dream, as though strings pulled him along. Quietly, he slid off his boots so that he'd make no noise when he stepped in the room. He took an undue amount of care in standing them on the porch, beating down his conscience even as he sat them side by side.

One of his hands was wet and grainy when he moved it from the boot. Some of the concrete, he thought impatiently, wiping his palm down his jeans leg. Then he sucked in a deep, steadying breath and reached for the knob.

The door rattled an instant, and he finally understood that it was locked. He had no key. Preston had it, maybe. The growling was back in his throat before he realized it. Then the old, thin screen in the window beside him pulled quietly and neatly out of a corner of its long frame with only the urging of his fingers.

He bent to step through the opening he'd made, letting the screen drop back in place, and came silently to his full height, in the room now, with just her.

He wished for the key again. If he'd had it, he would have thrown it away for good.

Breathing hard, he stood still, waiting for her to stir and order him out, or pull the covers up over herself indignantly.

But she didn't.

"Lainie." He was begging. If she woke up now, he might calm down. Get a grip. Remember why he couldn't do this.

The sound of his barefooted steps to the bed was hidden by the buzzing fan.

The candlelight seemed to spread and diffuse its light, widening its glow, inviting him to see more of the treasures it guarded.

She was on her back on the sheets and atop some kind of pajamas that were crumpled under her shoulder. Her head was turned away from him, leaving only her profile and the long slender line of her throat for him to see. On the snowy pillow, the dark strands of her hair were pure silk. One of her knees was bent outward.

She had no covering except a flimsy towel, worn thin from years of service at the Magnolia. It wrapped her diagonally, concealing only enough to drive him mad.

Brown, smooth arms.

Flat belly.

The hint of satiny legs and tiny-ankled feet somewhere in the darkness beyond the range of the candle.

One breast hidden . . . one revealed.

He could not have stopped himself if it meant he would die to continue; he'd just have to die, right here, tonight.

His hand shook when he reached out; it wavered; and it veered suddenly, to snuff out the waiting candle.

The darkness pulsed with his own wanting. Just her and him, alone, here where nobody watched. The two of them, and the whirling dervish of light at the end of the bed that insisted he do something.

Some last shred of willpower made him shake the bed.

"Lainie," he said, one more time, and didn't even recognize his own voice. He was strangling with passion.

Something slid from the bed, hitting the floor with a thud. He bent to fumble for it, and when he found it—a bottle—a pungent liquid spilled out over his hand as he picked it up.

Gin.

Just how much was inside her and how much he'd just spilled on the floor, he didn't know. But this close, he could smell it as it mingled with her delicate soap and the clean sweet smell of her hair. He set it beside the candle, his movement rough.

The quick flash of his anger momentarily tempered the desire he was battling. Lainie didn't drink. She had no business even coming here tonight, and her getting stoned-out drunk was just another example of how much damage had been done to her this summer.

His Lainie, naked and drunk, waiting in a hotel room for a man.

He wanted to stay angry, or better yet disgusted, but the hot surge of pure lust that the thought stirred in him was far, far stronger.

He'd shake her awake, that was all.

Instead, his fingers touched her unerringly right where the light had anointed her skin . . . on the gentle swell of her breast.

Too dark to see much.

He could hear, though, hear himself panting in the quiet room.

He could still think: this was very, very wrong.

And he could feel. Oh, God, he could feel. Silky skin, warm and firm; thrusting nipple, startled and hard against his palm.

She stirred and murmured a laugh that made him jerk his hand away and freeze, as still as a stone statue.

He'd heard her laugh a hundred times, husky and not quite sure, and he loved it.

He loved her.

Right here, at his fingertips, was all he ever wanted. Just his, just tonight.

She had been waiting for another man, his conscience argued. In this state, she might never know that he hadn't come.

She wouldn't know who had stood over her like this, dying for her, wondering why he could never have her.

And the next thought was so huge, so logical, that it had him in its grasp at its inception. He surrendered to it without even a struggle.

It was why he was here, why he'd blocked the other

man's way to her, why he'd wanted them locked in this room together. It was why he'd taken off his boots, so that he wouldn't awaken her until it was much too late.

He would take Preston's place.

He would be her lover for this one intoxicating night.

And he had been.

The memory let go of him for one merciful minute, and Colley was in the present again, at the Magnolia in the bright sunlight.

She and Way were still there, and the yard was full of people intent on cracking open the cellar door.

The world rushed back around him. So did his own guilt.

God forgive me, and you forgive me, too, Lainie. Please.

19

She heard the sudden shout, but she didn't understand what was being said.

She heard the cry of a man. James Rawlins.

Why would he be crying? Out of joy, because his son wasn't there?

Voices, the voices of a thousand people, it seemed, roared around her.

Sheriff Roberson came closer and called to Way, "We found him. You were right. It's over."

"What?" she whispered, her lips numb.

"Lainie, listen to me," her cousin said firmly, but she heard the alarm in his voice. As the world spun, he grabbed at her. The sky that should have been blue was turning red and black. Breathing deep, clasping Way's arms, holding on to consciousness by sheer force, she laughed.

Way stared at her, letting his fingers clutch her shoulders tightly, letting her reach her own trembling fingers to him and hold on in a panic.

But before he could offer any answers to the questions on her lips, another cry was heard from the direction of the cellar. It was barely distinguishable.

"—gun! There's a gun here, too. Look at this, Way!"

Way released her and turned back to the crowd at the corner of the house.

Lainie couldn't see the men in the backyard, but she could see Susan, who'd stepped out on the side porch of Olivia's house opposite her and the Magnolia. The big woman laid a hand on Deborah's arm as the two of them stood in sick horror at sight of what had been pulled from the cellar.

"Get this body covered!" the sheriff was roaring at his deputies. "Where is that damn ambulance we called for?"

"Oh, God, oh, God, my boy!" James was keening. "What will I tell his mother?"

"This gun—it's at least fifty years old. Almost in mint condition, if the water hasn't ruined it. It has to be the murder weapon." The private investigator was making it clear that the local force might have found the body, but he knew his stuff. "He's been shot, once right at the heart and once low in the groin."

Lainie clapped her hand to her mouth to stop her own cry.

Colley Rawlins came up off the ground in a surge of movement.

"Catch him!" the detective said sharply.

"Get your hands off me," Colley told the man who'd dared to make a grab at him. The agent's hand wavered, and Colley went past him, straight to Lainie. He didn't ask; he just pulled her from Way, hugging her up tight against himself, and pushed her head down to his chest to shield her from what was happening.

"He's dead. He's really dead," Lainie said to him blankly.

"Be careful with that gun," somebody ordered brusquely,

and at that moment, Jerry headed for Lainie's corner of the hotel, the gun held cautiously in front of him in his gloved hand. It was still dripping water. The detective fell in behind him.

"Don't touch it, but look. Have either of you ever seen this before?" Jerry asked the two caught in the quiet embrace.

"No." Colley's answer was quick and blunt.

Lainie wished hers could have been, too. She hadn't seen it before, not with her eyes, anyway, but she knew it.

It was large and silver, and it had an ornate pearl handle with a silver *B* engraved in it.

She turned her face into Colley's torn dirty shirt and shivered.

"Lainie?" His arms tightened. "Don't be scared. There's no need for you to be afraid."

"Let me . . . let me see that." The voice that spoke came from the backyard. It was rough and choked. Colley reacted to it with a quick twist toward the sound. Lainie felt his movement as she leaned against him, and she looked up to see Devil standing at the corner, his overalls heavy around him.

"Sure, Mr. Rawlins," Jerry said in agreeable surprise. "It's a Colt .45. They used to call them Peacemakers."

"I know what it is," the old man said raggedly. "But that one never made any peace. Never."

Susan had drawn closer and closer from the house next door. When she spoke, she was just beyond them. She said resignedly, "You'd best put that thing away. It's caused nothing but heartache since it turned up again last week."

"We found this gun under Preston Rawlins's body," Jerry said flatly. "Do you know where it came from?"

Susan tried to answer, but her words got swallowed up in the noise.

An ambulance came roaring down the highway, its blue lights flashing, its sirens wailing as it pulled up in front of the Magnolia. Behind it, like always, were two or three interested spectators in their cars.

But nobody in the yard did more than glance at the ambulance. Susan McAlester and Albert Rawlins held center stage. Deborah walked closer to the fence to hear, and the way she kept deliberately turned from the backyard just beyond, it was clear that she, like her daughter, had no wish to see what remained of Preston Rawlins if she could help it.

"Whose gun is this?" the sheriff demanded of the tall woman.

"Once it belonged to Lansing Blackburn," she said steadily. "He used it to—"

"He used it to keep me out of his hotel," Albert finished when Susan couldn't.

"Deborah, what's this fuss about?" Olivia herself stood unsteadily on the side porch, clinging to the rail. In her soft white dress, she was an airy spirit.

"Livy," Albert whispered, the name a harsh moan.

He knows, too, thought Lainie, and she wrapped both her arms around Colley's narrow waist just to have something solid to hold on to.

Susan took a hurried step toward Olivia. "Now, Miss Livy," she called, "you know you're not in good health. Don't come all the way over here. You're liable to get dizzy and fall if you don't go back inside and lie down."

But Olivia took a slow step off the porch into the yard. "Oh, fiddlesticks. All this noise would wake the dead." Then she saw the gun that Jerry held and she went still, her face blanching. "Why, that's Father's gun," she whispered.

"Yes, ma'am, it is," Susan said hurriedly. "Now, let's you and me—"

"I knew I had it, but I . . ." She frowned. "I don't remember what I did with it. I had to take it with me when I made up my mind to go with Albert. I was afraid if I left it, Father would follow and hurt him."

"He hid the letter from her," Lainie burst out, pulling from the haven of Colley's arms to plead with his gray-faced grandfather. "She didn't even know you had written it until the storm last week, when we found his strongbox. It was in it."

"She gets confused about time. She tried to come to you Friday night. She didn't know it was sixty years too late," Susan finished reluctantly.

"NO."

The one word that came from the old man's throat was a hoarse cry of agony. "Don't. Don't do this to me," he said harshly, and his hand reached for the side of the hotel to brace himself against the misery. "I'd rather you killed me than for me to find out it was all in vain. My whole life, in vain?"

Olivia caught the fence that separated the two yards, and her fingers looked young as the sun danced on them. "I remember . . . coming across the yard. But Albert wasn't there. He was instead. I knew he was bad. He was the one who stole my whistle. Remember, Lainie?"

"Preston and Colley had an argument over a whistle in front of Aunt two weeks ago," Lainie tried to explain to the listeners.

Olivia frowned, trying to remember. "He wanted you, Lainie. He said to me, go get her. I told him no. No. Oh, he got so angry." She was shaking all over, her voice a whimper of fear. "Susan, please, help me."

"I'm right here, Livy," Susan said soothingly, walking to her, wrapping her arms around her protectively. "So are Deborah and Lainie. Nobody's going to hurt you."

"Are you trying to make us believe," the detective said sharply, "that this fragile little woman did Preston in and then hid him in the cellar afterward?"

"I was keeping watch over her that night," Susan said emotionlessly from above Livy's head. "If I hadn't fallen asleep, she wouldn't have left the room. It's that one there." Freeing a hand, she pointed to a window high in the side of Olivia's house. "I woke up and saw her out here in the moonlight, saw him trying to pull the gun from her. I ran as fast as I could, but it was too late. I did all I could think of to do. I dragged him to the side of the cellar. The door had been blown half off during the storm. It's solid oak and rusted metal, but I got it open and put—I put him inside in the water. Then I dragged the door upright and stood it in its place again. I'm six feet tall. I weigh one hundred and ninety pounds. I can assure you, I can do it."

The detective looked at her tall, heavily shouldered figure, and capitulated. "What about the car?"

"After I got my poor Miss Livy back to bed—she was hysterical—I gave her one of her tablets. When she finally went to sleep, it was nearly dawn. I drove the car to the quarry. It was hard to handle, but I knew if I got it there, I could get rid of it. I knew the gate was open; Lainie told us it was, the morning after she fell in. I put the car out of gear and rolled it right to the edge. It just . . . it just kept falling. Took forever to hit the water. Then I walked back across the field that you can see beyond the cellar. It leads straight to Lo-Joe. I got here in time to tell Hargis to get concrete and seal the door." Susan's throat worked a little. "I know it was wrong. I know Preston Rawlins deserved better. A life, or at the least, a Christian burial. But it was all I could think of to do. I have asked God to forgive me every moment since."

"But you didn't tell anybody."

"No. I was too afraid of what they'd do to Olivia," Susan whispered. "Whatever it is, they have to send me with her. I did more wrong than she did."

The investigator meant to say something else, but two ambulance attendants with a stretcher came around the side of the building. Between them, they carried a long bulky shape that was covered by heavy white sheets.

Lainie gave a cry and backed away from Colley, right into the porch post.

"You damn fools, take that around the other way," the sheriff commanded sharply.

One of the attendants shrugged apologetically as they obeyed.

"Was that . . . was that a dead man?" Olivia asked in quick fright, her face shocked. She looked from her niece to Susan. "He tried to pull the gun from me. It made a horrible sound. Did I—did I hurt that man?"

She clutched at Susan's arm in a panic.

Lainie could barely breathe, and even the face of the detective was beginning to show pity.

"You didn't mean to hurt anybody," Susan whispered brokenly.

Olivia pushed from Susan's comforting hold, putting her hands to her head in confusion, shaking like a leaf in a storm. "I don't remember. I don't. Oh, please, where is Albert? Why isn't he here like he said he would be?"

"Livy." Her name on the old man's lips was half entreaty, half tears.

"No, Aunt." Deborah caught at the old woman, but Albert Rawlins stepped forward awkwardly, his stiff leg pronounced.

"Let her come. I'm here, Livy," he said huskily, and he pulled off his cap so that the sun shone on his hair, white as snow. It glittered off the tears that spilled down his wrinkled face, as well.

"Don't hurt her," Deborah whispered as she let Olivia slip from her grasp.

"I never could."

Olivia looked at him carefully before she smiled. "You've been gone a long time."

"I'm home now."

"So I see." She took another step, and another, and finally laid her hand on his shirtsleeve. He carefully put his over it.

"Let's walk back to your house, Livy," he said unsteadily. "Leave all of them to their talkin'."

"But Mr. Rawlins, your grandson."

Albert looked over her head at the investigator. "He's dead. You think I don't feel it? My heart hurts through to my back."

"This woman needs attention. Something will have to be done. She'll have to be examined and formally questioned. There are institutions—"

"No. Please, no, not Miss Livy," Susan begged, taking an imploring step. "That's why I hid what she had done. She can't live away from the Magnolia anymore. She won't last a week."

"Then she'll live here," Albert said, letting his hand lift to brush Olivia's hair, as white as his. "Whatever has to be done to let that happen, we'll do it. I'll pay for whatever or whoever she needs. Money is the easy part. I wish it was all of it. I'll be payin' for the rest of my life."

"I don't understand," the agent protested.

"I don't expect you to. You couldn't know the truth, that I caused most of this. I'm as much to blame for . . ." He couldn't finish for a moment. "I'm as much to blame for my grandson dyin' as she is." Then he looked down into the scared face under his, and his voice softened. "Now, Livy, let's take that walk on home, where you can rest."

Lainie watched them go, Aunt Olivia's soft dress like cream against Albert's overalls, him hitching sideways a little with every step, his cap dangling in his hand opposite her just like a schoolboy's.

20

"*We're going somewhere to talk,*" Colley said firmly as the old couple vanished inside the house opposite. "Somewhere alone." He caught her hand up from her side to pull her with him.

But Lainie had something else besides talking on her mind. She knew. Had she always known, and just not faced it? Or had everything fallen into place at once? The minute she'd let herself be pulled up against him, had heard his heart beating, had measured the familiar span of his waist with her arms, she understood it all.

She flattened herself back against the wall of the Magnolia, and with its bulwark behind her, she spoke, her voice strained and her eyes dark with shock. "You. You were the one."

Unable to finish, she just stared at him, her face accusing.

He flinched, but he didn't turn loose of her hand. "I tried to tell you."

"You just walked in on me and you—"

In the pulsing silence between them, Way's shadow fell. "I don't know if I'm here at a good time or not," he said, and it was plain that he didn't care whether he was or wasn't, "but I've got something to say. Your boots, Colley. They told me where to look. They made me realize the truth, that Preston never got near her last Saturday night."

"Way—please."

"Stay out of this, Lainie. I watched you this morning, Rawlins, when you were in the room at the station with her. I don't know when it hit me, but it was like having a house dropped on my head. Your cousin didn't come to the room. He was already dead. Somebody else did. Somebody who'd stepped in the concrete that Preston was already walled up inside."

"I was the one," Colley cut in flatly, looking directly into the other man's angry eyes.

"You damn son of a bitch. I should have known you'd never stand for anybody else to have her."

"You should have known," Colley agreed wearily.

"I'm going to break you into so many little pieces that they can't put you back together again," Way rasped, stepping between him and Lainie.

"Way, stop it," she said hurriedly, pulling at her cousin's arm.

"Lainie, he—"

"I know. But I'm not about to let you bruise him up until I get the chance to," she protested. "I'm the one he—well, never mind what he did. But let me handle it."

"You're a girl!"

"I realize that fact. If I weren't, I wouldn't be in this predicament," she retorted, her face pale. "Don't cause a scene. Haven't we all done enough damage to each other and each other's families for one day?"

Arrested, Way took a slow step back before he said finally, "You better make things right with her any way you can, Rawlins."

"That's what I'm still standing here for. Whatever she wants, I'll do it."

Way straightened his gun belt, looked from Colley to Lainie, and strode off.

The minute that he was out of sight, Lainie twisted from Colley and ran. It was childish, but she couldn't stop herself. Not to the cellar anymore—she swerved away from it—but she could hide in the kitchen.

She ran up the back porch steps and pulled the screen shut behind her. Then she fumbled for the latch. It was a feeble defense; he could pull it open with one strong hand. She didn't think he would.

Huddled in a corner of the kitchen, she waited for the inevitable. She saw Colley when he stepped up on the porch. He reached for the door, and when it wouldn't open, he let his hand drop. In another second, his eyes found her.

"I swear before God that I know what wrong I've done. I didn't mean it to happen. I meant to watch for Preston and to send him away if he dared to show his face. But I was waiting behind the cellar. I saw you go past, to the room and I—I lost my mind. You were—"

"I don't want to know what I was," she flared.

"Then I won't say it. Open the door, girl, and let me—" His husky voice broke as he raised his arms to brace himself with a hand on each side of the door facing. Through the shadowy screen, she could see the high, hard line of his cheekbones.

"No," she whispered. "You just reached out and took."

"I didn't," he denied vehemently. "I asked. You know I did."

She remembered; she remembered that instance so clearly she could hear his voice in her ear again.

"You deceived," she substituted with a gasp.

His forehead dropped forward until it was resting on the screen. "That's true. I deceived. And I've paid for it. I thought you knew me. You whispered my name. But when it was over, you called me Preston. It was me, Lainie, me. How could you not know that?"

"It's too late to worry about what I feel. You didn't stop to ask me about it Saturday night. You can't just get in bed with a woman because she's there."

"I wouldn't."

"You did."

"You. It was you. I couldn't touch anybody else the way I touched you," he pleaded. "Let me make it right."

"Make it right!" Lainie came out of her corner furiously. "How do you think you can do that, Colley?"

"I can give you everything I've got. Marry me."

Marry him. She could just marry him.

"I'm not sure I want a man like you," she whispered.

He didn't move for a minute, then he let his hands drop from the facing. "A man like me?"

"You're—"

"We've done this before. I didn't kill your father. I might have, but I didn't. Not that it makes any difference now."

"In a way Papa was right," Lainie burst out. "He said you wouldn't let any other man near me. They're all afraid of you."

"And that's damn good," Colley suddenly exploded, and he reached for the old door handle. With one hard pull, the flimsy latch broke, and he yanked the screen open and stepped into the kitchen.

"See what I mean?" she cried, backing for the corner again. "You're—"

"An animal. That's what you're supposed to say next. You're right. Where you're concerned, I am. A wolf fights for his mate. A stallion will kill another stallion for coming too close to a mare he's staked. What's wrong with that?"

"I'm a woman, that's what."

"I said that. Hell, I know that."

"No, you said I was—I was—"

"Mine." He took a long step right to her, reaching out to catch her face in his hands. "Is there something wrong with that, too? Isn't it the truth? When we were kids, when we were in the cabin, you were mine. But it works two ways. I'm yours, too. It's the only excuse I have to offer for what I did to you Saturday night."

"I don't remember—"

"I do," he said instantly, his dark eyes hot on her lips. "Let me do it again. You'll remember the next time. You'll feel the truth, that it can't be wrong when it's us."

"Colley! Stop!" She pushed his hands away furiously, her face dyed crimson. "This is what I mean when I say you're not civilized."

He pulled away from her, breathing harshly. "Then let's talk about what's civilized. You tried to go to bed with Preston, and you hated his guts. I was right there, yours for the asking. You wanted me. Me, not him, but you invited him into the Magnolia. Is civilized better?"

"You know why I did it."

"And you know why I did what I did."

She couldn't bear to look at his accusing face. Folding her arms protectively across her, she turned away, staring blindly at the Frigidaire emblem on the old white refrigerator.

"I want you to go away," she said finally in the silence.

"I've been away from you most of my life," he protested.

"I have to think. I need time."

"Time! Well, that's one thing the Magnolia has. It holds all the time that Olivia wasted here, waiting for Devil, and all the time you've been running from me. How much more of your life are you going to live like this, Lainie? How much more time do you have to waste?" he demanded brutally.

She turned in a flame of anger right into him. "Maybe you could take that from me, too, while I'm asleep."

"You weren't asleep. You were drunk. You had to get drunk to stand having Preston in your bed," he shot back at her, reaching out to grab her by her arms.

She might not even have noticed the hold. "You're not sorry you did it at all," she accused hotly.

"Hell, no. I'm sorry you couldn't feel how much I love you. But I'd do it again." The anger in him was flooded away by a darker, richer emotion. He groaned, "Lainie," and pulled her to him.

Her mouth turned to his, clinging to his lips. This was the kiss he'd burned her with that night. This was more than she could bear, but she couldn't bear to end it.

Colley was the one who broke the contact at last, but he didn't release her. He held her up tight to him and whispered, "I'd only change one thing. I'd have you invite me to your bed, want me, know it was me, make love to me. Not some shadow. Not Preston."

Then he released her as quickly as he had caught her up. It felt nearly cold without his arms about her.

"And that's the whole problem. That's the difference in me and the animals. Even Devil Rawlins's shantytown grandson wants the woman he goes to bed with to know who he is. I want you to love me."

He gave her a chance to speak, but she couldn't make her tongue shape the words he wanted to hear. Not then. Not yet. "You either want me—me, Colley Rawlins, just the way I am, or you don't. Decide. End it, or begin a life with me. No more in between. I'll give you what you want this one last time, because I owe it to you. I'll stay away for a few days, until you've made up your mind. You're right. You ought to be able to think for yourself."

Before she even knew what he was doing, he had pulled open the screen and stepped off the porch in wide, strong strides.

She came out of her daze in time to run outside after him. "Colley!"

When he halted and turned out on the grassy yard, a tiny, midsummer breeze blew his black hair across his cheek. "Just don't take too long deciding, Elaina Marie. The whole world shifted today. If it shifts again, one of us may not be here the next time the dust settles."

The town had another field day after the discovery of Preston's body. "Well, as long as those two families confine theirselves to killin' each other, instead of the rest of us," Ben said ironically, "maybe they expect it'll all work out."

"One thing's for sure," Davis Boles put in disagreeably, "nobody's goin' to prison for anythin', not as long as Devil's got the money and the power to keep 'em out. It ain't right, but it's life."

"Just who would you send to prison?" Bella demanded. "The old man? The old woman? They might live to serve five years at best, and neither one of them set out to kill anybody. It seems to me that the Blackburns and the Rawlinses should try to put this behind them. They'd do better to take to marrying instead of fighting."

Lainie would have agreed to the solution. If she'd known where Colley was, she would have gone to him almost as soon as he was out of sight. One afternoon was all she needed to understand that she had to be with him, no matter what. But nobody, not even Devil, knew the whereabouts of Colley Rawlins.

The world really had shifted.

A specialist came the next morning to work with Olivia, a pleasantly gruff, fortyish woman from Vanderbilt Hospital, and another woman to help Susan take care of her elderly charge. Susan fairly bristled with resentment, but she stayed quiet. She knew what the alternative for Olivia might have been.

Workmen showed up at the Magnolia the second day, and a Nashville architect came along to design plans for a renovation. When Deborah and Lainie protested, the old man delivered his ultimatum. "Either tell the workers what they need to know and let them do their job," he said brutally, "or I'll pay the back taxes on this place in my name and then you'll have nothing at all to do with it."

To Lainie, right in front of Deborah, he had more to say. "If my grandson ever shows up again, it'll be because of you, I reckon. He'll come where you are. I never saw a Blackburn yet that didn't cling to the Magnolia. So I'm doin' this for Colley, too. He's likely to spend a good part of his life here if you'll have him."

"I'll have him," she answered steadily, and the words were for her quiet mother as well as Rawlins.

"Albert's an old reprobate," Susan declared in indignation, but Lainie wondered if maybe they weren't all as relieved as she felt down at the bottom of her soul to have Devil and his boundless money at their disposal. Who else could have commanded a doctor from Nashville to attend Olivia? Who else could have kept her out of an institution or, worse, a prison?

"It's scandalous," Bella told her firmly when they met at

church the next Sunday. "Almost like a man taking care of his mistress."

"She's eighty," Lainie said, her face full of laughter. When had things been funny? It had been a long time.

"I hear there's going to be a big advertising campaign across the state to get people to visit the Springs and the Magnolia. Albert's doings, too, I reckon. I certainly hope that none of you expect the Magnolia to do much business, even if it is going to be a showplace again."

"Why wouldn't it do business? You'll come, won't you?"

Bella gasped at Lainie's dull-wittedness. "Lord, child, of course I will. I understand these things. But I'm local. Other people—the ones who'd come to spend some time—those don't go to hotels where they're afraid they might wind up sleeping for a lot longer than a night."

"You mean because of the accident."

"Accident!"

"Maybe you're right and visitors won't come for a while. But twenty years from now, they'll come because of it. I don't like that, but it's what will happen."

"Twenty years! Are the Blackburns expecting to be around these parts that long?"

"With any luck at all."

"That's a commodity that some of us have a little more of than others. Poor Preston Rawlins was a mite short of it. Now there's one who got more than a night's rest. Much more. He took sleeping at the Magnolia dead serious."

Bella wasn't so funny, after all.

"What did happen to him exactly? All we heard was that Olivia mistook him for an intruder and shot him. Did he fall in the cellar? Hargis Lowe didn't sleep a wink for two nights after they found Preston. He didn't have an inkling that anybody was there when he sealed it with that concrete. I told him Olivia probably didn't know it by then, either; it'd be just like her to forget the whole thing."

"Something like that," Lainie said elusively.

Bella gazed at the girl in frustration. "Preston was buried yesterday, the *Tennessean* said, at Mount Olivet Cemetery in Nashville. The other grandson appears to be gone, too, for good."

"He'll be back," Lainie said quickly, and a little worry hammer tapped at her temple.

"Will he, now? I'm glad to hear it. It's for the best. The old man needs him, and this place is as dull as dishwater without Colley Rawlins to keep things stirred up." Bella's unexpected words were dry, so dry that Lainie laughed before she could stop herself.

Bella eyed her. "Hmph. I know somebody else who wants him back."

Lainie flushed involuntarily and mentally kicked herself all the way home for giving Bella her next bit of gossip: that she was pining for the witch boy.

The trouble was, she really was pining for him.

Way kept watching her, too; that made it even worse. "What in hell went wrong?" he finally demanded. "He said he'd do anything you wanted."

"He did. I told him to go away and let me think."

"Think!" Way exclaimed, shoving his thumbs down into his back pockets. "Think!"

"I know. I was upset, and it made me stupid. He said he'd come back. Well, where is he?" She kicked one of the rockers on the porch of the Magnolia.

"If he said he would, then he will."

"When? When I'm as old as Aunt Livy? Would you look at her and Devil? He brought a buggy and a horse after lunch today, right to the house."

"An honest-to-God buggy?" Way demanded in surprise.

"He bought it off somebody with the folk medicine show. Now they're out for a Sunday afternoon ride."

"Surely you're not jealous?"

"Aunt Olivia deserves happiness, even if it is with Devil Rawlins. But maybe I am, just a little."

"Let me guess: you want Colley to come back and put you up in a buggy and take you—"

Lainie grabbed hold of the high back of the rocker. "No. You think you're smart, don't you? You know what I really want? If I could get my hands on him, I'd haul him right up those stairs and tie him to the bed so he couldn't get away again and treat him exactly the way he treated me that night."

Way's face flushed right to the roots of his sandy hair and his mouth dropped open. "Huh."

She refused to show embarrassment, but frustration she couldn't help. "Men make me so mad. They walk while we wait. But someday—"

Way reached up to loosen his collar. "You been going to the library to those meetings Alma holds every month about women's rights?" he said dubiously, the color still high in his face.

"No. I've been sitting around, missing Colley. But I'm finished with the languishing-lady routine. I'm going to start choosing wallpaper and paint for some of the down-stairs rooms this week. Devil's fancy decorator says I have an 'eye for color,' and the man who came with James Rawlins, the detective, called and asked if we ever catered parties down at the marina. I said yes. So I'm going to stay busy."

"Good," Way murmured. "You're probably less danger-ous that way."

*   *   *

"They say we always wind up right where we started, and I'll be damned, boy, if you didn't come close to doin' that."

Devil's laconic words made Colley jump and drop the log that he was carrying into the open truck bed with a loud clanging noise. I knew somebody would find me sooner or later, he told himself as he turned around, and I knew that somebody would probably be my grandfather.

The old man looked better than he had two weeks before at the Magnolia.

"You found me," Colley said at last to break the silence of the overgrown yard that lay around them.

"It took awhile. I never thought of the Thorne place. It's terrible quiet out here at this dead end; I reckon you're as well hid here as you'd be anywhere." Devil strolled over to the truck and looked in at the limbs and stumps and general debris. "You're being mighty neighborly, cleaning the place up just so you can sleep here."

"I called the man who owns it. He's a doctor out of Cookeville. I asked to rent it. He was happy to have the offer. The house is falling to ruin. Maybe it's a good thing. The longer I stay here, the more I see that there's too much of John Thorne in the place." Colley didn't know why he was talking so much, and so civilly, too, except that he'd been fourteen long, long days by himself, and that was lengthy even for a solitary sort like he sometimes was. Besides, the old man seemed different.

Devil looked at the sagging porch on the corner, and the honeysuckle vines that had overtaken the side rail. Then he looked back at his grandson.

"You're no more short of cash than the forest is of trees," he said bluntly. "And this old truck—is it the doctor's, too? It's not yours."

"It sort of came with the place."

"Why are you foolin' with it? You've got a shiny new one

sittin' in the barn. You got a home, too, one that needs you more than this one does."

"The farm belongs to you and James. Not me."

"It's more yours than anybody's, just by right of knowin' it and touchin' and workin' it, Colley. But if you need to know, I changed the deed last week. It's yours."

"I wasn't asking you for the farm," he said shortly.

"Then tell me what the hell you are askin' for."

"I don't know anymore," Colley admitted helplessly, resting on the open tailgate of the truck. "I know what I want, but—"

"You want me to list them for you, the things you want?" the old man demanded. "You want Lainie."

"That's true."

"Hidin' out here won't get her."

"I told her I'd give her time to think," he said tiredly, reaching a hand up to massage the top of his shoulder. "I reckon I'm scared she's going to say no when I ask her again to marry me. Some people just don't get to be together. Not you and Olivia, not Brodie and Colleen. Why would we?"

Devil slid his hand behind his bib; how many times had Colley seen him do that? "I'll be damned if I'll turn pious in my old age."

"No, don't," Colley said with a shudder.

"Still, I know truth when I see it. I wasted my life, Colley. I spent all those years hatin' Livy, and the woman I married—I did her the most wrong. I can't hardly even remember her name. I used her, and you, and James, and Preston all to keep the hate alive. Brodie found the one escape from me."

Devil squinted up into the sun. "Now my life's nearly over. James is gone as good as Preston is. He's taking Teresa and they're moving to D.C. He kept wantin' to prosecute somebody, anybody, for Preston's dyin',' until that investigator of his turned up some things about Preston that might have come out at a trial. I made a deal with him. I gave him money to let it go, and Teresa finally agreed. James went along with her, like he always does. Someday, if he's got half as smooth a tongue as his son did, and if she keeps pushin' him, he'll be in politics. I wish him well."

"He didn't belong in the Springs," Colley said reluctantly, and he was talking about Preston as much as he was James.

"No. But you do. Half the town wants to know where you are."

"They hate my guts in that place," Colley said shortly.

"Some do, and some don't. That's to be expected when a man's got as much power as you do. Not many of 'em know you. They just understand that you're the Man now. No, don't tell me you're through again. You're not. You're just gettin' started. There's the tobacco crop; I called about gettin' another warehouse and goin' more into the buyin' and sellin' end of it. I should'a done it long ago."

"I'm not going to let you use me again," Colley said forcefully. "If that's what you're here for, hire somebody else to build you bigger barns."

"I reckon it's your turn now to use me. Use my money." Devil's dark eyes bore into his grandson's. "Run the farm and the crops and what's left in Nashville how you will."

"Don't try to tell me you've quit. Not you. You'll tell death what to do."

"I ain't got that much money," Devil said dryly, "no matter how much I've made, and that's a lot. I just can't figure out what I made it for. I ain't exactly one to spend it on clothes and cars. Neither are you, but you're young enough to have more wants than I do. You know something? Fixin' the Magnolia for Olivia is only the second time in my life I ever enjoyed spendin' a part of those millions in the bank."

"The second time?" Colley asked warily. He knew the old man wanted him to ask the question, and he still fell right into the trap.

"The first time ain't what you might think. It ain't the money I spent buyin' you, although I never regretted that. Colleen made it hard for me to take pleasure in the purchase." Devil reached up and pulled off his cap, wiping sweat from his forehead. "Damn, it's hot. What was I sayin'? Colleen. That husband of hers wants me to let her be buried beside the quarry whenever they turn loose of her remains down in Nashville. Maybe I will. I keep thinkin,' she was your ma. And she fooled me, too, didn't she? She couldn't leave you and Brodie after all. But this talk ain't about her. It's about how the first time I ever had pleasure in spending money was when I bought the horse."

Colley didn't know what he had expected; Devil's answer wasn't it. "Black Horse has made a lot more money back for you. I guess there's pleasure in that."

Devil twisted the cap in his hands. "James and Preston would have said he gave a good return on my investment. They'd be right, but not in the way most people think. See, Colley"—he looked away in a kind of awkward embarrassment—"I bought him for you. He was my investment in you."

Colley didn't answer. He was beginning to hear what Devil was really saying, and he didn't know how to respond at all.

"I seen how you hung around the barns and the nags I used to keep while you lived with Charley. It got me to thinkin' that I'd better be gettin' a fancy one, one to take a boy's eye. I ain't sayin' I didn't do it out of selfishness. I was figurin' that when you got older, it'd be a lot easier to hold you on the farm with a fine piece of horseflesh—hell, it turned into a whole barn of horseflesh—than it would with a tobacco crop. I can't say I ever met too many boys who're overly fond of workin' tobacco."

"You never even noticed me back then," Colley protested.

"I thought I did. But maybe I didn't see enough. You sure knocked me flat when you turned up with Lainie Thorne's whistle. If I'd only known how to play that card, the girl, I might could'a saved my money where the horses were concerned," Devil said wryly. "But I got a lot of pleasure out of watchin' you with —'em. An' I got what I wadn't expectin', what James wanted: I'll be damned if you didn't make a fortune right there in my barn. I tell you, Colley, I ain't got much luck with women, but I can flat turn out the money. So can you."

Colley stayed silent. What could he say?

"Come home." Devil was abrupt as he pulled his cap back on. "How many times do I have to beg you? I'll do it. Or bribe you? I'll buy you a whole damn stable of blooded horses if it'll do the trick. You and me, we're the Rawlinses now. All of it. Do things your way. Marry Lainie Thorne. She'll have you, that's plain. Sell the tobacco base and sell the horses and live at the Magnolia for all I care. I just want you to come back."

"I—"

"No. Don't say nothin' else just yet. Think about it. If you show up, I'll know what you decided. If you don't, then so be it. I'm through movin' you around, Colley."

Devil Rawlins would never say he loved his grandson. Not out loud. He'd come as close to it that day as he ever would.

But he was a man of action. Maybe he'd acted out his feelings all along more than Colley realized. Once he'd even killed John Thorne to save his grandson.

Colley thought about that, and it was good thinking. He couldn't say out loud he loved Albert, either, but he missed him. He wanted to go back to the farm and the stables.

His farm. His stables. He would be the only boss now. That was scary, but it was exhilarating, too.

He would have it all, more than a man could ever hope for, if Lainie agreed to marry him.

Devil was sure; he said she would.

Had she told him that? Colley felt happier than he had in days thinking of the possibility.

A little softness—hers—mixed in with his life would be paradise.

He threw the gloves in the back of the truck. The heat of the July day was dying; it was time to stop work and get cleaned up and go into town.

It was time to hear what she had to say.

The house had electricity to run a pump for a well that still had water. Colley was grateful for both as he stood under the shower nozzle and let it spray the dirt and sweat off of him.

He pulled on underwear and worn, clean jeans and was reaching for a shirt when he heard somebody in the living room. "Devil?" he called, frozen in the act of sliding one arm in a sleeve.

"Rawlins! If you're here, show yourself!"

It was Way Blackburn's voice.

Colley stepped barefooted into the room. Way had his back to him, looking down the hall. "I'm here. What do you want?"

Way made a quick, startled turn. "Don't go sneaking up on me, Colley," he groused as he relaxed. "What in thunderation are you doing here, anyway?"

"It was an empty house and nobody ever comes, not until today, anyway. I didn't have to see people like you," Colley retorted, sliding his arm into the other sleeve.

"I thought that was Devil's truck coming from this dead end," Way said in satisfaction. "I figured if anybody could find you, he could."

"He really is getting old," Colley said flatly, "if he let you follow him."

"Or he wanted me to find you." Way looked the other man over speculatively.

Colley started to button the shirt, but his hands dropped at Way's expression. "What?" he demanded warily.

"You're all cleaned up and shaved. That's real good," Way said in satisfaction.

"What in the hell is wrong with you?"

In answer, Way drew his gun and pointed it right at Colley's head. "You're under arrest, that's what."

"Under arrest!" Colley took a step back. There was a fiendish glee in the other man's face that told Colley he wasn't quite serious, but the big gun was. "I can't be. I didn't do anything. And besides, I've already looked down a gun barrel and seen the jail once lately. I've got better places to go, like the Magnolia."

"Well, that's convenient. That's going to be our first stop." Way fumbled at the back of his belt, brought out a pair of handcuffs, and tossed them to Colley, who instinctively caught them. "Put those on."

"Are you crazy?"

The gun went right to Colley's head. He heard the trigger being cocked not far from his left ear. "No. If you expect to see Lainie sometime tonight, just do as I say. Put on the damned handcuffs before I shoot you. It wouldn't be hard to see you bleed a little, Colley. All I'd have to do is think about you climbing in bed with her when she didn't even know her own name. Put them on."

He hesitated, then slid the silver cuff around one wrist and snapped it shut.

"Now the other one."

"If I don't get out of these when we get to wherever we're going, you're the one who'll be bleeding," he said darkly as he fastened the other cuff.

Way uncocked the gun, slid it into his holster, and took the link between the cuffs, pulling Colley's arms up to his waist. "That was easier than I expected. I figured I'd have to knock you unconscious and then put them on you. You know what I think? I think you've got a guilty conscience, Colley."

"Where are we going?" Colley demanded impatiently.

"I told you—the Magnolia. No more questions. Just get in the back of the patrol car."

There wasn't a man alive he would have put these shackles on his wrists for except Blackburn. Way wasn't the sort to pull rogue cop tricks.

So what exactly was he up to?

Maybe Colley should have been afraid, but he wasn't. He'd seen Way in a fit of rage a time or two, but it wasn't tonight.

Lainie had put him up to this.

Was that it? Nerves were jumping all over his skin, and he was shivering as if he were cold. It was ninety degrees, and he was anything but chilled. He felt more like he was being burned at the stake.

He wanted to ask Way, but what if he was wrong?

When they pulled in at the side of the Magnolia, sweat began to bead on his back. His tongue felt so thick that he had trouble talking; his body was heavy, too heavy to move.

Way opened the door of the car. "Get on out."

Putting his pinioned hands out first, Colley ducked his head and stood.

The grass tickled his feet. Way hadn't even given him time to find his boots.

Where was she?

Colley let his eyes search the darkening grounds, and Way knew instantly who he was looking for. "She's not here," he said with a quickly smothered laugh. "She doesn't even know you're coming, but she will."

He motioned to a set of steps, the same ones that Colley had climbed two weeks before to get to the sleeping girl. "I reckon you know the way."

"You want me to go to—"

"Right to it. Move, Colley, or I'm gonna get me some help. Don't worry. You won't be up there by yourself for long."

The tingling had turned to downright, unmanly quivering. His whole stomach was shaking as he went up the stairs, Way right behind him, and down the porch to the door. Way stepped in front to open first the screen and then the creaky door.

Colley remembered that creak.

"Go on, Rawlins."

A lamp burned on the table, holding off the gray, shadowy dusk, and the same fan that had tried to cool his passions the last time was still in the window, where it whirred away. Its breeze was just as useless as it had been before. Sweat was dripping off his back, and he rubbed it off his bare abdomen with the palms of his hands as he twisted the cuffs against each other.

"Come on, Way, get me out of these," he said sharply.

"Sit down. No, not there. The bed."

And right there was where Colley finally balked. "I don't think so," he said ironically, standing perfectly still. "I'm not your type."

"No. You're a damn sight too ugly for me," Way retorted, "but I've got this cousin, and you told me you'd do whatever she wanted. The other day, when she wasn't too happy about you, she let me know exactly what it was. Being a nice girl, except for her weakness for shantytown boys, she probably wouldn't repeat it to your face. But we're gonna get it for her, tonight. If you meant what you said. If you love her. If you don't, get out of here right now and save me the trouble of trying to kill you later."

The two of them measured each other, circling a little.

Then Colley said with dark humor, "All I wanted was for her to marry me and live with me and give me a few kids and maybe sit on the porch with me when I got old. What does she want?"

"I'm a naturally shy man, so I covered my ears during part of it, but it was something about tying you to the bed," Way drawled, watching Colley's stunned face burn red.

"Jesus."

"I'd pray, too, if I were you. Now sit down and hold out your hands."

He went where Way shoved him, right to the head of the bed, and watched him unfasten and refasten one of the cuffs, locking them around the thick middle spindle of the cherry headboard. He couldn't hear, see, or think for the sparking current that was roaring through him.

Way stalked back to the door. "You better not hurt her, Colley. I'm trusting you when I send her up here."

His voice was as thick as porridge. "Me, hurt her?" He tugged at the cuffs.

The other man grinned suddenly. "I'll warn her that

you're fragile in this condition. I wouldn't want you to die of a heart attack right in the middle of . . . things."

The door shut behind him, leaving Colley alone, chained to the bed in the corner room at the Magnolia, remembering too late that Way was taking the handcuff keys with him.

The irony of it all struck him suddenly, and he laughed a little under his breath. Here he was, the shantytown boy who had once been thrown out of the old hotel, and now he was chained to it.

How had this happened? He hoped the place didn't get blown down again while he was trapped in a position that wasn't exactly easy to explain.

Not until Lainie Thorne was through with him, anyway.

The preacher had unexpectedly dropped in while Way was gone, and before he got halfway into the living room, the Reverend Masters had him cornered.

"I haven't seen you in church in a while, Wayland," the preacher said reprovingly.

Lainie had just entertained the man for an hour, so she was in no mood to help her cousin. "Oh, he asks about the services a lot," she said cheerfully. "I was explaining to him the sermon about tithing that you preached last week, but I think I had part of it wrong. Could you explain it to him again, while I go help Mama in the kitchen with supper?"

"Lainie," Way said desperately, but she avoided his hand as it caught at her arm and breezed past him.

He didn't escape the preacher until Mama had supper on the table and the man took his leave. "Come and eat with us, Way. There's plenty. Susan and Olivia ate earlier," Deborah said. "I know it's late, but we've been busy today. We've had company out our ears. They want to know about the Magnolia, and Olivia, and everything else, and I finally left the house awhile just to get away from it all."

"Where's Reverend Masters?" Lainie demanded evilly. "Didn't he stay to eat?"

"I hope not," Way said fervently. "I gave him twenty dollars for the offering to shut him up."

"Better you than me," she retorted, but with a touch of gratitude. "You were right, Way. The town tells everything. Now the reverend thinks I need guidance because I met Colley at the cabin all those years ago. He's trying to make me respectable again."

"He'll quit once you're married. Can you really see anybody saying anything about you to Colley? Or Colley letting them?"

Lainie stilled at his casual remark.

"Eat," Deborah said firmly.

"Lainie doesn't need to eat. She'll get fat," he said.

"I'm hungry," Lainie exclaimed. "And I am not fat."

"Colley wouldn't like a fat woman."

Lainie, blushing, hissed furiously, "Shut up! What's wrong with you tonight?"

What really was wrong with him? He rushed through the meal and urged her to do the same. She had barely touched her plate before he was up, pulling on her arm.

"You'd better put him out of his misery," Mama said.

Lainie resigned herself to whatever Way's problem was. She wasn't really very hungry, anyway, no matter what she'd told him earlier. "What is it?"

"I want to show you something over at the Magnolia."

"Can't it wait?"

"No, it can't. Not another minute. I hope the place is still standing."

His grip on her hand was too tight as he pulled her from the room, and the house, and the porch, out to the far corner of the yard. Dew had fallen, and fireflies danced through the trees. An unexpected blackberry bramble caught her leg below the shorts she wore.

"Ouch."

But he didn't give her time to inspect the scratch. "Look." He twisted her so that she could see the corner window. There was lamplight shining from it.

Her hands went to her mouth.

"I couldn't find any rope on the spur of the moment, so I had to make do."

"Wh-what?" Her idiot cousin had done something. *Please, God, please, don't let it be that.*

"I used handcuffs. I had to pull a gun on him to make him put them on, but they did the trick."

"Way!"

"He's been there awhile. I bet he's worked up a temper, too. If you hadn't sicced that preacher on me, I'd have told you about this when I first got here."

Sounds were huffing out of her mouth, but she couldn't say anything. She knew what the sounds were supposed to say: I'll feed your body to sharks. I'll take your firstborn and hide him in a cave somewhere. I'll—

But when she finally managed something coherent, it was, "Is he really there? Does he love me still? How do I look? I want to be pretty tonight."

"Thunderation, how should I know? Ask him. Oh, here."

It was a key he was pushing into her hand, the one to the handcuffs he usually carried.

That was when her heart really started a panicked jerking.

"I should kill you," she managed.

"This time tomorrow, you'll want to thank me, honey."

Colley looked quiet enough through the screen door as she tiptoed to it. He lay on his side, away from her, and she had time to drink in the sight of him in the warm pool of lamplight.

No, she wasn't angry with Way anymore. She adored her cousin. Look at what he had brought back to the Magnolia for her.

His arms were pulled up above his head. How was she going to explain those handcuffs to him? she wondered hysterically before she noticed how the posture revealed the long, sleek lines of the muscles in his brown arms. The side of his ribs and part of his back were naked, too, because the short-sleeved shirt he wore hadn't been fastened and it fell open, pooling at the small of his back, leaving the exposed skin to glisten like rich satin. The old jeans were loose and worn; they rode his hips low, gapping away to let the white cotton of his Jockey shorts show above their denim waistband.

She had him.

From the top of his dark silky head to the soles—the bare soles—of his agile feet, the witch boy was hers, a captive right there in her bed.

Mine, mine, mine.

She was no different than he was when it came to passion and possessiveness. She was no different when it came down to what she meant to do now that he was there.

Her hand reached for the handle, and the door swung open. Even over the sound of the fan, he heard her. Colley rolled like a cat to his back, the shirt nearly falling off him, his arms twisting above him, and he saw her there at the door.

"It's about time, girl," he rasped, his voice nearly unrecognizable.

"Were you waiting for me?" she asked chokily.

"Ever since you were eleven years old."

That wasn't what he was supposed to say. He wasn't supposed to be so poignant and direct, and he wasn't supposed to make her cry.

"That's a long time." She had to try twice before she could speak.

"Most of my life. Shut the door."

The room was small when the door closed, and the air felt tight.

"Are you . . . are you mad because Way brought you here?"

"You mean because of these?" He gave a tiny, wry tug on the silver shackles. "Not as long as you make an honest man out of me tomorrow. If you'll do that, I reckon you can do whatever else you want."

She had to hold to the tall post to stay upright at the foot of the bed. He strained to lift his head, the raven hair brushing his shoulder, to keep watching her.

"Maybe I'll do the exact same things you did to me here in this room."

His chest rose and fell sharply. "I thought you didn't remember."

"I remember enough."

"But you didn't—" His body jerked a little as her hand found the bottom of his foot and traced its outline. "You thought I was Pres—"

Lainie moved fast to cover his mouth with her hand. His skin was hot.

"Don't say it. Forget him," she whispered. "I'm sorry he's dead, but I don't want to hear his name again."

His eyes watched her above her hand, and his tongue caressed her palm, startling her into pulling it away. "I won't say it again, then," he promised roughly, "but don't turn out the light. Keep looking at me, Lainie. This is me."

"It was you, then, Colley. I cried the next morning because I thought I had wanted you so much that I imagined it was. I wondered if it was a whiskey dream, and if I could stay drunk the rest of my life so that it would go on being you."

"Lai—"

But she cut off that word, too, this time with her mouth, bending over him to open his lips with hers. He strained up to her, the muscles in his arms tight and furious at her head, trying to reach for her.

She ended the kiss at her will, pulling from his lips even when he tried to hold her, ignoring his sound of protest. Her hands touched his face, traced the uneven line of his nose, his distinct black eyebrows, the line of his cheeks.

Then she found his throat, brushing the silky hair away with her palms, bending to adorn him with a necklace of kisses to match the one he wore that held the whistle. He was cursing, repeating her name in a pleading chant.

"How good was Rachel Harding, Colley?" she whispered when she reached his ear.

He heard her. He stilled. "No, Lainie, please—"

"And the others? I know there was somebody when you went away the first time. You came back different. I didn't know why until I was nearly grown."

"I don't even remember her," he gasped truthfully.

"You left the creek, and the river, and me, and you tried to forget us."

On her knees beside the bed, he could see the heart-break in her eyes. "I tried, but I couldn't. I never have been able to."

She sucked in a sobbing breath. "Then tonight is your punishment for all of it."

"I might not live through this, Lainie," he groaned as her hands found his chest, soothing over it, too. She traced the scar, his rib cage, the thin dark line of hair that led to his navel, and then bent to place a kiss in the tiny indention.

"Girl, have some—have some mercy," he gasped, trying to twist away when her hands found the waistband of his jeans. "Let me touch you."

"Did you have any on me? You could have left me alone, but you didn't."

He couldn't answer at all.

She grasped the band and gave it a hard jerk. The snap flew open, and she released the zipper by yanking it apart.

Her mouth was dry, her legs felt like weak rubber, her hands were trembling.

"Help me."

Fastened to the headboard as he was, Colley was awkward, but he obeyed, lifting his hips to let her slide the jeans in jerks down his long legs and over his feet. She paused to look at him again, the legs, the chest, the face. The boy of all her childhood adventures and her teenage fantasies. "Colley, you really are beautiful," she choked out.

"You're the beautiful one," he said huskily, watching her face. "The first time I ever saw you, nothing but black curls and blue eyes, I thought, she belongs in that tree house, up there close to heaven."

For a moment, she thought she would be all right. But the words hurt too much. There was no place to hide. With a muffled cry, she slid off the side of the bed, buried her face against his warm smooth stomach above the white shorts, and burst into tears.

The sound froze him into stillness; her shoulders heaved against him, and he felt wetness on his skin. Pulling his head up, he tried to reach the soft waves of her hair, finally giving the rings at his wrists a furious yank, all to no avail.

"Lainie, what's wrong? Unlock these handcuffs and let me hold you," he demanded in a worried panic. "What are you crying for? Let me loose."

The weeping girl didn't answer, but she pulled away

from him and wiped tears away from her reddened cheeks with the back of her hand. Still jerking a little with the force of emotion, Lainie came to her knees on the carpet beside the bed, fumbling in her pocket.

Without a word, she pulled out the key and leaned over him to fumble with the lock. Her throat was just at his lips, and he closed his eyes to let the sweet, warm scent of her body engulf him.

His arms hurt and felt weak when the release came, but he made them grab for her before she could slide away, and the left handcuff, still caught around his wrist, hung momentarily on the spindle before he pulled it free and tossed it off somewhere on the floor.

"No, you're not going anywhere," he warned huskily as he wrapped his arms around her waist and pulled her up on him even more than she already was.

"Colley, you've made a big mistake. I'm not any part of heaven." She dropped her face to let it rest in the hollow under his chin. "I wanted you locked up tonight so you wouldn't run when you stopped to think how terrible I really am."

"How terrible are you?" he whispered, with a tiny half laugh of relief.

"How can you want me? I hate what I've done," she whispered miserably, laying her hand against his cheek.

"Maybe you'd better tell me what that is," he murmured against the top of her head, using his free hand, the one not occupied with pressing her to him, to push them both up on the pillows.

"I let us drift for three years, and I would have stayed away from you forever, no matter how jealous I was of Rachel."

"I'm glad she served some purpose." He pressed his lips against her forehead. Now he could hold her completely, pull her body so tightly against his that he could feel her jerky breaths.

"I loved you, but I meant to go to bed with Preston. I thought about his money, and mostly, how it would hurt you. I deliberately got drunk. I let a man se-seduce me, hoping the whole time he was somebody else. You." Her confession was ragged and painful.

"Lainie, look at me." With his hand under her chin, he tried to pull her face up.

But she resisted, pushing his hand away. "My soul has great big scars on it. What if you look at me and see them?"

This time he made her turn her face up so he could gaze down on the smooth cream of her skin, the way her wet lashes lay against her cheeks, still hiding her eyes from him. "I'm looking. I don't see anything but the girl who loved me when nobody else did. She's capable of that kind of love. She loved John Thorne enough that she couldn't forgive herself for hurting him, or me, either, even when she wanted me. I knew you wanted me. That's part of what's been eating me alive. It's why I kept hanging around."

The eyelids lifted and she looked at him. "Why? Why, Colley?" she asked anxiously.

"I came to your house before you went to meet Preston to offer you every bribe I could think of to make you forget your father and your plans, and come to me. You turned me down cold for your father's memory. I want that kind of love for me. I want Lainie Thorne to say no if somebody offers her the whole world to turn her back on Devil Rawlins's bastard grandson. I'm not afraid of that kind of strength; I don't want a woman with a lukewarm heart. What you are is what makes you worth the having."

"And Prest—"

This time it was his hand over her lips. "We said we wouldn't talk about him."

"But I—"

"You got drunk to sleep with him. You didn't get drunk to come here tonight," he pointed out quietly.

"No." Her cheeks stained pink, but she kept looking at him. "I don't feel like a whore tonight, either."

"Lainie," Colley protested painfully, shifting her suddenly so his hands grasped her arms high near the shoulders. He held her in front of him, their faces only inches apart, their bodies pressed close together. "There's no whore about you. What's between us is love. I was your first man, your only man. I sinned to make sure of that."

She looked into his serious black eyes and read his own regret. "Don't look sad. You'd do it again," she accused with a ragged tenderness. "Even if sinning is what costs you heaven."

"I told you, you're my heaven. The only one I ever hope to hold."

In the eternity that they faced each other, remembered wrongs and ancient heartaches slipped away. They were the boy and girl who'd found each other in the cold, sparkling water of Widow's Creek.

And at last, they were more.

They were lovers.

Lainie didn't know why she hadn't noticed the scalding heat of the legs that wrapped hers until that moment, or how her breath was so uneven she was nearly dizzy. Her breasts hurt with a heavy ache as she pressed herself to him and felt his heart slamming against his ribs.

"Hold me now, Colley," she moaned, reaching for him, clutching at the dark hair at his shoulders.

"Forever," he promised, twisting her under him, covering her body with his. The whistle trapped between them pressed the echo of the word into her skin.

Night was falling quickly. Out on the dusky porch, a summer breeze blew a reluctant rocking chair into a tiny sway, passing on to ripple the moonstruck water of the creek . Then it danced farther, flipping the silky tassels of Miss Olivia's sweet garden corn into a gentle tangle.

The old hotel wrapped its arms around the two high in the corner room, shooing the impudent breeze away. Forever, they had said. The Magnolia knew about forever.